STEEL DEVOTION

Dylan Hubbard

Larryram Press—Warren, RI
Paperback ISBN: 979-8-3303-0978-8
eBook ISBN: 979-8-3303-0980-1
Title: *Steel Devotion*
Author: Dylan Hubbard
Digital distribution | 2024
Paperback | 2024

This is a work of fiction. The characters, names, incidents, places, and dialogue are products of the author's imagination, and are not to be construed as real.

Published in the United States by New Book Authors Publishing

Dedication

iii

For Tricia and Kirsten, the lighters of my creative flame.

And for Les.

Chapter 1

The past was something that recently started to intrigue Dawn Bell. Not everything of course. She never needed to be reminded of the time she had fallen flat on her face in front of her entire fifth grade class during recess and how awful it had felt, both physically and emotionally. Or, a few years back in middle school, when she finally stood up against that little bitch Sophia Wilkinson, who had been teasing and spreading false rumors about Dawn and her friends the entire year. It would have been a positive memory for her, had Sophia not started slapping her and pulling her hair before she could even get out her first sentence. *It's always the hair girls go for isn't it?* Dawn thought as she had waited in the nurse's office for her grandmother to pick her up, secretly proud of the few hits *she* had gotten in.

No, those were parts of her past she wasn't very fond of and didn't like thinking about. Especially when they resurfaced while she was trying to fall asleep and she had to forcibly think of something, anything, to take the place of those dreadful past embarrassments. "Again," she would often say to the empty room when her brain decided to show her her previous failures instead of something better. "Yet a-fucking-gain."

The past she really liked was a past that she never actually had. The ideas and scenarios she imagined when she found herself with nothing to do were the ones she often thought of, and liked, more than the ones she had experienced herself. Walking to the local ice cream shop with her dad, him carrying her when her feet started to get tired, having to stand on her tiptoes to see over the counter. Dawn liked to imagine herself younger, usually six, sometimes seven, running around with him when they had finished eating. Him playing the horrible monster and her being the brave hero who would slay it. Then the two would simply lie down to end the outing, the prickly but comforting feeling of the grass on her skin, the warmth from the sun beaming down on her, wearing her father's sunglasses to try and get a better view of the sun without going blind. Having to squint as hard as she could and still barely make out a circle. But eventually she would do it. She would see the sun. He made sure to tell her not to stare at it for longer than five seconds at a time, he also told her numerous times to not look at it at all, but she often tried to push her luck. And he never got angry enough to scare her into keeping her eyes off of it. She made sure he never did that.

"I see it, Daddy! I can see the sun! The whole thing!" she squealed, her squeaky voice beaming happiness with each and every word about her wonderful "Sun-Seeing."

Then the sun started to speak.

"Dawn? Hey, Dawn. You okay?" the big, fat circle of heat inquired.

The voice sounded awfully familiar although she couldn't quite pinpoint the owner. The booming sound above her snuck its way through her ears and rattled the brain inside her head. Dawn's smile dropped and she sat up, never taking her eyes off of Earth's largest heating system that just asked her a question.

"I'm okay, sun," she said, and just because her parents always told her to be polite when meeting a stranger, she added, "how are you?"

"*What?*" the giant ball of gas responded.

Definitely a female voice now. The voice's identity still remained murky however, like something floating just below the surface of water; almost recognizable but too blurry, wobbly and contorted to make out what it is. Or in this case, who.

"Are you on something?" the sun asked. Then, in a much quieter voice, it continued, "Is there any left? Because you need to get rid of that shit if there is."

It was then that things began changing. With every passing second the grass became harder and harder, significantly less prickly and much more flat. The sky started getting closer to her and turning an odd creamy color with strange, swirly patterns covering the entire thing. Even the talkative sun started to morph, becoming smaller and duller and easier to see. With these weird things that looked almost like boat paddles sticking out of it. It got closer and closer, getting more and more dreary, with the disembodied voice growing louder and more distinguishable. Dawn covered her eyes, no longer in the mood to try and challenge her eyesight. She wanted to be home where she felt safe, with Mom and Dad. They'd protect her from this bizarre transformation the world was experiencing. She didn't like the sun anymore, and didn't like the way it kept saying her name, like a broken record. She wanted to be home. She wanted to be in her room.

Her eyes shot open and that was exactly where she was.

The first thing she noticed was her ceiling light and accompanying fan, which was casting each blade's shadow, long and slanted, across her off-white ceiling. A ceiling that had a varied wavy patterns that covered the top wall of her room like a tablecloth. Or a sky. Her bedroom rug hurt to lie on and she was sure that she would have an imprint of it on every part of her body it pressed against. Her clothes wouldn't stop that, they would just make it less pronounced. Her upper back, rear and heels were numb. The only part of her body pressed against the carpet that wasn't numb was her head. The back of her head, which felt far worse. She removed her arms from where they lay, forearms rising up to meet where her hands, right resting on left, draped across her stomach, and wiped a few beads of sweat from her forehead. She didn't know how she was sweating when her room was as cold as it was today but the evidence was on her palm.

It took an unfortunate and enormous amount of strength for her to lift her head up. It felt as though her brain had turned into wet cement and had completely hardened at the back of her head. She began to sit up and had to put her arms out behind her and prop her hands on the dirty, hard carpet to keep her from having to sit up straight. The cement pulled her head back and she yanked it forward again, and in doing so she met the worried eyes of Zoey Kay, perched at the edge of the bed and sticking her head out like a dog staring at a potential threat.

Dawn went first. "Hi." A long pause. Dawn decided to continue. "Zoey," she said apprehensively. "What's up? Why are you staring at me like that?"

Zoey sighed. "Jeez, don't scare me like that, Dawn. I thought you were going crazy or something."

The smile Dawn gave her confused Zoey, but it was something she desperately wanted to see so she offered one back.

"Not yet," Dawn said, still smiling.

Zoey saw her smile leave and her eyes squint and dart from left to right, although it was apparent she wasn't looking at anything in particular. Zoey was well informed on what this meant, after all they had been friends for years and Dawn did this "Zigzag Look," as Zoey liked to call it, very often.

She's thinking hard again, Zoey thought. *Why does she need to move her eyes like that though? It looks like they're trying to find a place to hide.*

As if in response, Dawn's eyes settled and turned right to Zoey's again.

Zoey pulled her leg up and rested her chin on her knee. "Whatcha thinking about?" she asked, eyebrows raised. Any number of responses could result from this question and that encompassing umbrella excited Zoey.

"How long—" Dawn slightly shook her head and looked down. "Do you know how long I was out for?"

Zoey took out her phone and Dawn saw Zoey's features light up a bit as the screen brightened her face. She could almost see her screensaver but it didn't matter. Dawn knew what it was; the two of them from that day last summer they went to the beach together. No adults tagging along, for the first time it was just them.

She stole her dad's keys. And I was the one who had to drive us there. Two hours on the road, traffic, wrong turns and we could barely find a place to park when we finally found it. She wrinkled her nose. *And the water, God that nasty damn red tide water. We weren't even planning on going in but that sealed the deal for sure. Ugh and it was windy and freezing, even though we went in July. What a nightmare!*

It was without a doubt one of the best days of her life.

"I think, like, fifteen minutes. That was when you laid down and when I started doing that thing you always say I do. When I talk a lot," Zoey said. "I stopped when I looked at you and saw you giving that hundred-yard stare. I tapped you with my foot."

She bent her toes up and down for emphasis.

"Waved my hand in front of your eyes."

Again, for visual aid, she brought her right hand to her eyes and waved it back and forth.

"And then I just started calling your name."

No action was needed to personify this step.

"I really didn't know what to do. I mean, you weren't even *blinking.* And then you called me your *son* and I don't know." She moved her arms up to her head and dropped them into her lap. A *who knows* gesture. "I guess I thought you were on some sort of drug." Zoey's shoulders jumped up to conceal her neck then fell back to where they were. "I mean, it's not *that* crazy to think right?"

Dawn realized she had been looking down and decided it would be a good idea to keep eye contact with Zoey, to prevent her from thinking she had zoned out again. Dawn's eyes slowly crawled up to meet Zoey's and as soon as she saw the bright hazel eyes that belonged to the most important person in her life, more than her other friends, more than her mom, more than her boyfriend, Dawn felt a wall of heat come up and wrap itself around her like a blanket despite how cold it was in her room.

"No, no it's not," Dawn said. She was fighting to keep her eyes on Zoey's and it was a fight she was losing. Zoey was beautiful, no doubt about that, but Dawn hated seeing her look so shaken and upset. She was afraid, probably on the verge of tears, and it was Dawn's fault.

"Sorry," she said and she noticed that her gaze was starting to drop from Zoey's eyes. From nose to chin, breasts, or more accurately, where her breasts came up, circled around and went back down her low cut shirt, belly button ring to the snowflake pattern on her leggings.

Come on, don't break the gaze! You can do it! Just climb back up Mount Zoey and get to those eyes! One body part at a time! You can do this! Just get to that sweet hazel sanctuary and we'll be fine! You can do this! You CAN do this.

No, I can't. It's over. We can't even see her anymore, we're at floor level again. Back to staring at this germ covered rug. I can't believe we were lying on that earlier. We need to get a vacuum in here sometime soon.

"Hey." Zoey got off the bed and kneeled down next to Dawn.

Dawn continued to keep her eyes locked to the floor. She put her right hand on Dawn's right cheek and turned her head to face her. It, surprisingly, didn't take as much effort as Zoey expected it to. Which almost made it worse.

"You have nothing to apologize for, okay? You didn't do anything wrong and I don't want you to feel like you did." Zoey's voice was stern but it was welcome.

It reminded Dawn of how a mother would talk to a child who thought they had done something bad. Dawn took Zoey's hand off of her cheek and interlocked their fingers. It was harder than it should have been. Zoey was wearing those long, fake fingernails that Dawn thought would make better spoons, but eventually their fingers were grasping each other's hands.

"Zoey, I'm sorry."

"Stop it!" This one wasn't stern, this was sympathetic.

"I know, I don't mean to." Dawn could feel her breathing quicken, and knew she would start tearing up if she kept talking. But that didn't stop her. "I just don't know what else to say."

She closed her eyes tight until the tear rolled out and down her cheek. It would do what they all did; travel down to her chin, hang there for a few seconds and drop off. But this one didn't. It didn't even make it near her mouth when Dawn felt something small and smooth stop the tear and wipe it away. She opened her eyes to one of Zoey's nails holding the tear. It hadn't even melted away yet, it was just sitting there, balancing on the plastic claw coming out of Zoey's finger. She looked at Dawn with her trademark smug grin.

Dawn knew what came next. Zoey had a comment she assumed would crack Dawn's miserable shell.

Dawn was correct. Knowing that Dawn wasn't crying for a legitimate reason, adding to the fact that Zoey was no longer scared of what might be happening to her, she was right back to her regular self.

"I know what to say." Zoey held up her hand with her tear catching fingernail extended. "Told you these nails were for more than just show."

Dawn smiled at her as she flicked the tear off to its terrible carpeted fate.

"Turns out they make good tear removers, too. Who would have thought? Let's just hope we won't have to use them for that purpose anytime soon."

I know I'll *certainly hope for that,* Zoey thought.

After scanning Dawn and making sure she was getting back to normal too, Zoey pulled her phone out of her pocket to check the time. Her parents had told her to be home by 9:00, but Zoey knew her parents better than that. She also knew what she could get away with (which are the two most dangerous things a teenager can know). Home at 9:00 to her parents meant home at 9:30 to her, and that was only if things were getting boring and she had no other choice. But they all agreed no later than 10:30. They told her it was because they would be afraid of where "their precious little girl" was, but Zoey knew it was really because they would both be asleep and didn't want to be woken up by her arrival. The lie was dirty, the fact that she knew them well enough to be able to see through it was even worse.

She had a feeling that if she ever arrived home an hour or two after her curfew, the house would be black and silent. The two of them would be shut out completely, unless her mother's insomnia decided to greet her again, and Zoey would walk to her room without a single noise or notice from either passed out parent. They may say something the next morning, her father certainly would, but they wouldn't be able to complain that night, they wouldn't be able to stay awake until she got home. They didn't care that much.

Or maybe they weren't lying. Maybe they would stay up, every light turned on, waiting for her to come home. *That would be even better,* she thought. Let them stay up if they wanted to. Then when she got home, the arguing could start sooner and end sooner. And she would really see just how frantic and scared she had made the two of them, if her mother really would be pacing the floor like she always told Zoey she would be, if all of the threats her father promised would really be dished out. She would learn why they were so worried or angry, most likely for making them stay up late instead of their fear of her being in danger, but she would learn just the same. And of course, though she didn't know she wanted this and would keep it a secret from herself if she did, them staying up and waiting for her and arguing with her when she finally showed her face meant that they were concerned. And they would have no idea how much that would mean to her. She herself would have no idea. Zoey would just walk in and argue with them until they gave up and she would go to bed, completely unaware of just how satisfied she was. And how happy.

She turned on her phone and never thought she would be so shocked and panicked to see her and Dawn on the beach.

"Son of a bitch!" She stood up.

"What? What's wrong?" Dawn mimed her motion.

"It's eleven oh-six," Zoey said and a feeling she was not very used to came over her.

Her stomach felt empty and her heart felt like it had grown five times its size. The beating and banging against her chest made her think it was about to pop right inside of her. It wouldn't really matter what time she got home then would it? Was it fear, or was it more shock that she had spent so much time with Dawn? Either way it gripped her throat and dug its teeth into her sensitive heart.

It was easy to roll her eyes at the threat of arriving past curfew when she always made it home on time. But now she was late and the instantaneous panic was just as confusing as it was unsettling.

"Really?" Dawn asked. "It seems like—"

"—Yes, well, whatever it seems like is just going to have to wait until tomorrow, okay?" She didn't wait for a response. "Good."

Dawn said, "All right, Zoey, calm down. I mean, they're your parents, what are they going to do? They can't hit you or anything, right?" *Please say right.*

Zoey paused for a moment and two vertical lines formed on the side of each eyebrow, just above her nose. Dawn was right, they *couldn't* do anything. Even if they were still awake, which was the case Zoey was now rooting for, what could they do to her that she'd actually be afraid of? That would actually make her life harder? She started to form a list in her head.

1. Ground her? Please, she was in her room more than any other part of the house. Whenever she wasn't at school or a friend's house that was where she would be. What kind of punishment is that?

2. Forbid her from seeing her boyfriend? This one nearly made her laugh out loud. They didn't know who she was dating. Hell, they didn't even know if she *was* dating. Which was ironic, considering she had done a whole lot more than "date" up in her room with a few special guys. And she knew there was far more important things in her life than the guy she was planning to pick next. She nearly squealed at the thought of them using that one.

3. Take away her car? That would be the worst outcome but even that one was only bad in concept. She had had her car for what, two months now? It wasn't exactly the most "up to date" car, unless 12 years old with a barely functional brake pedal was the most top of the line vehicle in existence, which seemed unlikely. Not to mention that Dawn brought her to school every day and Zoey could go weeks without driving with ease. That threat also wouldn't change very much.

Dawn had known Zoey long enough to know when not to talk to her. When she was thinking or angry. And right now Zoey's face told Dawn everything she needed to know. She was both. Dawn sat quietly on her bed and let Zoey finish riding this train of thought to wherever it was taking her. It was only when she heard her whisper something she couldn't quite make out that Dawn thought it might be safe for her to rejoin the conversation. And she did.

"What did you say?"

"Those...clever...bastards!" Zoey said, getting louder with each word.

Dawn didn't mind the volume. Her brother was out, fuck knows where, and her mom was passed out on the couch and could only be woken up if someone was jumping up and down on her face. Wearing cleats. Dawn may as well have been home alone. She looked at Zoey and the first thing that came into her mind was the only thing that needed to; *She's got that look in her eyes again.*

Zoey looked at Dawn and started from the top, her words coming and going as quickly as a blink. "You're right. They can't do shit to me! There isn't anything they can dish out that I can't handle. They scared me for no reason. What *is* the worst they can do?" She looked at Dawn and Dawn looked back with drab expectancy.

She's not done yet. Give her a second, Dawn thought.

She had also known Zoey long enough to know that whenever she went on one of her famous "Talking Sprees" the first pause was more about her catching her breath than it was about getting any actual feedback. What Dawn was supposed to do, what all of Zoey's friends were supposed to do whenever they found themselves in this situation, was let Zoey catch her breath and continue with whatever she was rambling on about. Once she paused a second time she would most likely be done and *then* came the time to actually talk to her and try to understand what she had said. And right now Dawn understood at least half of what Zoey was saying, which was a pretty damn good start.

"Ohmygod I can't believe I *fell* for that!"

There it is. One down, one to go.

Zoey's words shot out like bullets. "What *can* they do! Lock me in my room? I'mthereallthetimeanyway. Fuck with my love life? Theydon'tevenknowthatexistss. Take away my pieceofshit car? That doesn't change anything! AmIright?"

She had said piece of shit, but Dawn had heard pizza shit.

Not a long enough pause. She's still got some gas left in the tank.

"Now I *really* need to get home and foil this little scheme of theirs."

All right, that's long enough. She's done, it's safe now, Dawn thought. "So, you're going home?"

Zoey made a face that said, *Were you even paying attention?* (little did she know, the general consensus amongst her friends was that it would probably be easier to outrun a missile than it would be to figure out whatever information she was trying to convey during a "Talking Spree"). This time it was her who broke their gaze and started shooting her eyes around the room.

"Of course I am. That peaceful little house is gonna be blown into—" She looked at Dawn again and was suddenly brought back down to reality.

She sat next to her on the bed and put an arm around her back and a hand on her shoulder. "Well I don't have to leave *now*, I mean if you still need me I'll stay longer." She was hoping Dawn would tell her to go home. Dawn was her best friend and she held a bigger place in her heart for her than anybody else, but she really couldn't wait to come home and cause the power dynamic of her house to crumble to the ground. She was slightly shaking with excitement and anticipation and it was something Dawn took notice of.

Even though she would have preferred Zoey stay longer, though in truth she really would have preferred that Zoey never leave at all, Dawn knew she couldn't get that. She shook her head and put on a passive smile. Sometimes being a friend was putting your wants aside for theirs.

"Just go, Zoey. It's late, I'm exhausted and..." She scanned Zoey and grinned. "You're clearly teeming with happiness about the *idea* of going home. I'll be fine, now go and...rock the house or whatever you said you were going to do, all right?" She gave her a hug and Zoey hugged back.

It was the best feeling in the world for both of them. Interactions with their boyfriends, while some good but most sufficient at best, didn't compare at all to the warmth and love Dawn and Zoey felt when they wrapped their arms around each other. Whenever the two came together like this, the sense of belonging and feeling needed was almost palpable. Everything else melted away and all that remained were the two of them. Just them in each other's arms. Their heads nuzzled into the space between the others neck and left shoulder. The best place either one could be. And they ended every hug with their own special statements. The wedding vows of their friendship.

"I'm always here," Zoey said.

"No matter what," Dawn replied.

Zoey broke the hug and jumped up, not to Dawn's surprise. "All right, now I'd love to stay here but I have jaws to drop." She started for the door and stopped just as she had almost left. She looked back in the room where, maybe fifteen minutes before, she thought her best friend might lose her mind. It seemed so silly thinking about it now, but she still felt the unease hiding in her body just the same. "Bye."

"See you tomorrow," Dawn said through a fake smile. She wondered if Zoey would notice it and, for a second, it seemed like Zoey did, but the way she took off down the hall, down the stairs, through the door and into her car before Dawn could even drop the smile gave her a pretty clear answer.

Dawn was sure she'd hear all about whatever Zoey was planning on doing to her parents on their drive to school tomorrow (she wouldn't), but right now all that mattered was that she was alone. And that was the worst thing she could be. She hastily brushed her teeth, spitting the foamy toothpaste into the sink three times exactly, changed clothes, making sure to get her bra off as fast as she could. Her breasts were already bigger than she would like and she really didn't need these old small bras pressing them together and making them even more uncomfortable.

I'll go out and get some new ones eventually. Make sure they fit because, in this case, bigger is better.

But she couldn't go with Zoey. If there was one person who actively bought smaller sizes than she needed in order to look better, it was her. And that was the opposite of what Dawn needed right now. She turned off the ceiling light and her little sun died out. She climbed into bed, pulled the covers up, closed her eyes and let out one long breath as she let her muscles and brain relax.

Remember Sophia Wilkinson? Remember how she kicked your ass?

"Yet again," she said to the darkness, her top row of teeth welded to her bottom. "Yet a-fucking-gain."

Chapter 2

Zoey Kay drove home like she was trying to outrun a rockslide. People, buildings, trees and cars whipped by as her pitch black Honda Accord zoomed down Main Street. At this time of night there were barely any cars left on the road so Zoey didn't have a problem getting to her house. Oh, that house. She had never wanted to get there so fast in her life. That boring but now amazing place that held a couple too many adults who thought they were real sneaky in thinking they could pull one over on Miss Zoey Kay. She'd prove that wrong, oh yes indeed she would.

She was getting closer now, passing the elementary school, the library, the bank and all the while thinking about how empowering it would feel to prove her parents wrong. To watch their expressions change; to feel the power and control drain from them and flow into her as their harmless punishments bounced off of her skin and she walked away completely unharmed. She was experiencing it now, while she thought about it. She could sense it flowing through her body, through every nerve. Giving her that fantastic sensation of adrenaline pouring into her bloodstream and making her feel indestructible. She turned down her street and her car moved with the curves in the road until she made it to her house. Her wonderful, beautiful, soon to be very different house. She wasn't particularly confrontational, but she really couldn't wait to walk through that door and see how badly they argued with her.

And, her real subconscious motivation, to see how badly they cared for her.

But something wasn't right. Not at all. Both cars were in the driveway so her parents were *home*, but the house looked less lively. Then she noticed it and stomped on the brakes. It was hard enough so that anyone who wasn't prepared would certainly suffer from whiplash, but Zoey knew her car's brakes needed this harsh treatment. She learned within the first week of driving her car, that she had to step on the brake as hard as she could or it wouldn't stop for the next thirty feet. Just a slow grind that would come to an eventual halt. Like a train.

The house was dead. No warmth, no life, not one single light. It was completely dark. Not empty, but it was obvious no one was awake inside. "You're kidding. You're fucking kidding me," she said. Again she was oblivious to the volume her voice was rising to.

Now it was *her* jaw that hung open, not theirs. Not the two who tricked her into thinking she needed to come home by a certain time or she would suffer the consequences, but her herself. *She* had been tricked and that was the real bitch of it. She noticed her mouth and snapped it shut, hearing her teeth click as she did it. She turned off the car and got out, slamming the door.

Why bother being quiet now? Maybe I'll wake them up so they can realize I'm home late, she thought.

She walked up the front yard, ignoring the stepping stones her father had put in, leading from the front steps to the driveway, and trudged up to the front door. She put her hand on the doorknob and turned it, expecting to hear the click of the lock, but instead the knob turned and, with one eyebrow raised above the other, Zoey opened the door and stepped into a place that suddenly felt very unknown.

She walked into the kitchen, making sure to step lightly on the linoleum tiles. Although now it didn't matter. They were asleep and the fluctuation of power (as well as the acknowledgment of care) was going to have to wait for a future day. The linoleum became carpet as kitchen became hallway. Now it was smooth sailing down the hall and then to her room, where she could think about how this situation had fallen apart so quickly and so spectacularly.

It's honestly kind of impressive, Zoey thought.

But right before she made it into the hallway she heard the click she assumed she would hear from the doorknob, but it sounded different. It was more of a *flick* than a *click*. At the same time she heard this *flick* a light popped on behind her and lit the wall against her gray shadow. She spun around and the sight of her father made her jump back and smack her head against the wall the shadow of herself had just appeared on. She recovered, forcing herself not to think about the thudding she wanted to press her hands against, and glanced at her father, who got up from his seat by the light switch and looked at her in a way she was not familiar with. It wasn't anger or shame, two expressions she was *very* familiar with, this was more of a lustful vengeance. Something she now prayed she'd never become familiar with. The look made her stomach churn. All she wanted was for him to stay where he was and let her go to her room. Let her go to her room and forget that indescribable look. *Oh, that horrible look.*

There would be no acknowledgment of care tonight.

"Try not to make any more noise," Maxwell Kay muttered to his daughter. "Your mother is asleep."

He waited for the sarcastic remark he would often get from his much too egotistical child, and a few seconds later, he got what he was expecting.

Zoey scoffed and shook her head. "Yeah, well the only noise I made was because of you so…" She made sure 'you' went out of her mouth with the most venom it could carry. She turned to follow the hall to her room—

This isn't what I wanted. One won't be enough. Especially not if that one is him.

—and her father's voice, much clearer, firmer and louder, cut through the air like a guillotine; speeding towards her, ready to slice off her head in one fell swoop.

"Stop."

Zoey's head shot down an inch, as if ducking a blade, eyes closed tight and biting her bottom lip. It was hardly noticeable but it still made her scowl.

Mom definitely heard that. She must have. She'll be up too now, it's just a matter of time. She'll walk out of the bedroom, robe tied securely around her waist, rubbing her eyes, her hair a mess and come to my rescue.

What Zoey didn't know was that her mother had taken three Temazepam tablets before bed to help with her insomnia. She would be out for the entire night and no one was coming to Zoey's rescue. She'd have to do this alone. She circled around to face her father again and noted that he was getting up and walking towards her. Slowly.

"Where were you?" he asked, the lanky man getting gradually closer and taller. And as he walked farther and farther away from the light he had turned on, his features became more and more dark and shadowy.

"Dawn's house." Closer.

"Really? Until quarter past eleven?" Closer.

She did pride herself on how fast she got here, but she had to table that thought for now. Right now she had something else that needed her full attention, despite how much she didn't want to give it. She cleared her throat but didn't look him in the eyes. She didn't want to risk seeing that look again. She instead watched the rug. Much like her friend had done a half hour or so previous.

"Yeah, we had some stuff for English to work on and I guess I lost track of time." She peeked over at him and was taken aback by just how close he had gotten, less than a foot for sure. She tried to look him in the eyes to help convince him she was telling the truth, although it would have been a better idea to try that *while* she was talking as opposed to after, but what she saw when she looked at his face was merely a shadow. The light behind him lit up his outline but his visage remained hidden. Her eyes dropped to the ground.

"You got a boyfriend, Zoey?" her father asked, and it was clear from the tone of his voice that he didn't care about what the answer was. He had his own answer and was certain his was right. "Is there any one special guy for you right now?"

"No," Zoey responded quickly, saying it as if it were pronounced with two syllables. "I haven't had one since Eli." She looked up at the towering shadow, stone faced. "Remember that?" Another question that didn't require an answer. That memory was glued to her brain forever, whether she liked it or not.

She didn't understand why she reacted the way she did, maybe because he was her first, maybe because things hadn't gone on as long as she wanted them to and she had wanted to figure a few more things out and now couldn't. He was remarkably sweet and genuine, and almost had an air of femininity to him given his sensitivities and presence with her. She felt like she had consoled him far more often than he had her, but she had enjoyed that. And if she had known she wouldn't have a relationship like the one she had with Eli for months and years following, maybe she would have fought a little harder when he decided to sit her down and talk to her.

Regardless of the reason, regardless of the fact that at sixteen years old maybe she should have found a less dramatic way to react, after separating from her boyfriend of the past six months, Zoey had spent most of the day in her room crying. Her mother had spent some time consoling her but had to leave to make it to work on time. But before she left, she took her daughter's chin, picked up her head so she was at her eye level, and whispered the words *her* mother would tell her when she felt bad.

She looked into her daughter's puffy, wet, yet beautiful golden eyes and said, "You're better than you think and stronger than you know."

She wiped away the most recent tear that had escaped Zoey's eye, kissed her forehead and hugged her. Zoey watched her mom leave her room, and immediately felt more deserted. She buried her face in between her knees and began to sob again, still not precisely aware of why she was doing it. It wasn't like she had really loved Eli. She only stopped when she heard her father's voice. But she stopped out of confusion.

She didn't even realize he had skulked over to her room, she simply heard his voice, cold and monotone, say, "You're going to have to get used to this if you keep acting the way you do."

She raised her head from its hiding place between her knees and looked at him, standing in the doorway, leaning against where the door's lock clicked, hands in his pockets. And the static, unemotional face of someone she loved that looked back at her almost made her cry harder than anything. Zoey didn't think of herself as overdramatic and, even though she didn't quite understand why she was taking this so hard, she knew that in this situation she should be given a bit of a pass for an overly emotional response. But instead of screaming at him or accusing him or getting violent, she cleared her throat, inhaled sharply and asked, "Acting how? *How* do I act?"

Having a scapegoat to send her anger felt good, but what followed did not.

Her father looked down at her body (she could swear she heard him sigh), and back up to meet her eyes. He said, "I think you know. There's a reason why guys really want you. And I think you know exactly what it is."

And without looking at her again, he backed into the hallway and closed the door. Zoey looked down at herself, feeling even worse than before, and wrapped herself in a blanket. She didn't think about Eli for the rest of that day, or any day after.

Until today.

"So you say you were at Dawn's?" her father asked, ignoring her previous question.

Zoey's jaw tightened. "Yes." It was half a word and half a breath.

"It was just me and her."

Her father took a few steps back. Now she could at least see his left eye in the light. That was all she could see but she never took her eyes off it. She watched it scan her body, down to her shoes and start back up, stopping momentarily on her breasts, and ending where they started; on her eyes. Almost *through* her eyes.

"Right," the tall shadow croaked.

Zoey could have reached out and grabbed the disbelief if she wanted to. He walked past her and started down the hall, only stopping once.

"Shut off the light before you leave." He walked into the bedroom his wife was still fast asleep in, and closed the door gently behind him.

Zoey worked up the strength and fought back the urge to shut off the light without smashing it, and mirrored her father's actions; walking down the hallway, quicker than he had, and closing her bedroom door as soon as she was inside. Again, doing this much faster than her father had. The only thing she did that he didn't do was lock the door, and that was of great importance. She would make sure that door stayed locked.

She stared at the door, specifically at the turned lock, and slightly shook her head, wanting to scoff but not finding the breath to do so. *He would never hurt me. He would never do something like that. Or something worse.*

The other side of her mouth responded, quick and curt. *You're sure? You are absolutely, one hundred percent certain of that?*

She said and thought nothing. The lack of a response gave her chills.

Without letting another moment pass, she crawled into bed and buried her face in her pillow. She'd change clothes tomorrow morning. The last thing she wanted to do now was take off anything. She was hoping she'd fall asleep soon but she knew you could never tell when that was going to happen. You simply stood on the edge of the chasm, swaying back and forth, until the strength left you completely and you dropped off the edge of conscious thought and fell into the wonderful middle ground of sleep. Not consciousness but not quite unconscious either, it was the slim yet ever expanding area that separated the awake from the unreachable.

Zoey was there in minutes.

Chapter 3

Her phone's obnoxious preset alarm and screen, brightly illuminating the once dark room when turned on, awoke Dawn from her slumber with harsh, unpleasant thoughts swimming through her head. Her hours of peace were over, at least for now, and it was time for her to carry on living her life. She hit STOP on her alarm and, upon even glancing at her screen, pinched her eyes together with her thumb and index finger. It felt like she had switched on a flashlight and shone the light directly into her eyes. The next step was to turn down the brightness, which she did with no hesitation, and begin getting ready. She glanced down at her phone through numerous blinks in an attempt to get her vision back, and saw the time; 5:00.

All right, good, she thought, *but I need to start now so it can last as long as possible. The second alarm is going off at six, I still need to be ready to leave by seven and that monster takes about an hour all by itself.* She pushed her covers aside, sat down on the floor, back held straight against the bed stand, and began her morning meditation.

This was something she made sure to keep to herself, she didn't need anyone thinking she was some sort of hippie. Because she wasn't. She didn't light an incense and breathe in the smoke, sitting in lotus position and holding her thumb and index finger together with the other three stretched out, continuously speaking some kind of mantra or saying, "Ohhhmmmm" like she saw in movies and TV shows. She simply took a seat on her still yet to be vacuumed carpet, legs crossed, back straightened and took long, slow breaths. It was a time for her to unwind, think and get a clear image of the day she was about to encounter.

On the rarest of occasions she thought that she heard things, but she assumed it was as unimportant as her dreams, just her brain filtering through her thoughts and clearing out what wasn't needed.

Let's see, gym is first, and we'll probably play indoor soccer again. Just stay out of everyone's way and if you manage to touch the ball, make sure you kick it as far away from yourself as you can before you get trampled to death. Then it's algebra. Pretty sure we have that test on the quadratic equation today but I know it well enough. Let's make sure to look at our notes beforehand, just to be safe.

She could feel the world she was surrounded by start fading away, as it often did when she meditated. She continued on, a small smile starting to form.

Next is history.

The smile died.

Most likely going to be another forty-five minutes of listening and doing nothing. Just daydream or something to keep from having a mental breakdown. Long period is ceramics.

And the smile was resurrected, longer this time.

An hour and a half of nothing but talking to Zoey, Steph (not Stephanie, she hated when people called her Stephanie), *and Luke.*

The thought of her two best friends and boyfriend being in her favorite class with her made the smile stretch and she felt herself begin to rise; begin to float upward.

What are we making this time? The, uhhhhmmm... the bowl! That's it! The bowl! Oh, I'm basically finished with that already. Now it really IS an hour and a half of talking. Jus pretend to work whenever Ms. Prinn comes by. Then we've got science. I think we're doing a lab but you're gonna have to wait until you have the class to find out. Can't fucking remember. And then last period is... what was it? Uhhhh it was... dammit! Ummmm....

But it was too late, she was gone. She had floated miles above her body, her house, even the world. She felt weightless; she had become a balloon, going higher and higher, leaving everything behind, with no end in sight. She used to wonder where her meditation took her, where exactly she was, but eventually she figured it out. Or, rather, she came about as close as she could manage to figuring it out, given the fact that she didn't particularly care anymore. As far as she was concerned, she was among the stars now; the wonderful, quiet emptiness of space. She was in love with it. It was only her. No responsibilities, no people, no noise. She heard herself sigh, breathing out all of the toxicity that came from the world she once belonged to. She could stay here and continue to float against the black sheet that covered everything she saw, for as long as she wanted. She saw herself, rising in this dark sanctum, closing her eyes and giving herself up to it. Giving herself

—BEEP BEEP BEEP BEEP—

Her beautiful, empty paradise shattered like glass all around her. She began plummeting back to earth, through the atmosphere, through the roof of her house and rocketing back into her body. Her eyes snapped open and she jerked back upright, having started leaning to the right with drool leaking out of the corner of her mouth. She snatched her phone, turned off that goddamn alarm and checked to see how she was doing on time. It was 6:00, right on schedule. It was time to begin the laborious process of getting ready. She cringed in the dark at the thought. Time seemed to speed up when she meditated.

After what seemed like two days of brushing her teeth, getting dressed, brushing her blonde, ratty hair into the smooth, wavy version she was a much bigger fan of, pulling the locks of hair from her brush and throwing them in the trash and finally putting on, contouring and layering her makeup properly, powering through the pins and needles her feet were experiencing because of the way she sat while applying it, she was ready to leave.

She stood up, ignoring the pain from her feet, and turned to look at herself in her full body mirror, purposely standing sideways and arching her back to get a better view of the certain parts of her anatomy she liked to add a little something to. Nothing big, but maybe she would put on underwear that was a little more cheeky than the other pairs she owned. She only did it for Luke, and maybe just a tiny bit for herself, but she liked to make him happy. Pulling up her jeans and watching them jump back down and bounce a little immensely satisfied her, maybe more so than it should have.

She wouldn't be able to handle looking at herself in the mirror tomorrow.

Despite what she would tell people, Dawn liked how she looked. She would never brag or show it off, but she was happy with how she turned out. From her hair that resembled wavy lasagna sheets, down to her dainty size six feet. She loved everything except for her nose. God she *hated* her nose. Protruding from her face and looking more like a forty-five degree angle than a natural part of someone's appearance, it was the one thing that would always keep her from looking, in her opinion, perfect. And she could never get rid of it. She had put a considerable amount of thought into certain procedures to eliminate as much of it as possible, rhinoplasty being the one she thought about most often, but the cost was larger than that of her car, so she decided to live with what she had. Whether she liked it or not. She stepped away from the mirror, grabbed her bag and headed out of her room and into the rest of her house.

She passed her brother's room, not stopping to check if he was there. She knew he wasn't. He should be, but he wasn't. In passing through the living room she was met with another unhelpful family member; her mother, who lay in the exact same spot on the couch she had been on for so long before. Dawn looked at her for an indeterminate amount of time, not thinking very much nor moving very much, simply staring. She didn't know if anyone thought differently but she found no similarities between her face and that of her mother's. And she didn't know whether to be happy about that or not. She looked away, feeling like she had to rip her eyes away from her mother's limp body, then quickly grabbed her keys, went down the stairs, and out the front door. The February air was cold and sharp, but Dawn didn't mind. She liked the feeling of the icy air on her warm skin. She got in her car, made the engine growl and drove off to pick up Zoey, an imaginary chain loosening around her neck with each passing foot she put between herself and her house until it fell off completely, clattering against the cement.

But it would be back. Dawn knew that. A bitter taste in her mouth grew, although she hadn't eaten anything yet. It would wrap back around her throat and drag her back as soon as she got close enough. But, for now, she was getting farther and farther away and the chain got smaller and smaller every second.

It was 7:00, her schedule still being followed to the minute.

She pulled up in front of Zoey's house about fifteen minutes later, the chain now a forgotten memory, and texted her the same text she sent every time she picked her up: *I'm outside.* And Zoey sent back the same text she always responded with: *On my way.* To pass the time, Dawn decided to look into her rear-view mirrors to check if anything was out of place on the outside of her car. She was still checking the blue exterior when she heard the passenger's door open, felt the weight dip slightly to the right, and heard the door close shut.

"How do I look?" she heard the voice ask. It was wonderful to hear her again.

Dawn frowned and her eyebrows came together. It wasn't very often that Zoey asked for Dawn's opinion on what she wore, her own judgement was more than enough for her when it came to that topic.

Still looking in the mirror and examining the car she asked, "What do you me—" She turned to look at Zoey and got the answer to the question she hadn't even finished asking.

Dawn started with Zoey's straight, shiny black hair and followed it down to her neck, like a slide covered in a smooth layer of tar. Zoey wore a thin black choker around her neck, a harmless fashion accessory but one Dawn had always found to be a little strange, bordering on kinky. Below it, her breasts looked as if they were trying to jump out of her skintight, black crop top. This one wasn't low cut, it was severed from her shoulders completely, showing every inch of skin from the half circles bulging out of the top of her shirt, to her choker that suddenly looked far higher than it had appeared before. Her belly button ring gleamed against the small amount of light the sun gave it and her dark blue jean short shorts looked like they hurt to wear. Rips in them, before they were cut off mere inches under her waistband, revealed thick, tanned skin that was practically oozing out of every space they could find. It wasn't an outfit Dawn favored, and definitely not something she would ever wear (Luke's happiness as well as her own weren't worth her legs going numb and possible frostbite taking off her arms), but she knew Zoey and even though it was a bit much, even for her, Dawn read her expression and knew she wasn't going back in to change.

"Wow."

"Do you like it?" As if it would matter.

"You look great," Dawn said cheerfully. She chose to answer Zoey's first question rather than the one most recently posed to her. "What made you wear that today?" She nodded her head at Zoey's body to imply she was referring to the entire outfit, there was no individual thing. This was a perfect storm and every element was needed to get the optimum outcome.

Zoey said, "Brandon," and the inflection she gave the word made it sound important, which made Dawn look away. She started doing her "Zigzag Look" and when she turned back to Zoey she had stopped smiling. Her mouth had become a perfect horizontal line with her eyebrows raised and eyes half open.

Dawn shook her head. "Brandon?"

"We were talking about him last night, remember? Brandon Finley?" Zoey hoped the name would register in Dawn's mind but it was also when she started talking about Brandon last night that she had thought Dawn had started zoning out. The continued "Zigzag Look" Dawn wore made her certain of her theory. "I think you had zoned by the time I started mentioning him," she added helpfully.

Dawn looked at her steering wheel and slightly tilted her head to one side. *That wouldn't be surprising,* she thought.

She had trained herself to be able to "Power Down" (a saying she liked much more than zone out) whenever Zoey started to talk about guys, whether it was the ones she was with or the ones she *wanted* to be with. She didn't talk about it often, thankfully for Dawn, but it was still something she didn't need Dawn to be there for. It was more like she was thinking out loud, and she always came to the conclusions herself. Dawn simply found out how to tune it out one day, and had done so ever since. She got to think and Zoey got to express her thoughts without anyone interrupting her. They both got what they wanted.

"That's likely," Dawn said, smirking, as she put her car in drive and accelerated down the street. They still had two more people to pick up and she wanted to make it to school on time.

"Well," Zoey said, a hint of slyness in her voice, "he plays on the school's football team. Not now, obviously, but when it's in season he does. Anyway, I've been dropping hints that I'm into him but he hasn't made a move yet."

Dawn nodded and kept her eyes wide, focusing on the road.

"So hopefully this will act as a little extra incentive for him. The ball is in his court now."

"You really like him? You think this'll work?" Dawn asked, although the answer was clear as day.

Zoey's eyebrows became two slanted j's, sliding down above her eyes and slightly curving up at the ends. "You think it *won't?*"

It was a question that was phrased more as a statement. Dawn didn't answer.

"Come on, have some faith in me. I know what I'm doing."

Dawn knew that. That was the problem. She also knew that Zoey had chosen, much as she herself had done, to answer one question and conveniently ignore the other.

Zoey shifted positions and sat on her left leg. "Do your thongs ever get uncomfortable?"

To anyone else, a question like that would be confusing or alarming, but Dawn was used to questions like this from Zoey. She barely batted an eye. "I don't wear thongs." She occasionally would get a little risky, like she was today, but never that far.

Zoey's head whirled to face her. "Seriously?"

Dawn could feel the utter perplexity in her voice and she decided to humor her. "I don't need to, I've got Luke. I don't have anyone to show off for."

She barely got to finish her sentence before Zoey's voice drowned her out.

"Honey, that's exactly who you show off for."

Dawn shrugged, hoping things wouldn't get any deeper than this. As worthwhile as this wonderful conversation was, she really didn't need this turning into an argument. "Maybe for you, but I've never found a reason to wear one. Probably never will."

There was a short pause before Zoey sparked the conversation again, thankfully no longer interested in underwear. "What class is long today?"

Dawn thought back to her morning meditation. The memory made her smile and the recollection of the class the two had long that day only made it grow. "Ceramics."

"*Fuck!*" Zoey shouted and Dawn's car shook from side to side for the next few seconds as she tried to get it back in the right lane and, more importantly, recover from the temporary ringing in her right ear.

After Dawn finished leveling out the car she gave Zoey a quick glance, but it wasn't actually to look at her. It was more to see if she had fatally injured herself or something else that would warrant such a response. She was completely unharmed, which annoyed Dawn even more.

"Jesus, Zoey, what was that?"

"Sorry, I'm just getting tired of Prinn. Like, I finished the stupid bowl, back off. I'll start the next assignment when *I* want to."

"I don't think it works that way. Oh, we're here," Dawn said excitedly as they pulled up in front of Luke's house and beeped the horn.

Zoey, upon hearing the horn, opened her door, got out, and hopped into the back, sitting diagonal from Dawn.

Dawn twisted her body to look at her, grateful that Zoey knew to do it on her own. "Thank you," she said.

Zoey smiled at her and noticed Dawn's gaze shift and her face change into an expression quite different. Without moving an inch,

Zoey knew Luke had left the house and was walking to the car. And a few seconds later, the door swung open and he entered it.

"Hey," Luke Bradley said to the blonde haired, blue eyed beauty who had made his last few months the best of his life.

He leaned toward her, lips puckered and was immensely satisfied to see her doing the same. They met each other halfway and gave each other one long kiss, which gave him a feeling unlike anything he'd ever experienced. Except maybe for the time he was 10 when he accidentally broke a window of his grandmother's house with a rock he was trying to get to land on the roof. The shock to his body mixed with the instinct to act fast was the closest thing he could compare to the way Dawn made him feel. And even *that* wasn't doing her full justice. The sensation of her warm hand brushing against his dark skin made him want to stay with her forever. It was perfection, or at least, what he defined perfection as in his very limited experience. His perfection, however, didn't last too long and it only took one female's voice to eliminate it entirely, for the time being.

"Awwwww," Zoey's voice seemed to echo through the car, "you guys are so *keee-yoot* together."

The two had forgotten they had a certain someone else in the backseat, watching them like a child watches an IMAX screen; eyes wide, mouth open, fists clenched tightly together against their chin. Or, rather, they had forgotten just how vocal and unabashed she was. Neither of them knew how sincere Zoey was being but they both knew she wouldn't tell them if they asked.

"And there she is, right on cue," Dawn said.

"Yeah, I walked into that one," he responded. He cleared his throat and turned his head sideways to look at her through the corner of his eye. "What's up Zoey?"

"Hey, Luke," she said, intentionally drawing each word out for a few seconds longer than she needed to. "Do you taste anything different on Dawn's lips?" Her goofy smile looked like it would split her face open.

Luckily for Dawn, Luke was comfortable enough with Zoey to expect these kinds of comments from her and he knew exactly how to get around them.

"I'm good, thanks," he replied smugly.

Dawn, again, put the stick that separated her and Luke into drive and headed toward the final passenger's home. It was 7:30. They had half an hour before school started.

The ride to Steph's house was significantly shorter than the length it took to get to the previous destinations and a few minutes after pulling away from Luke's front yard, the trio had pulled up in front of Steph's and Dawn honked the horn again. She only texted Zoey. Everyone else got the horn. A few seconds later Steph (not Stephanie) Warren left her house, not bothering to make sure the door was locked, and headed towards the car that belonged to her amazing friends. She didn't wait for them to begin the greetings.

"Morning, Dawn."

"Morning, Steph."

"Morning, Zoey." *You're gonna freeze to death wearing that.*

"Hey, Steph."

"Morning, Luke."

"What's up, Steph."

Once Steph was seated and buckled in Dawn, for the fourth time in thirty-five minutes, pushed the stick to drive and the four headed off to school. The peaceful silence was, yet again, ended by Zoey.

"Luke are you aware that Dawn doesn't wear thongs?"

"Zoey!" Dawn snapped.

"Sorry, but you know you'd do the same for me."

"I most definitely would *not*!"

"What're you talking about?" Luke asked, eyebrows raised and eyes locked on Dawn's. If he didn't see her blush before, he'd have to be blind to miss it now.

"Your girlfriend here told me—"

"—In *confidence!*" Dawn growled through clenched teeth.

"I'm plenty confident. Anyway, she told me that she doesn't wear thongs because she doesn't want to show off for you."

"I said I didn't *need* to...show off...for...him," Dawn retorted, her voice getting smaller with each word said, until eventually "him" was nothing more than a barely audible mumble.

Zoey continued. "What do *you* think about that, Luke? Don't you agree if someone is gifted with an ass like Dawn's, that they should use it to their advantage as much as possible?"

Dawn needed backup to get her out of this conversation. "Steph," she whined.

Steph kept her eyes glued to the world passing by. "I'm not getting involved in this. You three just keep talking." But she could never truly remain unbiased. "And honestly, Dawn, wouldn't it be more embarrassing for you if Zoey told Luke you *did* wear thongs? I'm just saying."

"Yes, thank you. See, Dawn, Steph gets it. I'm only trying to help." Her voice sounded innocent, but Dawn knew of the hundreds of words one could use to describe Zoey Kay, innocent was far from the most accurate.

Dawn gave her the fakest smile she could make as they pulled into a parking spot next to R.I High School. She turned off the car and turned to face her favorite person on Earth. "Do me a favor, will you? Try less." She got out of the car and the rest followed suit.

While most people their age dreaded going to school, Dawn, Zoey and Steph didn't mind so much. Dawn liked being anywhere outside of her house, Zoey loved getting attention and saw school as a useful vehicle to obtain it, and Steph liked to learn and found a lot of joy in doing it. If they had known what would await them less than ten minutes after entering the building, Dawn would have stopped them where they stood and taken them all back home.

Once they pushed through the double doors that led into the school, the four knew exactly where they were going without having to even look at one another. They'd go to where they always stood in the morning before the bell; right by the doors to the gym. It was the perfect place for all of them. Everyone passed by there on their way through the school when they didn't want to wait in home room, so Dawn and Steph could say hi to their other friends, who didn't stand with the three, Zoey got to chat with the guys who went into the gym for a little quick practice before the school day had to start and Luke was one of the guys who got in some early practice as often as he could. Especially with football season months away, he needed all the exercise he could get. Except for today. Today he had to go see Mr. Shaw and talk with him about his grades. He tried his hardest, but still couldn't get a firm grasp on chemistry. The entire science seemed to elude him. He bid farewell to Dawn and gave her another set of kisses which, again, was interrupted before it could even get started. For the two of them time might have felt as if it had slowed down, but for Zoey and Steph it dragged like an anchor.

"Okay!" Zoey said.

And Dawn pulled her soft, wet lips off of Luke's and turned them, with assistance from her arched eyebrows, into a hard, dry glare aimed at the walking interruption. Ending their physical farewell meant that Dawn could drop back to her normal height and it was nice to not be on her tiptoes, which she always had to be whenever she kissed Luke given their six inch height difference, but that slight ease didn't cheer her up too much. For some reason, Zoey had little patience when it came to Dawn kissing Luke beyond a little smooch.

"Bye," she heard Luke say and she turned to see him walking down the hall, creating more horrible empty space between the two of them.

She opened her mouth and closed it just as quickly. He wouldn't have heard anything she chose to say. She turned her glare back to Zoey who put her arms up defensively.

"Sorry to break it up but when you start going at it with him you don't stop until someone intervenes. And that's my job."

Besides it's just a phase, she thought. *You'll get tired of it. Everyone does eventually. Usually it stops after a couple weeks, though. I've never seen it remain this strong after four months. There's got to be something really special in those lips.*

Steph laughed and Dawn's glare, as well as whatever irritation she felt, disappeared. The routine had been followed and they were exactly where they needed to be; standing against the wall to the right of the gym's main door. Seeing other friends, chatting with each other, even standing in the same positions. Steph with her hands in her pockets, Zoey with her arms crossed tight below her chest (it didn't take a genius to figure out why), and Dawn holding her left elbow with her right hand. For one moment everything just *fit*. Everything felt *right*.

That moment was fleeting.

Zoey felt a force that almost seemed like a wall, slam against the back of her left shoulder and knock her into Steph. Steph caught her and propped her back onto her feet, seemingly with no effort whatsoever. Zoey's shoulder now pounded with pain she chose not to show and she looked in the direction of the, had to be, door that nearly sent her sprawling to the ground and was met with the terrifying, sinister glare that belonged to Amy Cooper.

Now *this* was a glare. Eyebrows almost twitching, skin coming together in perfect, hateful harmony, mouth that curved up and down in just the right places to perfectly speak one word; Disgust. And eyes that made Zoey feel like she was less than dirt. Eyes that were darker than dirt, darker than night. Eyes of metallic coal that fueled Hell's eternal fire. This made Dawn's glare look safe and loving. Zoey felt herself suck in a breath which made her shoulder pound harder. Suddenly a swinging door didn't seem all that bad. It became welcoming the more she thought about it.

"What did you *hit* me with?" Zoey demanded, staring into the girl's hands and seeing nothing but closed fists.

She thought she saw something that almost looked like a smile cross Amy's face but it passed before she could consider it. Besides, it couldn't have been. In the ten years she had known her, she had never seen Amy Cooper smile. Not once.

Amy backed up a foot or two so she, along with her boyfriend Evan Mitchell, the only person on the planet who she offered any level of respect, could get a better view of the three worthless sacks of flesh parading as humans. The Slut, The Black One and her favorite. The Slut was who she focused on first. She had asked her a question after all and Amy wanted to give her an answer. She licked her lips and snarled, "I *bumped* you. With my shoulder."

Yeah you should *look confused. You* are *that weak. I know* I *was confused when you launched your nasty body five feet away after I embarrassed myself by touching it. Confused but certainly not surprised.*

She looked down at Zoey's breasts and felt a powerful urge to rip them off of her, but pulled it together and kept going. "Why don't you take your cum covered ass back home to the strip club? You won't have to worry about falling down then, will you?"

If you answer that question, I swear I'll push the bone in your nose straight into your barely functioning brain. As deep as it can go.

Zoey didn't answer.

Good little whore.

She moved on to the next girl in the row.

Amy could feel the want, the *need*, the *urge*, the *drive* to hit her coming from The Black One. It was a feeling that was nearly overpowering. She used to fight against it too, in a time that seemed like decades ago, but one day she let it consume her and never regretted it. The want was pouring out of her and Amy smelled it. Smelled it and used it. She moved closer.

"Hit me. I dare you."

My god you're practically shaking aren't you? You can't hide it, I can see it. And feel it. The need to lash out is boiling beneath the surface of your skin. Just like it was for me. Allow me to turn the heat up.

"Come on, you think you're tough? Then prove it, bitch."

You can't. You can't and you won't.

Then she noticed something that she found to be simply delicious. "Oh, look at that cute little glare," her voice's light and jovial tone acting opposite her callous expression. "You think that scares me? That's nothing. *You're* nothing."

She shifted her deadly eyes to the next one waiting in line. She was Amy's favorite, and Amy loved playing with her more than anyone else. She got even closer, now practically standing on Dawn's toes.

Dawn would sooner rip her hair out, strand by strand, then break off from the harmless white panels that lined the school floor and look at Amy, but she knew she had to at some point. Amy had done far worse to people who had done far less to her.

But Amy didn't want Dawn to look her in the eyes. That would spoil the fun.

Amy looked down at her, the closest to showing a smile in public she had been in a long time though it didn't remotely show on her face, and asked the trembling girl one question she didn't want an answer to.

"You ready to look me in the eyes yet, Poodle?"

She had become so used to this nickname to describe the girl's wavy fluffy hair, slim face and long snout of a nose that she had forgotten what the girl's name actually was. She didn't mind though, she liked "Poodle" a lot more. Poodle was silent and her eyes stayed looking where they were.

"Good. Let's keep it that way." Amy backed up to admire her handiwork and all she saw were a few pathetic, little worms wriggling hopelessly in the burning sunlight, desperate for any water, that could help bring them back to life. But Amy was their sun, and she would make sure this drought lasted an eternity. She turned to leave and, brushing her fiery orange locks of hair out of her eyes and tucking them behind her ears, took Evan's hand and led him down the hall to find more unwilling prey her predatory senses could hunt down. *Let the worms have a few drops. At least for now.*

As soon as she was out of sight, the worms used every last ounce of them.

Dawn saw Steph move towards the two and she shot out her hand

and grabbed Steph's wrist, as instinctual as flinching at a loud noise or covering your face when something is coming towards it. "Just let them go, okay? It's safer that way."

"I'm not afraid of him. Or her," Steph grumbled, pulling her wrist out of Dawn's snakelike grip.

Dawn heard the uncertainty behind Steph's voice but chose to ignore it. "I know you're not afraid, but you are smart. You know it's better to leave it be."

"It's not fair."

"I know it's not."

"She's asking for it."

"I'm sure she is," Dawn responded calmly, "but you know what she's capable of. And I don't want anything bad to happen to you. That would be on me." She motioned her head toward Zoey. "On *both* of us."

Zoey patted Steph on the shoulder. "Yeah you don't want to end up like Kaitlin Simon. Remember that?" she asked as if any of them didn't. As if anyone in the school didn't.

At the beginning of the year, less than one week in, the three of them were in their English class, which also housed Kaitlin, Evan and Amy. Kaitlin had always been a talker, though she oftentimes had very little to say. Apparently Kaitlin's talking was too much for Amy to handle and Amy was not the kind of person who could simply count to ten and take in a few deep breaths to calm herself down. As far as anyone was aware, there was no way to calm Amy down. So Kaitlin had continued to talk about a topic no one would even remember by the time that class was over and Amy silently got to her feet and made her way towards her, nearly floating from the right side of the room to the front, where Kaitlin sat. Some might have noticed, some might have known where things were going, but no one said anything. Everyone just hoped she would take it easy on her. They all knew if you got in Amy's way, you were the next in line. And Evan simply watched her go. He didn't even look at her as she got up.

Kaitlin was cut off mid sentence and her story was abruptly ended by Amy throwing her out of her chair, pinning her down with just her legs and pounding and slamming her fists down on her face while Kaitlin cried and begged for Amy to stop. Everyone, Dawn, Zoey and Steph included, was forced to stare as Kaitlin's blood poured onto the floor of the classroom. Their teacher had tried her hardest to remove

Amy but even when she attempted to pick her up, Amy would not budge nor stop until the dean came in and carried her away, using an unsettling amount of effort. Kaitlin was rushed to the hospital with a bloody, broken nose and a swollen, puffy black eye and Amy was sent home for ten days. As if that would be enough. If anything Amy came back worse. And Kaitlin didn't come back at all. Better, less dangerous schools existed for her.

She remembered the scenario with far too much clarity, but Dawn especially remembered how Evan just sat there and did nothing. He sat there and let Amy wail on Kaitlin. As if he had no other choice, as if he was just passing the time. Just another day at the office.

Dawn shuttered as the nightmare fueled memory surged back into her mind. Steph closed her eyes and tilted her head down, attempting to hide the tear that was trying to reveal itself. *I'm sorry, Amy, please!* Steph could still hear the shill, shrieking voice of the girl who was getting her face beaten in and couldn't even move. *I'm sorry, Amy, please!* That was the last thing Steph heard her say. *I'm sorry, Amy, please!* Over and over and over. *I'm sorry, Amy, please!* She heard it echo through her head every so often, like someone screaming into an empty, seemingly endless, cave. *I'm sorry, Amy, please!*

"What's her fucking *problem* with us?" Zoey asked while rubbing her shoulder. She didn't like how her friends looked now and decided to move the conversation away from Kaitlin. It worked.

Steph gave a small grunt and responded. "Simple. The bitch is crazy. As for us?" She sighed. "You never know who she'll target next, you just get down and hope it's not you. We got down this time, like always, but this time we weren't lucky. This time we were noticed. We just have to wait it out, wait for her to move on to someone else."

Zoey squinted, a physical manifestation of her thought process at work. "Yeah, but is it just me or were there a couple less psychopaths with Evan and Amy than there usually are?"

The three stood there looking at each other, all silently refusing to speak the remaining two names. Dawn eventually gave up, closed her eyes and spoke the names of the two they were all thinking of. "Heather and Trevor."

Zoey made a face that looked like the words insulted her. "Yeah. *Them.*" An appalling thought rose high above her and crushed Zoey into the ground. "And when we have English tomorrow we're going to have to deal with the four of them first thing in the morning." She felt air leave through her mouth and thought she might deflate right then and there.

"What a great way to start the day," Steph said, almost spitting the words out of her mouth.

The bell rang, meaning it was seven fifty-five. They had five minutes to get to home room or they'd be marked as late. Steph took notice of this, gave Dawn and Zoey a hug goodbye and left to get to her home room on the other side of the school. She made it through the door with seconds to spare.

The day moved by pretty fast, as it often did for Steph. When you liked to learn, the school day was oftentimes over in the blink of an eye. And a particular event made the last class of the day whiz by even faster. Her drawing 2 teacher had called Steph up to her desk a few minutes before class was over and showed her a drawing she had done of a teakettle placed in between a few cups and bowls earlier in the year.

"What about it?" Steph asked, a bit confused, extremely thrilled and a little scared.

"This is good. This is *really* good," her drawing teacher, Mrs. Clifford, told her. "I think you could have a future in this."

She wanted her words to have an impact on Stephanie. Far too often her students told her they'd peruse an art field, before dropping it and ignoring their calling all together. She didn't want that to happen to Stephanie. But, since it seemed like Stephanie was self-conscious about her own name, there was no telling what other self-esteem issues she could be facing, including an inability to believe that compliments posed to her were legitimate. She knew she'd have to get her message through to Stephanie and getting her to understand what she wanted from her. And Mrs. Clifford knew how to do it.

Steph saw her open her bottom left drawer and take out a paper she hadn't seen before. Mrs. Clifford waved the paper in front of her face and said, "This is an application for an arts internship taking place over the summer. A few different things, actually. Not just sitting and sketching, there's some museum work and events to help put on. I want you to take this home, read it over, have a parent sign it, and bring it back to me, where we can discuss it further."

Steph was overjoyed, without the words adequate enough to express that. "Wow, okay, thank you. Thank you so much. I will. I absolutely will."

Melody Clifford smiled. All of a sudden it seemed absurd to think that Stephanie would feel self-conscious about anything, much less her art. "I look forward to continuing this conversation. Remember though, a parent needs to sign it. If you're not eighteen a parent needs to agree to let you do this. It can't just be the two of us. And it needs to happen today, I'll need the paper signed by tomorrow. It's a competitive internship and the deadline is already getting too close as it is. I'm sorry it took so long to give this to you, it took me weeks to get them to send me any applications at all, but this last piece really showed me what you're capable of. Do you think you can get that signed today?"

Steph's smile widened, "My mom gets out at one o'clock. She'll be home when I get there and I *know* she'll approve of this."

The ball rang and the day was over.

The energy her student was displaying before her eyes was the reason Melody started teaching in the first place. *That's what it's all about,* she thought as her Stephanie hovered out of her class and into the hall, still holding the paper. *The inspiration.*

Steph still had the paper on her mind as she was driven home with Dawn, Zoey and Luke, though she had folded it and hidden it in her backpack before any of them could see it. Although they would react positively to the news, she didn't know if they would really take her desire seriously.

And serious she was. As far as Steph was concerned, this paper could be the starting line for a complete new future for her. And it had little to do with pursuing a talent she wanted to get better at or wanting to do what made her happy. Those things were important, yes, but Steph didn't think she would be spending her life doing either of those. It was just too unlikely. Besides, this paper, this future, was about a lot more than simply doing what made her happy. This would set her apart, this would prove she was different, she was better.

That was the front that kept itself hidden behind the fake veneer of doing this to pursue the career she wanted. This was all motivated by something else. She knew that and she was fine with it.

As she had grown up, Steph had learned how to live in silence and cope with unhappiness. Most of that unhappiness came from the screaming between her mother, father and older brother and sister. It seemed like they only ever stopped when they went to bed and Steph very quickly, despite still caring for all of them, ended up dreading their arrival at the house. They always had something to complain about and the only way she saw to avoid it was to stay out of sight as often as possible. And things stayed that way for a while. Her sister would argue with her mother over clothes or responsibilities or something and Steph would simply stay in her room and block it out. Her mother and father would argue...whatever it was that they got into, Steph hardly understood it at the time nor remembered it now, and she would stay locked up in her room waiting for it to end. It had reached a point where it even sounded like the rest of the family was getting tired of it as well.

And then Hazel, the older sister who wanted to be taken seriously as an adult and wanted her parents to take her seriously as well, disappeared.

Of course, they all knew what had happened. Even Steph put the pieces together as she listened to her mother and father really start to go at it now. Hazel hadn't gotten kidnapped, she wasn't being held for ransom, not that there was much money in the house anyway, another common argument, she had simply run away from home. Steph thought she was eighteen when she left, but that was nothing more than uneducated guess, a hope.

And then, not only did the arguing start up again, but now fingers were pointing and blame was being shot back and forth. And now they really didn't stop. Steph would sneak out to make it to the bus stop and hear their voices echoing from the house for a few dozen yards or so after she had closed the door behind her, she would recall little nuggets as she sat in school and tried to focus.

Great job you did raising her.

Somebody had to do it and it's not like you're ever here.

The only reason I'm not here is because I have to make money so we can afford to stay in this shitty house.

She made her way into the kitchen to get herself food and heard them in the living room. She played outside and heard their screeching voices berating each other.

They had seemed to forget about both her and her older brother, but apparently Caleb had a plan in mind for that. Or he was motivated by something else completely, Steph didn't know and never would. She would never speak to or even see him again. She didn't know what prison he was being held at and they couldn't afford to pay the bail. Maybe they didn't even want to. Or maybe one of them did and the other didn't. That certainly didn't help cap the overflowing geyser of screaming in the house. She had little concept of time when it came to her family and when certain things happened, mostly because every day seemed to feel the same. It could have been two weeks or a year and a half, but Steph Warren became the only sibling living with her parents by the time she was eleven.

One night she was in her room trying to recover from a stomachache that seemed to have come out of nowhere. She spent several hours lying in bed, trying to ignore it, taking tentative sips of water and all she could think about was how badly she needed a hug or a head scratch or something physical and real and warm. After a while, once she couldn't quite take it anymore, she made her way to her feet and went out to the two of them, their voices continuing to grow louder, amplified, as she closed in on shaking legs. She walked into the living room and stood there until they noticed her, hoping she wouldn't vomit and would just be able to get some help for her aching stomach.

Her parents were standing on opposite sides of the room, pointing at each other and yelling and neither noticed her for upwards of a minute. They just went back and forth like they always did.

"We could have paid it and you know it. We could have gotten him out of there if you fucking wanted to."

"What would be the point in paying to get him out just so he can put himself in there again in a month or so. We'd be wasting our money."

"He's your son, not a goddamn check."

"He made his mistake and he has to pay for it. It's not like he'll be in there for life, Alaina."

Her mother almost shrieked with laughter. "Oh, that makes everything okay. Maybe if you had spent more time raising him, he wouldn't have turned out this way.

"And maybe if you had just given Hazel what she had wanted we might still know where she was or even if she was still alive."

"Jesus, Micheal, how many times will we have to go over this?"

"Until you can actually look at this from someone else's perspective."

Her mother shook her head and turned to find Steph still standing near the hallway. But before she could say anything, before either of them could say anything, her father was already making his way towards her, and not gently either. He got down on his knees in front of her and the sight of his angry, dismal face made Steph's stomach clench even tighter.

"And what do you want? You want to confess to something you've done, too? You commit any crimes you want us to know about? You planning on following in your siblings' footsteps right into an early grave?"

Steph couldn't find anything to say, she was still focusing on not vomiting. Especially now, the last thing she needed was to throw up directly into her father's face. She didn't think she could get him to stop acting so angry and scary these days, but she knew if she ended up showing him what she had eaten, things would get far worse than they had been. For her, anyway.

Her mother swept by her side before Steph even noticed she was moving and yanked her away from her father's shadowy face. "Get away from her, she's only ten. She hasn't done anything yet."

He got to his feet and slowly strolled back over to his recliner. "Give it time, Alaina. She'll be just like them. Not every fruit that grows on the tree is fresh."

"Wow, what a goddamn poet you are," she muttered over her shoulder before turning to Steph and attempting to look calm. Her haggard face and exhausted eyes made that difficult for her and a little intense for Steph, but they both ignored it. Steph had also ignored the fact that she was eleven. "What's the matter, honey, huh?"

She didn't know why she felt a need to, but she whispered her problem so only her mother could hear. "My stomach hurts."

Her mother nodded close to furiously and her head darted around a little bit as she spoke. Steph didn't understand the reaction, but later on she thought her mother was just happy to have found a problem she could actually solve. "Okay, well, I think we can do something about that. Come on, let's go back to your room first, get you off your feet." She took Steph's hand in a grip that was a little too tight and led her back into her room and onto her bed. Steph made her way back under her covers and answered the stream of questions her mother had for her.

"Have you thrown up at all yet?"

"No."

"Do you feel like you have to? Or like you will at some point?"

"Yes."

"Do you know what to do when you start feeling like you might?"

"Yes."

"Is there anything you need?"

"Can you turn the fan on?"

Her mother slapped the switch up and the droning buzz of the overhead fan began to bore a hole into Steph's head.

"You should try to get some sleep, Steph. It's already close enough to your bedtime."

She didn't even know she was going to say it until her wavering voice carried it out of her mouth. "I've been trying. It's too loud."

She looked up at her mother, shocked by herself and waited anxiously for whatever response she might get. Her mother took a few seconds and said nothing, then dropped to her knees, barely even bracing her body for the impact against the hardwood, and ran her hand through Steph's hair as she spoke.

"I'm sorry about that, honey. Things are just a little off-center right now. But you know that your father and I both love you, right? More than anything, even if we don't show it, we love you."

Another impulsive thought turned itself verbal and darted out of Steph's mouth as she lay beneath the soothing massage of her mother's fingers. "Do you still love Caleb and Hazel?"

A longer pause followed this and even out of the corner of her eye, Steph had now decided that her ceiling had gotten particularly interesting to look at. She could see the glimmering shine of tears sticking to the bottoms of her mother's eyes before she wiped them off and coughed a little. "I...we do. And you should, too. I don't know when we'll see either of them again, but I don't want you to ever forget about them or stop loving them, okay?"

Steph nodded and her mother got up with what looked to be a lot of effort for a woman in her mid-thirties. "All right, I'm going to go lie down too. I'll be in my room if you need me for anything. You all set?"

"Yes."

"Okay. I hope you feel better. Goodnight, honey."

"Goodnight."

Her mother closed her bedroom door and Steph simply lay frozen for what seemed like a while to her. A lot had happened within the past five minutes. A lot she didn't understand and unfortunately a lot that she thought she did. But what she remembered the most, what followed her into her dreams that night and nestled itself into her subconscious for the foreseeable future, was her father's voice. Her father telling her mother that not every fruit that grows on the tree is fresh.

She took that with her long after her parents had decided to separate, surprising no one. She ended up with her mother, something she wasn't unhappy about and even though she still cared for her father a part of her was somewhat relieved that things could start over. No other siblings, no more screaming, no more rotten fruit, it could just be her and her mother.

And it was, for a short while, before her mother met someone else. Someone who certainly argued less (he did everything less. Work, talk, care) but wasn't much better than her mother's first attempt at love. But Steph wasn't thinking about him just yet, even as she was being driven home, she was still over the moon with excitement. Eventually Dawn pulled up alongside her house and Steph had never been so happy to see her house. So happy in fact that she didn't even cast a glance into the driveway and see whose car was there. And whose wasn't.

She said her goodbyes to the three of them and tried not to run into her home as the scenario began to unfold in her head. Mom would sign the paper, Steph would give it to Mrs. Clifford and the two would talk about her future in art. A future Steph assumed would be fun but short and unsuccessful, though she would enjoy and take advantage of every second of it. She was inside, walking up the wooden stairs now, and couldn't wait to turn left, see her mom on the couch, half paying attention to the TV and explode with good news. She curved left, smile ready to be seen, walked into her TV room and stopped dead. Her smile did too.

The TV was on all right, that wasn't the problem. The problem was who was watching it. It wasn't her mother, it wasn't her younger sister Emily, it wasn't a rabies infected coyote. It was worse. Sitting in her mom's spot on the couch was Arnold, her stepdad of, so far, five years. It had been that long since he came into her life and Steph still had nothing to offer him except contempt. Her memories of her first father, the one she had known for eleven years, were a hazy mixture of good and bad, though of course the rotten fruit she and her siblings were in his eyes ended up being what she remembered the most about him. But as ambivalent as she was about him, she already knew that Arnold was worse.

Where her father had lost more and more of his happiness the more and more Steph could remember him, Arnold had never had any happiness to share with her from the beginning. She was more of a minor wound in his life than anything else, he was here for her mother and would have to put up with her until she left. But what really pushed Steph over the edge into rooting for more adversities to come into Arnold's life was Emily.

Her mother and Arnold had gotten married when Steph was twelve and popped out a new child that same year. And whether it had just been a mistake on his part or the fucking idiot had forgotten how to use a condom or whatever reason he could throw out, Steph could already tell that the way he felt for her was the way he felt for Emily. Even though she was far younger, with a much smaller and far less biting vocabulary than Steph. She hadn't done anything to deserve this kind of treatment. Yet she received it just the same, though Steph didn't even think she was aware of it. Six year olds have a pretty positive outlook on most things. She could go up to her father and ask him to play and when he shrugged her off without even glancing at her she would merely carry on blissfully with whatever she was doing before. She was lucky in that respect, but Steph didn't think Arnold deserved a daughter who would look away from an attitude like his. When her mother used to work nights, Steph could remember numerous times when she had to lift Emily out of her crib and get her settled down when she started to cry while Arnold simply watched T.V. in the living room and waited for the screaming and sobbing to stop.

She could think whatever she wanted to about her father, and how not every fruit that grows on the tree is fresh, but she could at least say that he had helped her when she was sad or played with her when she was a kid. Her mother had lost a temperamental, opinionated banker and gained the disgusting, crusty eyed, loveless potato sack that sat a mere six feet away from her. Six feet that felt like a centimeter.

"Where's Mom?" she asked, hating herself for even giving him *that* much attention.

Arnold didn't look away from the TV. "She told me she had to take a few extra shifts at work. Said she'd be home around midnight."

Steph's future crumbled around her. All ideas and possibilities of future projects, artistic or otherwise, burned to the ground. Tomorrow's conversation with Mrs. Clifford would now be an apology for her failure to get one simple sheet of paper signed.

She could hear Clifford now. "Sorry, Steph, but you needed to have a parent's signature if you wanted to take this seriously. We've already hit the deadline. It's too late now, but maybe something else will come down the line later. Now go back to your seat." It sounded awful to imagine and the thought of being there and hearing it in person almost made Steph retch.

Arnold Sheldon glanced at his stepdaughter after a few seconds of silence, noted her unhappy expression and decided it didn't interest him. But he would have to put in a mild amount of effort to keep Alaina from getting on his case about not helping Steph. "She's coming back later. Why does it even matter?"

"It doesn't," Steph stated, quiet and bitter. "Not anymore." She looked at him, and immediately felt more angry.

God his gut is bigger than mom's was when she was pregnant.

"Well, what do you want me to say? She had to work late and she'll be home later."

Steph felt the venom, nasty and acidic, travel out of her mouth with the following words; "Yeah, well she wouldn't have to if some people pulled their own fucking weight around here." She glanced back at him and the look of utter shock he gave her made her feel a tiny bit better. It was still microscopic compared to how bad she felt, and the moment only lasted another second or two.

He pointed his finger at her and wagged it around. "Your mother has high hopes for you and I still can't figure out why."

Steph gave him an ugly grin. "Maybe because I was just considered for an arts internship this summer."

There was another small pause, but before Steph could wonder if he was actually gong to show some investment in her, he responded. "You couldn't handle that. You don't have the commitment for it. You'd get pissed off and leave before the first day was over. Your attitude would get in the way."

"It's not an attitude, it's how I am."

"We'll you should change it because it's ruining your future and messing up our family and I've gotten sick of dealing with it." He tried sending some of the venom back, but the desperation it revealed made

Steph chuckle.

"Yeah, *that's* what's messing up our family." She swiftly left the room before she could hear another pathetic remark from him and went into her room.

She threw her bag on the ground and saw the paper flutter out of it and land gently on the carpet. She picked it up and looked at it with new eyes. These new eyes saw the paper as a harsh, painful reminder of what her family had become and how it would never go back to the way it was supposed to be. All and then her first father was right, she wasn't meant to have a career in art or to pursue something she wanted to, she was mean to be just like her older siblings, wherever the fuck either of them were right now. They were rotten and so was she. It was the Warren family curse. Maybe Emily would be better off, would be luckier. Maybe Emily was the fresh fruit. But Steph's luck, the few hours or so she had of it, had now run out. Her mother would be out all night and she would leave early tomorrow morning. Hospitals needed all of the help they could get and her mother, helpful to a fault and also needing the money thanks to Arnold's lack of a job, would be there as early as possible. Steph wouldn't even get the chance to see her before she left for work and she knew Arnold wouldn't pass the paper onto her mother. She held the paper in her hands a bit tighter and fought back a need to cry. Her future didn't matter anymore. Not much did matter anymore. The only thing that made her perk up was her bed and how comforting and approachable it looked.

Without giving it another, more optimistic thought, she crumpled the paper into a ball and threw it into her trash can. Then she fell into her bed, turned on her phone and was lost in the world of technology. She was fast asleep by the time her mother got home. And was fast asleep when she left the next morning.

Chapter 4

Amy had become used to her early morning routine and as soon as six thirty rolled around, her eyes were open and the cool breeze from Evan's bedside fan was more noticeable. He always insisted on having the fan on, said he couldn't sleep without it, but Amy didn't care. It felt relaxing after a while and it definitely helped her get to sleep. And, when it was already freezing enough outside, it helped her wake up.

She reached over and pushed the OFF button, a saddening feeling infecting her, then pulled her hand back to grab Evan's arm that had fallen off of its usual spot around her waist. She twisted against the blanket and turned her body around to face him. It was too dark to make out his face, but Amy knew where every part of it was. They had been together for two years, seven months, two weeks and four days. She had memorized his face by now. She loved his face. She loved his dorky brown hair that began curling when he refused to get it cut. She loved his peaceful, deep voice, his odd but captivating tan eyes, his calming presence when she needed it and his silence and subservience when she needed that too. She needed him just as much as he needed her. He was the only person she had ever met who she felt genuine love for. He was the only one who deserved it. He treated her like royalty, listened to her complain, helped her when she asked for it and was always there to take her away from bad situations she found herself in.

One of which she could tell was coming.

She couldn't explain it, but stroking Evan's hair and rubbing her hand up and down his back helped her quiet her mind, close her eyes and attempt to make some sense of it. Whenever things came together in the sickening way they sometimes did, Amy felt herself begin to fall off the edge. She still made conscious thoughts and actions but they were driven by something greater; something she couldn't understand. All she did understand was that when her anger became too much for her to handle, and the seething lava began to spill down the sides of her inner volcano, she had to do something to silence it, or at least let it simmer down for a few weeks, until the next inevitable boil began. Before her fury and the heat became too powerful to control, she would often feel something cool inside her tell her it was coming back and to batten down the hatches, like a fuel light in a vehicle when you're running out of gas. She always felt it the same day her inner volcano erupted. And she felt it now. Amy didn't tell anyone about this, besides Evan. But the secret she kept only with herself, was how she felt about this special feeling that always looked out for her. She didn't think even Evan would understand that. The thought of Evan yanked her eyes back open. It was time for him to wake up.

Amy leaned in and gave him one of her long slow kisses that covered his mouth. She thought it was what it would feel like to kiss a dead body. "Hey," she whispered into his ear, hoping that it would bring him back to her calmly. "Remember me? It's time to get up now, okay?" She felt his weight shift, smelled the morning breath that he blew into her face that she somehow never got tired of and leaned back as he stretched and turned his head to look at her.

"Hi," Evan said. He motioned towards his lips with his hand. It was dark but Amy's eyes had adjusted enough to see what he was doing. "Can I get another one of those?"

Amy licked her lips and gave him another, moving her hand up and down his shirtless chest and letting him pull her, hands locked around her lower back, to his lower front. She wanted it, she wanted it now. The two made sure to have one of them always ask the other if they wanted to do it before they did, but this time she didn't want to, and didn't think she even needed to. But she also knew where her priorities lied. She had a schedule to keep and didn't want it to be interrupted. No matter how thrilling and pleasurable the interruption would be.

She separated their lips, pried his hands off of her back dimples, climbed out of the bed and stumbled to the light switch on the other side of the room near the door, her finger ready to flick it up. "Lights are coming on." And the next second, they did.

Evan cupped his hands over his eyes and rapidly blinked them as they adjusted to the new orange light that had erased the darkness he had been so used to.

Amy smiled at him, though he couldn't see it. "I'm going to go get ready. I'll be back."

His eyes adjusted to the new light a few seconds after she closed his door behind her and he got to his feet, wobbling a bit, ready to start his own routine, which mainly consisted of getting dressed and blundering around on his phone.

And, as per usual, He was sitting on his bed, shirt and jeans slapped on and bouncing his gaze between his phone and his door like a dog waiting for its owner, in three minutes flat. But Amy would be a while. She was getting a surprise from the eldest member of the Mitchell family.

Amy always snuck some coffee to drink while she got ready. It helped her wake up and it felt like it sharpened her senses. She poured a relatively small amount into Evan's mug, another secret he didn't know about, and took a knife from the drawer to stir the black liquid with. She didn't need creamer, it was way too sweet for her. Though that didn't stop her from stirring the coffee anyway. She liked hearing the noise if the knife on the ceramic mug. The *ting* put Amy at ease, which didn't last long.

"Amy?"

She whipped her head around, firing on all cylinders, with the knife held behind her back, blade pointed down and ready to stab. The first two were instinctual. The third was a force of habit she picked up from seventeen years of living in her house. She let out a breath of relief and loosened her body a little when she saw it was just Isabella, Evan's mom.

"Sorry," Isabella said, raising her hands and extending her arms in front of her chest. "Just thought I heard a noise in here and wanted to check it out and..." her sentence trailed off and died before it was complete. She nodded her head at Amy and put her hands on her hips, turning her head slightly to the right. "Are you all right, sweetie?"

Amy readjusted her position and stood blocking the mug. She slowly and quietly set the knife down into the cup, but couldn't ignore the seemingly deafening sound the metal made as it hit the ceramic rim. Shaking her head with her eyes closed she responded as honestly as a lie could be. "I'm fine, Mrs. Mitchell. You just startled me."

Not Mrs. Mitchell anymore. From now until I join him, I'm Widow Mitchell.

Since raising her own child, Isabella Mitchell had picked up on the numerous ways you could tell when one was lying. This one seemed to be checking off all of the boxes. She approached slowly and carefully took her hand. The girl's face smiled, but her eyes didn't.

"I'm here for you. You know that right? Whatever you're having problems with, you can always come to me. Whether it's Evan, school," she moved in closer and held Amy's hand with both of her own, making the single hardest and scariest decision she had ever made in relation to Amy Cooper and choosing to mention the one word. "*Family*." Truthfully, she had no idea if her family might be the problem, mostly because she knew nothing about Amy's family. For the two years she had known her, Amy had rarely ever mentioned them and Isabella assumed Amy didn't spend nearly every day at the Mitchell house because she liked the feng shui.

Isabella wished she knew how things were at Amy's house, she would have loved to have the confidence to ask, but she also knew that Amy had a bit of a temper. She often heard her voice rip through the entire house and wondered how he could put up with it for so long.

She had spent enough time with Amy during their various trips to New Hampshire and Vermont and New York to know that she wasn't always angry. Isabella was often more angry during these trips than Amy was, though that was because it was hard to enjoy a vacation when she knew she was only hosting it as an apology to Evan for her behavior after her husband's passing. But regardless of her emotional state, Isabella took great notice of Amy and found that, once she was comfortable enough to let her guard down, Amy had a content and, often, sweet side, which was something Evan very much needed at that time. But what Amy lacked in consistency she made up for in intensity. And the intensity Isabella heard racing through the house occurred when Amy was moderately irritated with someone or something. Isabella assumed that being forced talk about a family situation that Amy was probably far from okay with would bring out the worst of her anger. And the idea of facing her when she was screaming and swearing and pacing with her hands probably rolled into fists and her face an unhealthy beating red was a little too much for Isabella to handle. It was a secret she kept to herself and would certainly not admit to anyone who she wanted to take her seriously, but her fear of Amy, minor as it was, still controlled how she spoke to the girl and what she spoke to her about. And this one time mention of her family was going to be exactly that. It was just easier and safer that way.

The word made Amy close her eyes and search her mind for

anything else to think about. It was far too early for her to be reminded of that aspect of her life and she didn't think she had the strength to handle the emotions that would come out if that topic was probed for too long.

She took in a breath, refocused her mind and opened her eyes to see a concerned, forty-something, hairdresser who read one too many parenting books staring back at her. *I do not fucking need this shit right now,* she thought. She decided, though, it would be better if she kept that quiet and let the fake, peppy side have a turn to speak.

"I know, and I will if something ever gets out of hand."

"Good." Isabella turned and walked back into her room, but before she left the kitchen she looked back at Amy and said, "You know you can take as much coffee as you want. I'm the only one who drinks it anyway."

Amy chuckled and her boyfriend's intrusive mother disappeared down the black hallway. As soon as she was out of sight, Amy dropped the smile and took the mug into the bathroom where she would spend the next few minutes getting ready and enjoying the hot bitter taste running down her throat.

Evan watched Amy come back into his room and was instantly concerned. He jumped up and met her before she could even close the door. It was that look again. He had seen this kind of look cross her face before, and he hated it. She just looked so *small*. He put his hands on her shoulders and rubbed them up and down, hoping it offered some form of unspoken support. "You got that feeling again?" He asked, slightly afraid to hear the answer.

Amy looked up at him and nodded. "Yeah, I do. Something is going to happen today, Evan. I know it is. I can just...*tell.* It's something inside."

He nodded and tried his best not to let his own internal feeling of dread be present in his voice or face. She had gotten *that feeling* the day she had attacked Kaitlin. As far as he could remember, she seemed to get it every morning before something big happened. Before she ended up scratching someone until they were left with dozens of bleeding claw marks, or nearly strangling someone into unconsciousness because of a poorly timed glance in her direction. She had even lashed out at him a few times during the earlier months of their relationship until she was able to put a cork on that and could aim the bottle at someone else instead. He assumed, though never told her, that the only reason she had ever attacked him at all was because she was still under the false assumption that he would leave her and was trying to get ahead of him so the inevitable punch wouldn't be as hard. Amy could throw all the punches she wanted, she could revel in the eyes that refused to meet hers, she could enjoy the sight of people making their way to the other side of the hallway when she came around as if they had been pushed there, but Evan didn't think even Amy herself knew just how scared and timid she really was.

He also didn't think she knew just how often he woke up in the middle of the night to hear her crying.

Of course, though, whether she thought he would leave her or not, and despite how many times she asked, he was still here and wasn't going anywhere. "Look, you're going to be fine, okay? I'll be with you whenever I can. When I can't, just shoot me a text and I'll be in your class before you know it. I'll pull you into the hallway and talk you down out there. But no matter what you do, I'll stand by you. I promise." He didn't like to lie to her but he knew deep down that he wouldn't stand by anything necessarily. He took out his phone and checked the time. "We're leaving in… four minutes. I'm going to go use the bathroom and then we'll go, all right?" He took one step and looked back at her. "You can beat the feeling, Amy." She nodded and he left.

She appreciated his devotion but, truth be told, she never said she wanted to *beat* it. Or even that she didn't *like* it. She actually wished that the feeling telling her to prepare herself would go away. It was more enjoyable not knowing when she would burst. The sudden internal spill of lava was much more enjoyable when a pesky, "take cover" feeling didn't get in the way. And as she thought of her inner volcano, she gave herself an idea that she didn't even think about before agreeing with.

She slithered over to the bottom drawer of the cabinet Evan kept his clothes in, opened it as quietly as she could manage, rummaged through pairs of pajamas that definitely didn't fit him anymore and found the one thing he probably though he kept secret from her. It was probably only for protection so he didn't use it very often but, as far as Amy saw it, there were a number of untapped possibilities that this little thing held. Far many more than simple protection. It just needed to be held in the right hand. Evan wasn't right for this sort of item, but she was. She had gotten used to blood by now. Closing the drawer and making sure it looked untouched, Amy slid Evan's failed secret into her back pocket, left his room, wearing the same face she had walked into his room wearing, the face that perfectly faked the minor jitters he expected her to show, and met him in the hall on his way out from his last minute piss.

"Let's go," she said. Her forced upset voice was painfully noticeable to her, but to Evan, it was perfectly genuine.

The ride to school never lasted long, but Evan liked to drive and hated using the school bus so it didn't take much convincing for him to support driving to school with Amy. It was especially easy for him when she stayed the night, which Evan thought happened a little too often. Not that he was against it or wished she would spend more time at her own home, but the fact that she went to her house only one or two times a month was concerning. He never asked her about it though. The tears that had been brought to her eyes when he last questioned her made him promise to never mention it again. They were still a few miles from the school when Evan noticed a very distinct person walking down the sidewalk, head wrapped in a hood and backpack slung around one arm, although it had both straps.

"Holy shit, it's Trevor!" Evan exclaimed and Amy flinched.

Trevor Logan was Evan's longest friend and a member of his and Amy's little group of four. He was of average height and larger weight and had been that way for as long as Evan knew him. That was almost what led Evan to like him so much to begin with. He seemed to have given up on being taken seriously even back in second grade or so, so he decided to simply be a court jester of sorts. At any mention of saying something or doing something no one else had the courage to do, he would do it instantly. And Evan had found that a rather fascinating (and extremely funny in the right situation) trait. It had seemed to depart from Trevor as he had gotten older, but occasionally he came out with a stupid little comment that reminded Evan of who he used to be. Who they both used to be. Those reminders felt like being injected by a syringe filled with acid.

His stomach hung only an inch or so off of the waistband of his tan khakis, but one inch was more than enough for him. His small, black rimmed rectangular glasses sat awkwardly on a head that was, at the same time, too big for his face but too small for his body. His permanent buzz cut was concealed by his various hoodies that were pulled on top of his head wherever he went and his earbuds, things that had become essentially sewn to his skin, dangled from his ears, swinging back and forth with each step he took.

Evan slowed down the car and didn't notice Amy's glare that had once again colored her face, as it always did before she entered her school (it was her own make up in a way), and turned to face him. Trevor was in theory her friend, and a ridiculously loyal one at that, but this was supposed to be her time alone with Evan and she didn't need Trevor getting in the way of that. Which is why when Evan asked if they should bring Trevor along with them, Amy cut him off with a sharp and pointy, "No."

"Really?" He stopped the car, still at least thirty feet behind Trevor, and looked at her. Her eyes were locked on the road in front of her, but not on Trevor who continued to walk on the side. Just the road.

"He could use the exercise." And before he could respond. "You know it's true."

A long pause ended Amy's statement and the car didn't move for the entirety of it. Evan only put his foot on the gas when Amy looked at him, finishing her staring contest with the road, and uttered two words that sounded both threatening and passive. She managed to sound like that a lot when he started pushing against her. "Now drive."

Evan drove.

"I just don't want him to get pissed if he sees us drive by and know we didn't stop to pick him up," Evan said, a whiny tint accidentally escaping out with his words.

Amy turned back to look at the friend they had left to trek the remaining mile and a half alone, and scoffed. "He's got his earbuds in and is staring at the sidewalk like it's talking to him. I doubt he even knew we drove past."

Evan nodded in a failed attempt to reassure himself. Then a thought popped into his head that he only said out loud to move away from Trevor, mentally and physically.

"You think we'll see Heather before we get to school, too?"

Amy shook her head. "No, she's probably still asleep. You know how she's always late."

"Yeah, why is that? Have you ever asked her before?"

Amy sighed, thinking back to it. Thinking back to Heather in general. "She said something about 'Too many people. Not enough cars.' She phrased it in some stupid Heather way."

Evan pulled into the parking lot and parked as close to the school as he could. He knew Amy didn't like the cold and they both wanted to get in there as soon as possible. As he was turning the car off he reminded Amy of something he was sure she'd get angry about.

"We have English first, you know."

He saw her freeze and turn to look at him. He turned to meet her gaze, expecting to see the beautiful glare she had spent years getting to look just right and was instead met with something that made his skin crawl.

The distant, unnatural combination of eyebrows, eyes and a smile Evan looked at, as if it were all controlled by a puppeteer who was yanking the strings in the scariest variation possible, stared back at him and spoke three words that made him shrink into his seat and made the figure grow even taller, reaching through the sky and leaving him a mere speck.

"My favorite class."

Mrs. Gardiner's English 11 class was bitter sweet for Dawn, Zoey and Steph. But as soon as R.I High School's very own Four Horsemen of the Apocalypse came through the door, the sweet was captured, strangled to death and devoured by the bitter. The four had come to an agreement that they wouldn't go to Gardiner's class until they were all present, that way they could all make sure they'd have multiple people to talk to. But the intimidation factor wasn't lost on a single member of the group.

"Nice of you four to join my class," Mrs. Gardiner stated with immense frustration at the four unruly students who had arrived late. Again. It was only by a few minutes this time, the class hadn't even really started yet and the students were mostly chatting with each other, but committing a small crime is still committing a crime. She shifted eyes to the rest of her class. "I have to run to the printer to get your assignment so no one do anything you wouldn't do if I was here." There were a few students she was talking to specifically, even though she knew they couldn't follow simple rules if it meant saving their own lives. She left the class, passing the four of them without a sound and hurried down to the printer before anything major could take place in her classroom.

Not that she would have been able to stop anything anyway.

Like a pack of fucking wolves, Steph thought as they passed by, their thundercloud clapping loudly above the twenty other eleventh graders. Everyone watched them head to where they all sat; on the far right side of the room in a group of ten desks that were intentionally turned ninety degrees to the left, facing Zoey, Dawn and Steph, who sat on the opposite side of the room and whose desks were turned ninety degrees to the right. With a clump of tables clumsily placed in between the two, facing straight ahead. *We get to see their cheerful faces all year and they get to see ours! We both win. Oh and don't forget about the poor middle group who has to sit helplessly in the middle of this war between our seven pairs of eyes! Great seating arrangement, Gardiner!*

There was a small, internal gasp among the class when everyone realized that Jason Eddly was sitting in Amy's seat to get closer to his friend who sat just to the side of the four. He murmured a lot and all Jason had wanted to do was hear him a little better. He was going to move on his own when asked, or more likely demanded, but he never got that luxury. He saw Heather sit down and smile that awful, sinister mug at him. He looked to face her and the smile grew. Almost like she wanted him to look at her. So he couldn't look anywhere else. And especially not at the person who was slinking up behind him.

"Have fun." The statement sounded happy, almost excited. Before he could ask what she meant he got his answer.

He felt a cold hand slam down on the back of his neck and squeeze it until the pain made him bend his head back, eyes closed, and contort his shoulders in a desperate attempt to make it smaller.

"Out," a cold female voice growled.

Another hand, just as cold and just as forceful, reached under his left arm and gripped that arm until it, too, felt as though it would be ripped right off. For a moment he was moving up, then down and he finally hit the end of his journey when his head connected with the floor and an audible *thump* echoed into every pair of ears in the room. He got up, dazed and seeing dots, with a hideous pain screaming from the right side of his head and slowly lumbered over to where his desk sat, looking more and more unpleasant with each painful step it took to get there. There was no point in doing anything about it. It was safer this way. Safer to let it pass. Hopefully the throbbing in his head would pass but right now he almost considered himself lucky. At least he wasn't bleeding.

That stone caused the ripple in the pond of their lives. His head hitting the floor and the dull drumbeat that came from it was the candle being lit near the curtains, the swimmer inching closer to the current, the sickening sound that people can drag behind them for far longer than any image they might forget. That changed everything, for the better and the worse. Though mostly for the worse, sadly.

Tiny stones affect large bodies.

As she watched him shuffle to his seat and rest his head in his hands once he made it, Dawn felt something rise up inside her that she hadn't felt before. It was calming, yet chaotic. Loud and soft. Fast, but slow. She liked it, it felt cool in her veins. She let it control her as she stood up and stared across the room at the person she had gotten very sick of as of late. It was time to let it out. For Jason, for Kaitlin, Zoey, Steph, her and everyone else Amy had been allowed to step on for as long as she had gotten away with it. Years by this point. She didn't even know what her voice might sound like when she was angry, would it be low, would she scream? Dawn wasn't exactly the emotionally immature type, she didn't think so at least. And yet here she was, taking in a deep breath and finding that she didn't care how she sounded or how important it was for her to practice abstinence with her more stormy thoughts. All that mattered was the sound Jason's head made when it hit the floor. It still continued to pound in her head.

"What is *wrong* with you? You couldn't have just asked him to move?" Dawn wasn't looking for a response. And she would have interrupted one if she got it. She continued to let the feeling pour through her body and help her speak. Her voice, not that she was even paying much attention to it, came out smooth and sure and crisp and venomous. "What makes you so special that we have to put our lives in danger every time we show up to this goddamned school? What, because Mommy left and Daddy wasn't enough for you?" The look Amy gave Dawn would ordinarily have caused her to back down and "go to the bathroom" to catch her breath, the strange sort of shocked and furious recognition in Amy's face made Dawn think she might have actually hit a little closer to the bullseye than she was aiming for, but this time backing down was not an option. Because she still heard the sound of his head smacking against the floor. "Well guess what? *All* of our lives are fucked up in some way or another. The difference is, however, everyone else has a high enough IQ to know to leave the bullshit at home. Maybe you should take a step back and actually think about if *we*," she motioned her hands at her other classmates, "should have to put up with *your* issues, just because you're too weak to handle them like a normal person."

"All right, Dawn, that's enough."

Dawn's eyes followed the voice down to her left towards its corresponding body and saw that Steph had leaned over and was wearing a face of grave intensity.

"No it's not," Zoey shot back from Dawn's right.

Dawn looked down at her and Zoey beamed back up. She had never been more proud of Dawn in her life. And something about the way Dawn looked, or maybe just the confidence that was radiating off of her, was exhilarating. It was something Zoey just wanted to grab a hold of and completely envelope herself in. She pushed the odd visual out of her head and brought herself back to these, very interesting, current events. This was the most fun she'd had in Mrs. Gardiner's class all year and Steph wasn't about to throw that away.

Steph leaned back, away from Dawn, so she could talk to Zoey without Dawn's thighs interfering. "Look at Amy."

Zoey did and wished she didn't.

This is it, Amy thought, eyes firmly closed and breathing slowly. *It's here. It's here and it's time.* She could picture her inner volcano starting to cough and sputter, small bits of smoke puffing out of the top. *My cold feeling was right. It's happening. It's taking over.* She let her volcano continue to rumble and fume. It would come, soon enough. *The fire is here.* She began to shake. Not in her head, physically in her chair. *The wick is lit.* She could feel her breaths grow heavier and she could smell the smoke. She breathed it in and it hurt. She choked and gagged and coughed on it but let it fill her system anyway. The volcano's pain was just another part of the process. The lava began to rise within her. *I'm falling off the edge. I'm falling in. Don't hold back, let it flow. Let it surge through every inch of your body. This is how it should be. This is how it should always be. Don't be stupid. Don't resist it. Let the cold feeling leave and the hot one replace it. LET GO AND GIVE IN!*

She did.

The volcano erupted. Lava shot miles into the air and came down like thick, scalding sludge. The burning liquid covered everything in sight and melted it all away into nothing. The lava flowed down into Amy's body and turned her blood to a boil. If such a phenomena were possible, she would have expected steam to emanate off of her skin.

She distantly heard someone's voice. A male's perhaps. She could almost remember but she didn't bother. The voice called out, quiet and scared, "Amy, are you okay?" She laughed it off and felt the orange goo continued to drown and destroy everything it touched. She wished she had that power. Maybe one day she would. She turned her mind away from the future and let it settle on the glorious, burning present. It was Heaven. She never wanted it to end.

Evan did.

He had first noticed she may be getting that feeling of hers when her skin had started turning pink. That only happened under two circumstances; when she was laughing a lot and when she was enraged beyond the ability to coherently think. And one of those happened far more often than the other. The shaking was when he called it off. That's what got him to his feet to pull her out of the class and calm her down somewhere safer, like they had agreed upon. When he asked if she was okay, she only turned a hint brighter and shook a bit more. Her hands were cemented at two corners of her desk and he had a bad feeling, however unrealistic as it might have been, that she could very well rip the two corners of the desk clean off if he continued to let her sit here and shake in her uncomprehending rage. But it was when he touched her that he decided he was willing to drag her out, kicking and screaming, if he had to. He put a hand on her forehead and he may as well have touched the engine of a running motorcycle.

Amy felt something cool press against the outer wall of her raging volcano. The volcano contorted slightly and then stretched taller than it ever had, sending out another wave of the acidic flaming liquid. The entire interior of her head was drenched in her lava and the rest of her body was following suit and the lava sunk down to burn the rest of her inhibitions.

Evan watched as a small trickle of blood ran down Amy's left nostril, falling in a perfect vertical line and hid in between her top and bottom lip. Her grimace softened, her eyebrows relaxed and she smiled, the blood sliding down her tooth and dropping onto her tongue.

"All right, that's enough," Evan said. He grabbed her arms,

God, she's so hot! Why is she so hot?

slung one over his shoulder,

Should I take her to the nurse? What good would that *do? She's never been so pink for so long before.*

and walked her into the inviting corridor that awaited the two on the other side of Gardiner's door.

As soon as the door that led to Gardiner's room was closed, Evan grabbed Amy's head and jerked it around. He could feel the skin on his hands getting used to Amy's new intense temperature, but *he* still wasn't. He was terrified. "Amy. Amy!"

She opened her eyes, with the expression of someone being rudely awakened, and the pink spilled out onto the floor and was refilled with a much more muted apricot. Evan heaved out a long sigh and embraced the girl he was afraid he might lose. Lose to what, he didn't know, which one made him hold her tighter.

"I know what I have to do," Amy remarked coolly, not completing her half of the hug. Evan let go of her and looked into the eyes of blind and soulless contempt.

"What do you mean?"

"I just got that feeling in there."

"Oh you don't fucking say," he touched his hand underneath his nose and Amy did the same, feeling a peculiar sticky substance. She looked at her fingers and saw fresh blood dripping down them. *Interesting,* she thought as she wiped it away onto the white sleeve of her sweater. That was new.

"I know what I'm going to do now. And I know exactly who I'm going to do it *to.*" She gave the door a glance that had enough fire behind it to burn it to charcoal and looked back at Evan, another smile starting to show. "Do you want to know?"

He nodded, though still too scared to bring himself to smile. "Tell me all of it. Every last detail."

Of course she couldn't tell him every *single* aspect. She knew his anxiety and irritating overthinking would get in the way and he'd try to talk her out of it. But she gave him the toned down version which was more than enough for him. And ideal for her. They didn't go back to class.

Dawn sat at her desk, having powered down, and spent the rest of the class thinking about nothing. She heard someone gasp and she was pulled out of her empty thoughts and looked across the room at Heather, Amy's and Evan's seats still empty. Dawn watched her show Trevor her phone, and listened to an entire conversation happen between the two without either one opening their mouths. Dawn couldn't understand how they did it but while she thought about it Heather's big, wide, golf ball eyes flashed over to meet hers.

She didn't need to wonder what Heather was thinking, she could hear it in her own head, in Heather's own voice with that atrocious callous grin that could only belong to Heather Grey, the scariest member of Amy's group.

A part of it may be over, kid, but something much worse is on the way.

Tiny stones affect large bodies.

Heather winked at her and Dawn felt sick.

Chapter 5

"Jesus, Dawn, that was fucking awesome. You knocked her ass out of the park without even *touching* her!" Normally, Zoey's giddiness would be infectious and make Dawn relax. Normally, but not this time.

Dawn's body walked to her next class with Zoey and Steph, but her mind was still sitting in her seat in Mrs. Gardiner's room, recalling the entire event and playing it repeatedly in her head. She had felt the energetic feeling leave her body after Evan and Amy left, and she still felt bad about the way the situation had unfolded.

She hadn't even wanted to speak, and a powerful, long gone feeling had given her a microphone and pulled her onto her feet and she couldn't even remember what she had *said.* She just remembered Evan leading Amy, her eyelids fused together through thin pink skin, out of the class. And she, of course, remembered the red liquid Amy had coming from her nose.

I didn't want any part of that and I ended up making her bleed.

Technically she bled on her own. You saw her shaking, it was probably just a way for her to let out some—

—Shut the hell up! I did something I shouldn't have done and I regret it.

"Do you think she's okay?" Dawn asked.

Zoey made a *pfft* noise. "Who cares? I hope she's not. Fuck her."

Steph's elbow jammed into her left arm sent a jolt of pain through her body. She recoiled and grabbed her bruised limb. "Dammit, Steph, what? You're the one who said she was asking for it. I'm just trying to let you guys know how you should be feeling about all of this and *I* get hurt?"

Steph looked at her, stunned. "What you need to *get* is an off switch."

Zoey shook her head. "Whatever, I just wish she could have gotten worse. Remember when—"

Her sentence was cut short by a certain tall, brick wall of a football player who came up behind her and separated the trio, his hand now connected to hers. Zoey looked at the telephone pole that had taken Steph's place and instantly forgot what she was talking about. And it didn't matter.

She had forgotten to mention to Dawn how Brandon had made a move yesterday and how they were going to hangout at her house after school. Though she didn't think she would have told Dawn the latter, mostly because she knew she would get the same exact response she got every time she told Dawn she would be hanging out with a guy at her house alone.

That's great, just be careful, Dawn would tell her and Zoey would internally roll her eyes and give Dawn a great big toothy smile. How little faith did Dawn have in her? Sure, she was a little promiscuous, but she was still smart. She always made sure the guys were protected and she always checked herself out afterwards and nothing had happened yet. What was one more going to do? It wasn't like she had gotten pregnant and, even if she did, she loved babies. Her aunt had recently given birth to quite the little chubber and when Zoey had gone over to meet him, he had snuggled against her as if he knew exactly who she was. She could handle babies, she would be fine. Besides, this was all just another cog in a larger machine anyway. Maybe this time something would change. Maybe she would finally feel what all her friends *told* her she would feel but hadn't yet.

Zoey gave Steph and Dawn a goodbye and went down a separate hallway with Brandon, keeping his hands with hers. The grabbing and squeezing would come later, when they were alone. Let him wait for it. They talked a little on their way to her next class and when he dropped her off, they even shared a few small kisses before he had to go or risk being marked as late. Zoey stood outside of her classroom, watching him walk away and letting her smile fade with each distant step he took.

Nothing, Zoey thought, disheartened.

Once the future wall crawlers had gone off on their own path, Steph moved closer to Dawn and filled the gap between them. Steph knew where Dawn's next class was; the gym.

Good. Gym will give her time to think.

She knew Dawn's mind had been elsewhere since leaving Gardiner's class and she wasn't surprised. She *needed* to think about what had happened. It was so unlike her to explode like that. Prior to this, the most anger she had ever seen out of Dawn was when she stubbed her toe or got a sunburn. And that was nothing more than a whispered curse or two. Something so loud and out there and public was something even Steph wouldn't consider doing. And certainly wouldn't consider doing to Amy of all people. Steph liked physical confrontation much more than the lesser, more verbal alternative. The rest of her family didn't, they all hid behind their voices, but she was not the same.

Not every fruit that grows on the tree is fresh.

She looked down and minutely shook her head as they reached the, now very unattractive, main doors to the gym and Steph grabbed Dawn's arm.

"You going to be okay?"

She took Steph's hand and removed it from her body. The last thing Dawn needed right now was anyone touching her. "I'll be fine, I just...need some time to clear my head. I don't have any more classes with her (Steph didn't need her to clarify. She knew the *her* Dawn was talking about) and who knows? Maybe she'll forget about it."

Steph gave her a look that said *You know that won't happen* but she kept her mouth shut. Dawn's arm felt cold and Steph could tell she needed space, which she was happy to give her. At least for a short while. She almost looked like she was afraid of herself, and Steph could understand why. If *she* had spontaneously burst into a verbal assault targeted at one of the most dangerously unhinged people in their school and had no idea where it came from or what might happen afterwards, Steph expected that she would be a little confused and frazzled too. If she allowed herself to believe in the supernatural, Steph might have even considered momentary possession as a cause of their recent events. It just wasn't Dawn. "Text me if you need me."

"I will."

She decided to overstep just a bit to see if things really were just as dark on Dawn's side of the tunnel. "You really have no idea why that just happened?"

She heard his head smack against the ground again and Dawn sighed and ran a hand through her scalp. "All I know is that I wish it didn't. And I really don't want to talk about it anymore, okay?"

"Of course." Steph let Dawn walk through the doors to the gym and the second they closed, cutting Dawn off like some bizarre horizontal guillotine, she felt incredibly uneasy. She couldn't explain why.

Which only made the feeling and the unrelenting surety of it all the worse.

Maybe that was how Dawn felt.

Amy had spent every subsequent hour since her volcano erupted and filled her veins with lava ignoring her schoolwork and texting any one of her three closest and only friends. Evan's texts were for support, which was cute, but Heather's and Trevor's were to inform them on the plan. Evan may get in the way, but it was nice to know that the other two would be all in. Trevor was essentially Amy's pet, and Heather? Amy had acted and interacted with her long enough to know she would be behind her for anything. They could kill the fucking Poodle and Heather would still stay up with Amy until the early hours of the morning digging the grave. The thought disgusted her.

Heather had always put Amy's senses on high alert. Ignoring the innate disdain she had for most of the girls at her school and how satisfying it always was to put a few fresh bruises on the ocean of sluts who surrounded her, Heather was her own brand of abnormal. Something about the way she acted, the way she was almost *too* willing to go along with whatever Amy was planning on doing, made Amy want to run into Evan's arms and hide. There was just something about her that made Amy think she was...off. Like someone whose brain didn't release the right chemicals, a brain that was almost normal but just beyond repair and sent out the wrong messages to every part of the body. And it was impossible to forget about her mud brown, baleful eyes and that creepy smile of hers. Amy wasn't afraid of her, but she'd prefer to be locked in a cage with a hungry tiger, than be alone with Heather Grey any day of the week. At least with a tiger you knew what to expect.

Who gives a shit? The important thing is she's on board. Trevor is, too.

And Evan?

He'll be with me until the end of the world.

Yeah, cute, but let's be realistic. You know he won't approve of the part of the plan he doesn't know. So when he gets in the way—

—IF he gets in the way, it won't matter. I'm not going to hurt him but I won't let him ruin this for me.

We'll see. How much time until your little plan anyway?

Amy gave the wall clock a quick glance.

It was almost time. Evan would be waiting outside her class, they'd go get Trevor and Heather and wait for their prey. A special little dog whose bark had gotten far too loud for Amy to put up with. A disgusting, worthless, prim little bitch who thought she could get away with disrupting the natural order of things.

The blonde cunt, this filthy, disrespectful, trashy whore was everything Amy despised in her fellow female students embodied into one pathetic host. The big tits, the round ass, the repulsive walk like a perfect virginal princess when she probably went home and took it in both holes at the same time. The superiority and the arrogance and the inflated sense of self, thinking she was better, that she deserved better. It was enough to make Amy want to break glass with her bare hands, suffering through the stinging cuts. The innocent smile she always wore and fake giggles whenever a particularly thick skulled guy was talking just to make sure she could fuck him later on and the clothes that squeezed and suffocated her body to get everybody to look at her. All of it, everything about her, about her little Poodle, made Amy sick. She was just like The Slut she hung around with, but The Slut cared little enough to be upfront about the kind of filth that she was and didn't pretend to be better. But she didn't realize all of that until now. Because before, looking at Poodle and taunting her and playing with her had been fun, mostly due to the fact that she was so scared to even look at Amy that Amy didn't even know her eye color. But now that had changed. Now she went after her, she decided to stand against Amy and try to beat her. And now, seemingly out of fucking nowhere, her slutty little Poodle had the balls to stand up and say things no one should have ever thought they could say to Amy and get away with. And, even despite the warning from her colder feeling that morning, her little Poodle had still gotten an upper hand on her and managed to genuinely shock her. And that was simply another lit match tossed into a bonfire. Amy would have expected such a ridiculous retaliation from The Black One, even The Slut, but not Poodle. But regardless, Poodle had messed around in the wrong animal's cage and she was going to suffer for it. Worse than anyone Amy had ever placed a finger on. She was going to bleed and cry and scream as Amy looked her in the eyes and saw the overwhelming pain and misery and regret, she would make sure her disobedient Poodle learned her lesson. Amy thought about what she would sound like screaming and it brought the smallest flicker of a smile to an otherwise tight and rigid face.

The bell rang, and Amy's plan began.

Evan found her, they found the other two and within a few minutes the four were waiting outside. Hidden of course. Amy had sent the three of them to wait where they would take Poodle, and she waited to the right of the double doors alone. She wanted to see her Poodle first. The thought of it brought a real smile to Amy Cooper's face. But it was one that still struggled to hold its weight against the monumental fury building in the girl.

The flow of lava ran through her, stronger, ticker and hotter than ever. It had been burning in her all day and she was ready to let it out. She needed to.

Dawn sat in the bathroom stall and tried to slow her breathing. She had snuck in when school let out to think things over again, calm herself down and try to get as much space between herself and Amy as she possibly could. She heard the door open and her heart almost stopped beating. It continued, though, when she heard Zoey's voice.

"Dawn? You in here?"

Dawn stood up, a momentary feeling of nausea gripping her stomach. She jumped out of the stall and sent Zoey up in the air about half a foot. "Sorry."

Once Zoey had landed, she shook her head. "It's fine, don't worry about it. So, what's going on? Why was it such an emergency that I came here?" The only reason she would ever go to the bathroom in her school was if she was having a little problem down south and needed a certain product for it. And, given Dawn's little speech earlier in the day, that possibility now held more weight than Zoey would have thought.

Dawn took a breath, hating how it felt in her body, and explained. "Okay, so I don't want to be a bitch but...do you think that you can get a ride home from someone else? I've already asked Steph and Luke and they're fine with it, but I want to make sure that you have someone you can fall back on right now."

Zoey nodded. "Yeah, I can find a ride, it's okay." Dawn sighed with relief and Zoey pushed her luck. "Are *you*?"

"Yeah, I'm still just a little shell-shocked from what happened with Amy this morning. I just want to lay low, you know? Make sure she's gone before I leave."

"You want me to stay with you? Keep you company?"

Dawn replied almost instantly. "No. No, I don't want you to—

get hurt

—waste your time. Just go home. I'll be okay."

Zoey watched her for a few seconds, examining, but once she was sure that it was what Dawn wanted, she nodded her agreement and, after another few seconds, smiled.

The juxtaposition of emotions made Dawn feel both better and worse. "What?"

"I know who I can get a ride from." There was a pause.

"Would you like me to ask who from?"

"Yes, please."

Dawn exhaled. It was louder than she meant it to be but, truthfully, she wasn't in the mood for Zoey to be so...Zoey right now. "Okay. Who from?"

Zoey's smile got bigger. "The who it is from is Brandon Finley." Dawn's face looked happy and surprised but Zoey could tell she still didn't know who he was. Regardless, she continued. "We're hanging out at my house today." Dawn's next smile was one of genuine happiness and Zoey noticed the difference instantly.

"That's great. Just be careful." She saw Zoey close her eyes but just before her eyelids blocked them, Dawn saw her hazel irises and black pupils roll up. The smile she gave Dawn, the same smile she always gave Dawn when she told her to be careful, contradicted the irritated story her eyes were telling but she ignored the possible correlation. Her mind was still elsewhere.

Zoey nodded through her loving annoyance. "I will, don't worry. Speaking of which, he's probably waiting for me so I should go." Dawn's face begged her not to so Zoey waited a bit longer, trying to get rid of this miserable feeling both Dawn and Steph had been entertaining for far too long. "I'm sure that whatever you're nervous about isn't even going to happen. Just get outside, get to your car and you're safe. It'll take one minute. Okay?" Dawn nodded and Zoey, after giving a quick hug that Dawn didn't quite reciprocate, left.

After she stepped out of the bathroom she felt a ugly feeling seep into her body. No, not ugly. Bad. A bad feeling. A feeling that seemed to scream *DANGER*. And it only hit her once she was away from Dawn. If Zoey had mentioned it to Steph, she would have understood the feeling perfectly. She felt the same way the last time she saw

Dawn, too.

After Zoey left, Dawn counted to ten, making sure it took as long as possible, and started her long, slow crawl to the doors she entered her school every day through. The only doors you could use to get in or out. Every step she took made the rope in her gut tie another knot, slower and slower but tighter and tighter and after this dismal death row trudge she was standing opposite the double panes of glass completely alone. Upon further inspection, she couldn't see Amy or anyone else lingering nearby. Of course the doors only went so far until the walls of the school blocked off view of the outside world, but even the nearly deserted parking lot didn't quite ease her. Fear spoke in many tongues. She took a deep breath, felt the knots squeeze ever so tighter, pushed open the doors and started walking the small, but seemingly endless, distance between her and her car.

Which would not take one minute.

Amy saw Dawn pass and her vision was suddenly dripping, pouring, spurting and flooding with orange. The lava was scalding in her bloodstream.

"Where are you going, Poodle?" Some excess lava came out with her words and singed the concrete at her feet.

Dawn turned around but continued walking to her car, staring into the eyes of someone who was beyond reasoning with. So Dawn didn't bother.

"I'm not afraid of you anymore." Something Dawn knew was a lie, but something that nonetheless sounded convincing enough. Seeing Amy shake and start bleeding was alarming, but it wasn't without realization. Maybe Amy wouldn't fight back if you instigated the fight. Maybe she was better at starting them than finishing them. Right?

Wrong.

Amy spoke just loud enough for Dawn to hear. If she got any louder she wouldn't be able to control the volume of her voice. "I don't want you to be afraid of me anymore. I just want to hear you scream."

The words dove down Dawn's throat and ripped her vocal chords out. She began backing up a bit faster. She didn't care if she tripped, she didn't care if she fell and broke her arm. All she cared about was getting away from Amy. It was the only thought her mind could process. Her car couldn't have been more than ten or fifteen yards away from the door, she had to have made it at least half of that distance by now. If she turned and ran, unlocking the door while she did so and locking as soon as her ass touched the seat, she would be safe. Amy couldn't break glass with her hands. And even if she could, all Dawn had to do was turn a key in a lock, put the car in drive and slam the gas pedal. She just needed to find the right time to turn and run.

Though, unbeknownst to her, Dawn's time had already run out.

A large, thick arm wrapped itself around Dawn's neck and her only plan died with the rest of her thoughts.

The arm yanked her down and her feet gave way, but she never hit the ground. The arm dragged her backwards and she tried to pull it down to keep herself from losing oxygen. She was wheezing and heaving as she was pulled away from her car and watched Amy start to follow, close behind.

She ignored Dawn's car. She wanted *her*.

Already Dawn's breathing had slowed down drastically and her panicking didn't help matters. She inhaled for no more than a second and exhaled not much longer and the arm only got tighter. She stopped kicking and the world began to darken. She saw a row of trees block her view of Amy and felt slightly relieved. If she passed out, she wouldn't be able to see Amy. The relief grew even more when the arm let go of her neck and the world came back. She was able to snatch up a few uninterrupted breaths but her relief quickly transformed into fresh, new fear as Amy came behind the trees to meet her and Dawn felt two pairs of hands, one considerably stronger than the other, latch themselves onto her arms and drag her to her feet. A third, more familiar set of heavy arms grabbed the bottom of her shirt and launched it upward, covering Dawn's head and her vision in a thick layer of fabric.

"Check out *this* set," Dawn heard a voice boom from behind her. "She makes your rack look like nothing, Amy," Trevor Logan sneered.

"Fuck off," Amy said, sounding surprisingly indifferent. This part of the plan belonged to everyone else. Amy would wait for her time. *Let them have their fun, so that I can have mine.*

Dawn heard another voice to her left and instantly knew who it belonged to. The girl's voice matched her smile when it came to recognizability.

"They are beautiful."

Dawn felt a thumb lightly press into and rub her half exposed breast. She was wearing a bra that showed off quite a bit, which ordinarily she wouldn't have worn to school but it was the biggest one she had and she wanted as much comfort her bras could give her. Now Dawn would have gone back in time and burned the bra into a pile of smoldering fabric for even considering it.

The thumb turned downward and pushed its nail deep into Dawn's skin. Dawn twisted and turned to try and escape the pain but the arms held her in place. She felt Heather's nail bury itself farther and farther into her chest, certain it would draw blood, and she let out one desperate yelp. A tear fell from of her eye and spread out on the shirt in front of it. She heard a *hawwk* sound that she knew very well from growing up with an older brother and felt a warm, thick sludge-like something fall onto her other breast and slowly drip down it.

Heather didn't brag or goad or ask Dawn if she liked the way the spit felt on her tit. Heather didn't plan on saying much at all. She enjoyed to watch just as much as Amy enjoyed to act.

Amy ripped the shirt off of Dawn's head and dropped it back where it belonged, taking a few unwilling strands of hair with it, and marveled at how Dawn kept her eyes on her shoes. Amy twitched and her vision turned from orange to red. This little slut, this filthy little holier-than-thou *skank* was still too scared to look Amy in the eye. After everything she'd done.

It wasn't fun this time.

Amy swung her arm as far back as it could go, letting her internal magma fill each finger, and slapped Poodle across the face with it. She watched her head swing to the right, exposing her bright red cheek, but it wasn't enough. "No, not anymore," Amy growled. She leaned in to speak directly into Poodle's ear and whispered through closed teeth, "Look. At. Me." No response and Poodle still kept her head down. *"LOOK AT ME,"* Amy roared and felt the slightest bit of satisfaction by watching Poodle recoil in agony. Though she was far from finished.

Dawn felt her hair tighten and shoot down, yanking her face up. She thought her entire scalp would peel off. It was the worst pain she had felt so far but that was quickly topped when she looked into Amy's eyes and was nearly brought to tears. Like a scared child, too frazzled and afraid to express how they felt in words. She had never seen Amy's eyes so close before. Even when she had berated her she hadn't really been looking into her eyes, they were too far away. But now they floated mere inches from her own, like twin black holes.

Christ, those eyes!

As she gazed at them, she saw Amy lean her arm back and Dawn prepared herself for the blow that would follow. It didn't help at all. She felt Amy's fist smash against the hair just above her ear and the whole world was black for one single second. Just like how it looked when she meditated. She wished that second would never end.

Another hit followed. And another. Bashing in her bottom lip, cracking against her nose, bruising her cheeks. Every hit thumped, battered, hammered and pummeled a new part of her head, and a new feeling of pain came and rose with every punch. She whipped her head back from the powerful blows and every single time, Trevor grabbed her head and yanked it up to face Amy once again. Smash, whip, yank. Smash, whip, yank. Heather giggled like a child being tickled with each and every impact. Dawn could feel blood running down her nose and into her lips, and could taste the cold, copper filling her mouth. Amy delivered a devastating hit to Dawn's stomach and when she lurched forward, gasping for breath, she saw her own blood splat against the grass and drip from her fat lip and sore nose. Amy lifted her back up again and pushed her face back to Trevor to hold. She flexed her fingers and closed her fists again. She was risking four bleeding slits digging into her palm but Amy didn't care. She wouldn't have even felt the pain.

This was where the plan ended for Evan. As far as he knew, the four were supposed to grab Dawn, drag her to where no one could see them, and rough her up a bit. But Amy was going too far. He didn't like the fact that they were already making her bleed and it looked like Amy wasn't going to stop. He thought about how to phrase it and came up with the perfect sentence; one that wouldn't make him look weak and would make Amy back off a bit. He turned his attention to his girlfriend and said, "All right, Amy, calm down." He intended to continue but the way Amy turned to glare at him, as if her eyes had pulled her head in his direction, made him squeeze Dawn's arm tighter to hide his fear and momentarily forget where his sentence was leading. His mind was like a car with a bad engine; you turn the key and only get sputtering. He tried to find his sentence and only got a bunch of *ifs* and *yous*. But eventually the engine started up and he remembered what he had planned on saying; "You keep hitting her like that and you'll knock her out."

"Oh, I'll kill her," Amy said, still fuming at Evan for interrupting but turning her glare to look back at the slimy cocksucker that was held down in front of her. She knew Poodle was dating Luke Bradley, just one in the ocean of idiots at this school who needed to rely on sports to get them through life because their intelligence sure fucking wouldn't. She was sure she'd gotten piped a few times by him. Probably by the entire football team. She and The Slut she hung around with presumably took turns riding each dick then topped it all off by screwing each other.

Dawn Bell was a virgin.

"I'll kill you, you hear me?" she screamed in Dawn's ear, "If you close those eyes for anything longer than a blink you'll never open them again!" Her knuckles lashed out against the bone between Dawn's cheek and eye and hesitated before delivering the final, strongest hit, against her jaw. Dawn's teeth bit down on her tongue hard enough to make her think it might bleed, but her mouth was already painted with the stuff so she doubted that she would notice.

And Amy still wasn't finished with her little, bloody Poodle.

Dawn's head throbbed, her face now aching and her nose and mouth dripping with blood. She looked up at Amy whose hair, now highlighted against the afternoon sun, made it look like her head was on fire. Black eyes and a flaming head, a living demon. She decided to close her eyes to try and keep herself from crying.

"Don't stop," Heather snapped at Amy through quick breaths. "Keep going."

Amy felt an odd, sexual energy radiating off of Heather. Evan was often the only person with Amy when her volcano unleashed her on someone so this was a side of Heather that Amy was unfamiliar with. The side of her that was witnessing what Amy was capable of instead of hearing about it after the fact. Not that this side of her mattered to Amy in the least. It was nothing more than a quick, pointless interruption. She looked at Evan's slightly worried face and said, "No, it's done. You want me to let her go, I will. But first," she rotated her hate back towards Dawn, grabbed the girl's head and shook it around vigorously, making sure she would be fully conscious for this next part. Dawn opened her eyes and the lava flowed, yet again, through Amy's body and out her mouth.

"Okay, tramp, from now on whenever you look at me I want you to think of two things." Amy extended the index and middle finger on her left hand while her right moved to her back pocket to grab Evan's failed secret. "What you *really* are," she brought her hand up to Poodle's line of sight, finger on the switch, "and how I *showed* you." Her thumb went forward, the switch went up and a cold, steel blade shot out of the hilt of Evan's knife. The smallest hint of a smile crossed Amy's face and she didn't hide it. She wanted Poodle to see it. The smile glowed with malicious intent.

Evan's eyes widened and his jaw hung slightly open. *How did she know about that? When did she take it? What's she gonna fucking* do *with it?*

He didn't want an answer to the last question. This had gone on long enough and Amy was already completely unhinged. And an unhinged person with a knife is a very dangerous duo. It was an old piece, his grandfather's in fact, and it hadn't been used in the decade that Evan owned it, but age didn't seem to affect the blade.

"Amy, I don't think this is a—"

"—Close your eyes then!"

He did.

Told you he'd get in the way.

Fuck you.

Dawn didn't want to cry, and her aching, pulsating head certainly pushed her further towards it, but when the sharp, metal knife came out and she followed it up to Amy's equally dangerous stare, she couldn't help herself. And the potential help from Evan that was destroyed just as quickly as it had surfaced only made it worse. She pulled away from Heather and Evan, yanking and contorting her arms in ways she had never done, using strength she never knew she had, and the hands only tightened around her skinny arms.

Heather dug every nail she could into Dawn's soft, squishy skin and the urge to have her nails go into the girl's arm and wiggle around underneath was almost too strong to resist. But she managed.

The tears streamed down Dawn's face, merging with her blood. "Evan, please, please don't let her do this to me." Despite her begging, he didn't open his eyes and she turned from him to someone there was a much smaller chance of getting mercy from. She tried to reason with her, knew it was hopeless, but attempted to nonetheless.

"I'm sorry about what I said, I'm sure it's not true, I won't do something like that again. I promise." She wished she could be at home, with Zoey's arms folded around her, or with Luke, or alone, or, shit, even with her mom and Cole. Anything was better than this.

A look of utter distaste replaced Amy's smile. A look that was very easy to read: *You're pathetic.* Any doubt Amy might have had left her body and mind when Poodle started blubbering. Nothing was more deplorable to her than not being able to take your punishment when you so rightfully deserved it. She pulled Dawn's shirt back up to reveal her stomach, the tits were for the rest of the group to play with, and she gave the shirt to Heather to hold, which she did happily. She stared at her Poodle's stomach and saw nothing but a place where dozens of guys had flung their jizz. She desperately wanted to make it her own. And she would.

"Amy, Amy, please! Please don't! I'll do anything!"

"I know."

Heather's hand, rough and fast, seized Dawn's throat and pushed against it. The hand still held Dawn's shirt.

Amy pressed the blade against her Poodle's stomach with immense pressure, slowly moved it down and a red line followed. A red line that soon began to trickle. Many more red lines followed, all tricking seconds after they had been made.

It was hard to scream with Heather's hand around her neck, but Dawn managed to just the same. It was hard not to. It felt like her stomach was being sliced into ribbons with the hot end of a fire poker. The tears came again and didn't stop as she moved her stomach left and right like an amateur belly dancer, trying to avoid the knife and never managing to do so. As soon as she felt the blade ease up, it was forced down again as her skin was separated by another wall of red and a new stream of blood fell into her jeans. The only thoughts she could form begged for it to end soon. It was all she wanted.

What she wanted would have to wait, for Amy hadn't finished the word yet.

A cold sheet of wind scraped against the five of them and, in spite of the brief shiver most of them faced, Amy didn't move a muscle. She didn't even get goosebumps as she continued clawing into Dawn's stomach.

Dawn found herself losing the ability to scream as the pain took over her voice and could only manage to silently bawl and try not to taste her own blood as Amy continued to cut into her.

Evan took a wary glance at Dawn's stomach, the top of her jeans looking dangerously purple and put a stop to Amy's plan, answering Dawn's plea to little and too late. "Oh my *God*, Amy!"

His voice infuriated her. She had hoped he'd keep his mind out of her business and she was sorely disappointed with his horrified tone. He had too much of a heart for this kind of thing and too little an understanding. But that would change in time. She would make certain of it. She whipped her head at him, eyes shaking in their sockets and spewed lava all over him. *"Shut up, Evan!"*

Silence fell on all of them. No one moved, besides Dawn who was still shivering in the biting, thirty degree air. Her skin now taut and shaking and covered in goosebumps with most of her shirt pulled up and the wind cutting every mark on her stomach.

Amy looked at Trevor and said, "Come on." She tilted her head to the right, began walking away and threw back, "And bring our little Poodle. It's time to send her home."

Trevor picked up Dawn, cradling her like a baby, and after wrestling with Heather over Dawn's shirt, he took off after Amy. He heard the girl start to cry softly and felt her rub her face into his shirt sleeve, getting blood and salty tears all over the cheap fabric.

Once they had stopped walking and Amy turned around, the look she gave him brought a glare to his face. Though, of course, the glare didn't rival Amy's. "What? What did you want me to do? I *had* to carry her like this. I didn't want to stretch out her stomach."

"Just shut up and give her to me." Amy's arms were outstretched and for a few seconds nothing was put in them. A look of surprise flashed over her face for an instant and her eyes became slits. "Now."

He gave Poodle to Amy and was blown away by the lack of effort it took Amy to hold her. They couldn't have been more than fifteen pounds apart but Amy held her like an empty duffel bag. He watched Amy lift Poodle up and he winced as Amy slammed her down on the trunk of her car as if she were trying to crack a coconut.

"The next time you think about opening your mouth to do anything other than take a dick…reconsider," Dawn heard Amy mutter. She could only hear it, though, because she kept her eyes sealed shut. She didn't need to see that face ever again.

Amy gave Poodle a hard slap on the stomach, which made her squeal with bright new pain, wiped the blood off on the blue trunk of her car and took off toward Evan's truck, not waiting for the other three. They would follow. They always followed.

And they did.

Dawn stayed there, skin burning against the freezing cold exterior of her car, for what seemed to be a long time. Though, eventually, she decided that she had to head home and slowly made her way off of her trunk. But as soon as she got to her feet the pain in her stomach dragged her to the cement in a curled up heap. When she crawled into her car she found that she couldn't wear her seatbelt, she could barely even wear her shirt. She got home eventually, but the pain never lessened.

Heather insisted she be dropped off first and as soon as she was, she ran into her room. She locked the door, flung herself onto her bed, removed her leggings and underwear and stared down at her "special place." She had only touched it to clean up her period blood. *Blood.* The word made her special place tingle. She had never touched it for the same reasons she assumed other females did, like when they watched porn or even thought about a guy they really liked. Heather simply didn't understand the attraction to it, but wanted to give it a try. She never had done it before and for someone her age, she assumed that was impressive. She took her right middle and index fingers and slowly pushed them into her special place. Down to the knuckle.

Nothing.

She moved her fingers back and forth, in and out.

Nothing.

She decided to take a different approach.

She leaned her head back, feeling it sink into her pillow and thought about Dawn. But not the *person,* instead she replayed the new thoughts she associated with the name. She thought about the blood, the pain in Dawn's eyes, the screaming she heard from her and something down in her special place begged for her to continue. She did. She thought about taking Dawn back to the row of trees where no one would be able to see them; where the two could be alone. She would take the girl and force her against the bark, pressing and rubbing every inch of her silky smooth skin.

Keep going, her special place shouted.

She didn't care if the girl wanted to. In fact, she preferred it if she didn't. She liked thinking of Dawn fighting back, pushing against her with all her might. And Heather would absorb it like a plant absorbs sunlight. She would take her fingers and smear the blood all over the girl's stomach.

Keep going.

She would spread open the cuts and shove her fingers deep inside of them. The girl wasn't attractive, the pain was. She wouldn't stop when the girl screamed, or pleaded, or cried out for mercy. Those would only help. She would revel in the screaming, the pleading, the begging for mercy. Especially since the girl would get none from Heather. She could hear the screams now, a helping hand from her special place making them crisp. Heather would have her for as long as she wanted.

Keep going.

She moved her left hand underneath her shirt and found her left breast. It was much smaller than the girl's but it would do for now. She took her thumb and shoved the nail deep into her bosom, harder and harder without slowing down. She hadn't gone as brutal as she could have into the girl's tit, but she did for her own. She bit her lip and closed her eyes. She was getting something in her special place. She was getting closer.

She felt something in her boob give way as her thumb shot through the skin and a healthy gush of warm liquid brushed against her finger and slid down her body.

Keep going.

She moved her hand, now one finger wetter and redder than the rest, to her forehead. A poorly made minefield of red and yellow acne with each claymore sitting above the dirt. It would finally be useful for something. She knew it would. She dug her nails, all but the thumb, into the right of her forehead and, without thinking, slashed them across to the left. Skin came off under her fingernails and fresh blood and pus oozed down into her eyebrows and ears. She didn't cry out. The pain made it better. She was feeling something she'd never felt. She was "getting off", "reaching her climax." Phrases she had never said or used before flooded her head and made her smile. She pushed her fingers in deeper, moved them faster, and made them rougher. This was it; Heather Grey was having her first, and miles from her last, orgasm in, as far as she was concerned, the best and only possible way.

Luckily, Heather had been alone when she burst through the front door and up to her room. If any of her numerous other family members were home, they may have wondered why she was screaming. They might not have heard the horrid joy in it either.

"Am I a bad person?"

The question made Evan turn her over, so she was facing the ceiling instead of the wall, and stare at Amy in the dark. This was worse than the volcano. That was a passing monster that he had avoided unscathed, but the sad thoughts that followed it were the ones that stuck with him, for a long time. He almost wished she was asking out of a genuine willingness to hear the answer, but he knew her better than that. It wasn't that she thought she was a bad person or had gone too far, she was just afraid of what she was always afraid of; being alone. This was a test for him, a test to see if he still cared about her. And he did, more than anyone else on the planet he did, but he really wished she actually wanted an answer sometimes. She had gotten lucky so far, much more lucky than anyone had any right to be, but eventually that would run out and Amy would do something too big to simply ignore and move on from. And it was almost certain that she would be alone then. Even if he went down with her, prisons kept the genders segregated.

He brushed the hair out of Amy's eyes, finally feeling like he was touching skin and not the burner of a stove, planted a kiss on her forehead and told her what she wanted to hear. "Absolutely not. You just...lost your temper. Happens to all of us. Sometimes you can't keep all of the feelings bottled up and you need to find some way to let them out."

She knew what he meant. Her bottle took the form of her inner volcano after all. "Thank you."

"No problem. Now let's get some sleep. We've had a very interesting day." He reached over her waist and grabbed her hand. "I love you."

"Love you, back," Amy said. She really did, which made her all the more afraid to think about how he would react to her next statement. "Evan?"

"Yeah?"

"There's something I haven't told you. About what happened with Dawn."

Hearing Amy say her real name made his eyebrows come together and his tone fuse with apprehension. "What about it?"

"Evan," she sighed, "I liked it. A lot. And I want to do it again. The beware feeling is gone and the anger hasn't left. I don't know if I can control it anymore."

For one split second, Evan Mitchell was terrified of the girl he lay next to. He thought back to his knife. He had thrown it in his downstairs trashcan, but that wouldn't suffice for long. If Amy had found it once, she could find it again. Especially if her rage was no longer going to be taking a break. He hardly understood her anger and her beware feeling at all and to know that now what little he knew was going to be changing filled him with something far too close to dread. He cleared his throat and hoped his fear wasn't noticeable when he spoke. "Let's deal with that later. Like, Sunday or something. That's two days away, which will give us time to think. We can talk about it then because right now,

I'd rather die.

I just want it to be the two of us. Here and happy."

"Okay," her shaky voice responded. "Sunday."

"But I think we're going to need to spend that time separated."

Amy froze, understanding what he was really referring to and intentionally choosing not to say. Immediately she felt her eyes swell with tears that he thankfully couldn't see in the dark. She was too scared to argue and all she would allow herself to say before the tears threatened to choke her was, "Are you sure?"

Evan nodded and tried to hold her hand a little tighter. "Yeah. Just until Sunday. We both need time to think. I'll take you home tomorrow and pick you up the next day, okay?"

She turned over so her face was to the wall and Evan silently sighed his relief that she wouldn't be putting up a fight. Though he knew the only time she didn't fight against something she disagreed with was when she was too scared to bother.

And knowing that almost made him feel better.

He didn't sleep well that night.

Dawn liked showering. Something about the warm water falling against and rolling down her skin, washing away sweat and grime, was somewhat therapeutic for her. But this time the shower only highlighted the problem.

The warm water felt like acid on her stomach. Eating away her skin and stinging when touched. She still hadn't looked at it, but the urge was getting too strong to resist. Especially now that she was as bare as the bark on a tree. She washed the rest of her body thoroughly, also attempting to wash away the recent events, which failed, and she checked her breast to see if there was any blood.

There wasn't. Just a deep, poignant imprint of a crescent moon.

She stepped out of the shower, towel wrapped around her like a clumsy hug, and inch by inch, uncovered her wound. She looked down at her stomach in the mirror and coughed out a chuckle at the sloppy penmanship the mark displayed. But that awkward chuckle was short and painful.

Carved into her slim pale stomach, with odd and viciously intentional imprecision, just above her bellybutton were the letters:

WHORE

They were there, forever, a permanent brand forced upon her. A word that didn't even describe who she was. A wave of self deprecation, harsh and unrelenting, washed over Dawn and she fell limp to the rug and cried. Harder than she had all day. Harder than she had in all her life. But after half a minute or so she pulled herself back up, as she always did. There was a greater problem than her emotions. She would have to set that aside, which she also always did.

Reaching up and holding back a yell from stretching her cut up stomach, Dawn grabbed a roll of gauze from the closet and began wrapping it around her wound, like a kid who uses toilet paper to become a mummy. And with each loop, she felt more tears slide down her face and more snot fight to come out of her nose. She threw her jeans in the trash, the waistband much too purple for her liking, put on her pajamas and looked at herself in the mirror.

She had never thought she looked more ugly.

Her eyes left her reflection and looked down into the sink as Dawn thought about something she couldn't remove from her head; *Those eyes.*

She still thought about them, the hours that had passed had done nothing to dull their clarity. Usually something as minor as someone's eyes she'd forget about in less than an hour. She never thought it would be that noteworthy. Or terrifying. But this time it was. This time they were cemented into her mind as if they were glued to her eyelids, always seeing them whenever she closed her eyes for longer than a blink. Irises like black marbles, where others would be blue or brown or green, Amy's matched her pupils so closely that it looked like one giant black dot standing in the middle of the pure white in each eye. She had been forced to look into them and saw nothing but her own reflection. They were polished, they were shiny, but a certain nonexistence lay behind Amy's eyes. Just a deep, black, circular ocean that seemed like it could darken the world and swallow her whole. A wave of goosebumps washed over her, flowing from her legs to her hips, then covering her back and rising to the sides of her face. It was then that she realized the bottom of her vision was turning streaky, shiny. Another tear rolled down her cheek and she quickly wiped it off with the sleeve of her shirt.

No, not again. Never again.

She didn't want to give Amy the satisfaction of crying. She had taken too much already. Dawn turned off her bathroom light, hovered into her bed and tried to fall asleep. Although she knew that all she would see when she closed her eyes were the permanent, pitch-black marbles that seemed to burn a hole straight through her body.

Those eyes.

She longed for the memory of Sophia Wilkinson.

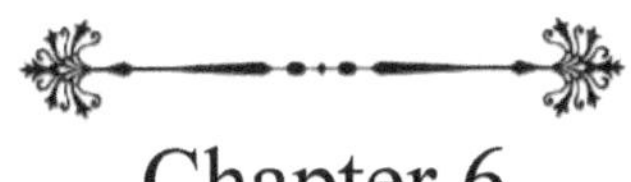

Chapter 6

Zoey liked to think after sex. Oftentimes, right after. She saw it as a time to go over what she had experienced and reflect on it's impact. But after Brandon rolled off of her and began catching his breath, instead of immediately trying to figure things out, Zoey chose to wait. Overnight. She wanted to sleep on it before analyzing their time together. She hoped that extra time would help her come up with an answer but, she was wrong. As she lay in her bed, blinds blocking out the ever rising sun, Zoey realized that sleeping on it did her no good in terms of better understanding why this kept happening.

Yet again, she had felt nothing. No satisfaction, no pleasure, no passion. At least she was happy that she didn't feel used but it would have been hard to feel that way when she knew just how much she had used Brandon. Had used all of them.

He did what the rest of them did, he grabbed the parts of my body the rest of them grabbed and he lasted about as long as the rest of them had lasted. So why do I still feel zip when it's supposed to feel amazing? I didn't do anything wrong, I don't even know how I could have done anything wrong. All I did was lie on my back and make the right noises, but it still didn't do anything for me. Add his name to the list, one more cog is in place.

She wondered if she would ever be able to enjoy sex and wondered how many more times she might have to force herself to have it before she did. The thought was horrid enough to drive her out of her flimsy nightwear and into a much more concealing outfit.

The bright sunlight forced Trevor Logan's eyes open and the first thought he had was the first thought he had every Saturday morning; *I hate weekends.* The thought of spending forty-eight solid hours cooped up in his room doing diddly-shit was nothing short of torturous. His home was a prison, and his room his cell. He had grown to loathe the four walls that separated him from the rest of the house, and the sunlight shining through his window only served as a painful reminder of the world he couldn't explore. Because what was the point of going out if you had to do it alone? Amy and Evan were the ones who came to him with the plans and information and he always gladly agreed to go along with it, desperate to break the monotony of the two 'S' days that so rudely interrupted the school week. And Heather? He really didn't want to be alone with her.

She was hot, absolutely, but sometimes she got a little too intense for him, a little too offbeat. Whenever he was alone with her it felt like she was waiting to pounce on him. Like at any moment he could say the wrong thing, or the right thing, and she would attack.

As far as he was concerned, he would be alone for the next two days, as he always was. The next ceaseless two days.

He got up slowly, practically rolling onto the floor, and went into the kitchen to find something to snack on. He heard his mother following him, but made no motion to acknowledge her. She was his prison guard.

"We're going to your father's today." Her voice was firm, but he knew that could be changed if the need be.

He tried to appear unfazed but the frustration itself was clenching his fists independent of his mind's command. She frequently attempted to get Trevor to go to his father's house and, luckily for him, it didn't take much willpower from his end to get her to drop it. His mother had been slightly coerced into doing and becoming a lot of things because of his father, and she still had some of the bruises to show for it, so when he got angry enough with her she shrunk away and let him be. Perhaps seeing the same anger she had seen in her husband, perhaps not wanting to upset the last person she was living with, it didn't matter much to him.

He kept his voice clear and slow, it was the voice he remembered hearing his father take with his mother right before she would leave him be. "No I'm not. Feel free to go alone, but don't wait up for me."

"Jeremy is going to be there."

He froze in his tracks and turned to face his prison guard who suddenly looked much nicer. And much more smugly satisfied. She knew she had him. "Are you serious?"

"Yep. We leave at noon." And Trevor was alone in the kitchen with his hand on the cereal box, thinking about all the ways he would make this day last. Not just for him, for his younger brother, too. *This* weekend would be nothing like the rest.

"It can't be. I won't let it be," he said to the cereal he held that he was no longer hungry for. For the first time in his life, he willingly ran into his room. His cell looked very inviting right now. He had quite a bit to think about in the time before he left.

His parents had been the textbook case of a couple who had no patience. Dating, having a child, marriage, it had all come to them far too soon, before certain traits and behaviors could be noticed or snuffed out by the other person. For his mother, it was her willful attitude towards what she believed. For his father, it was how little he could stomach an ideology he disagreed with. And neither of them were aware of the hidden traits in the other person until it was too late to simply break up.

Trevor had a few years to watch them before they were married and as little as they fought, one of them always managed to leave before things could get out of hand. Which, to some extent, solved the problem before it could become a problem. But after they had gotten married and they depended on each other and one of them simply couldn't leave and go to their apartment to cool down, the problem was not so easily solved. And not so verbally either.

Usually he was good at tuning them out, mostly due to the fact that they never yelled when they fought. They had an unnerving amount of control over the volume of their voices, even at their most furious. Which was apparently counteracted by the astoundingly small amount of control they had over their bodies when they argued. They simply spoke to each other, their voices angry but never loud, until a hand had to be used to signify the end of the argument. And his mother's hand flew almost as often as his father's did. They certainly shared that part of their marriage. Maybe it was in their vows, *For each of my hands that hit you, yours may hit me.*

Somehow, despite their inability to control their bodies when talking to each other, they rarely ever lost control when having to discipline him and once it became just him and his mother, she hardly punished him at all. Either because she didn't want to drive him away or because there was some shared sort of symbiotic relationship between her and her ex husband and, once separated, they became weaker. It was an idea that Trevor wasn't against,. Having to watch or even hear his mother and father hit each other until one of them simply couldn't take it anymore wasn't something Trevor wished on anyone.

Nor were the countless times he wondered if they were ever going to realize he was listening and take their physical anger out on him, always assuming that they eventually would. He had gone to bed most nights tense and ready to run if he had to.

And that, he figured, was the worst part of all of it. The changing, the flipping, the not knowing how they were going to handle solving their issues when they were dating or married or divorced. And not knowing how, after the marriage and divorce, they were going to start treating him. At first they cared about each other, then they attacked each other when the arguments got too intense and now neither ever spoke to the other and his mother rarely ever raised her voice or hand. His mother went from confident and stubborn to violent and stubborn to submissive in the space of a handful of years. And if he had known or seen or heard from his father for longer than a few minutes at a time over those same few years he wouldn't have been surprised to notice the same thing with him. And those sort of emotional acrobatics left whiplash on a child's brain and on their emotions. And as he sat in his mother's SUV and the distance between his half and the other half of the family shortened, he began to think about his younger brother. The one who had been too young to remember anything about his parents' slap fight of a marriage. The one who hopefully didn't have the same emotional marks that Trevor did.

How long has it been since I've seen him? Trevor thought with both excitement and slight dismay. *His ninth birthday party?* Trevor choked on the number. *Four years ago. But damn was it fun. The pranking, the laughing, the water balloons that didn't even break when you hit someone with them. They just bounced off and popped on the grass. God I wouldn't trade that day for anything.* His smile got bigger and he felt his glasses get slightly higher above his nose, then slide back down, a bit lower than where they usually sat. He pushed them back up as the vehicle slowed down in front of a familiar yet alien house and an unnatural sense of anxious urgency sunk down into his stomach. A feeling of warning, of cautioning, of admonishing. Steph and Zoey would have understood it perfectly. He ignored it though, and was inside before his mother had taken the keys out of the ignition and was in his younger brother's room, growing horrified, by the time she walked into the house that belonged to her ex-husband and second born son, intent on fully ending things today.

Jeremy Logan was virtually unrecognizable to Trevor. His bowl cut hair had been turned into a head with no hair on one side, and seemingly all of it on the other, flopping down and almost covering the boy's right eye. He had grown at least a foot since Trevor had last seen him. His optimistic gaze had now become one soured with animosity. The boy's clothing had also changed, getting much more muted and dark from his ninth birthday when everything he wore had no less than three colors splashed onto it and he looked at Trevor the same way a child looks at a needle. Trevor's ideas for how he would spend the two hours he had with the brother he never saw, fell out of his mind and shattered on this thing calling itself Jeremy Logan's floor.

He did what they did, what both of them did. He was Trevor's familial lifeline and now that final vein had been severed as well. Apparently it was just some horrible curse of this family. He had changed just like their parents had. He took what he should have been, how he should have acted and carried himself and looked, and had completely shifted all of it around and sent Trevor for yet another loop of emotional surprise. What was so difficult about simply keeping things the way they should be? Why couldn't the people in this family just stay the same? Why had he been able to when the rest of them couldn't? Was he doing something wrong?

No, he wasn't, he knew that. He would defend that. He wasn't the one constantly flipping his appearance and outlook and attitude like his mother and father and now his brother. He was smart enough to know to keep things the way they should be, to keep things safe. And if Jeremy didn't understand that or refused to believe its importance, then this half of his family really may as well be strangers to him. Not that his mother was particularly better, but his mother was someone he couldn't get away from. With these two, he could.

But not yet. This visit was meant to last two hours.

Every ten minutes, five seconds went by. He tried to start some conversation, albeit nothing very deep, but he never got a conversation out of it. He would ask what Jeremy was into now, how he was doing in school, if he had any friends or hobbies and he would be met with either one word answers or the names of games he had never heard of. And upon admitting his lack of familiarity with them, he would get little more than a grunt, showing that Jeremy had heard him but was not interested in teaching him anything.

It was a mentally exhausting couple of hours and he felt like he had finished running a marathon by the time he and his mother left the house that belonged to two people he never wanted to see again. But he had been right. So far this *was* nothing like his other weekends. This was far worse. His other weekends hadn't made him lose all hope for his family, or anyone in it, to be the same.

"So, did you have a good time with your brother?" Judy Logan asked her son as they pulled away from the house where she had spent far too much time explaining to Noah Logan that the spark was lost for her and he'd have to move on. They had separated years back and he was still fawning over her. Maybe once she changed her last name back he would get the hint. *He may say he's changed, but I have the scars and bruises to make his promises moot. I'll never go back to that pig. At least I was always pulling my punches.*

"I don't want to go back there anymore."

The straightforward and emotionless response her son gave her, made her eyebrows almost touch her hairline. Though she felt the same way, she hadn't expected a similar response from him. "Why not?"

He struggled to put his feelings into words and every time he tried to, he heard the voice of the umpire. He had only played baseball for a few years in elementary school but the umpire had still made quite an impact. The strangest people often do. "I di—"

—Strike One.

"He's nahh—"

—Strike Two.

"I cuhh—"

—Strike Three. All right, Logan, back on the bench. Hustle.

He stopped trying and stared out the window, looking at a horizon that had looked much more promising the last time he passed it, going in the opposite direction. He couldn't talk to his mother about this, she was part of the problem. He needed someone else. He needed anyone else. He scoured through the pages of his inner friend list and, to his astonishment, had reached the end almost exactly where he started. There were no more than three names he could turn to and he knew two of them were doing their own thing and wouldn't be able to help him. Only one was left; the only person he'd really rather not go to was the only person he had no choice but to see. He told his mother to take him to her address and before he knew it, he was heading to see her. Alone.

Miles away, Steph Warren was having much better luck with *her* younger sibling.

"Stephie, why don't you like Dad?" Emily Warren asked, crayon in hand. She had spent most of the day with her older sister in her room drawing and every time she made a picture of her family, Stephie always forgot to tell her to color her dad. She had finally worked up the minute amount of courage it took a six year old to ask any question and was now patiently waiting for her sister's answer. Though her patience wouldn't last long.

Hearing Arnold be referred to as Steph's *anything*, let alone *father*, was enough to make her grind her teeth. But this was Emily, who didn't know anything about the life Steph and her mother had before Arnold. Steph wanted to change that, wanted to tell her about Steph's other father and their other siblings, but she knew she wouldn't. Maybe once Emily matured a bit. Maybe when her age reached double digits. "It's complicated."

"What does *commlicated* mean?"

She asked the question with a half interest in the answer, clearly the drawing and coloring took top priority. Steph smiled at her and brought the girl's attention back to her drawing. Something they were both more interested in.

"It doesn't mean anything important to you right now. Now come on." She picked up another crayon and put it in her little sister's hand, not paying attention to the color. She just needed to get Emily's mind on something else. "This one will look nice on the...whatever it is your drawing."

"It's Dad. I'm gonna give it to you to keep in your room. That way you can look at it every day and eventually it'll make you like him," Emily said, her voice strong with the confidence only a six year old who barely understood a situation could have. Steph laughed at her sister's blind optimism and, as much as she wished she could try and get Emily to understand that Arnold was not worth her love, she did realize that she was talking to a six year old. And, regardless of what she said, it would be forgotten by the morning. Emily held out the drawing to her once she had finished it and Steph internally swore she would keep it. After all, it looked more like a zombie than a human. It captured Arnold perfectly.

Steph Warren had a new picture on her wall that night.

Chapter 7

"That's terrible. I'm so sorry, Trevor. Really, I am."

"Thanks, Heather."

Her fabricated sympathy was lost on him. Which she greatly appreciated. She understood his situation, but by no means felt the slightest bit sorry for him. Heather Grey was a stranger to all human emotion. But she was very proud of her ability to replicate them. She looked back at him, keeping the smile she wanted to produce inside, and said, "At least you only have one sibling to worry about. I've got three to keep out of my hair with a couple of adults to top it all off. And they always stay the same, as annoying as can be." She was hoping to get the emotion she wanted out of him from saying that. She did.

The feeling of knowing his family would never be the same was brought tears to Trevor's eyes, which he then gave to his hands to hold. He didn't care if she told anyone he'd been crying, the confusion and the exhaustion and the pain were too much for him to hold in. And now that his family was at the forefront of his mind all he could think about was the fear he used to feel so often and the ninth birthday party and the happiness that day brought him that would never be replicated. A brother he was hardly related to who seemed to want nothing to do with him. He cried.

If he had seen the smile spreading across his friend's face however, he would have promised to never drop a single tear again.

She brought his head to her shoulder and held it there, a common trick she had seen countless people use to console others. She may have painted her family in a negative light, but Heather wouldn't trade them for the world, or anyone else in it. They were hers. They were her living experiments. And she wasn't done testing them yet.

Heather was the third born of four. And, as such, she received the least amount of attention or focus. The oldest, Violet, took their pride, Heather's older brother Daniel, owned the disappointment and the youngest in the family, Mason, kept every ounce of care. Three emotions, four children. Heather knew those were the only emotions her parents could express and the only feelings they could bestow on their children so Heather learned to come to terms with it. And the day she unintentionally started a fight between Violet and Daniel, after spotting Violet's diary in Daniel's closet, she began to use her lack of apparent existence to her advantage.

Whenever she got bored, she would take one of her siblings aside, and tell them about something another sibling never said or did. Sometimes it took longer for the fights to erupt but Heather would always be there when they did. She watched a lot of fights take place growing up and the knowledge that they wouldn't have come to be without her only made her want to create more. And she did. Taking on harder tasks and more difficult scenarios to maneuver through, by ten her feelings had become a desert and she controlled her family's emotions and feelings for each other singlehandedly. She controlled their actions and this experiment required arduous and continuous tests, regardless of how many times nasty insults were launched or siblings and parents left for days or cried themselves to sleep.

She wished she could have gotten them to fight physically, knowing that she had the potential power to break bones would have sent her over the moon, but that was not the case quite yet. Apparently her forty year old parents and twenty-some year old Violet and Daniel had little interest in physically assaulting each other nor their fifteen year old brother. But the future was bright, maybe the right nerve had to be severed and words suddenly wouldn't be enough. She would only know if she waited, which she was more than willing to do. She had been doing this for years, sometimes needing to devote days or weeks to get one sibling to start turning on another. She knew quite a bit about waiting.

With age only came more motivation and knowledge. She learned more about her siblings and parents and kept it all written in her secret notebook, along with a list showing all of the previous times she turned them on each other, what the "problem" was that led to it, and a corresponding date. She looked at it to marvel at how powerful words and extreme neglect could be when put in the right hands. She planned on adding another title to her list today, with a new name next to it.

She closed her eyes, fell deep into the part of her mind that always knew exactly what to say to get the pain pouring, and spoke in a voice that sounded the same to Trevor, but cast a long wide shadow of ulterior motives over the boy.

"I can't believe your parents would *do* something like that to you," the voice hissed.

"What do you mean?" Trevor asked, though he was afraid of the answer. The pain in Heather's voice sounded real and regretful and he didn't want that spreading to him.

Heather used her sad voice the most. It was her favorite. She worked hard to keep it perfect and loved to show it off every chance she got.

Yes, what do I mean? Come hither and find out. Learn what I mean and feel *what I tell you to.*

Hearing her sad voice at work brought a smile to her face, that she quickly removed. This was her first time using Trevor and she didn't need him noticing and ending her trial run where it started. The tears he shed weren't enough, she had to make him angry. Angry at someone who didn't deserve it. That was when Heather would stop; when she could reach out and feel his rage. The rage she used to have in her early, more confused years, before it perished with every other feeling she used to feel, and was buried alongside them in her emotion cemetery. Then she would send him on his way to do something he didn't want to, to someone who wasn't at fault. The same way she had always ended her discussions with her lab rats.

"I mean, some people just don't understand how important it is to keep things the way they should be. Your parents, all knowing as they think they might be, are exactly those people. *They* did this to you and him. *They* separated the two of you and killed your relationship. They could have stayed together and tried to make it work for you and your brother, but that was too much work for them. And you weren't important enough. Not to them, probably not to your brother either."

She let the pause sit for a while, letting her words take effect. When the time was right, she began again. Trevor's stunned silence was music.

"But, hey, this kind of thing happens. Usually not like *this*," she let that word stand out from the rest. She let it sound personal, "but some people go through this stuff. I just wish I could be more helpful. No one should have to fight through something as awful as this alone." And then she saw it in his face and felt it in his body.

There it is. The anger, the hate, the loathing. Not pointed at me though. I just get to sit here and let it consume me.

Her breathing increased.

The feeling was invigorating.

For Heather, at least. It was agonizing for Trevor. He realized she was right.

He had fallen victim to her just as the rest of her family had countless times before.

"They really don't care about me." He phrased it in a bizarre combination of a question and a heavy realization. He got up and Heather slowly rose after him.

"I didn't say that." *I implied it but* you *said it.* You *came to the conclusion on your own. As long as you think that, I've gotten what I need.*

"You didn't have to." He felt tears start to form again and stomped on them with his disgust. "I need to go."

Good, you're useless to me now. Die for all I care. She kept her internal smirk chained up and let her beautiful sad voice continue to work its magic. "You really should stay and think about this, Trevor. Maybe bounce some of your ideas off me."

He looked at Heather and heard an air of happiness in her voice. But he didn't care, his parents had destroyed his relationship with Jeremy and got off Scott free. If they only could have tried to get help, tried to stay together, tried to be better, none of this would be happening. "No, I might take some accidental anger out on you and that's not fair. I don't want to hurt you." He was looking down, mind elsewhere, and didn't notice her sardonic remark.

"You're too kind." *And you couldn't if you tried.* "You want me to give you a ride or something? You don't live too far away." She begged for him to say yes. She could imagine herself now, alone in her mother's or father's car, having just dropped Trevor off at his home, putting her fingers into her "special place" thinking about his pain. And how he'd take it out on whoever was unlucky enough to be chosen. She could feel her fingers inside of her and the sensation almost was strong enough to make her moan. She was pulled into the present when she heard him mumble something that was just a little too soft to be processed.

"Say again?"

"I said, 'no, I'll walk.' I have a lot to think about and it might help. Heather," he looked over at the girl who and realized that she might understand him better than anyone else he knew did. He could see himself spending the whole day with her here. Though he was a bit unsettled by the marks across her forehead. They almost looked like a long ragged scratch, but before he could get too distracted by them, he moved his gaze from Heather's forehead to her wide, dark brown eyes. "I've never been this mad before. I've been pissed before but my body has never damn near shaken with anger. I don't know what to do with all of it."

Heather did.

"Use it against those who caused it. Against those who deserve it. That's all anger is, an internal drive to accomplish a goal your mind doesn't want you to overcome. The best way to satisfy your anger is to let it control you."

"And that works?"

Though she didn't find lying as sacrilegious as others, this time she opted to tell him the pure blank truth. "Believe me, I know from experience."

"Okay, I will."

She smiled. To him it looked understanding. Just like it was supposed to.

"Thank you, Heather."

His heartbreaking sincerity almost made her smile drop. But, to her, it was just another slight vocal shift, and nothing more. Her smile remained stitched onto her face.

"Anytime."

The second he left she reached under her mattress and felt around until her fingers touched a very familiar leather and string. She latched onto it and pulled her notebook up to get a better look. She kept it hidden for almost a decade from the four guinea pigs that ran rampant throughout her home and it was the only thing she felt the need to protect. She unraveled the string that tied around it and opened it to the page she'd written on last, a mere two days ago. Grinning but feeling nothing inside her change, she added SATURDAY FEBRUARY 22 to the left and, to the right of the vertical line, she wrote, with eyes glimmering and teeth showing, TREVOR: FAMILY SEPARATION.

This newest entry was her three hundred and forty-fourth. She jumped back to the beginning and read over each one, her smile becoming more and more painful to wear, which only made it grow and stretch farther across her face. She had a lot of nostalgia to relive and was very excited to do so. And even more excited to think of new ways more could be added.

She could almost hear their voices, could hear them screaming at each other, swearing at each other, breaking each other's belongings when screaming would no longer serve. It was a symphony of memories.

It was twenty minutes later, and she was on entry 109, when her phone rang. She grabbed it, glaring that something had taken her out of her childhood, and was filled with another tingle from her special place when she read Trevor's name.

She controlled herself and scrolled through her voice collection to find one that fit the situation. She eventually settled on *interested and/or concerned*, which was in the *care* file. She took the call, cleared her throat and she heard her voice, in a perfect duplication of what she knew about interest and concern, say, "Hey, Trevor, what's up?" What he said next made her fake voice die and her real one take over.

"I've been thinking and...I don't really think I should take my anger out on anyone in my family. I don't know it just...doesn't seem right."

"Yes it does!"

The volume of her voice made him yank the phone away from his ear as if it had been pulled by a rope. *Christ, she sounds possessed.*

Heather calmed herself down, the hardest thing she had ever forced herself to do, and brought her fake voice back to life. "It's perfectly fair to give them what they deserve. *They* did this to you, and they should pay. *Someone* should." That last part wasn't supposed to come out, but she was too angry to contain herself.

"Someone will. I've already thought about that."

Heather's burning glare cooled down a bit. "And?"

"*And,*" he said mockingly, "I'll be able to let it out without having to do any of the thinking or planning myself. Amy has already found her next targets, so I figure, why not save it for them? Why do they deserve to be so happy, why shouldn't they be taken down a peg? If they look at me like I'm a plague, why should I act like one?"

"Can you at least give me a hint?" She didn't need one, but she wanted to hear him say it.

"Bark, bark," Trevor said and ended the call. That was all she needed to know.

Heather looked down at her phone and turned it off. She said it aloud, hearing the words as if they were the first she ever spoke. "Bark...bark." For the first time in her life, Heather Grey felt something inside of her get warm. She didn't know what it was, but she liked it. She put her notebook back under her mattress. She had something much more important to think about.

Chapter 8

Evan had taken Amy home first thing Saturday morning to give them time to clear their heads. Maybe he needed to, but Amy didn't think for one minute about Dawn, or the knife, or what happened on Friday at all. All she thought about was one thing; the future of her and Evan's relationship. She knew he was different from her, in terms of mental state and keeping his temper under control.

Although after what happened with his dad, I'm surprised he's not worse than me, Amy thought as she paced back and forth in her sister's empty room. It was where she went when she felt stressed, which was the biggest reason why she stayed out of her home as much as possible. She ended up in her sister's room more than her own. She turned to face Elizabeth Cooper's old bed and ran her hand along the mattress, sheets still clinging to it like a desperate hug.

She would have stayed that way for a while but the sudden blast of music she heard ripped her hand away and pushed her against the wall. She finally started breathing again when she realized the music and accompanying vibration was coming from slightly below her hip. She pulled out her phone and felt a sigh of relief and fear pour out of her mouth as she answered.

"Hi, Evan, what's up."

"I'm on my way to pick you up, okay?" His voice sounded devoid of a heart, of a pulse. She had never heard him talk like that before and it made her shudder. The voice continued. "Let's go for a little drive."

Usually that would make her smile. She loved driving around with Evan. Feeling the wind in her hair, watching the world zoom by, getting to let out whatever she was thinking and knowing it would stay between the doors of his truck. She wanted to smile, but she knew there was something else causing this. Some other reason, and not a good one, that led Evan to want to take her out with him today. The same reason he had dropped her off at her house yesterday. He was making a decision and couldn't have her around while he came to the conclusion. He couldn't have her influencing his decision. He was going to end things.

No, no that's not true, he can't. I can't. I can't handle that. No, Evan, please don't.

"Amy? Are you still there?"

She pinched her stomach to hide the tears she just knew he would hear, and replaced them with a calm, happy tone. "Oh, yeah, sorry, umm," it wasn't working. She pinched harder, rubbing her fingers and twisting her hand. She gritted her teeth and stomped on the carpeted floor to try and relieve the horrible burning pain and, in doing so, killed the wariness in her voice. "Yeah, sounds good. Where are we going?"

Please just say 'to a movie' or 'out to eat' or, fuck, even just say that we're going to sit in the truck and not speak to each other at all. Say anything other than what I know you're going to.

"I'll be there soon," the robot voice said, then Amy heard nothing on the other end. She heard nothing at all, barely even her own breathing or her soft, rapid heartbeat.

I'll have to get used to that, she thought. She closed her eyes and held in the sobs that were scratching at her mouth to be released. *Not now. Not here, in Liz's room. Don't ruin what's—*

"—What are you doing in here?" A tone dripping with anger spat at her. Her eyes opened and fell to the floor. *You can do this, just keep your eyes on the floor. Whatever you do, don't look at him. Wait for the storm to pass. God, what I would give to be deaf.*

She turned, eyes still burning a hole in the floor, to look at her father. Or, more accurately, the shoes of her father. That was about all she could handle looking at. "Nothing, sir." It disgusted her to have to call him that, but that was the title he demanded he go by in their home, always had been, and tempting him by choosing to omit the title didn't strike Amy as a smart idea. And she had more important things to focus on, like trying to slow her breathing. She saw his shoes move forward and felt a shaking hand grab her forehead and push it against the wall with a gentleness that didn't comfort her in the least. Her eye-line rose and the second she saw her father's face, she immediately felt herself shrink down and the urge to cry had never been harder to resist. Except for the night her mother had left. That night she hadn't been able to resist it at all.

She had spent what felt like a few straight hours watching her tears slide down her bedroom window as she pressed her face against it, staring as far down the road as she could, waiting for her mommy to come back home and put her to bed. That was six year old Amy's favorite time of day, when day had left and night returned to bring her and her mother together for a few minutes to chat before bed.

But this time there would be no nighttime chat or tickle fight or snuggle time. Two cold hands grabbed Amy under her arms, dragged her to her bed and dropped her onto it with no care for how she might land.

She wailed, her face moist and her head throbbing, "I want Mommy! Where's Mommy?"

He crouched down next to his daughter and looked into the red soaked eyes of a girl who had, at such a young age, ripped his wife away from him and left him alone with two children and no answers. *This one*, he thought, *shouldn't even exist*. He glared down at the little home-wrecker crying and pounding on her bed in front of him. "Your mother is gone."

"Why?" The little girl asked. She saw something new look down at her then, something she had never seen before. It wasn't her daddy. It looked like him, but there was some kind of monster underneath what she saw. And it made her squeeze her favorite stuffed animal, a bright pink pig her mother had won for her at a carnival the previous summer, even harder. The monster walked over to the light switch near her door and Amy felt cold at the thought of being alone in the dark. She needed her mommy's kiss to protect her from the monsters who lived in her room, and especially from the one that looked so much like her daddy but just *wasn't*. The girl couldn't explain it, but she could tell.

"Don't ask me that. You already know the reason." The monster snapped off the light, shut the door and the six year old girl who had lost both parents that night dragged herself back to the window and continued staring out at the empty road and black sky until she fell asleep on the floor. But that wasn't where it ended.

"You know you're the reason your mother left," her father said, his voice booming through her ears. She had heard that sentence at least once a week since her mother's leaving and had become used to the words she was supposed to follow it up with.

"Yes, sir." The words were simple noises to her now but she still hated saying them, even all these years later.

"*And* your sister."

You'll never get me to admit to that. Not once as long as I live. She'd have to be crazy to say any of that out loud, but she straightened her back, took a long breath through her nose, smelling his cigarette smoke, and said with her eyes still on the ground, "Elizabeth left for college."

"She left because of what you did. Because she couldn't take living here, with you, anymore. She was just waiting for a good excuse to jump ship. Haven't you ever wondered why we haven't seen her since she left? What has it been, two years?" He knew how long it had been. Knew it down to the minute, but he wanted to hear her say it. To give the guilty a chance to confess.

"Three years."

"EVEN WORSE," he shouted and the volume pushed Amy back to the wall and shook her.

Just hit me, please. Slap me, break my arm, cripple me, I don't care. Just do something that hurts less and heals quicker. For once, just hit me.

James Cooper had never laid a finger on his daughter. In anger or otherwise. The only people who had hugged Amy in the past ten years or so, were her sister and Evan. James didn't think physical abuse was right, despite how much she deserved it. Instead, he leaned closer to her and delivered some new information. Because if he wanted to hurt her, there were much better ways to do that.

"I never wanted you. It was your mother who wanted to keep you. I told her it was a bad idea, that one was enough, that it would be too much work and we would barely be able to afford it, but as soon as she found out you'd be a girl, convincing her was a lost cause. She would have you no matter what. And look where that led her, look where *you* led her. She put up with you inside of her for nine months, only to run away when she knew I was right. Because you ate her alive. Always crying and whining and demanding, you just took and took and took until she couldn't handle it anymore. She had to leave this house and abandon this family just to be her own person again because you took so much of her."

What also took so much of Lily Cooper was her husband's miserable constant insistence that she get rid of her baby. The unwavering willingness he had to set up the appointment, the refusal to listen to her side of things, it had opened her up to how selfish and unreasonable he really was. To an extent, she gave birth to Amy out of spite and was just as upset as her daughter was the day she decided to leave. She didn't want to take Amy with her until she had a well enough life to support the two of them, but moving states and starting over and changing her name to make sure her dangerously persistent husband wouldn't track her down wasn't as easy as motivational quotes made it seem. And even now, more than ten years later, Allyssa Mayer was living far worse off, hardly able to support herself, and assumed her daughter wouldn't want anything to do with her at this point.

James began drifting away from Amy and started talking to himself. "It was the worst decision she ever made. It's amazing how so much can be taken and ruined…" He was back in the present with his daughter and the anger rushed back, "by one…single…accident." The look his daughter gave him made it all worth it. She thought she knew pain? She couldn't dream of what he had been through, having to look after the girl who had torn his family apart and never even apologized. He left. Being in Elizabeth's room was something he couldn't handle for more than a few minutes and he was plenty beyond that.

As soon as he was out of her sight, the tears poured down Amy's face. Her legs could no longer support her and she fell to the floor, laying there and sinking her tears deep into the rug. Her breaths were wet and ragged and shallow and she wished she would choke on them. She had barely begun letting out what was inside her when she heard a horn honk outside and sucked the tears back into herself. Although if her outing with Evan went the way she thought it would, there would be many more tears on that rug when she got back.

Evan had been waiting for longer than normal, and was ready to go inside and take care of this there, when Amy burst out of the front door and ran to his truck. She looked perfectly normal. He knew that would change soon, although he didn't want all of the tears. *But you're definitely going to get them*, he thought. She got in the car and, before doing anything else, she leaned over and wrapped her arms around him. It felt different from the hugs she usually gave him. This one had an aura of panic and desperation, as if she was holding onto someone who had just saved her from drowning, but he still returned it.

"Tell me you love me."

"What? Amy are—"

"—Please. I just...I need to know you do." *His tone will paint the picture. He just needs a brush.*

Evan moved her head off of his shoulder and put her nose touching his. She looked completely exhausted and, again, he assumed that this outing wasn't going to help with that very much. His voice was soft and slow.

"Amy, I don't know why you constantly think I'm suddenly going to stop loving you and I don't know what I could possibly do to put you at ease. So, all I'm going to do is tell you, yet again, that I'm never going to suddenly leave you, okay? You've done a lot of things, some worse than others, and yet we've always ended up in the same bed at the end of the day. You're the best thing I have, you're everything I have and I would never want to hurt you, sweetheart." *Not the best I can do but hopefully it'll be enough right now.* "You want me to keep going?"

She smiled but he could still see sadness behind it. "No, that's enough." She sat back in her seat and strapped on her seatbelt as she thought about how odd he was acting. He called her sounding like he was being held at gunpoint yet spoke to her like he hadn't seen her in months.

The two drove off to Evan's previously determined destination in silence, thinking about completely different things. Amy finally broke the silence and asked Evan something she knew she would get some sort of emotional response out of. "How are things at home?"

Evans fists clenched around his steering wheel until his knuckles were white. "It's fine. It's," pause, "the same." He saw Amy shaking her head in his peripherals and turned his head towards her while still reading the environment he drove through. "I'm not lying, Amy."

"Why do you hate them so much, Evan? Is it because of your dad?"

"Don't talk about that. Not now, while I'm driving." *Or ever, for that matter.*

"That was the first time I've ever seen you cry." *And it was beautiful.*

He took advantage of the red light and looked at her. "And it's going to be the last." *There aren't even any tears left in me.*

After the parade of *I'm Sorry's* had filtered out of his room, he had gone down to the basement, called Amy and told her—

—"I need you to come over."

Amy sat up in her bed, wary just by the sound of his voice. He had a deep voice already, but this was worn out and cracked and exhausted and she knew that whatever he was talking about was worth taking seriously. Which only made her more afraid that she wouldn't be able to get to him

"Right now?"

"Yes. I'll be downstairs." Again, completely empty. This was really the same boy she often heard singing in the shower? A boy she felt comfortable enough to be honest with and give her virginity to?

"Can you pick me up?"

"That wouldn't be safe."

She didn't want to make him feel worse than he already was so she left that topic there, despite his response bringing on an entire new wave of questions.

Besides, now she had a problem that needed dealing with before she could help Evan. Because if Evan couldn't get her and they lived too far apart to walk, the only person who could take her to his house was her father. And suddenly walking six miles at eight o'clock at night seemed much more approachable. "I'll be there as soon as I can, okay?"

"Bye."

He hung up and she sat on her bed with her phone still against her ear. She briefly wondered if her time was better spent thinking about the fact that he had hung up without more than one word or how he still didn't sound particularly human or even alive. But before thinking about either of those things, Amy did what she always did, what got her into trouble so frequently. She acted fast and tried not to process things.

She slid her phone into her pocket and made sure she didn't need anything else before leaving. She assumed her father wouldn't give her the time to go to her room and get anything if she did. Walking out to the living room was difficult and waiting for him to address her was no less. He was sitting on the left couch, the one that was aimed towards her, he could see her even without use of his peripheral vision, yet unsurprisingly he made no motion to acknowledge her presence. So, taking in a tiny breath, she made him.

"Can you take me somewhere?"

He said nothing, hardly moved at all and Amy thought about what might be happening to Evan right now, what had already happened to him to throw him into the horrid state of his emotional daze. And at the thought that she was being kept from him and from helping him because of her father and his petty childishness, her hands clenched behind her back. And she used the word that she knew would get his attention. And she was right.

"Dad, I—"

His head yanked to face her and his features were slightly hidden by the lamp behind him. "Never call me that."

Now his eyes were on her and, despite how weak and shaky it made her, she lunged at the attention. "Sorry, sir, but I need you to take me somewhere."

He seemed to size her up and sighed, as if ashamed that she still looked the way she did and had the gall to still live in this house with him. "Why do you think you deserve that?"

Expecting such a question, Amy had her response ready and she even felt somewhat empowered by the answer she would give him. It wasn't one he would be able to argue against. It helped them both. "Because then I'll be out of the house for a few days, you won't have to...deal with me. Isn't that what you want?"

That last sentence went a little too far. She felt it at once and she knew her father did too when he stood up and his long slanted shadow crawled against the floor until it met her and seemed to grab at her ankles, holding her in place.

"Don't you ever tell me what you think I want. After everything you've done to this family, the last thing I need is you telling me what I want. You understand that?"

She nodded and dropped her eyes to the floor. "I just think, sir, that if you take me where I want to go, you won't have to deal with me for a few days. I thought it would be nice."

"It's not enough is what it is."

They both said nothing for a few seconds, him mulling over his options and Amy waiting to hear his response and she had the time to think about just how angry all of this was starting to make her. Her volcano had erupted a few days prior and she had taken that out on someone she couldn't remember so she shouldn't be getting so unstable so soon but, when it came to her father, she wasn't surprised to find him to be an exception to the rule. And, God, it was so tempting. He was even close enough for her to reach him, any part of him. She thought if she could just launch herself at him one time she would be able to get him to the floor and everything she hadn't let out on all of her disgusting dipshit classmates would explode into a fury she didn't think she herself would be able to stop. Then, instead of some jackass who had the nerve to try and test her on a bad day, he would be the one with the swollen eye or the broken nose or the limp that was so bad he needed a crutch. And then things would change around here and she would never hear him say, *You know you're the reason your mother left* again. How blissful that would be. And how simple it sounded.

"Where are you going?" he finally asked, sulking like a child who didn't get their way.

"A friend's house, sir."

He scoffed, as if the idea of her having friends was too outrageous to believe. "Where?"

She gave him the address then added, "It's only thirteen minutes away." He gave her a glance that shut her up and again she fought back an urge to shove him down the stairs.

"We're going now."

She nodded, beyond grateful that she had brought her phone with her, and followed him into his car.

She was thinking about Evan for most of the ride so it didn't feel especially long, even in the utter silence. And when they got down the street leading to Evan's house and a little more than half a dozen cars were shoved up along the front yard, her fears deepened. She still didn't know what happened but if half the family needed to be together for it, the news was either great or terrible. And she had a feeling she wouldn't be surprised when the time came to find out.

The car stopped in the road once it lined up with the front door. "Get out."

She was too deep in thought to really bother with her father so all she did was unbuckle her seatbelt. "Thank you." As she tried to bring her hands to the door, he grabbed her wrist and she whipped around to face him. This may have been the first time he had touched her in years. She had forgotten how strong he was. And all at once the idea of her jumping on him or breaking any of his bones seemed impossible. He could probably kill her with one hand and no weapon if he wanted to.

"This doesn't change anything. And I'm holding you to what you said. A few days. I don't want to see you at any point before that."

She managed to look him in the eyes for a few seconds, noted his raw severity, nodded her agreement and left the car once he let her go. She could hear him speeding off down the road as she walked up Evan's front yard but he didn't matter to her anymore. Because now there were other problems to worry about. She walked into Evan's house, his mother and father had told her she didn't need to knock because she was as close to family as she could be, and made her way downstairs. She held her hands together and wondered what she was about to walk into and how long this whole situation might linger in her mind.

She turned left once she opened the door to the basement and found Evan sitting on the couch doing nothing besides breathing and possibly blinking. He hadn't turned the lights on and it was too hard to tell. She took in a breath and walked over to him, hoping that her fear wasn't showing. She stood in front of him, not yet willing to crouch down and see exactly what was going on inside and behind his eyes.

"Evan, what's going on?" Even her voice was shaking a little. She wondered what his voice might sound like if he spoke, seeing as how he looked like a limp puppet without a puppeteer, and she pushed the thought away.

"Evan, I need you to tell me what's going on? Why are so many people here?" No answer again and this time she started to feel the fearful tears scratching at her eyes. "Please, Evan, you're starting to scare me. Did something happen to Henry or your mom or your dad?"

He blinked harder and twitched a little, as if she had prodded him in the ribs with something sharp and she realized that this memory was going to stay with her for the rest of her life.

Then, without a single word or sound, he started to cry. And Amy finally knew how he must have felt when she did the same. The only difference was, she did it in the middle of the night so he wouldn't hear her. Most of the time he didn't, but when he did he simply held her until she was empty and until she fell asleep. She was ready to do the same for him but she couldn't. Not yet at least.

She did hold him for a while, hoping he might slip up and let her know what was going on, but he never did. And after what felt like fifteen minutes of standing with his face buried in her stomach, he started to dry up a little bit and Amy explained things vaguely, so as not to disrupt what was already a faltering metal state. "I need you to stay here for a few minutes, okay? I'll be back as soon as possible."

She made her way upstairs, her fear still eating through her stomach lining, until she found Evan's mother in her room, staring at her bed. Amy said her name a few times but she didn't move until Amy lightly pressed her hand on the woman's shoulder. Then she whipped around as if given no warning and lightened up a bit when she saw who had scared her.

"When did you get here, Amy?"

She shrugged and tried not to read too much into Isabella's horrible wet and tired eyes. All she needed to know was that the problem that was affecting Evan was also affecting her. "A few minutes ago. Evan called me. Can you tell me what's going on? I've tried to ask Evan but he won't."

Isabella nodded, sat Amy down on the bed and explained everything she and the rest of the family knew so far. Which wasn't much. All they really knew was where he had done it, how he had done it and that he was successful in doing it. But that was enough, she didn't need or want a full blown medical report explaining the details. She could barely handle thinking about it and she had to stifle sobs as she explained it to Amy.

Once she heard the news and put it in the context of Evan's behavior it made more sense. And the first thing she thought, horrible as it was, was how different her reaction would be if that ever happened to her father. Once the selfishness passed and after she spent a few minutes consoling Evan's mother, she made her way back downstairs, not making any eye contact with the rest of the sniveling silent family she may have met at one party or another but couldn't remember right now. She closed the door behind them and sat beside Evan on the couch. He hadn't moved. She took his hand. He barely gripped it.

"Do you want to talk about it?"

He shook his head.

Amy nodded. "I'll be listening if you do. And I'm not going anywhere. I'll stay here for as long as you want." *Much more than a few days,* she thought. They stayed downstairs in the dark for a while before the rest of the family left, then they went up to Evan's room and went to bed. Evan did at least, she assumed he was exhausted, but Amy had a bit more difficulty falling off.

He was gone. The first of Evan's parents she had met, the one she was much more nervous about making a good impression on but the one who immediately put her at ease. The one who told her, while she was running her fingers back and forth on the dinner table, that she could be a pianist with form and precision like that. She hadn't believed he was being serious, but she remembered compliments when she got them. And now he was gone. By choice.

She really didn't know if she wanted Evan to ever talk to her about it. How could she help him? What could she say?

He had tried to explain it to her a few times, both the following day when he thought he would be able to process things a little clearer as well as weeks and months afterwards, but he never quite got her to fully understand. She could nod and *mm-hmm* all she wanted but Evan knew it wasn't something Amy was going to comprehend out of the blue one day. He didn't even know if he comprehended it himself.

He still remembered that day, that night, what had happened before Amy had shown up at the house. And he remembered, after his mother had told him the news and before he was able to call Amy and get the actual support he wanted and needed, he was forced to sit in his room and let each and every member on both sides of his family hug him and say the same thing over and over; I'm so sorry. The words alone made him want to smash something and Evan, rather quickly, grew to loathe all of them and their desperate need to help.

If he had needed any help that might have been appreciated but, after the first week, once it had fully settled in, he knew he had to move on and took strides to do that. But they wouldn't let him. Whether it was them sending him texts telling him how much they love him or it was one of his grandparents who didn't quite understand boundaries simply asking him if he missed his father out of nowhere. One week he had tried his hardest to block out included each of his six aunts coming to the house, one each day, with their foolproof strategy of forcing him to confess his feelings, from endlessly talking about his father to sitting next to him and saying nothing until he had no choice but to start talking to telling him how he should be feeling and not hesitating to mention just how abnormal his grieving process was.

He always said as little as possible, knowing better than to trust any of his chatty, gossipy family members but their endless interference still did a hell of a good job making him feel sick with them and sick with himself. There was a reason he didn't cry and it was one he knew none of his family members would understand. He kept his tears for Amy. Amy didn't try to get him to cry or force him to open up to her or blatantly ask him loaded questions and catch him off guard. Amy listened and Amy didn't always respond. She didn't force her help upon him, she offered it and took what he was comfortable giving. Which was how he thought help should be offered.

He may as well have had the house to himself for the few weeks following that night. Amy stayed with him every day but even her presence began to become almost unnoticeable. She sat with him and talked to him but for the most part, she let him do a lot of the thinking and understanding on his own, so it was harder to remember that she had been there at all. When his mother wasn't at work, she spent every waking second in her room with a blanket tied around her. Her eating was occasional, her speaking was less frequent than that. Evan answered the door, signed off on flowers from people no one in his family even knew, fed himself, put together a new ten foot bookshelf for his room with help from Amy and all the while feeling his father's lingering presence in every room, like food that someone had burned. He became a slave in his own home. And this slave was being haunted. Time and again he wished he could ignore his father and concentrate on something else, something that would make him more happy and all he could think of in those moments were the voices of family members who tried to force him into their grief circle, regardless of his own method of venting. His hatred was interrupted by Amy's voice.

"Evan, why are we at school?"

Amy's voice was brimming with anxiety and her left leg was slightly bouncing up and down, but Evan ignored that as he parked the truck in the same place he parked on Friday. When they had their little skirmish with Dawn. He turned off the truck and said, "Come on, I want to show you something." He got out and Amy didn't.

She could feel her body getting colder and her stomach dropping. *I'm not ready. I can't do this. Please, please don't do this to me, Evan.*

Her internal turmoil was interrupted when Evan opened the door, pulled her out and carried her over to the spot where they had carved into the girl. He set her down onto her feet and stared at her. If Amy had looked at him she would have grown even more horrified at the rigid, unwavering decisiveness in his face. But she didn't look back. Because Amy was too busy wrestling with herself.

Don't cry. Don't you dare drop a single fucking tear. Nothing has even happened yet. There's still a chance, we still have hope. I feel that tear coming. Kill it. Now.

"Amy, do you remember this place? Do you remember what happened here on Friday?" His voice remained calm and without expression. He, of course, knew Amy remembered. How could she not?

Amy nodded, afraid to say something that could lead her to tears. Which, at this point, was almost anything. She could hardly breathe. Evan continued.

"We've both had a few days to think about and process everything that happened and now I think it's important that we talk about what it means for us."

Amy's tear ducts gave way.

Her eyes became a fountain and she fell to her knees on the hard frozen grass. It hurt a bit but she didn't notice. She bawled into her hands and coughed on her own saliva. Her head felt hot and the rest of her, uncomfortably cold. For one awful moment she saw herself in her house, alone, with only her father to keep her company and to constantly remind her of the terrible thing she did to their family. She always contained her tears until she was in one of her very few safe spaces, but the knowledge that the only person who kept her tethered to sanity was following in her mother's and sister's footsteps and leaving her alone was unbearable. And what did it matter if he saw her cry, it was the last time he would see this side of her anyway. She cried harder. It felt like she was vomiting, but she knew she wouldn't feel any better once this was over.

God dammit, I knew this was coming. Why couldn't you just let me finish, Evan thought while watching Amy spill a waterfall onto the same grass Dawn's blood had soaked into a couple of days prior. He, despite knowing it was wrong, found appreciation in watching Amy cry. It was nice to be reminded every now and then that his girlfriend was human. The occurrences were few and far between and they often took place at night when he couldn't see her, but that only made it better when it happened. "Amy, get up."

The voice remained dry. She hated the voice. Through coughs and a banging head, Amy replied, "Please. Please, I...I can't." It hurt to speak and Amy wondered if she would die here, from a broken heart. That always sounded melodramatic and stupid to her, but maybe it was possible after all. Or maybe she would just cry herself into a state of dehydration.

Again, Evan picked her up and set her on her feet. Her entire face was wet with tears and the shining light from the sun made her look plastic. Like a doll.

Evan sighed. "Amy," his voice sounded more raw but it was drowned out by Amy's coughing. "I'm not leaving you."

The words kicked her coughing to the side and took root in her ears. Though it still took a few seconds for her to process them.

"What?" Her voice sounded as if it were put through a tornado and Evan smiled.

"I've made my decision. I'm staying with you, no matter what. I tried to imagine my life without you, and I couldn't take it. We need each other. With everything we've both been through, we're the only people we can say anything to and I'm not going to leave you alone. I care about you too much." He sometimes wondered how he might have ended up if he didn't have Amy alongside him while he made his way through those harder few weeks. And he had a bad feeling he wouldn't have ended up doing much before falling into his father's footsteps.

She took a deep breath, let the cool air fill her lungs and made a sound that was half a laugh and the other half a cough. She cleared her throat, shot some spit onto the ground and returned Evan's gaze. "Really?"

Evan's eyes rolled above his smirk. "Yes, really. I promise, I'll stand by you for good. No getting in the way, no holding you back. Whatever you want to do, you'll be able to count on me. I mean it." Amy forcing him to think about his family had affected him more than she probably expected. He could still feel that anger, as raw as it had been years ago, like it had never gone away, and wondered if Amy's method of releasing the aggression that built and built and never went away was really so crazy.

The sun was starting to come out for Amy Cooper. It had been cloudless throughout their entire expedition but this was the first time she felt the warmth fold around her. She wiped the layer of water off of her face and embraced Evan. It felt like she was doing it for the first time. The vision of her future died and a few more tears, these ones carrying happiness, fell onto Evan's shoulder.

Once the hug ended and they were facing each other again, Amy's face was dry and she was back to her confrontational ways. "So is that the reason you dragged me out here? To screw with my head?"

Evan's color darkened a little and he looked down into the grass again. "No. I want you to know that what you…what we did on Friday, is probably the worst thing we've ever done. And I figured if I could tell you that I still wanted to be with you here, where it happened, then we would both know I meant it. And I do want you to know that it was a mistake. You know that, right?"

Amy wouldn't have called it such a word, but she nodded. She always found it easier to get away with lying when you didn't talk.

Evan nodded back and seemed to lighten up a bit, in both attitude and pallor. "Though I was hoping your face would stay dry while we did this, but that was a gamble I suspected I'd lose. Now we can go." He put his arm around her and led her back to his father's truck.

"Have I ever told you how much I appreciate seeing you cry? It sounds morbid but—"

"—No," her voice cut in, "I think I understand what you mean." And she did.

The two drove home in peaceful silence and spent the rest of the day together. Amy could tell Evan was more angry now than he had been before, prodding him about his family was the presumed reason for that, and she could tell, just from his rigid body and his occasional sigh at nothing, that something was building in him. Fast.

She knew he was never going to get in her way again.

And she smiled.

Chapter 9

Dawn woke up Monday morning feeling the same rough, cramping pain that she had felt all weekend. Except this time she couldn't lay in bed and try to let it go away on its own. She had to be up and in school in mere hours and the pain had not gotten any easier to deal with. In fact, the thought of going to school and having to sit with it, mentally and physically, only made her stomach strain even more.

Can't it just give me a break for a goddamn day? she thought, while getting up and feeling the gauze rub against her stomach and make the pain even worse. She went into the bathroom and changed her makeshift cast, while keeping her eyes away from the wound that still felt as if it were forced into her ten minutes ago. When the final wrap around was done and the gauze peeled off of her tight skin she wanted to cry but she kept her promise that she never would again. It was the new Dawn Bell law. And that law was strictly enforced.

She tried to meditate, but every time she inhaled she felt new pain from her stomach rise up through her body. She couldn't get lost in her wonderful black paradise anymore. Whenever she got close, the pang from her stomach dropped her back into her room. Her new markings had taken *that* away from her, too.

After a few stressful minutes of attempted peace, she gave up and, moving as slowly as possible, got dressed. The idea of wearing anything even remotely tight around any part of her body was enough to make her cringe on prospect alone. Even with the new bandages she put on after taking off the old ones, she didn't plan on taking any risks. Taking risks was what put her in this situation to begin with. She thought for a second if she would ever be able to wear something tight again, but tried not to come up with an answer. She threw on a sweatshirt and sweatpants, which still irritated her cuts through the layers of gauze, but less so than her other options would have. She began moving the waistband up and down to see where it would hurt the least and that was she heard a loud noise come from the kitchen.

She accidentally released her hold on her waistband and snapped it to her stomach and the furiously ache she felt rip up through her body nearly made her drop to the floor. She held onto her dresser though, and when she went out to see what had caused her to interact with the excess pain she was met with the sight of her older brother rooting through the fridge like a raccoon through a trash can. He had come back after his latest week long adventure and seeing him made Dawn feel relief and disapproval.

"Where the fuck have you been?" This she had to hear.

"Out with friends," Cole Bell responded to his sister's random interrogation.

"For a week?" It was a question that she turned into an insult. It didn't matter what he said next, nothing could be justifiable for this.

"What's the big deal? I'm alive, aren't I? It's fine, Dawn."

"The big deal," she said, making quotes around the latter two words, "is that you left without saying anything, didn't say anything the entire time you were gone and left me here alone with Mom. You know how she's been recently."

"All right, I'm sorry I didn't say anything. I'll make sure to do that the next time I leave you with the house to yourself." He said this like he did nothing wrong and then his eyebrows furrowed. "Wait, *recently*? Since when have things changed around here? Let me guess, she's still laying in her second bed in the exact same position she was in when I left?"

Dawn took an apprehensive glance toward the couch and, just like her brother had predicted, their mother was still lying where she had been for the past seven days. *She must have woken up at some point,* Dawn thought while staring at the statue on the couch. She looked back to Cole and said, "It doesn't matter. You just need to let me know when you're about to go on one of your unplanned excursions. That's all I want." She pushed her luck and continued. "And maybe go on them a little less frequently. You know, like, *less* than twice a month."

"All right, Mommy," Cole said with distaste. He didn't need to take this responsibility speech from his little sister. Though warning her the next time he was leaving seemed fair. Given how on edge she was acting, it might help calm her down if he gave her that much. Then he looked down and noticed her bandages peeking out from the bottom of her sweatshirt and looked back up at her. "Or should I say mummy. Is something going on there?"

Dawn felt down to her gauze, ripped it away when she felt her stomach scream at her and looked back at him while pulling her sweatshirt down to cover it. "It's not funny." And his faux caring tone wasn't very funny either.

"Okay," he said, putting his arms up, "but whatever's going on there, just don't die from it." He had closed the fridge that had been opened for Dawn's entire investigation and began heading back to his room. "By the way, this was taped to the front door," he said, handing her an envelope she couldn't read in the black room. The sun had only barely risen and it would still be about twenty minutes until she could discern anything outside. She took the envelope, waited for his door to close and, once it had, turned on the kitchen light, adjusted her eyes and read two words that came with them a feeling of colossal sorrow.

Stamped on the front of it in red, were the words EVICTION NOTICE. Nothing else mattered, the details were, at this moment, irrelevant. She swiftly headed to where her mother lay, still asleep despite the new burst of light.

She put one hand on her mother's shoulder, the other on her head and shook, her frustration and forcefulness growing until Natalie Bell woke up to her daughter mumbling some sort of nonsense she couldn't understand. "Wuuhh? Wuhizzit, honey?"

"Mom, did you pay the housing bill this month?" *Just tell me you didn't and stop looking at me like you've never seen me before.*

Her mother replied, through a dry voice, "No, not yet hun, but there's still time. I got the money, just gotta give it to the bank people." She smiled at her daughter who did not return it.

The "bank people" huh? "Where did you put the money?" *God, tell me you have the fucking money.*

"Isssn my purse, over on the counner." She tried pointing to the counter near the kitchen and, alternatively, whacked her daughter square in the stomach.

The pain burst like a firework and Dawn, tired of the conversation and the woman, threw herself backwards and crawled through the pain to get the purse. She grabbed it off the counter and, sitting on the floor, dug through it looking for anything green. It was the only color she wanted to see.

It's like a nuke went off in here. Tell me you weren't lying. Tell me you have the money, because we're all screwed without it.

After what seemed like an eternity of going through her mom's junk, she finally found an envelope with the beautiful green paper in it. She let out a long breath, or what would have been a long breath if not for the sharp pain that cut it short, and brought it back to her room as she continued getting ready for school. She never dreaded going to school more in her life.

She performed her typical routine, keeping everything shorter if she could, and spent her last nine minutes resting on her bed and breathing through the hideous pain. It wasn't getting better and, against her will, a tear fell out of her eye. She wiped it off, got up, sat for a few seconds to let the stronger pain pass and went to begin what would certainly be the worst day of her life. But first, she had to go deal with the money and she'd done it enough times to know every beat that would play out.

Every beat did.

It was the first, and only, good thing that would happen to her all day. And even as she did it, all she could think of was her mother. Her mother who had been lucky enough to marry rich and had been unlucky enough to let that cushion her life. Dawn could remember when she was a kid, her mother used to jog around their neighborhood every morning and afternoon because she wanted to keep herself as healthy as possible. Now she barely got up from the couch. And why should she? Even though he didn't have to, Dawn's father still sent them money to keep them all from homelessness, so why bother getting up and taking action yourself? She wasn't like an alcoholic, who would fall down the bottle but would at least try to get back out of it for the sake of their family. She was down and stayed down, perfectly content living like a corpse.

At the very least, Dawn was relieved that her mother didn't try to handle the money herself because Dawn needed these experiences. She assumed she wasn't going to be getting the luxurious life her mother had, so learning the nuts and bolts of living would come in handy.

She picked up Zoey, Luke and Steph, all later than usual though none of them seemed to care, and all the while had to fight to contain the incredible pain from the tight seatbelt and the arch of her body. Even when she straightened her back, the torment from her stomach continued to needle her. She began wondering if she would eventually get used to the pain and learn to live with it, and that thought was enough to make her grimace. A face that was not invisible to Luke.

"Hey, you okay?" The face she had made nearly pushed him back. She looked like she was holding in a scream.

She wiped the grimace away and put one of surprise in its place. "Oh, yeah, I'm fine. I was just thinking about something that happened to me while I was getting ready." It wasn't technically a lie, she just omitted some of the more harsh details of the process.

She had decided soon after her markings were given to her that she would keep this mess to herself. She didn't know if she could go to the police without any proof that Amy had done this to her. When Amy attacked someone at school she was suspended for less than two weeks and that was when there were dozens of witnesses around. What could happen when Dawn didn't have any witnesses who would be on her side? When it was just her word, the word on her stomach and nothing else?

Aside from that, her family wouldn't care and despite the fact that she trusted Zoey Steph and Luke, she knew they would try to help. And that was the problem; they would try to help. They would get involved. And Amy had recently shown just how dangerous she could be and putting any of them in her path was something Dawn refused to do. She could handle her own pain, but theirs would be too much for her to deal with, knowing she caused it.

"What happened?" Zoey asked through passive interest. "I mean, you look normal. Maybe a bit underdressed, but not bad." *You really should stay away from sweats,* she thought. *Your figure is too perfect to cover it up with baggy clothes.*

"Cole came home this morning." A good enough replacement for the truth and not a lie.

"Where was he for the past, what was it, a week?" Steph asked. She made it sound like she wasn't certain, but she knew it was seven days.

Dawn scoffed and gave air quotes with both hands still on the wheel. "Out with friends. Which basically means he was any*where*, doing any*thing.*"

"You think he'll take off again?" Luke asked. Despite having never met Dawn's brother, he did not care for him. Anyone who would leave Dawn with no warning and no explanation was someone he didn't think kindly, or highly, of.

Dawn frowned, thinking back to their interaction. "Probably. I told him to let me know the next time he planned on disappearing, but you really can't break through to him. It's like talking to a wall. It's there, but you know it won't respond."

"Maybe you're just looking at this from the wrong perspective," Steph said, slightly irritated at her friend's dislike of being home alone. She would walk the entire Earth on broken glass to get the house to herself. "Isn't it good to have some time to yourself? To get to calm down and think or just do whatever you want? Maybe it's not so bad."

Dawn admired her positive outlook on the situation, but it wasn't as easy as that. Not to mention that Steph thought her mother held a job and was gone for several hours each day. No one knew about her mother, whenever someone came over Dawn would say she was sick or exhausted. It was less embarrassing to lie.

"Maybe that's how it is for you, but things aren't that easy for me." Her stomach gave another yell and she bit down on her lip to keep from answering it with a yell of her own. "Can we not talk about this right now? Please?" She thought back to the chain that awaited her in the road near her house. That awful, cold, predatory chain.

An awkward stillness fell over the car. A stillness that brought with it a sense of unease, worry and suspicion. Dawn continued to think about her mother, Cole and that awful chain, despite her mind telling her to stop, and everyone else in the car was thinking about Dawn.

Something was wrong with her but they all knew she'd never admit to that. They could almost hear each other's thoughts and with a few passed glances and a few sent text messages, they all agreed to meet up and talk about it. Everyone in the now voiceless car collectively, and privately, sighed with relief once their school was in view. The desire to get out of Dawn's car gripped all of them.

Except for Dawn.

Chapter 10

All that the four wanted to do was go to their usual waiting place by the gym doors and stay there until the bell.

That'll help her. Once she's with us, where we always stay, that'll help her, Zoey thought as they walked to their waiting point. She continued glancing at Dawn and noticing how she walked as if it hurt. At almost every step her eyes would flinch and tense up, like she was waiting to be hit. *She'll be fine when we get there. And maybe we're wrong. Maybe she's just sore from something and we're reading too much into it. Please, just be sore, Dawn. Maybe she and Luke got a little more intimate over the weekend and she—*

—"Give me a fucking break."

Steph's outburst brought Zoey out of her thoughts and back into the school where, a few seconds later, she understood the cause of Steph's oral spasm.

Standing in the places where the three girls stood while Luke was in the gym, were Amy Cooper, Evan Mitchell, Heather Grey and Trevor Logan. And if looks could kill, Dawn, Zoey, Steph and Luke would have dropped swatted flies.

There was a deep powerful hostility living behind the eight eyes that watched the four walk by, and it still burned when the four left. As Amy had expected, The Black One put up the biggest fight, but it was one that stayed between her and her friends' eyes. None said a word and none made a move. The Slut also had eyes that wanted them to stay and stand their ground, but Amy knew she would trail behind the rest of the group and be gone in seconds.

Poodle kept her head down, also no surprise, and Amy kept an intense eye on her stomach but saw no blood and no bandages. It was possible that it healed over the weekend, but she doubted that. Not to mention that Poodle was clearly walking through the pain. Amy could tell and was slightly impressed by her little dog. Poodle's boyfriend went into the gym, but he was of no concern. He didn't matter to Amy or anyone else in her group. It was just the three of them who held any importance. Watching them pass, biting their tongues and dragging their feet, made her feel good, but it wasn't enough. Amy didn't want them subservient to her, she wanted them to be whoever they wanted to be. Individuality was something Amy took pride in breaking down and stripping away from people. And she was ready to do that to all three of them; leave them as nobodies. As empty shells, timid and shaking, weak against the wind.

Just like her father did to her.

The three passed and were soon gone.

"That felt good," Trevor said. "Kind of empowering."

In accidental unison, Heather and Amy said, "That's not enough." They looked at each other and smiled, though Amy's was little more than a shadowy smirk, but it was the closest to a smile she ever let out in public. Amy continued. "They've gotten off too easy for too long."

Heather, staring down the hallway after the three, added, "What do you say we change that?"

"That's the best idea you've ever had."

Obviously, it wasn't Heather's idea, but Amy didn't need to point that out. They were all on the same side and, as long as they kept their mouths shut and their teeth bared, Amy would be able to focus on what was important. And, on the off chance that she ever needed their help, help they would. Whether they liked it or not. For one passing moment Amy wondered if she would have been where she was, doing and thinking what she was, if it wasn't for her father. Or her mother or sister or herself. Blame was tricky like that, it was unwieldy.

After a few more seconds of watching people swing around this corner of the school and being thoroughly disgusted with most of them, Amy realized something. "I hate standing here," she growled sourly.

"You want to go somewhere else?" Evan asked.

"No," Amy spat.

"Excuse me, Zoey? Zoey!"

She, along with Dawn and Steph, turned around and met their principal, Mr. Cleveland, heading toward them with a student none of them recognized. Once both of them had caught up to the three girls, they all collectively moved over to the side of the hall to avoid the stream of classmates.

"This is a new student." He motioned toward her with his hand as if showing off a prize. "Myah Rowland. I thought it would be a good idea if you, as well as Dawn and Stephanie…" The two glanced over at Steph and saw her clench her fists but it was clear she wouldn't say anything. They looked back to their principal who was oblivious to Steph's anger. "…show her around the school. You know, tell her where her classes are, help her become more comfortable here, that sort of thing."

"Oh, yeah, we can totally do that," Zoey said, smiling at Myah, who gave her a smaller and more feeble one in return.

"Excellent," he said. Then he turned to face Myah, who had to slightly tilt her head back to meet his eyes. She was only five foot two and her new principal stood before her at six foot one. "I hope you find this school and its people very welcoming."

She smiled at him. "I will. Thank you."

With another nod to the three girls who now had a new errand to run, he left for his office.

Without much hesitation, Zoey started talking. "All right, Myah, let's see that schedule. Where are you going first?"

The small girl blinked a few times then shook her head, like she had zoned out. "Oh, um, here." She took out her schedule and handed it to Zoey who snatched it so fast it made Myah's hand retract like she had almost been bitten. "You guys probably know more about it than me." The three girls stood staring and reading the schedule, sharing a few glances with each other and pointing at certain parts of the page until eventually Zoey looked back at her, shocked. Which made Myah nervous. "What?" *Don't tell me something's already screwed up. I've been here for ten minutes.*

Zoey smiled with glee. "You have one of us in every class you're in. Well, except for English but you don't have that today so we'll deal with that tomorrow." She lowered the paper and looked off at nothing. "That's probably why he wanted us to help you."

Myah raised her eyebrows as the nervous feeling fell back. "Oh, that's…" She stuck her bottom lip out and looked at each of them, one at a time, before bouncing back to Zoey, trying to find a word to say. "…Cool."

Zoey shot out a louder than normal "Yeah" and Myah recoiled a few inches and her eyes became wider. It wasn't until the girl to Zoey's right started talking that Myah's eyes started to shrink back to their normal size.

"You're going to have to excuse her," Dawn said while pointing a thumb at Zoey. "You know what happens when you down an energy drink and you get that crazy rush?"

"Yeah," Myah said, although she had never drank one of those in her life. Stuff like that would be brutal to her teeth and body.

"Well, Zoey is like that pretty much all the time." She closed her eyes when her stomach hit her again, but recovered quickly and opened them.

"Really?" As loud as Zoey was, Myah found herself already starting to like them. Or maybe she was just happy to find people who wanted to help her.

Dawn sighed. "Yep. She doesn't even drink them. Her bloodstream is just full of caffeine and energy drinks." When Myah laughed, small but genuine, Dawn felt her stomach give her the only small release of pain she had gotten over the past few days. "I'm Dawn."

"Myah."

Steph introduced herself as well and, because of the nerves that hadn't quite gone away, so did Myah.

"Well, I'm sorry but, I can't help who I am," Zoey responded. She took out a pen and began scribbling on Myah's schedule. When she was done she waved her over. "All right, Myah, come look at this."

Myah came over and saw her schedule with one of three names, Dawn, Zoey and Steph, written next to each class.

"The classes you have with me have my name next to them. And the same system applies for Dawn and Steph. So here's how this is going to work." She backed up a bit and created space between her and Myah.

Steph grabbed her shoulder and quietly said, "Go slow."

Zoey removed the hand. "Yeah, yeah."

Zoey began.

"Your first class you have with me. Then when it's over I'll drop you off at your next class that you have with Dawn. Once *that* class is over she'll bring you to your next class, which you have with Steph. And this whole passing of the baton thing will go on for the entire day so you don't have to wander around the school like a lost puppy. Then when the two thirty bell rings, school's over and we're done. Sound good?"

Dawn and Steph could tell that Zoey had fallen into a "Talking Spree" and by the end, neither of them understood what she had said after 'Steph.' They were ready for the raised eyebrow most people gave Zoey when she finished one of her "Talking Sprees" and instead, their own eyebrows simultaneously rose with Myah's response.

"Yeah, that sounds like a good idea. I just don't want to get in the way or anything."

Steph said what they were all thinking before Zoey could jump scare Myah again. "You won't be. School is pretty uneventful and this is probably the most interesting thing that has happened to any of us all year."

Dawn looked down and Steph was reminded of her failed arts internship but neither of them let their distaste become visible to Myah or each other. Steph continued.

"We want to help. I think we can all agree that the first day in a new school is pretty fucking terrible. And it being halfway through the year doesn't really make it any easier."

Myah cocked her head to the side and leveled it shortly after. "You're not wrong." This being her first time in a public school also didn't help ease her very much.

Steph went on. "Exactly. So we can help you and you can ask us any questions that you have. It's difficult making friends," her eyes widened and she looked down, "in general, never mind being new, so you can think of us as your friends. Until you get tired of us at least." At the word 'us' she gave a sneaky point to Zoey that only Myah noticed and it brought a much more normal looking smile to the girl's face. A smile Steph enjoyed seeing. "Right guys?" She cast a look at Dawn and Zoey.

"Yeah."

"Of course."

Myah smiled at her new "friends" and for the first time in these last few hectic and busy days, she felt all right. "Okay. I will."

Zoey spoke next. "Great. Now, let's show you as much of the school as we can before the bell rings." They took no more than five steps before the "get to class" alarm blared through the school. "Son of a bitch," Zoey snapped. She looked at Myah and smiled. "I guess the tour is going to have to wait. So you're going *where* first?"

Myah looked down at her schedule and at the first class she had. A class that had 'Zoey' written next to it. "Psychology."

Zoey nodded approvingly, having already known where Myah was going, and led her away from Dawn and Steph. "Good. Let's go."

They headed off to their class and Zoey turned her head to face the two girls she had left in the hallway. Part of her mind was still concerned about Dawn but she couldn't do much about it now. "Bye, guys," she called and Myah gave the two a wave.

"See you in ceramics," Steph called back and turned to Dawn who looked better, but still didn't look quite right. "And I'll see you in ceramics as well."

Dawn smiled and said, "You can count on it." Steph walked down the hall they came from and Dawn dropped her smile and let out a gasp of air that held a significant amount of pain in it. She headed to her first class with the only thought going through her mind being *let the day pass quickly. Or let the pain go away, at least for a little bit. Just give me either one. I don't care which. Just one.*

She was given neither.

The day lasted an eternity and the irritation stayed with her for every second that scraped by. It was almost impressive how six classes and one lunch, a schedule that often felt too short, now felt like a life sentence. She was behind invisible bars with only her aching stomach to be her cellmate.

There were small moments when the soreness took a break, but those were few and far between. Short enough for her to inhale one time without the need to cringe before the pain resurfaced and her stomach felt like it was trying to rip itself apart. She tried putting on her normal face in ceramics and she thought she hid the pain from the, now four, people who kept her company well enough. She *thought* she did.

If anything she only made Zoey, Steph and Luke more certain that something was wrong with her. When she was passed the Myah baton to take to their next class she tried to make small talk on the way, but her mind was too full with the thoughts of the throbbing sensation near her bellybutton to pay complete attention to Myah. All Dawn heard was that Myah had been transferred to their school because her old private school had closed down and her parents needed somewhere to put her while they looked for the next school that they approved of, but that was where she lost the thread. Her mind was on her stomach for the rest of their conversations. She felt bad about ignoring her but she knew when school was over it would be easier to give Myah her undivided attention. She just had to make it to the end of the day without crying.

Once the beautiful two thirty bell finally rang, Dawn met up with Zoey, Steph, and Myah and headed to her car to take them home. Luke told her he was going to get a ride home from one of his friends and teammates but that didn't bother Dawn too much. Sometimes Luke wanted to be with his guy friends rather than his girlfriend and her female friend group and Dawn could understand that. She didn't like it but she accepted it. And at least he still said goodbye to her before he left.

Luke leaned toward Dawn and spoke so only she could hear. "I'll see you as soon as I can, okay? And remember, we're your friends. You can tell us anything."

She hated the way he said that and the way he looked at her. As if she was this wimpy, troubled girl who constantly shut herself off from the world and wouldn't let anyone help her. If he had known what Dawn had been through recently, the look he gave her would have had a much different feeling behind it. And there certainly wouldn't have been anywhere near as much pity as she could see on his face now. Instead of letting her annoyance become noticeable through her voice, she nodded her head and told him what he wanted to hear, what everyone would want to hear. "I will. I promise." Even when she kissed him she could tell he was kissing her like it was the last time he would ever see her. The ridiculous passion behind it almost made her take a step back. It was the worst kiss he had ever given her. Even worse than their first, and neither of them had ever kissed someone before that. Once their lips separated and he walked away with his friends, Dawn looked at the three girls who stood watching and asked, "Did you guys see anything wrong with Luke just now?"

Myah gave a quick and soundless head shake, her brown hair wobbling around her head. Zoey had informed her on why they were all suspicious of Dawn and that she must be hurt in some way and Myah had decided to try to be helpful while keeping her nose out of it for as long as she could.

Which wouldn't be long. She would meet up with Zoey, Steph and Luke to talk about Dawn the next day.

Zoey was a bit more vocal about the situation. "Not with *him*, no." She unintentionally put more emphasis on 'him' than she wanted to but she didn't regret it. She did get aggravated when Steph looked down and mumbled, "Jesus, Zoey, subtle."

Steph looked back up at Dawn and tried to reassure her. "Nah, I'm sure he's fine. He's probably just thinking about something that doesn't have anything to do with you. You said he was failing chemistry, right? That might be why he didn't seem as...invested as he usually is. But I'm sure it has nothing to do with you." *I stumbled a bit at the end there but it could've been wor—*

Steph felt something slam against the back of her knee and she folded to the concrete like a house of cards. At first all she saw was the gray and white patchy sky. It wasn't very pleasant, but it became much more approachable when Heather's head rose into the top of Steph's vision and covered most of the sky with that terrible grin of hers.

Before Zoey could help her up, she was pushed back from Steph by Amy and felt a hand slap against her ass. She jumped away from where it came from and watched as Trevor scanned her up and down, licked his lips and continued past her. The sight made her want to throw up.

Dawn kept her view down when the three walked by and could feel Amy's burning stare start to drill a hole in between her eyes. It wasn't until Amy muttered, "Pathetic," and bumped Dawn's shoulder as she walked past that Dawn felt another urge take over her. The same one that appeared when she told off Amy a few days previous. The same one that led to her new markings. The same one that made her feel strong for a second and weak for an hour, the same one that she no longer enjoyed or wanted. She whipped her head around to face the backs of the three of them and, with no ability to stop herself, shouted, "Fuck you, you psycho bitch!" The way all three of them stopped dead and motionless made Dawn's new urge disappear yet again and leave her alone against Amy with no confidence. With nothing at all but regret. *What's wrong with me?*

Amy turned to face her Poodle and was pleased to see the horrified face of the girl who still didn't know how to keep her mouth shut. She decided it would be a good time to let them know what the new status quo would be. She walked toward the group and began to let the lava drool out of her mouth. "I've been pretty easy on all of you for a while. Now that's going to change. Get in my way and you'll wish you were dead." She leaned closer to Poodle and whispered, "But you already know about that, don't you. How's your tattoo holding up?" She reached towards Poodle's stomach and her hand was slapped away.

"Don't touch me."

It sounded firm, but Amy could see right through it and into

Poodle's fear. She scoffed, moved her head to the right and that was when she noticed someone she had never seen before. Her eyes burned like a forest fire. "Who is this?" A small smile bent across her face as she started towards Myah. She loved getting new students, especially when they were already friendly with the wrong people.

Zoey stepped in front of Myah and blocked Amy. This wouldn't happen, not so soon, that wasn't fair. "Give her a break, Amy, she's new."

The heel that smashed down into Zoey's toes, sandals suddenly seeming like an awful idea, made her feel as if she had put her foot in a trash compactor. The snapping and crunching that came from her bones dropped her to her back and she screamed as her toes stayed in their dented, crooked position, refusing to move. Amy's eyes stayed locked on Myah.

Myah, now close to screaming herself, tried to keep the peace. "I'm Myah." *Now go away unless you're going to call 911.* She glanced around for help and saw very few people surrounding them, as most students either jumped in their cars as sped off for home as soon as they could or jumped on buses that picked students up at another side of the school.

Amy's smile grew in length, but by very little. She paid no attention to Poodle and The Black One, who had gathered around The Slut. "Well, I'm Amy," she motioned to her left, "this is Trevor" and to her right, "and this is Heather."

Myah already didn't like Amy and just by looking at the other two she could tell her feelings wouldn't change. The face Heather made brought a shiver to her spine and she could almost feel Trevor's hands on her body as he looked her up and down.

Maybe Mom and Dad were right about private school.

The three closed in, Trevor and Heather grabbed ahold of Myah's arms and Amy stood right in front of her. And Myah, already shorter than average, had to look up to meet Amy and her bright, blazing hair. Myah was taken by her eyes. They almost looked completely black. They called to her. She felt herself getting sucked into them; the black empty space was hypnotizing. Oddly serene.

"So, you're new here?" Amy asked, despite the answer being obvious. "It's your first day?"

Myah pulled herself out of Amy's eyes and nodded. "Yeah. They've been showing me around." She moved her head towards

Dawn, Zoey and Steph, wishing she could go over and help, but Amy's eyes stayed on her.

"Good. It's important that you understand how a place works when you're new to it. Wouldn't you say?"

Amy's face wore a smile but her voice reminded Myah of a snake and how fast they could move. How fast they could wound. Or kill. She pushed the similarity to the side and kept talking, trying to keep Amy busy until she had her fun and left. "Yeah, I guess you're right."

Amy's eyes burned brighter. "Good. Now let me give you some insight into how a place like this *really* works." She put her hand under Myah's shirt and pressed her nails against the far left of the girl's back, holding them in place as Myah jumped and attempted to back away. Her nails weren't very long, but Amy always worked with what she had. She dragged her nails slowly across the girl's back, drawing blood if she could and certainly leaving a long lasting mark. "As long as you're here, you're nothing. Not because you're *new*, not because you're *scrawny*, but because you're with *them*. If you're stupid enough to hang around with them, then you deserve all you're going to get." Her nails continued scraping the girl's back, almost halfway there. "Is that understood?"

Myah fought against the impulse to let her pain be known. It felt like her back was being ripped open and resisting a scream made her face turn red. She opened her mouth and spat out an angry "Yes," and Amy's nails tore from the middle of her back to the right in a second. Her skin burst into flames but Myah kept it inside. The only sign of any pain was in her eyes, that snapped shut and shook for a short time before opening again.

Amy's black eyes widened. "You're good at holding in your pain. I give it a week before I can change that." She backed up, Heather and Trevor followed, and the trio took off for Evan's truck.

Once their backs were turned, Myah let out a breath of anguish and moved closer to the three people she liked a lot more, dropping to her knees and rubbing Zoey's back without noticing herself doing it. "Who was *that*?" She had been thinking about Zoey and trying not to fall deeper into Amy's ravenously inky eyes when Amy announced herself so she hadn't picked up on the name.

Steph kept her gaze on the three and said, "*That* was Amy Cooper, Heather Grey and Trevor Logan. We try to stay away from them as often as possible. It's pretty obvious why." Her hand pointed to where they had stopped at Evan's truck. "And that is Evan Mitchell, Amy's boyfriend." She said 'boyfriend' in a way that sounded like she still couldn't believe it. Myah certainly couldn't. The four of them watched, Zoey found it easier than watching her toes turn a most unhealthy shade of purple, with bewilderment as Evan came out of the drivers side door and began giving Amy several little kisses. It didn't take long for Amy to start returning them and that was when Steph wretched and they all broke their gaze.

"God, how could you ever love somebody like that?" Dawn asked as she started helping Zoey onto her working foot. It wasn't easy, even with Steph and Myah helping, and her stomach sent out a few painful jolts before Zoey was able to stand.

As she wobbled on her left foot and tried to keep her right from moving at all, Zoey answered bitterly. "Maybe it becomes worth it when she's on her knees. The bitch probably has razor blades for pussy lips."

Myah recoiled at the thought before deciding to push Amy and the rest of her accomplices out of her mind. Much more important things required her attention.

They all helped Zoey into Dawn's car, easing her into the backseat with Myah. Myah was about to buckle Zoey in when Zoey took hold of Myah's hands and moved them away. "I can handle this part, honey."

Myah nodded, ready to apologize before noticing Zoey's cheeky smile and smiling back. She knew Zoey was in pain, perhaps the worst of her life, but it hadn't kept her down.

That was the moment when Myah realized that being a part of this friend group had gone from something she would accept to something she wanted. Maybe needed.

Dawn went to the wheel with Steph beside her and the four of them drove off to the nearest medical facility they could find.

Chapter 11

Dawn called Zoey's parents as the four of them walked into the Rhode Island Medical Center where, thankfully, walk-ins were welcome. When they got to the front desk, Zoey and Dawn sat in the waiting room while Steph and Myah explained their situation to the woman behind the counter. Zoey's breathing was rapid and short, perhaps being at a doctor's office made the situation more real to her, and Dawn took in a breath, inhaled the distinct smell of the medical facility, and tried to ease both of their nerves while pretending to just calm down Zoey's.

"Zoey, relax. You're going to be fine."

Zoey gave a dry smile. "Really? I'm going to be just fine, huh? Look at my fucking toes, Dawn. I'll be lucky if I leave here with any of them still attached to my foot."

Dawn shook her head at Zoey's blind pessimism. "These people know what they're doing. Besides, they'll probably just put a cast or splint on your foot and you'll be out by tomorrow." Zoey slowed her breathing down a bit and gave a jittery nodded. Dawn leaned closer and put a hand on her shoulder. "Okay?"

Zoey gave her a look that almost brought tears to Dawn's eyes. It was a look of utter defeat and terror. Like someone who was responsible for a family member's death. She took Dawn's hand off of her shoulder and held it in her own. "I'm scared. It feels like my foot's dying."

Dawn understood what Zoey meant but didn't say so. She just continued to hold her hand and, when Zoey rested her head on Dawn's shoulder, kissed her hair.

"It's going to be okay, I promise. And you'll have the three of us to help you out until you're back to normal."

"Assuming Myah isn't going to be scared away."

Dawn didn't respond to that, instead she remembered the phone call she had finished and told Zoey the good news. "Your dad is on his way. He'll be here soon." The reaction she was expecting was far from the reaction she got.

Zoey sighed and her eyes rolled up as high as they could go before she closed them. "Great."

The sarcasm leapt out of her mouth and pushed Dawn back in her chair. "What's wrong?" *Why does mentioning your dad make you sound like you want to jump off a cliff?*

Zoey took her head off Dawn's shoulder. "Nothing. It doesn't matter." Now wasn't the time to think about him and the way he made her think about herself. And it certainly wasn't the time to have a therapy session with Dawn about it.

Though Zoey's contradicting words only made Dawn more concerned and invested. But before Dawn could grill her further, Steph and Myah came back and sat next to the only two people in the waiting room.

Steph started. "Okay, so, here's the deal. They can't take you in and, ummm, *examine* you until a parent or guardian is present to take ownership. They can only treat people who are eighteen or older."

Zoey went next and leaned her head back until it hit the wall behind her. "Oh my fucking God!" Her volume, yet again, rising with each word. If this had happened to her in a few months, once her age had risen to the oh-so-important digit, she would have been set. But this day wasn't quite done fucking her yet.

Now it was Myah's turn. "But it's okay because," she leaned over to look at Dawn, "you were talking to her parents?"

Dawn was up. "Yeah, her dad is already on his way." She looked back at Zoey who closed her eyes and scrunched up her nose.

Myah nodded. "Great. So we'll stay here to keep you company until he shows up, then they'll take you in, check you out and your dad will take you home."

"Wait," Steph said and they all turned to her. She pointed at Myah. "You still want to hang around with us? Amy'll be after you if you do."

Myah looked at each of them, not needing to think about it. "Would me separating from you change that at all?" She watched the three of them look at each other and answered for them. "She'll be after me no matter what so I think I'll take my chances."

"Are you sure?" Dawn asked, knowing that Myah had no idea what she was signing up for.

"Yes." She didn't say any more and all three of them could tell from the look on her face that nothing more was needed.

"There's another problem," Zoey said and when they all turned to her she swung her head against Dawn's arm and hid it there. "I don't want to be with him. I want to be with you guys."

They all looked at her like she was a puppy they weren't allowed to take home.

Steph sighed. "Zoey, you can't be with us all the time. Like it or not, you need to be home in your bed to sleep this off tonight."

Dawn followed. "It's better this way. Your parents are probably worried sick about this and you're going to need some time to take it easy. We have a day off tomorrow for professional development day, so you should take that time to rest."

Myah ended the three parter. "And you can text us or call us and we can all come by and check on you if you want us to. But you won't go through this alone." She did what her dad always did when he finished a big speech and put her hand on Zoey's. She never wanted to partake in the hand to hand contact with her dad, considering most of his speeches were about how she couldn't do this or go there and the hand she had to touch always felt like it was touching hers out of obligation, but she wanted to help Zoey more than she wanted her next breath. Her palm rested on the back of Zoey's hand and before she could look at them, Dawn and Steph put theirs on as well.

The four of them felt something as soon as their hands connected. To Zoey, Dawn and Steph it felt like the polar opposite of the nauseating dread they all felt on Friday. An overwhelming sense of harmony seemed to fill the air between them all. Myah looked at their stacked hands and knew this was where she belonged. They all fit together and that was something every single one of them could understand, even if they wouldn't have been able to communicate it. The warm aura that flowed in between each girl and the all encompassing feeling of safety and security and tenderness was almost enough to make them believe in some higher being. Maybe this was what people experienced when they thought they had connected with God. Maybe that's what they were all doing right now. Maybe this God, this being, had brought them all together. Maybe things would be oaky.

Then it was all shattered when a voice that was very familiar to Zoey rang through their ears and pulled them out of their shared experience.

"Jesus, Zoey, you scared your mother to death," Maxwell said while walking toward his daughter and her friends. When he finally got a look at Zoey's toes, he almost stopped moving entirely. The purple, swollen, crooked and slightly bleeding toes that had one deep dent making a curved line through about four of them almost made him sick to his stomach. But he made sure to not let the alarming response to his daughter's definitely broken toes become noticeable, the last thing he needed was Zoey getting over dramatic. He kept his stride fast and was by his daughter's side, practically pushing Myah and her chair against the wall, in seconds. "What happened to you?"

One of her friends responded and it sounded like who had called him, probably Dawn. "We were moving a…uhhh." *God dammit, think of something. Think of literally anything.* Myah interrupted Dawn while she was spacing out.

"A fridge." She said it fast, before she could think of something better, and had to keep from sighing at her nonsensical answer. *This is the kind of shit my private school education is going towards,* she thought. *But it could still work if explained properly. I'd just need time to think it through.* Though she knew the time she had was very limited.

Zoey's father looked down at the girl he was almost smothering with his giant coat and noticed two things; he hadn't seen her before and he didn't want to see her again. "A fridge?" He spoke with the tone of someone who has had a bad day and can't catch a break and whatever this new girl said next ultimately wouldn't matter to him.

Myah shot the situation out as soon as the next part came into her head. "Yeah, we were on the way home and we saw someone with a truck stranded on the side of the road with a fridge behind them. It had fallen out. Anyway, Zoey said we should stop and help the person, so we did, and during the process of moving the fridge up and into the trunk, before we figured out how to properly do it, it fell on Zoey's foot. It could have been a lot worse." Once she finished she looked at her folded hands sitting in her lap and hoped all of the eyes she felt on her would move somewhere else. And, after a few long seconds, they did as Zoey's father moved the conversation back to reality.

"Right. Well, why are we still out here? Why hasn't she been taken in yet?"

"They wouldn't take her in until a parent or guardian could be here to take ownership," Steph said. "They can't see people under eighteen.

I think it's stupid too, but it's their rules."

Zoey's father grabbed his daughter and hauled her up. They needed to stop wasting time and get her toes fixed. He ignored the moan Zoey let out upon being forced onto her feet and when she nearly fell back into her chair, Dawn shot up to catch her.

As soon as Zoey looked at her, Dawn saw fear in her eyes. A look that said *Don't let me go. Don't leave me alone with him. Please don't leave me.* But she had to and, against her will, Dawn did. Zoey went hopping toward the front desk and down the hall to the right of it into uncertain and unfortunate territory. The air she left behind was cold and dry and, without saying a word to each other, the three remaining girls all got up and headed to Dawn's car. But they didn't start talking until they were driving away.

As much as Myah had wanted to help, and in spite of her mixed success in that regard, there was still a big question on the table she needed an answer to. "Why didn't we just tell the truth about what happened?"

Dawn and Steph didn't even need to glance at each other nor did they need to take much time to think up an answer. Dawn continued to drive as Steph explained. "If we told someone, and if they believed us at that, it wouldn't change anything. Amy has attacked people before, some people ended up worse than Zoey. If we tell, Amy might get suspended for ten days and after those ten day are over, she'll come back worse. That's the only outcome. She'll get suspended and come back and nothing will have changed aside from her having a much higher interest in us. If we could get her expelled, which I don't even think our school can do, the same shit would apply. She'll come after us outside of school and do something worse than what we've dealt with already. People have tried to beat her, to suspend her or expel her. They have their minor victory and then a week or so later they come into school with their arm in a sling. Trying to tell someone won't do us any good."

Myah waited for a few seconds, though not entirely sure what it was she was waiting for. Maybe for the punchline, maybe for the loophole, but it appeared that the ground had been set and she simply had to stand on it. "No one has tried to sue her family or anything?

Step laughed. She couldn't help it. "Look at the houses you're passing by. Do you think people who live here have thousands of unused dollars that they could put into a lawsuit?" She didn't wait for an answer. "People here swim in food stamps."

"So, we have to just keep letting her attack us?"

"That's how it's always been," Steph said, her voice as monotonous as her expression. "She's like a tornado. When she comes around, you just get down and hope the damage isn't too bad after she leaves."

"I think it's a little too late for that," Myah said as she turned away from the conversation and stared out the window as the car drove through a town that, now that she was looking for it, did have a few cracks in its veneer. Houses seemed to sag, weeds looked like they were trying to break in, the road felt more bumpy and every store seemed to have sales going on for anything somebody might want to buy. If the town wasn't dying, it sure was suffering. And was Amy the cancer that was killing it? Myah didn't think so but it sounded right just the same.

"I want you to take it easy, Zoey," the doctor said, slowly and much too clearly, as if she was insane and on the verge of some psychotic break. "You have three broken toes. Another one sprained."

Zoey used her hands and elbow to crawl back and lean her head against the wall, trying to get from a lying position to something that resembled a seated one. She was happy to be in a bed but her irritation that it had taken more than an hour and more than several experiments and adjustments to her toes to bring this doctor to his conclusion was much stronger.

"How long will they take to heal?" She couldn't see the damage or even feel any of her right toes thanks to the ice pack that had numbed them, but she would find out which were broken and which weren't later. As far as Zoey Kay was concerned, right now she just had to get out of here.

"The ones that are broken, the index, middle and fourth, will take around six weeks. The big toe, the one that is sprained, could take anywhere from two weeks to four." He tried to lighten up the mood a bit and added, "But the pinky one is in tip top shape." Zoey's face stayed stone and his colorless smile dissolved. "We put each of the broken toes in a splint, the fractured one doesn't require that, and once all three toes heal fully, you'll be able to take each one off. But until that point I would recommend crutches to better carry yourself and move around. W have a pair we can give you before you leave. And when you're at home, remember rice. Rest, ice, compression and elevation."

Zoey nodded a silent promise she didn't know if she'd keep and asked the million dollar question. "All right, when can I go home?"

The doctor gave a real smile this time, knowing Zoey would be pleased with the answer. She clearly looked like the answer would mean the difference between her living and dying and his smile grew as he said, "Well, you've got the splints on and your father has the medication you can take if your toes start to hurt, so you can leave whenever you want. Including right now." The face Zoey gave him told him everything he needed to know. And her actions that followed did the same.

As soon as he finished talking, Zoey got off the bed as fast as she could and felt no strength in her legs when her feet touched the floor. She began to fall and held onto the bed for support, saving herself from injuring another part of her body. Slowly, as she got back onto her working foot, she began to feel the blood flowing through her legs which gave her the strength needed to stand on her own. She refused to put her right shoe on but everything else was present and accounted for.

"All set?" The doctor asked.

She gestured around her. "The room is now all yours. Go nuts."

"Good, so if you do plan on taking the medication, aim to take it at least three times a day; when you wake up, around noon and before you go to sleep. You may also take it if the pain is too much to handle, but I don't recommend using it more than four times a day. This stuff is strong. Use it sparingly and in small doses. All right?" He was talking to Zoey but her dad answered before she got the chance.

"Yep, got it. Thanks, Brian." He extended his hand and the doctor, now Brain, took it and gave a meaty, quick and strong handshake.

Brian continued, saying the same thing he always said to patients. "I'm here if you have any questions or need anything and on that note." He opened the door, gestured them down the hall and, just like he assumed, they exited silently and were out of sight in a matter of seconds.

The walk to her father's car was the hardest part of Zoey's journey home, and her lumbering gait thanks to her new crutches didn't make it any easier, but the atmosphere between her and her father once the doors were shut was the thing Zoey disliked the most. Much more than the occasional burst of pain from her toes as she hobbled around on her heel. She was surprised that such small parts of her body could give her such a terribly large amount of physical grief. She sat in the passenger's seat only thinking about three things and not especially happy to be thinking about any of them; the aching pain in her toes, the unknown thoughts going through her father's head and which thoughts he would say aloud. She hoped he wouldn't say anything but she doubted that she would be that lucky. She almost scoffed at the mere concept. *Luck seems to have taken a break today, hasn't it?*

"How did you really hurt your foot?" he asked, voice dripping with disappointment and distaste.

"Toes." Her voice was soft but still defiant.

He waved the word away like smoke. "How did you actually hurt it? You don't really expect me to believe you were moving a refrigerator from the road into some stranger's truck." Now that he had been given some time to think about it and to think about it in the context of Zoey, who couldn't even be bothered to help bring in the groceries, the sequence of events he had been told seemed a little more difficult to believe.

She tried to hide her bluff but could feel blood stream into her cheeks and ears and was certain he would be able to tell that she was lying if he looked at her. He could always tell. "Myah was telling the truth. That's how it happened. You always talk about me like I'm a terrible person, maybe I was trying to do something good for someone else." Her last sentence held so much hate that steam was practically coming out of Zoey's ears. Her father took note of this and stopped it where it stayed.

He observed the red light he was approaching and slammed on the brakes and Zoey's foot launched forward and hit the inner wall of the car, just below the glove compartment.

The sudden spark of pain from her toes made her press her teeth together and close her eyes so tight that they hurt, but they took none of the pain away. She threw a glare at her father but her look retained an unwilling amount of fear and shock behind it. She saw the corner of his mouth move upward in the smallest, slightest, most minuscule smile he could show before he nodded and gave an "Mm-hmm," that sounded so very pleased with itself. The light turned green and they began moving once again.

"Well, this whole foot thing—"

"Toes."

"—will probably work out well for you in the end. Injuries are a surefire way of getting attention."

Zoey kept quiet but wanted to scream and she wished it was because of the pain.

Maxwell Kay didn't hate his daughter, he merely did not approve of the woman she was turning herself into. Whether she was flashing her figure every day through her outfits or acting all ditzy and bubbly when she spoke to a boy on the phone, it was horribly unattractive and not right for someone her age. The way she dressed and the way she acted was more fitting for a prostitute than a high school junior. He wanted the best for his daughter, but it seemed like she wanted something else. She refused to think things through and one day, with some boy she probably wouldn't know the name of, there would be a mishap and then she would be sorry for the illogical way she had been acting. And he would not be there to help. She would take her little mishap on all by herself. The thought of her and her mishap gave him an internal smile. The fact of the matter was that Zoey thought she ruled the world and the world needed to show her that she didn't.

The way home was completely silent. Both people under the inky black sky were thinking about Zoey, the kind of person she was and what her future would hold. One was enjoying it and the other was dreading it.

Before Zoey went to be that night she plucked off all ten of her fake nails, not liking the idea of Amy getting her hands on them first. It hurt to remove them but Zoey had a feeling she could be saving herself from much worse pain later on.

Chapter 12

"How do you handle all of your anger? How do you keep it concealed?"

Amy was shocked to silence by this absurd question. Evan had asked *her*, of all people, how she kept her anger inside. It almost made her laugh but she could see his head and arms were shaking so she decided to take him seriously. She could tell this was a new type of anger, one she had never seen from him before. This realization didn't scare her, if anything she was intrigued. He had looked at his phone a few minutes ago and, after turning it off, seemed to be a different person. She held his hand and put her other on the back of his neck, where his hair was curling. She chose her words carefully but didn't hesitate. "I don't."

He looked at her with an expression of sudden realization. She could see now that he had understood the contradiction of asking her how she handled her temper. Her words advanced. "Just tell me what happened and I'll help you through it as best I can. Okay?" He nodded and her curiosity peaked.

He recalled the events and fought the urge to punch the wall and no doubt break something in his hand as he did. He wanted to get a tattoo, that was all. Just a little permanent ink drawn onto his wrist. His mother was, for reasons he couldn't fill a sticky-note with, appalled by the idea. Maybe because he had decided he wanted it a few weeks ago and she didn't think that was enough time to think it over but, if that was the case, she didn't say that to him. It would have been easier for Evan to understand if she didn't have one herself on her ankle. It wasn't even something she had done when she was a teenager and regretted, she had gotten it last year. And seemingly out of nowhere.

The hypocrisy alone was enough to bring Evan's blood to a boil but, spending all day Saturday talking about how it wasn't that bad and the pain didn't matter and it was only one little thing and he would pay for it no matter the price, she had eventually cooled down and warmed up to the idea. The two even made a game plan; she would call the place she got her tattoo done and she would get all of the necessary information. How much it would cost, how long it would take, how much would it hurt, that sort of thing. Evan supported this plan and moved on, spending the rest of the day thinking about Amy, but not fully able to ignore the feeling that arose in him each time he thought about his upcoming ink. It was a great feeling. One of success and pride, things he rarely ever felt. He decided to keep it a secret from his friends and surprise them all on the fateful day. He could imagine the reactions. Trevor would love it, Amy would be a little shocked but would like what the tattoo represented and Heather? Well, he knew what two of them would think and that was more than enough for him.

She hadn't told him any updates yesterday but he was okay with that. He didn't know how busy her tattoo artist was so it could take a few days before her email got a response. He had been currently thinking about how he could get the tattoo without Amy knowing or becoming suspicious when the phone vibrated and he read his mother's text.

He couldn't get a tattoo. He was seventeen and it was illegal for anyone under eighteen to get one. And he knew if he had to coerce his mother into opening up to the idea of him getting one, then coercing her into letting him get one before the legal age was out of the question. All he wanted was his father's signature on his wrist and he couldn't get it. Waiting eleven months until his birthday was the only option he had and by that point, he probably would have forgotten about it altogether. What bothered him the most was the fact that she had texted him while she was at work, knowing how angry he'd get and not wanting to deal with it in person. Had she explained it face to face, she might have been able to settle some of his anger. She could promise that they would do it as soon as he legally could, she could explain that no places did under the table illegal tattoos for minors so that wasn't an option, she could sound like she regretted this turn of events. But, by texting him, he had no idea how she felt and it was all to easy for him to see the satisfied smirk of a woman who gotten what she wanted and knew her son couldn't do anything about it.

The shaking was still going strong now, after he had finished explaining the situation. In fact, it was even more noticeable than it had been before and Amy knew what this meant and knew what had to be done. It was time to snuff out his anxious overthinking, it was time for him to become exactly like her. Act now and don't think about it later. Evan was not violent by nature, he kept a lot of those feelings and urges inside, but Amy knew the danger of keeping those things buried and assuming you have control over it.

"Okay, first of all, we have to get rid of your anger and your need to hit something because I can feel it radiating off of you and it's unhealthy to force yourself to ignore it."

He looked at her. "How?"

Amy pronounced each word with a sharpness that could cut. "Let it out. Do whatever you can, just get rid of it."

Evan repeated his previous question but this time the word sounded distinctly more disturbed. She loved the inflection.

"Close your eyes, Evan." He did. "I want you to tell me how this whole tattoo mess makes you feel. Don't hold back and don't be afraid. It's just you and me." She kept her hand in his and was prepared for him to start squeezing it. She hoped for it. She needed to feel what he was holding in and how much damage it could do if it was properly harnessed. The harnessing would be her job later, but right now she had to know what she was working with. "How do you feel?"

He started slow. On purpose. Reciting the events were bad enough but mentioning how he felt about them made the vibrating grow and grow and become harder and harder to resist with each new word said. "Angry. Frustrated. Enraged." As he continued, the shaking in his shoulders began traveling down to his arms, hands (one of which crushed Amy's in its metal grip, which made her grin) and some of it rose up to his head. His breathing increased and his teeth clenched tighter and tighter every second. "Unsafe. Monstrous. Unlucky. Wronged." He stopped there, releasing Amy's bent, limp fingers and letting out a hint of a growl underneath each breath he passed through his clenched teeth. His head was still shaking and his vibrating collar bones were raging now. The rage fell into his bloodstream and traveled through his entire body. If he kept up his current thought process, he would not be able to fight the urge to hit something for more than another minute.

Amy could sense the violence he wanted to commit and acted fast to keep it contained. For the time being at least. His anger was more powerful than she was expecting. It might even rival her own. He was just like her, the only difference was that he was too afraid to act upon his own rage. And whether that was because he hadn't had the opportunity to or he was scared of the repercussions or he was simply weaker than she was, she would change that.

"All right Evan, calm down. I need you to keep those feelings inside right now." She put an emphasis on 'right now' that indicated his anger would be used later but Evan didn't pick up on the subtleties of her vocal inflections. His anger had almost taken away his hearing.

He got off of the bed and stood looking down at her. "You're the one who said to let it out. What am I supposed to do?"

She launched herself to her feet and was more than a little satisfied to see him take a step back. His new anger was fine by her, but it was still in his best interest to remember who wore the pants in their relationship. "Save it for a better time. I'll text Heather and Trevor and we'll find a better outlet for you. We'll pick them up and be on our way, okay?"

His expression remained the same, one of pure fury, but his voice sounded reassured. "Okay, fine."

Amy grabbed the sides of his face and pulled him closer to her. "I promise these feelings will be gone before the day is over. It's going to feel so good to let it out and afterwards, you'll only want to do it again." She gave him a long kiss and when she took her lips off he seemed to have settled down.

"Okay," he said. His voice sounded numb, tired.

"Good." She took out her phone. "I'll text Heather and Trevor." She gave him another long look, this one he didn't see. Within five minutes, the two Amy had texted were ready to be picked up and the hateful duo left Evan's house, his foot almost smashing through the gas pedal and the floor of the truck itself.

"So, what do we do about Dawn?" Zoey asked the three other people that sat across from and next to her at their table at Cafe Haven. "Because something's wrong with her."

"Maybe we shouldn't do anything. Maybe it's something bigger than we think," Luke responded. He thought something was wrong with Dawn too but putting her on the spot and meddling in her life might only make it worse for her. The logic was easy for him to process but the three glares from the six other eyes at the table made it clear that the logic didn't appeal to them. He shook his head slightly and looked from girl to girl. "What?"

"Luke, that's a terrible idea," Steph said with no hesitation. "We can't just ignore the problem because it might be something really serious. If anything, that should make us want to help her even more." She took a small breath and said something she didn't say very often. "Zoey's right. Something happened and we need to help her through it. Besides, could any of you really just sit back and hope the problem solves itself?"

Her rhetorical question was interrupted by the barista at the counter. The drinks the four ordered were done and ready to be given. "Dawn?"

The voice hit each one of them like a brick wall and Steph sighed and turned to Zoey. "That's really the name you chose?"

Zoey shrugged. "I don't see a problem with it. It's a rare name to hear and it puts our collective trains of thought back on the tracks."

"They haven't been *off* the tracks yet. We've been talking about Dawn the entire time we've been here."

Zoey made a matter of fact expression that bent Steph's eyebrows down. "Steph, it's about planning ahead. I did it just in case we *did* get sidetracked. And would you just look at what we're talking about now." Her matter of fact became a smirk. "See you...you just don't get it." She shrugged her shoulders and looked down at the table, feeling more than satisfied with herself.

Steph looked at the other side of the table where, hopefully, the two reasonable people would agree with her. Luke closed his eyes and shook his head, a *don't bother* gesture, and all Myah said was, "I'll get the drinks."

She sprang up, avoiding Zoey's crutches that angled against the table and made her way across the wooden floor to the counter.

She liked this place, this Cafe Haven. The atmosphere was relaxed and calming, it was quiet. She could see herself coming here regularly to do homework or to enjoy the serenity.

Myah took the tray of drinks and headed back to their table, hoping they were again talking about Dawn and not the name Zoey used for their drink order. She set the tray on the table, grabbed her vanilla chai tea latte and said, "Take what's yours," as she sat down next to Luke.

Luke's wasn't hard to determine. It stood taller and darker than the other two in the tray. Ordering a large black iced coffee with no ice and one sugar was in equal parts disgusting and baffling to Zoey, Steph and Myah. As it was to anyone else he was with whenever he ordered one. But, for whatever reason, he enjoyed the cool and bitter taste. He drank it while the remaining two stared at their final options.

Steph took her americano and Zoey took her breve caramel macchiato and Steph could only imagine how many thousands of grains of sugar were running down Zoey's throat. "How do you drink that shit?"

Zoey looked at her coffee and put her hands around it, protecting it, feeling her missing nails and grateful that none of them had asked her why she had removed them. She assumed they already knew. "What can I say, I guess I just want to drink something that's as sweet as I am," she said, giving a smug grin while her coffee warmed her palms. She tried repositioning herself on the booth she shared before shooting her head back, biting down on her bottom lip and letting out a small groan.

Steph's previously dumbfounded stare became full of worry. "What's wrong?"

Zoey shook her head and moved it to face the concerned people who surrounded her. She talked as the pain subsided, but her words were slow. As if she was waiting for it to come back and wanted to be prepared. "It's nothing…just that…sometimes when I try to move…my toes…to put it delicately…fuck me with pain." *Should have taken that damn medication*, she thought.

Steph put a hand on her shoulder and Zoey rested her cheek on it, smiling at her.

"So, what's the plan for Dawn?" Luke asked.

Zoey dove back into their old abandoned conversation. "It's simple. We just need the person she trusts most to…" She rocked her head side to side, but could find no better way to put it. "interrogate her about it. Get her to spill the beans."

Myah nodded but kept a straight face. "All right, who would that be?"

None of them said a word. Their eyes passed from one person to another and, while it looked like each of them wanted to say someone's name, no one did. It was as if their minds had sewn their mouths shut. At that point Zoey got an idea.

"Let's try this." She grabbed a napkin from the holder and rooted through her purse until she found a pen. She ripped the napkin into four pieces and slid one to each person at the table. "We're all going to write down the name of the person we think Dawn trusts the most. After you write a name, keep the napkin name side down. Once we've all written a name, we'll flip our napkins over and whoever has their name written the most has to do it. Fair?"

They all nodded and Zoey began writing. The pen moved from hand to hand and scribbled against the napkin's difficult fabric, making its way to Zoey sooner than she was expecting. She tossed it back in her purse and watched the napkin pieces close in toward the center of the table. "On three, we flip. One...two...three."

Remarkably, all four flipped the napkins over, Zoey was sure at least one of them would be too afraid to, and each one had the same name written on it in four various styles; Zoey. The lucky three looked at her and she kept her eyes on the four pieces of napkin that had given her the heaviest burden she would ever have to carry.

"You okay?" Steph asked. It wouldn't be an easy task to accomplish and Zoey could easily blow it if her heart and brain weren't giving one hundred percent. Despite her question though, Steph had great faith in her friend. Zoey always tried her hardest when it came to Dawn.

Zoey looked up with a face of fake determination that deceived Steph, Myah and Luke into feeling instant relief. "When should I start the interrogation?"

Trevor looked out at the world that was racing much too fast and his heart began to do the same. He tore his view away from the blurry window and turned it to Evan. "How fast are you going?" They were on a thirty-five mile per hour road and he knew Evan was doing fifty at minimum.

Heather also looked away from the streaky world and glared at Trevor for trying to ruin the fun. "Who cares? Just enjoy it." She herself didn't feel any enjoyment from the whipping world, but she was fascinated by the altered reality she was seeing through the truck window. She was beginning to get sucked back into it when Trevor's voice, again, pulled her out of it.

"Yeah, we're dead. All of us. We're going to die in this truck today. It's happening. It's over. We're done."

Amy's eyes climbed as high as they could go and then dropped back to down to where they started. "Shut up, Trevor, you're going to be fine." Her voice sounded confident but she did agree with him on the uncertainty of their fate. She waited until Trevor looked back outside and she put a hand on Evan's forearm and leaned closer to make sure neither of their backseat drivers would hear her. "Can you slow down a little? Please?" Evan's expression remained unchanged, still glaring, but he lifted his foot off the gas and the truck dropped down from the low fifties to the low forties. Amy leaned back into her seat and whispered, "Thank you," while quietly releasing an anxiety covered sigh. As the world became easier to see and distinguish, Trevor duplicated Amy's response and Heather looked down, disappointed.

"So, what are we actually doing? You asked us if we wanted to hang out, but do you have a location in mind or are we just wasting gas?"

Amy turned her body around to face Trevor. Couldn't he just shut up and stop complaining for one fucking minute? "Evan needs," she paused to pick her words, "to let out some anger." She noticed out of the corner of her eye that Heather was wearing that grin but she didn't pay it any real attention and kept focused on Trevor. "We're going to help him. *That's* what we're *actually doing.*"

Trevor turned his head to the right but his eyes stayed on Amy's burning black ones. "But how are we—"

"—IT DOESN'T MATTER!"

Trevor jumped and Heather's smile grew.

Amy closed her eyes and slowed her breathing as much as she could. "It doesn't matter how, we're just going to help him. Okay?" As she expected, Trevor nodded and she turned back to face the road ahead. She scanned the people they passed, considering each one but knowing they wouldn't suffice. It needed to happen to someone more personal, Evan wouldn't be willing to hurt someone unless it was someone he knew and someone he hated. After a few more minutes and miles, she spotted someone who filled both specifications. "Bingo." A smile had formed and she tapped Evan and motioned toward the person. Evan saw him, looked back at Amy and nodded. He tossed his head back, referring to the two behind them and Amy took the reins. "You see him? On the right? Alone?" Heather and Trevor looked where she had referenced and felt similar feelings of disgust.

"Jonah Dunbar." Heather said.

"The same," Trevor answered. "Fucking obnoxious asshole." They remembered him from middle school and how loud and abrasive he was to all four of them. As well as anyone else unlucky enough to cross his path. His family had moved to Polleyville before high school and the happiness from everyone in his grade was almost cult like.

Trevor's ironic insult, the pot calling the kettle obnoxious, was not lost on Amy but there were more important things to deal with right now. "You see where he's going?"

Heather looked at Amy and her grin returned. She could picture Amy's plan, what a wonderful plan it was. "Down the bike path. Alone. On an overcast weekday in forty degree weather."

Trevor understood it now, too. "Sounds like a tasty recipe."

Amy turned to look at Evan. "It will be." Then, softer, only to him. "Are you ready?"

He looked back at her and his glare hardened. "There's a parking lot by the park near there. We get in front of him, maybe in the tunnel, wait it out and when he comes by...we start."

He turned down a side street and parked in the empty lot. The four got out and hovered to the bike path.

Jonah Dunbar always walked on the bike path in times of excessive stress. It was a nice, quiet place for him to think things over, calm himself down and come up with an appropriate conclusion. The trees always seemed to give him unspoken support and the one tree he always sat under did that best. Countless times he had sat at the base of that tree and had found a solution in minutes. He was sure this time would be no different. He needed the tree now.

He had walked almost half of the bike path at this point. From Polleyville to Winno, almost four miles on foot. He wished he could just live in these woods with no one to drag him back into the uncomfortable real world. Thinking about having to get a job and stepping into a completely unknown and unusual part of adulthood lined up perfectly with the dark black tunnel he started heading through. A tunnel so black he couldn't even see the walls of it. He could imagine monsters and creatures lurking against those walls, watching him, ready to grab ahold of whatever they could get their claws on, but that didn't scare him anymore.

Besides, he was closing in. A few dozen feet through the tunnel and a few feet after it, there would be the tree and he would stay as long as he wanted; as long as he could. *Just a few more feet,* he thought to himself. The circle of light was getting bigger and he could feel the influence of the tree entering his system. His mind became clearer and he was already thinking about ways to get around this problem. *Just a few more feet. Just a few more feet. Just a fe—*

—you've been saying that for the past twenty four feet. I don't think

you know what number 'a few' stand for.

Who cares? There's the tree now, in a few more steps we'll be out of the tunnel completely, so this time there really is *only a few more fee—*

His internal argument was disrupted by a stick, about the size of his arm, that smacked against his forehead hard enough to split it in two and sent him colliding with the cement road beneath him. The stick belonged to a figure, one he couldn't identify but, although just an outline, it was a human and not a monster. Though that realization didn't do much to relieve him. Another figure stepped out from the other side of the tunnel and the two stood side by side, blocking Jonah from the tree and eclipsing what little light there was. Without daring to say a word, Jonah got up, ignoring the thudding above his eyes, and turned to leave, walking into the awaiting hands of two more figures. One of these felt like a monster just based on how hard their nails dug into his skin. They seemed to blend into the tunnel itself and they turned him around to face the first two figures who were moving closer and blending into the darkness as well.

"Wait, what do you want?" He got no answer. All he got was an ache in the back of his skull when they threw him against the wall of the tunnel and his head smacked the concrete. Despite already being dark, his vision started going darker.

Evan and Amy couldn't see each other in the tunnel, but they could feel when the other was looking at them. After Jonah was up against the wall Amy could feel Evan's stare, desperate for encouragement, fall onto her. She didn't need to say anything, she just gave the darkness a big slow nod and heard him step in front of Jonah. It was time to eat.

Evan's breathing became loud and heavy. He wound his arm back, thought about the one simple thing he couldn't get and everything he had lost and the people who made it even worse and he ran his fish forward.

The hit came from nowhere. The blacked out tunnel made everything impossible to see and he was unable to tense his stomach before the blow. It sucked the wind out of him and he wheezed for air. He could feel the hands tighten and tried to prepare himself for whatever hits might follow. Though, in the dark, that was near impossible.

Evan's hand hurt after the first hit and his arm felt like it was being ripped out of its socket. He didn't stop. He used the pain and anger and mixed it with the pain and anger he was already feeling. He grunted with every hit. Not from the hurt, but because he needed to find another way to release some of his rage. There was too much inside and a few hits couldn't get rid of all of it. Even after he finished there would still be a lot left inside.

Jonah couldn't breathe. Every punch took out more air and made it harder and harder to suck in the small amount he managed to find in between blows. They just kept coming and the growl from the puncher ended every one. He was convinced that he would die here and he would never get to see the tree or solve his problem. Suddenly having to get a job didn't seem like the worst use of his time.

After a while the beating slowed and then stopped. And when the punches stopped, he was thrown onto the dirty concrete and began catching any breath he could find. He heard a voice mumble, "It's still in me," and heard another say, "Then don't stop." There was a cold pause and Jonah didn't notice the figure getting closer. With no warning, a hard force smashed against his temple, cracked him against the cement and the black tunnel covered everything.

The impact echoed.

"Heather, check him out." Amy's voice was both angry and anxious. She didn't want both, angry was her preference, but both emotions were tangible when she spoke. Evan could have killed him and, although her eyes had adjusted to the dark, she had no idea if Jonah was moving. Or breathing. Getting the side of your head stomped on *that* hard and living was not something she would bet any money on. She saw Heather's figure move towards him and move her hand over his body. Heather's voice then called out, with faint sadness, "He's still breathing. Soft pulse though."

Heather heard something familiar and a fresh glob of spit splattered against Jonah's body. She stood up and backed away before any of Evan's saliva could hit her.

Amy relaxed. "Good. Heather, Trevor go to the truck and wait for us. We'll be there after we deal with this."

Heather and Trevor both wanted to stay, for very different reasons (Heather didn't care about helping them like Trevor did and Trevor didn't want to see what they would do with him like Heather did), but they both left the tunnel anyway, shielding their eyes from the light gray clouds that coated the sky and headed back to Evan's truck.

Evan was breathing normally again and after Heather and Trevor were out of sight he spoke about the unconscious lump in front of him. "Fuck him."

Amy considered removing Jonah, maybe bringing him to the secret path where he wouldn't be found for a while, but chose not to pursue that idea. In truth, she didn't care to. She was focused on more important things and more important people.

"How do you feel?" Amy asked as she took his arms in her hands and rubbed them up and down. "Any better?"

"A little."

She nodded, though not yet satisfied. "Enough to make it through the rest of the day without needed to attack anyone?"

He had to think about it and wasn't entirely sure his answer was the truth. "Yeah." After a few seconds, he asked, "But it still feels impossible to get rid of. Like trying to blow out a house fire. Is this how it feels for you?"

"It is now," Amy said. "I used to be able to relax for a few days, maybe a week. But now I feel the way you do, I feel…untethered all the time. But I'll help you live with it whenever we can't unload it. It's easier than you might think." It was for her at least after living with her anger and her volcano for years.

"I hope so," Evan said and he meant it. He felt both exhausted and excitable, like someone who can't fall asleep when they're tired and can't stay awake when they're up.

"It will be." She took his hand, it was shaking less. For now. "Let's go back."

They made their way back to the truck and jumped into their seats.

"So what did you do with him?"

Amy and Evan closed their doors, exchanged a confused look and Heather rolled her eyes. "Jonah."

Amy answered quickly, pretending she hadn't forgotten, "Oh, we just left him where he was. Keeping him in the dark is better than moving him to where he could be seen."

She didn't know just how important it would have been to move him into the light.

"And what if someone bumps into him?" Heather asked. "It's bound to happen eventually."

"That's not our problem," Amy spat.

"You don't think so?" Heather asked, a certain slyness in her voice that she hoped Amy would notice.

Her hopes were answered. But, instead of her slyness making Amy feel uneasy, it just did what everything seemed to do. It made her mad. "Shut up."

"Make me."

None of them knew where this retaliation was coming from aside from the one brave enough, or crazy enough, to instigate it, but all four of them had no idea what would happen next. The world itself seemed surprised and, as if in response to this shift in the group's dynamic, snowflakes began landing.

Evan, not even out of the parking lot yet, stopped the truck. In case he needed to act fast. He didn't even spare the second it would take to put on his wipers.

"You want me to?" Amy snarled, her nails scratching the leather of her seat.

Her glare could light a match but it didn't intimidate Heather in the least. Heather saw Amy more as a fun circus act than a threatening force to be reckoned with. "No, I don't. Just fucking with you."

"Don't."

"I'll do my best."

They stared each other down for a few seconds more before Amy turned back to face forward and turned on the radio. Sometimes, most times it seemed, she fucking hated Heather. After a few minutes on the road, once her anger subsided, a bit of unease began to creep into Amy's head. *Was* she just fucking with her? Did she know something? Would she say something?

Part of Heather was, indeed, fucking with Amy but another part of her thought that Amy's streak of torturing those around her was about to come to an end. And one impulsive glob of spit had the power to do it.

Heather had noted Jonah's weak breathing and slow pulse. What she hadn't noticed was the small amount of blood pooling from his head and by the time the four of them were dropped off at their respective homes, the weak and the slow had stopped altogether.

Jonah Dunbar was dead.

Chapter 13

"Hey, Dawn, do you mind if I come over after school today?" Zoey's question confused Dawn. She had never asked ahead of time if it was okay if she came over, she always just showed up. "Yeah, that's fine. Just you?" She gave a few quick glances at the other three people in her car who all either looked down or shook their heads. Either way, Steph, Luke and Myah remained silent. Zoey's was the only voice Dawn heard.

"Yeah, well, there's something I want to talk to you about, and it would be better if it stayed between the two of us." Zoey meant the first part of the sentence, but after 'about' she lied through her teeth. The idea of having to get Dawn to open up and tell her what was wrong with her sounded more difficult than anything Zoey had done in her high school career thus far. Though, seeing as how she was a B+ student with no qualms about public speaking, she hadn't done very much in her high school career that she would have described as difficult. But, regardless, the thought of this upcoming interrogation seemed insurmountable.

Her stomach felt empty and she got goosebumps at the mere thought of it. She knew she had to do it, for her, Dawn's and the other three's sake, but she really didn't want to have to do it alone. She had been getting nothing but positive reinforcement from Steph, Luke and Myah since the four pieces of napkin were flipped over and all of the 'You're gonna be fine' and 'I have faith in you' shit was only making her less confident in herself. And she hadn't even done it yet.

Dawn shifted, uneasy in the driver's seat, and tried to push away the strange feeling she got from Zoey's inflections. Something about it didn't feel right. Zoey *did* always go to her whenever she had a problem, that wasn't the odd part. The odd part was the feeling of dread that came from Zoey when she said "it would be better if it stayed between the two of us." The way she said it sounded regretful and, for a moment, Dawn wondered if Zoey had ended up having a little accident with Brandon Finley when the two hung out. But Dawn didn't let her fear become as palpable when she said, "Okay. Do you want me to take us to my house or do you want me to take you home and then you can drive over?"

Zoey's stomach lurched and she felt sick. "Oh no, I'll drive myself. It's okay."

"Maybe you *should* go with Dawn straight to her house," a bold, yet small, voice broke in.

Zoey turned to glare at the girl next to her and she met Myah's confident eyes. *Looks like she sucked the confidence out of me and injected it into herself,* Zoey thought. Before she could argue further, Myah continued.

"If this really is important, you and Dawn should take all the time alone you can get to find out what the problem is and how you can solve it."

Dawn may have been listening to the same words as everyone else, but she wasn't hearing them like Zoey, Steph and Luke were. Myah went on.

"I can find a way home. I'm sure Steph and Luke can, too." She broke Zoey's glare and looked around her. "Right?"

Luke spoke up first. "Yeah, I can get a ride home from one of my friends and we can probably drop you off, too, Myah."

Myah made a small face of revulsion at the thought. The last place she wanted to be was in a car with a bunch of jocks but, if it would help get to the cause of Dawn's issue, it would be worth it. She spoke through her teeth. "Yeah that sounds...great."

Steph heard the displeasure in her voice and moved the conversation away from Myah's testosterone filled future.

"And I can just head down town. There are a few things I need to take care of and a few errands to run. This'll be a good time to,

Think of any?

get those taken care of." She looked at Zoey's horrified and furious expression and Steph pointed down to her phone. She began texting the group chat the four had made shortly after Zoey's new mission was assigned and she sent them, *Myah's right. You'll need all the time you can get.* She expected a singular backlash that held the weight of hundreds and she got it.

Z: Easy for you to say, you don't have to do it.

M: Zoey, you're going to be fine.

No one noticed Zoey grit her teeth.

L: Just take it slow and be patient. You catch more flies with honey than vinegar.

Z: You're gonna catch my foot up your ass if you keep feeding me any more of this stupid fucking fortune cookie shit. This isn't as easy as any of you think it might be. I'm putting a lot on the line here. I'm putting my and Dawn's friendship on the line here.

M: If you two are as close of friends as you say you are, you have nothing to worry about. If you really are the most important person in her life, she's going to open up to you.

Zoey groaned and rested her head on Myah's shoulder. It was skinny and boney, but comforting. Myah smiled and tilted her head against Zoey's. Dawn heard the groan and was relieved to finally hear something other than the clicking noises from everyone's phones.

"You okay, Zoey?"

Zoey shot her head back up, throwing Myah's off to the right, and cleared her throat. "Oh yeah, I'm fine. Just, not really in the mood for school today. Especially with the day off yesterday, it's like my brain hasn't registered that it has to start working again."

"Apparently it doesn't register that very often," Steph said and Zoey smiled in response to the smirk Steph gave her.

"Fuck off."

She, Myah, Steph and Luke chuckled. Dawn wanted to but the threat of pain gave her only a longing smile to work with, and for the first time since yesterday, Zoey had a sliver of hope regarding the conversation she and Dawn would have later today. The hope was unfamiliar and a bit jarring, but it was the best thing she had felt over the past two days. Before she could even appreciate it, it was gone.

Zoey enjoyed school that day more than any other day all year, even in spite of the stupid crutches that she almost tripped over several times. She didn't enjoy school for her normal reasons today, she enjoyed it because it was one long interference keeping her from her future. Although, with every class she left, it became harder and harder to ignore the sickening wary feeling rotting her insides. Zoey wasn't used to being anxious, maybe that was why the hold it had on her felt so strong and tight.

By the time the two thirty bell echoed through the school, Zoey was nearly trembling and when she made her way outside, on crutches that had starting to feel like they were rubbing away the skin of her armpits, and saw Dawn's car, she wished it would explode.

Abruptly, the entire world looked horrid. She liked the cold and especially the snow, and there was a good foot of it covering the ground, but the smooth white blanket now looked deceptive and smothering and the cold air felt like it could cut her skin. She stared at it, at everything, and despite the rest of her peers suffocating her ears with their brief conversations, when Dawn came up behind her and said, "Hey," she jumped half a foot in the air.

Dawn backed up, eyes wide and smiled. "Sorry. Didn't mean to give you a heart attack. Is everything okay?"

Zoey searched Dawn's body and face and was amazed by how good she looked. No off way of walking, no pain behind her eyes, she wasn't clenching her fists or biting her lip. Dawn looked perfect. Zoey wondered if she could just call it off now, seeing as how it didn't look like anything was wrong with Dawn, but she knew she wouldn't be able to. She had made a promise. And it was possible that Dawn had simply gotten better at hiding what was wrong, which only made her feel worse. "Yeah, I'm fine. You just startled me." *In more ways than one.*

Dawn nodded her head and waited for Zoey to settle her breathing. Once she did, Dawn advanced. "Are you ready to go?" She saw an impromptu flash of mortal terror whisk by Zoey's face. Her voice tried her best to hide it but even in the one word she said, Dawn could tell Zoey was petrified. Of what, Dawn didn't know. But she would soon.

"Yep."

Dawn took a step closer and looked far into Zoey's hazel eyes. Eyes of a golden field on a harmonious sunny day. "Hey, don't be afraid to be honest with me. You can tell or ask me anything. You know that."

Zoey fought back the urge to say what she wanted to and instead opted to think it. *You won't think that in an hour.* She chose to say something much more pleasing and, to her surprise, almost sounded pleased. "Yes, I do. And I'm fine, really. Let's go." She took off for the car with her confidence rising ever so slightly. To her she sounded believable, but not to Dawn.

Her alarm was now expanding. Zoey was good at a lot of things, but lying was not one of them. The two drove into the high school traffic with an unnoticeable eyebrow hovering towards both themselves and each other. The talking was, at times, faint. At other times, deceased. When they passed by Steph walking towards the downtown area, the duo had an uplifting feeling sweep over them, but it was absent as soon as they passed her. If Steph could hear their thoughts, she would have heard a perfect harmony of *HELP*.

Unbeknownst to her, Steph would be the one begging for help before Dawn or Zoey could.

Chapter 14

"God, I hate the snow," Amy growled from the passenger's seat of Evan's truck. The cold alone bothered her, it upset her inner volcano, like the world itself was trying to extinguish her, and the snow was the white, freezing icing on this cake of displeasure.

Evan had a similar opinion with Amy when it came to most things, but the two were black and white when it came to the cold. "I don't know, I kind of like it." He didn't meet the glare he could feel and see out of the corner of his eye, he kept straight on the road.

"So do I," Trevor said, taking some of the heat off to Evan. Much to Evan's relief. "I like the idea of being able to wrap yourself in a blanket and make something warm to eat or drink. When it's hot, there's really nothing you can do to escape it."

Amy scoffed and turned around towards Heather who was watching the snow laden ground with a passion. As if she expected something to burst out of it. "And what about you?"

Heather turned to look at her and raised her shoulders. "I don't get bothered by weather. Hot or cold, there's no difference to me." She felt a small amount of satisfaction watching Amy be taken back a bit, this may have been the first time they had ever disagreed with her, even if for a stupid pointless reason.

She whipped her hair around and faced forward again. "How is it just me?"

"Maybe it's because of your red hair."

"It's orange, you bastard," Amy snapped at him. She hated when people called it red. Almost as much as she hated the few times she had been subjected to the 'gingers don't have souls' joke. A joke that always ended in blood.

Trevor shook his head. "Well, whatever color you call it, maybe *it* doesn't like the cold."

Amy could hear Trevor talking through his own amusement. The craving to jump into the backseat and knock him unconscious only subsided when she saw a familiar black girl with her frizzy hair pulled back into a screamingly tight bun walking up the road. Towards a main street. Where she would be safe. Amy muttered, "We can't have that," and the random sentence perked Evan's interest.

"Can't have what? The cold isn't going to leave just like that."

Amy didn't hear him. The lava was flowing again. In the past there would have been less in her, after Poodle and New Girl, perhaps so little that she wouldn't have had the energy to go after someone else until it refilled. But not anymore, now there would always be enough. "Stop the car."

Heather and Trevor looked at her, one excited and the other confused. Heather could read Amy's voice like a children's book.

"What?" Evan, not understanding why Amy thought it was so simple to stop in the middle of the road, spoke with annoyance. "Amy, I can't jus—"

"—STOP THE FUCKING CAR!"

Heather let out a barely audible snicker and Evan chose to pull over the fucking car as a substitute. They were still behind Steph when the quartet had stopped the truck and Amy got out before Evan could even turn the vehicle off. He watched her speed up the road and it wasn't until he saw the person in front of her that the pieces fell into place.

"Oh shit." He turned to look at the two that sat behind him, still in their seatbelts and, without saying a word, all three got out of the truck, slammed the doors in perfect unison and jogged to catch up with Amy. At this point they knew better than to let her roam free alone. Evan needed to be there to keep her from doing anything too stupid, especially since they were standing right beside a road that at least a dozen cars drove down every minute. He caught up with her, still fifteen or so meters behind Steph, and blocked her from advancing.

He put his hands on her exposed arms and ignored the blazing heat of her skin. "Amy, I need you to calm down." To his surprise and minor horror, she laughed.

She wiggled her muted pink arms out of his cold hands and thought about how stupid he could be at times. "Why do you keep trying to fucking stop me? *You* were the one who said," she put her fingers up in quotes, "I'll stand by you for good. No getting in the way, no holding you back. Whatever you want to do, you'll be able to count on me." She had remembered it word for word because of how special it made her feel and it felt good to throw it back at him with some volcanic matter added on. That was what real icing on the cake was. "You had your moment with Jonah, you know how it feels. Now get out of my way and let me have mine." She was ready to shove him aside when he kissed her, long and slow. Like the ones she gave him. It felt nice, but when the lava was flowing, as it was now, nothing could pull her out of her hate. He pulled his lips away and said something that, for the first time, almost stopped the flow.

"I'm not stopping you. I'm just telling you to think this over. We can't do this right next to a popular road."

Amy squinted her eyes, looked at their surroundings and altered the plan. "I'll take care of that. Now, are you finally going to be on my fucking side?" She watched his face and could tell, in a matter of a few seconds, that his thinking had left him and he was ready. He was probably thinking about his family. She moved him aside and took off after The Black One, who was getting farther away with every wasted second, leaving an invisible trail of an orange substance that ate through the sidewalk after her.

Heather and Trevor watched her bolt down the street and shifted their gazes to Evan, whose eyebrows had sunk to the resting place where Amy's always were. He gave them a cold glare and said, "Let's go." He ran after Amy and the two he left behind followed suit.

He was, indeed, thinking about his family, and it felt like he was never going to run out of material. He even put some of his anger into his footsteps, slamming his feet on the concrete as he tried catching up with Amy. Which was a more difficult feat than he would have expected.

For every foot closer he got, she seemed to separate herself from him by three. He was beginning to wonder if he would reach her before she got to Steph and he was relieved when she stopped walking and turned her head to the side, waiting for the rest of them. He caught up a few seconds later and tried to catch his breath before Heather and Trevor arrived. He still hadn't caught it completely by the time they showed up so he was thankful that Amy gave them a few more seconds to rest. It didn't look like she needed it.

Through heavy breathing, coughing and spitting Trevor asked, "Amy, do you even have a fucking plan?"

He was hard to understand while he wheezed in whatever air he could get and Amy ignored his unneeded question. "You all set?" Her eyes swam between each person and despite the overwhelming *No* coming from their six eyes, she couldn't risk letting The Black One get away. She gave them a few more seconds and said, without looking back, "We're going. Now." She continued on, walking this time. They were close enough to The Black One and the need to run was over. Walking would also help them sneak up on her better.

Evan, Heather and Trevor exchanged weak looks and headed off after Amy, thankful that they were walking now.

The weekend they had all been through, in addition to their interaction with Jonah yesterday, had changed them for the worse. They were watching Steph but not seeing her.

Evan saw his aunts, his uncles, his cousins, his grandparents, his tattoo, he saw so much that he could hardly focus. His anger almost made it hurt to breathe, hard to move.

Trevor saw his family as well but also saw dozens of girls who had disregarded him and acted like he was a piece of mold they found in their fridge. As if he had no right existing,

Heather saw a multitude of possible futures in which they tore into the girl they were closing in on and could have moaned at the thought.

And, because of this anger and, in one case, delight, they had no issue watching Amy take the belt out of her jeans, swing it as far back as it could go and, with full force, slash the metal buckle down on Steph's head.

Steph's mind had been on Dawn and Zoey for the entire school day and still was as she walked up the long road that led downtown where she would have no errands to run and would instead, begin the several mile trek to her house. Normally she would have been annoyed by the walk, but she knew she would be wasting time thinking about that when the future of her friends was much more important. She really hoped Zoey could pull it off.

It wasn't like Zoey to be so nervous but, then again, it also wasn't like Dawn to keep some sort of painful secret from them so Steph couldn't blame Zoey for feeling out of her element. She was thinking of the worst possible outcome that their conversation could lead to when she felt something slam against the top of her head.

She fell to her knees, seeing black spots for a few brief seconds until the beating pain from her head ripped them away and made her scream. It felt like her skull had been cracked open and she reached up to feel for blood. Her fingers were red when she took them away but she didn't have time to think about that before a hand grabbed her collar and yanked her backwards. She hit the concrete and smacked the back of her head against it, getting a duology of thudding pain from two parts of her head. Despite her heartbeat that was amplified in her ears, she could hear footsteps coming from behind her and hoped someone had seen her fall and was rushing to her aid. However, the voices she heard only made her head pound harder.

"Can't do this near the road." Evan looked at Amy and in spite of her glare, a glare that he had always backed down from, he didn't break her gaze this time.

Amy looked down at The Black One and snarled, "Get her up." Heather and Trevor wrenched her up onto her feet and Amy noticed, based on how limp her legs were, that she probably couldn't yet stand on them herself. "Follow me." She went past them and into the woods, eliminating any potential interferences.

She trudged through the ankle deep snow, not feeling the cold against her lava filled skin, and stopped after several dozen feet. When she turned around, the houses that stood opposite the woods were little more than slivers and slices of paneling and window in between the dozens, hundreds of trees that blocked their view. No one would be able to see them. She stood glaring, still clutching her belt. Once Heather and Trevor had dragged in their meat, her legs now trying to dig into the snow and stop her forward momentum, Amy could tell The Black One was more aware of her current situation. And the resulting glare Amy got from her almost made her smile. The struggling was another better example of icing on the cake.

She got as close as she could and spoke with lava dribbling out of her mouth and sizzling through the snow below them. "You still think you're tough shit? You still think you're strong? Go ahead and prove—"

Steph slammed her head into Amy's and knocked her back a few feet. She didn't think it would do her much good but she didn't care. It wasn't as if Amy was going to let her go so Steph figured she might as well give the bitch as much medicine as she was able to. The one issue with her outburst was that now the front of her head joined the top and the back in their pulsing assault. But the pain in her head was cut off by a pain in her stomach when Evan gave a hard blow that would have brought her to her knees again, had it not been for the two holding her upright. She could hear him in her ear.

"Don't you ever fucking touch her, you worthless shit."

She heard Amy say, "It's okay, Evan." She sounded more calm than Steph expected and when she brought her gaze up, she finally noticing the belt Amy was squeezing. And, as much as she dreaded how that would feel, a part of her was grateful. At least it wasn't sharp.

Amy looked The Black One in the eyes and tried something new. "I'll let the little *nigger* have that one."

It was a word she never used but found appropriate for this occasion. She even thought it possible that she might retire 'The Black One' and replace it with this more concise version if she enjoyed saying it. But, given how ugly it sounded when it came out, she knew she wouldn't. However, the reaction from The Black One, the nickname that would stay, made it worth it.

Heather and Trevor had a good hold on Steph, but she was much stronger than Dawn and when she lunged at Amy the two almost let go. She pulled and twisted her arms, making bull-like noises as she struggled against Trevor's thick fat arms and Heather solid immobile ones. She bared her teeth and extended her hands as much as she could and only relented when Amy swung the belt, metal buckle first, into the side of her head.

She went down, feeling a fourth area of her head join the other three in their drumming circle, and saw blood fall into the snow. It hit small, but spread far. She closed her eyes and could feel her heartbeat in her open wound. It was on the left side, probably above her eyebrow.

Amy spoke with forced restraint, which could almost be tasted in her voice. "How's your head?"

"Better looking than yours." It hurt to talk and the drumming circle only got louder.

"Not for long," she said, looking at the belt that now held a drop of red on it. Then, without warning or winding up, she whipped it without looking and smacked the side of The Black One's ribs. She groaned and Amy's grip on her beautiful black belt tightened. She knew the metal wouldn't be able to break bones, but she wanted to try regardless. *Life is all about pushing the boundaries,* she thought.

Heather kept her hands locked around Steph's arm but backed up to avoid any accidental friendly fire. The pain would be enjoyable to her, but she liked pain much more when it happened to somebody else. And the way Amy was swinging that belt and slapping it against the girl's skin would probably hurt too much to be pleasurable. Heather still enjoyed the show despite that. The belt flew through the air like a blur and only became noticeable when it connected with a part of Steph's body. Whether head or legs or torso, each smack that was heard was answered by a grunt from the body the belt was whipping. Some hits were more silent, some made a crisp slap and others gave an audible crack against the bone. At one point the buckle split her lip and Heather hoped Steph considered herself lucky. If her mouth had been open, that metal buckle could have very likely knocked one of her teeth out.

Heather began to wonder if the belt would break before Amy was done. It was as thick and as long as a regular belt, nothing really stood out about it aside from the red that painted the silver buckle, but if Amy kept going at this rate, Heather wouldn't have been surprised to see the force and speed snap the buckle off entirely.

But, after one final hit against The Black One's hip with another audible *crack* as the buckle smacked the bone beneath, Amy sighed, as if finishing a workout, pulled the belt back through the loops in her jeans and locked it securely in place.

She didn't wipe off the blood.

"Drop her," Steph heard Amy say and that was when she fell, front side first, into the snow. In spite of the white padding, she punched right through it and onto the hard dirt beneath. She could feel small twigs press into her but that wasn't her top priority. None of her bones were broken but it felt like they were. Her body was riddled with bruises and red marks and it hurt to move any of her limbs. She was bleeding from her temple and her swollen lip. The cold seemed to have no effect on her and she stayed put in the snow, hoping that they had gotten what they wanted and would go away.

They would. But not before one final message.

Amy bent down next to The Black One's body and dug her fingers through the girl's hair until she found her elastic hair band. She ripped it out and the bun melted around her head in one soft act, spreading out in every direction like a blooming flower. Amy tossed the hair band into the snow and stood up. Her hand was burning from the skin the leather had rubbed off. "We're done here." She turned and headed back to the road. The cutting breeze from the February air felt good on her singed hand.

Steph heard them leave and, when all footsteps had died, she got up. Her body moaned for her not to, but she swallowed the pain from her arms, legs and head and began back towards where she came. Back towards a main street. Where she would be safe. The word sounded heavenly; safe. She only thought of that word while she walked. She didn't think of her pulsing head or tenderized body, she didn't think of what had just happened to her, she didn't think of who did it to her, she didn't even think of Dawn and Zoey. All she thought about was the word safe. And once she reached the main road and that blessed safety surrounded her, she found the strength to smile. It was an odd smile and the sudden tears that ran down her face, tears Steph chose to ignore could have been attributed to happiness that she was safe or disappointment at how scared she had been, how little damage she had managed to inflict, how weak she really was, but Steph refused to pay them any attention.

She limped home, smiling and crying every step of the way. It took an hour and a half before she stumbled through her front door and her body was sore beyond belief but her smile stayed. As did her tears.

She washed off the blood that had stuck to her face and body.

Her smile stayed. As did her tears.

She went to her bed and collapsed into it, her muscles easing up and letting go for what felt like the first time.

Her smile stayed. As did her tears.

She listened to the banging in her head from above her right and left eye. *WOMM WOMM WOMM.*

Her smile stayed. As did her tears.

She thought about Zoey and Dawn.

Her smile left.

Chapter 15

The drive to Dawn's house seemed to last forever, as if they were traveling from one side of the planet to the other. Every building crawled by and every street stretched for miles. The ride was twelve minutes long.

What exchanges passed between the two were short and awkward and it didn't take one mile to pass before they both realized that it would be easier if they stopped conversing altogether. They were both too busy in their own thoughts anyway.

All Zoey's mind went to during the endless drive was what would happen when she got Dawn into her room. What would she say? How would she say it? She agreed with Myah that if she and Dawn were really as close as she thought they were, Dawn wouldn't cut the ties that held them together but, in her heightened state of anxiety, logic was thrown out of the sluggish car's window. She had almost considered taking Dawn to that secret path in the park, a place where they would have no interruptions, but decided against it. It would be better for Dawn to be as comfortable as possible, it might help ease her into a confession.

Zoey was so lost in thought that Zoey didn't even notice when Dawn pulled into her driveway and turned off the car. It was two forty-two. The only thing that brought her back to the real world was Dawn's voice, coated with fear.

"Zoey? You awake?"

Zoey blinked a few times, breathing stale air, and looked at Dawn. Her hands were still on the steering while despite having taken the key out of the ignition. Zoey nodded her head and tried on a smile that didn't fit. "Yeah, I'm here. Guess I just zoned out for a minute." Dawn gave a little smile and Zoey felt the weight of the moment ease up slightly.

"Good. And, by the way, zoning out is my thing and I'd like to be the only one with that talent."

They both laughed. Like they used to before whatever happened to

Dawn took that away. It felt refreshing and it lasted less than five seconds.

Dawn sighed, took her hands off the wheel and unbuckled her seatbelt. "You ready?"

Something was wrong with Zoey today. She wasn't acting like her regular self. Dawn had spent the drive home thinking about what it could be and hoping it didn't involve Brandon Finley but she couldn't come up with anything that seemed right. Zoey didn't get nervous about school, she didn't seem to be afraid of her parents anymore, she knew how to get around on her crutches and she hadn't mentioned any pain in her toes. Whatever it was, Dawn was sure she'd find out once they were in a more comfortable place to talk about it.

Her stomach still hurt but she had been getting much better at masking the pain. She was masking it right now and Zoey didn't seem to notice at all. Her blue eyes looked at Zoey and Zoey's hazel eyes looked back.

Zoey answered, sounding rather confident. "Yep. Let's go."

Dawn got out of the car and Zoey took a few seconds to send her text before following her. She got her crutches out from the backseat and trudged beside someone she could tell was walking slower to accommodate her. She would have thought that after two days she would get the hang of using them but it was just as difficult to maneuver now as it had been on Monday when she first put them under her arms.

They walked up Dawn's front yard and through her front door, the weight of the moment increasing as soon as Zoey stepped into her house. It sat on her shoulders and she felt herself caving under it. As she made her way up the stairs she felt her ass vibrate and she took out her phone, making what was already a challenging task even harder. She read her previous text to the group chat:

Z: Here we go. You assholes owe me one for this.

And read the new texts that followed it.

S: You're gonna be great. You can handle this.

L: Dawn trusts you more than anyone. You just need to have faith in yourself.

M: You're the best person for this job. We couldn't do this without you.

Normally she would have appreciated it, but now their attempts to make her feel better only washed over her like a stream over stones.

Then she got a text from the conversation between only her and Myah.

M: You're smart, you're strong and you're sweet. If she doesn't open up to you she won't open up to anyone. I'd say good luck but you really don't need it. Just be yourself.

Zoey put her phone back in her pocket as she entered Dawn's room. She set her crutches along the wall and closed the door behind her. Dawn was sitting on her bed and Zoey hopped over to it, passing the area on the rug where she had experienced Dawn zoning out a little less than a week ago. She longed to be there again. Her fear at that time now seemed humorous in a strange way. She sat next to Dawn on the bed, put a hand on her knee, took a deep breath and felt her three other friends sitting beside her. "Dawn, I need you to be honest with me. Can you do that? Please?"

"Of course."

The simple-mindedness of Dawn's response made Zoey scoff and shake her head. She looked Dawn in the eyes and didn't hold back.

"I know something's wrong with you. I don't know *what*, but I know something happened to you."

"That's not tr—"

"—Steph knows, too. So does Luke. Hell, even Myah figured it out." She didn't like to lie, but she was prepared to if it meant figuring this out. "We're all really worried about you, Dawn. We just want to help."

Dawn began to feel flustered. She could feel tears stirring in her eyes and lied through the truth she still refused to tell. They wouldn't be safe if they knew. "Zoey, listen to me. I'm fine, all right? I don't know what you've all seen, or thought you've seen, but I promise you that nothing is wrong with me." Dawn ran her hands through her hair and didn't feel her gauze peek out from its hiding spot beneath her shirt. She also didn't see Zoey lock eyes with it.

Once Dawn had finished talking, Zoey pointed at her stomach and looked at her with the eyes of a starving puppy. "Then what is that?" Dawn covered it hopelessly with her shirt and Zoey's eyes began to spill tears onto her cheeks.

"Dawn, please, we just want to help you. We're your friends." She backed away from that path and headed down a different one. "*I* just want to help you. But I can't do that unless you talk to me. How many times have we said that we can talk to each other about anything? That we're always here for each other?" Dawn started crying but Zoey powered through. "Well, here I am, and I need you to be here, too. Please, just talk to me."

They were both sobbing by the time Zoey was done and Dawn, knowing that there was nowhere else to turn and no excuse that would be believed, gave up. And it felt wonderful to cry again.

The coughing and choking made it challenging for Zoey to understand her but she tried as best she could.

"I'm sorry, Zoey. I'm so sorry. I didn't want you to get hurt and I didn't know what else to do."

"Dawn. What happened?"

Zoey thought about how beautiful Dawn was even now and restrained an urge to slap herself across the face.

"God it hurts. Zoey, it hurts so much. It happened on Friday and it still fucking hurts."

"Dawn, please tell me what happened." She was getting scared and Dawn was withholding the only piece of information left to be given.

The first word was all Dawn could bring herself to say before her bawling stopped her but it was a word that gave Zoey every detail she needed to know.

"Amy."

Zoey leaned back and her sympathy mutated into anger. "What *about* Amy?" But she knew she wouldn't get anything else out of Dawn right now. She was crying, she was moaning. It almost sounded like she was screaming.

Zoey took a deep breath and slowly moved her hand to the bandages around Dawn's torso. "Dawn, I'm going to take these off, okay? Will you let me? It's okay if you can't say it, but I still need to know."

Dawn nodded and was able to calm herself down, enough to stop crying at least.

Zoey unraveled the bandages, her worry growing as she got closer and closer to the center, and when she reached Dawn's stomach and peeled off the final layer, what she saw brought her hands to her mouth. It was lucky that she had been able to resist her initial reaction, which was to scream.

The five letters were still there, clear and legible, but they looked much worse than they did on the first and last day Dawn had seen them. The red of the letters had changed to a mix of black and brown across Dawn's stomach, with a few dried stray lines of blood running from the marks. The skin around the letters was a darker shade of red and when Dawn started to tilt her head down Zoey grabbed her chin and held it back up. The sight made her want to vomit so she had no idea how Dawn would react to it.

She took in a few breaths and came up with something. "Dawn, I've got a plan and I need you to do a few things for me."

Dawn sniffled and let out a wet breath. "What?" Zoey wouldn't let her look at her stomach and she both did and did not want to know why.

"I need you to lie on your back and close your eyes. I'm going to go get something and I don't want you looking at your stomach, okay? Promise me you won't look at your stomach."

Dawn stared at her for a handful of long seconds before she nodded and agreed.

Zoey got up, leaving her crutches against the wall, and limped towards the bathroom, hoping it held what she needed. What Dawn needed.

As soon as Zoey left Dawn pulled her shirt over her exposed stomach in a desperate attempt to keep her eyes off it. She felt more pain when she went down on her back and stretched her cuts but she put her faith in Zoey and did as she had said. Dawn slowed her breathing but it didn't seem to help. The pain was eating her. She felt a bit safer when Zoey came back, she had no idea how badly she needed Zoey's presence until she was gone, but the expression of *Don't hate me* that was drawn onto her face made Dawn's lip quiver. She had a towel in one hand and something hidden behind her back.

"This is going to help you, okay? Trust me, Dawn, whether you like it or not, I need to do this." She brought the white, rectangular bottle out from behind her back and wondered if Dawn recognized it.

She recognized the shape of the bottle, but not what was in it. "What is that?"

Zoey sighed. "It's rubbing alcohol."

Dawn shook her head. It didn't matter what the technical term for it was, all that mattered was that that stuff burned like fire on one cut and she had more than a dozen. She teared up at the thought of the pain and continued to shake away the possibility of Zoey using it on her.

"Dawn, this stuff will help the wound. It'll help the pain."

"All it's going to do is add more."

"I'm sorry, but I need to do this. And I'm not going to let you stop me and keep hurting yourself." Zoey put the bottle on Dawn's bedside table and went into her closet, bringing out the heaviest shirt she could find. She held the puffy sleeve, twisted it, one hand clockwise and the other counterclockwise, and put it horizontally across Dawn's mouth. "Once I apply it I want you to bite down on the sleeve, okay? It'll help."

That word; help. It was becoming one of Dawn's least favorites. What kind of help gives pain? How much help could it bring when she had to bite down on something to *ease* the pain?

Zoey folded the towel and slid it under Dawn's body to absorb whatever spilled off of her stomach. She took the bottle, unscrewed the top and the sickening, nostalgic smell made her nostrils flare and her eyes water. Zoey pulled up Dawn's shirt to reveal the wound, ignoring what word the wound spelled out for the time being, and gave Dawn a confident gaze that she suspected didn't quell her fear. "Try to stay as still as possible." Dawn nodded and closed her eyes. Zoey took Dawn's hand and poured the liquid all over her stomach.

The sleeve didn't help much, if at all. Dawn clenched her stomach and fought away a wail as the searing pain slid into each cut and stung the flesh beneath. It felt like acid. She kept her eyes closed, pressing her lids together until her eyes started to hurt as well. Knowing she couldn't handle any more pain, she snapped them open into a world that felt hot and wet and saw Zoey cringing.

Not at her though, Zoey was instead looking at her hand, which was bent and dented in Dawn's crushing grip. The tips of her fingers looked like four red blisters.

The cuts absorbed the liquid quite well, surprising considering their current state. The dried blood washed away and the brown-ish black lines almost began to fizzle. *This is good*, Zoey thought. *This is what's supposed to happen. She'll be fine. I might lose some fingers but she'll be okay.*

When Dawn's body went limp and she sunk into her bed, Zoey took her hand back, wiggling her fingers around and getting the blood back into them, before putting her other hand on Dawn's knee. "The worst of it is over, but not all." Dawn's eyes, that had been up on the ceiling, shot down to meet her.

She spit out the sleeve. "What's fucking left to do?"

"Dawn, we need to take you to a doctor or something." She barely finished when Dawn cut in.

"No. No way. Absolutely not." Her voice was a mix of stubbornness and fear.

Zoey stared at Dawn for a few seconds, unable to speak. Why was she being so difficult, what did it prove, what did she get out of it? Zoey didn't know and, right now, didn't care to know. All she cared about was delivering this important information through Dawn's skull and into her brain. Her eyebrows fell, her tone sharpened and she, for the first time in a long while, was pissed at the girl in front of her. "Dawn, you don't know what you're doing. You can't take care of this yourself, okay, because *that's* what happens when you do." She stabbed a finger at Dawn's stomach and felt an instant ache of regret when she watched Dawn recoil. She calmed herself down and, when she spoke again, her voice was much more reassuring. "What I did won't be enough. We need a professional to look at this and see if there's anything severely wrong with it."

Dawn shot her head up, too fast for Zoey.

"What do mean sev—" she stopped talking when she saw the wet skin below her shirt. The word had changed from a fresher red to a darker, more rotten shade with black blood poking out from each line. The skin around the word was lighter than the letters, but it was still red just the same. Dawn's breathing increased, which only made her stomach burn more, and the wail she had fought against before came out now in full force.

Zoey pulled the shirt over Dawn's stomach and crouched down so their eyelines would meet. "We need to go. For your own sake." She stood back up. "Where are your keys?"

Dawn mouth opened but she couldn't speak for a few seconds. "Zoey, you can't drive. You don't even have two working feet."

"Well, we're going. And if you won't drive then I will."

Dawn gave in again. Speaking without care of the answer, she asked, "Where?"

"We're both familiar with it." She helped Dawn up, put new bandages around her, wrapping them looser, and they walked back to Dawn's car. This time Zoey was going a bit faster. She watched with intensity as Dawn crawled into the driver's seat and put her seatbelt on. Zoey couldn't feel Dawn's pain but the idea of the seatbelt pressing in her cuts was almost too much for her to handle. The realization that Dawn had been suffering with this since Friday hit her now, and she grabbed Dawn's hands and held them.

"Please never keep something this big a secret from me."

Dawn ignored her attempt at a promise and thought about their destination. "Where are we going?"

Zoey let go of Dawn's hands and wondered if the rift between them was about to be formed. Dawn's tone seemed to suggest it. "The medical center."

Dawn started the car and put the stick into reverse. It was two-fifty.

Despite her newly awoken pain, Dawn felt better. She felt better as soon as she told Zoey what had happened but she had been too preoccupied to feel the difference until now. And at the thought of Zoey, Dawn stepped on the brakes. And when Zoey whipped her eyes to Dawn's, Dawn held them with her own. "Promise me that you'll keep this between us. There's a reason why I didn't tell any of you about this and I don't want any of you doing something you'll regret." She might have said 'any of you' but she was thinking about one particularly impulsive friend. And it wasn't Zoey.

Zoey broke their gaze and looked down, not wanting to lie to Dawn but not wanting to lie to the other three either. She knew she had no choice but to commit to one or the other and, deep down, she already knew who she felt more comfortable lying to.

"ZOEY."

Dawn's booming voice made Zoey's shoulders jump and her eyes slip back and drown in Dawn's double ocean.

"Promise me."

Zoey nodded and said, completely monotone, "I promise." She didn't want to break this one but what would she say to Steph, Myah and Luke? She wasn't a very good liar when it came to minor things and this was far from minor.

Dawn took advantage of the parked car and leaned her seat back into an easier and less painful angle. The driving was just as simple as it had been before and the two were at the Rhode Island Medical Center for the second time in three days in twenty minutes flat; at three ten.

Dawn walked and Zoey thumped down the same hallway and arrived at the same desk Steph had stopped at on Monday.

"Oh boy, it's never good when the same person shows up twice in the same week," The receptionist said with an old smile.

Zoey gave a fake one in return. "Well it's not me this time. I'm just here for support. It's her that needs the help." She cocked her head in

Dawn's direction.

The receptionist, Alice, made a face that neither Dawn or Zoey cared for. She looked back and forth between the two and eventually asked, "Do you two have anyone else with you who's eighteen or older? Anyone to take ownership? Because we can't see you without someone to fill that role."

Dawn and Zoey turned to look at each other, white as paper and just as weak.

"Your mom?" Zoey asked, hopeful.

"She's sick," Dawn said without a second of pause, hating how easy it was for her to lie to the person she was supposed to trust most.

"Shit," Zoey hissed.

Dawn's stomach gave her a hoarse cackle and she winced.

The two shrank back from the receptionist's desk until they were sitting in the same waiting seats they sat in two days ago, with Zoey's crutches jammed in the corner. Dawn was prepared to go back home but Zoey wasn't. She squinted her eyes and nodded her head. "Cole."

Dawn sighed and looked at a friend who had far too much faith in her family. "What about him?"

"He can come in and take ownership of you. He's legally an adult. I'll explain the situation to him and—"

"—He won't care."

"He will." She felt a bit of her anger coming back and silenced it.

Dawn stifled laughter but her stomach didn't. She closed her eyes and opened them when the laughter stopped. "Zoey, he won't come."

Zoey nodded and her own stubbornness took over. "Give me your phone." Dawn did so, her thumb having already unlocked it so Zoey didn't have to bother asking for the passcode. She flicked through the pages of apps until she found Dawn's contacts. She opened the app, scrolled to the C's, tapped his name and put the phone to her ear, giving Dawn a passive glance which Dawn responded to by raising her eyebrows and shaking her head.

Cole picked up after the third ring. "What is it, Dawn?"

"Hi, Cole." Zoey could hear him pause and could almost see his eyebrow climb down his forehead.

"Who is this?" He sounded concerned and Zoey smiled. Perhaps he cared a bit more than he let Dawn believe.

"This is Zoey. I don't think we've ever met in person but I'm Dawn's friend."

"Okay. Why are you calling me from Dawn's phone?"

"Dawn's hurt and we need you to come to the Rhode Island Medical Center and take ownership of her so she can be looked at." There was another pause. Zoey realized she had been squeezing the armrests of her chair with her empty hand and let her grip loosen. She left imprints on the green foam padding.

"I'm on my way." He hung up.

Zoey smiled again, did the same and gave the phone back to Dawn.

Dawn spoke without seeing Zoey's ecstatic face. "I told you he wouldn't care. Now can we leave? The smell of this place always creeps me out." She looked at Zoey and Dawn's face changed from that of disappointment to wariness. "What do you know?"

In contrast to Dawn, Zoey's voice was smug and certain. "Nothing, don't worry about it. I think we should wait here for a little bit though, just to think things through and get a clear view of all our options."

Dawn rolled her eyes. "Zoey, there's nothing more we can do. They can't help us. You poured your acid on me and I'm sure it'll do whatever it's meant to do, why isn't that enough? I've been doing fine hiding the pain and, I'm sure it'll go away. I'll be fine."

Zoey had been nodding while Dawn spoke but that didn't fool Dawn into thinking that she was getting through to her. And once she spoke, Dawn was given exactly what she expected.

"Let's just wait a bit. Let me think."

Their conversation ended there.

As the minutes went by, Dawn looked around the boring tan walls of the waiting room and speculated if it was possible to be kicked out of a waiting room if you were there for too long. It couldn't have been more than ten minutes but the question still lingered in her head. What would Zoey, in all her wisdom, do then?

Dawn heard the main door open about five minutes later and was taken out of her beige prison by a shocking voice that held even more shocking concern.

"Dawn?" Cole sped in, as if on wheels, and Dawn stood up at the sight of him.

"What are you doing here?"

He zoomed up to her and said, "Your friend Zoey called me and said that you were hurt and I had to come here and take ownership of you so you could get looked at." He threw his arms around her in an impromptu but well meaning hug and almost took her off her feet.

Dawn hugged back, but at a slow, tentative speed. At first it felt odd, like a joke, but after a few seconds, once she realized how good it felt, she held him tighter and put her hot forehead against his shoulder. Though she made sure to lean her stomach away out of fear of it giving her another cackle. This was the first time she had felt like crying for a reason other than the pain.

"What happened to you? I mean, you look the same."

"It's just a little scratch, that's all. But Zoey seems to think it requires immediate medical attention, so that's why we ended up here."

Cole looked at Zoey, who nodded, then back to Dawn. "Then let's go." Cole grabbed her hand and walked her to the receptionist's desk. He took proud ownership over Dawn Bell and within the minute, she was taken down the hall to be examined. It was three twenty-five. He walked back to the waiting area and took the seat Dawn was sitting in, next to Zoey. "So, you're Zoey." The smile she gave him made him feel warm.

"In person."

He looked down at her foot. "Are you okay?"

"I'm fine."

A small pause. And then, "Thank you for calling me."

"Dawn didn't want me to, you know."

He nodded. "That's no surprise. When she got hurt as a kid she would always take care of it herself. Most of the time we wouldn't even know anything had happened until we saw the band-aids. She's always been that way. She's either too afraid to ask for help or too proud."

He didn't need to tell her. "Believe me I know."

"But she was lucky you were there. Without you she'd still be in denial about the help she needed."

I'm always there, she thought. *No matter what.*

She felt another vibration from her backside, read the name of the person who texted her and remembered her new responsibility. She took a deep breath and thought over her situation.

Okay, maybe this is a good thing. Having to say it through a text is a hell of a lot better than having to fumble through saying it in person.

Yeah, but you haven't come up with a convincing enough lie. You actually haven't come up with anything at all.

Well, I'm about to.

She went to the group chat and read Steph's message.

S: Have you talked to her yet? Did she tell you what's up? Are you two okay?

One question I don't have the answer to at a time, please, was what Zoey wanted to say but she found the strength to refrain and let her fingers work independent of her mind.

Z: Yeah, I talked to her and she told me that she's perfectly healthy. Apparently she just had this weirdly strong stomach ache and it hadn't gone away yet. She said she was feeling better today, though, so I think she'll be all right by tomorrow. Friday at the latest.

She read what she sent and found it to be a good enough substitution. A stomach ache made sense. Technically Dawn did have pain in her stomach so it wasn't an outright lie. And if they asked Dawn about it, Zoey knew she would agree and shortly after, guide the conversation toward something else. She waited for their response and refused to think about what she would say if they didn't believe her. But, like usual, her friends didn't let her down.

S: Okay, that makes sense. But why didn't she just tell us?

Before Zoey could answer, Myah beat her to it.

M: She probably didn't think it was that big of a deal. Stomach aches are a pretty common thing.

S: I guess. But she's fine now, Zoey?

Zoey snapped back onto her phone and carried out her fib.

Z: Yeah, she said it was going away. She'll be good before the week is over, I'm sure.

L: And if you're wrong, then all we do is give her the time she needs to get better.

Z: Exactly. Is everyone okay with this? Just so you know, the answer is yes.

L: Yes.

M: Yes.

S: Yeah.

Zoey smiled as the puzzle was completed before her eyes. She knew they would bring it up again and she wasn't looking forward to lying to them in person but, with the excuse they were given and the way they seemed to be reacting to it, they would probably just mention it once to make sure Dawn was okay before putting it behind them.

Z: Wonderful. She'll be in school tomorrow. I'll let you guys know if anything changes.

Steph, Myah and Luke all agreed and thanked Zoey for her efforts and she put her phone away. She and Cole kept quiet but it was clear that it wasn't out of awkwardness. They were both thinking about Dawn and it felt redundant to both of them to re-establish what they already knew. They continued their harmonious thought processes until Dawn came back out at three thirty-five, only ten minutes later, which both confused Zoey and made her feel a bit secure. From his body language, Zoey knew Cole felt the same contrasting feelings, which helped her simmer down. Dawn came out looking the same and for a fleeting moment, Zoey thought she hadn't seen any doctor at all. That she instead went to the bathroom, waited a bit and came back. What Dawn said put her worries to rest.

"The doctor told me I'm fine. It'll hurt for another day or so, and," she looked down and put her hand to her shirt, "the scar will fade." She looked up again and Zoey wasn't surprised to see the relief on Dawn's face. "I'll be fine by Friday."

Cole sighed with relief and Zoey smiled.

"So, I'll take *you* home." Dawn pointed at Zoey then turned it to Cole. "And *you* can go wherever you want, but after I drop Zoey off, I'm going home, too."

"In that case, I'll meet you there." Cole read Dawn's content expression, said goodbye to her and her friend and left with a new appreciation for his younger sister and his cell phone.

Dawn turned to Zoey and flashed her keys. "Shall we?"

"We shall." Zoey was glowing with glee. Dawn was safe and all of her friends believed her lie. Everyone knew as much as they had to and was in the state of mind they needed to be in. Everything had gone right for once. She hooked her arms over her crutches and followed Dawn through the cold and into her beautiful sky blue car. She laid her crutches across the black leather seats in the back and crept into the passenger's seat beside Dawn. She glanced at Dawn's stomach and couldn't help herself but ask, "Did the doctor give you anything for your...marks?"

"No. She just said to take aspirin and that sort of thing. You know, medicine that people use when they have a little pain."

"Do you have a *little* pain?" She didn't know how much Dawn's marks hurt and Dawn hadn't said anything on the subject besides 'I'm fine,' which had recently been proven to not be very true so it was important for her to get as much information as she could.

Dawn stopped at the main road and, before checking lanes to make sure it was safe to take her left, looked at Zoey. "Yes, only a little, I promise. It really has been getting easier to handle. I mean, that acid you poured on me—"

"—It wasn't acid, Dawn."

"I know it wasn't acid. But it might as well have been. It hurt just as much. Anyway, the acid woke it up a bit, but it'll settle down soon enough. The doctor said the pain will go away in time, and it has, so all we can do is let time get rid of it completely." She stoked Zoey's internal conflict and decided to kill it once and for all. "Zoey, you can trust me on this. From here on out, no lies. I swear."

Dawn's powerful certainty put Zoey at ease a bit and she nodded her head, trying to believe her. "Okay. I trust you." Dawn gave her a quick nod and turned the car after only a few brief glances into the busy road. Once the two had been driving for a minute or so, Zoey asked another important question.

"What are we going to say when Steph, Myah or Luke ask about you? I told them you had a stomach ache that's just starting to go away."

Dawn shrugged, finding the answer in Zoey's question. "We tell them that. It's as good a lie as any other."

Zoey answered after a moment's wait. "Okay."

Dawn dropped Zoey off and felt an odd feeling when they hugged and recounted their individual sayings.

"I'm always here."

"No matter what."

It was a feeling that was much stronger than the one she usually felt for Zoey. And although she had already known that she cared more for Zoey than anybody else she knew, this feeling still had a different aura surrounding it. In fact, once Zoey left the car and began making her way to her front door, Dawn had to resist a sudden urge to get out, grab her and never let go.

You're just tired. Your mind is going wild, trying to comprehend everything that's happened today. Forget about this. We have a bigger day tomorrow.

She turned on the radio to drown out her outlandish thoughts and drove home, trying to think about nothing. And, no surprise to her, failing at it.

Chapter 16

Luke woke up late on Thursday morning, just like every other morning. He tried to get up by six o'clock sharp to give him time to get ready and relax with his phone but, for whatever reason, his body refused to allow it and he always woke up with the hour on his clock reading seven. Dawn never arrived later than seven-twenty so he always had to rush into whatever clothes he grabbed from his closet to maximize the amount of time he could spend on his phone before the day started and it was nothing but work until two-thirty.

By the time he had finished his morning cycle of getting dressed, brushing his teeth and doing his set of pushups and sit-ups, 30 each, he had seconds to rest before Dawn's car horn blared through the peaceful morning air and knocked him back a foot or two. He headed to his bedroom door and stopped at the shelf to the left of it. There, he grabbed the thing he kept with him each day and returned each night. It was a small thing, easy to keep in his back pocket, and, while not worth any money, was the most valuable thing he owned.

It was a polaroid photo, an inch or so snipped off of all four sides to better fit in any pocket it needed to go in. A man in his thirties, buzz cut and buttoned down shirt, was standing beside a young boy, seven. The two were smiling and Luke often wished he could go back in time and tell the younger version of himself to cherish that smile for as long as he could. It would be gone much too soon and for much too long.

Luke's father, Emmett Bradley, was shot and killed in Afghanistan. He had been aware of such a possibility and he had a wife and child who certainly made him wish that Operation Enduring freedom could carry on without him, but both he and Camilla knew it wasn't something you could run and hide from. He had taken an oath to protect his fellow countrymen and that oath was something he would live by. It wasn't a choice, there wasn't a discussion, it was a simple fact. This was his duty and he had an obligation to keep his country, as well as his wife and son, safe.

He promised them that he would return, one part of him believing it and another part not, and Emmet Bradley, a mere pawn in the chess game of the war, was gunned down in minutes once the led began to fly. His final thoughts were of his son and the smile he had forced himself to wear as the two had said their goodbyes.

Camilla Bradley was notified of her husband's death several hours later and, despite her intense emotional state, she had been able to put on the stone face she had been preparing to use since the first day Emmet had become a part of the infantry and she explained their new living situation to her son. She took him to his favorite spot on the couch, a spot that used to squeeze him right in between her and her husband, and explained what happened in the safest and least detailed way she could. He listened but there were no tears, no screaming, no denial. Luke just nodded along with her, hugged her when she grasped for him and, when all was said, went upstairs to his room.

Luke's world had been altered, he knew that, and while he wanted to cry, he had to be brave like his father. It was hard to do, he had no idea how his father could have managed to be so restrained when met with news that was so shattering but Luke remembered his grandfather's funeral and remembered how his father hadn't dropped one tear. He had to be like that now. Whether his father would have wanted him to be brave or react in a way that was healthier Luke didn't know but he had made his decision and would stand by it. In a way, the decision kept him as close to his father as he could be.

As time moved forward and days rolled by, Luke forced himself back into his old routine. His mother did not approve of him returning to school the next day, but home was the last place Luke wanted to be.

Over the coming months, Luke and his mother took gradually different approaches to the new way they were living. Luke carried on and tried to not let the thoughts of his father get in the way of his school work or social life. And they didn't. Once he was with his friends, he found it easier to smile and forget the thoughts that tried to infect him. School was his sanctuary but it was a sanctuary that only lasted a quarter of the day. And his home, where he spent his other three quarters of every day, brought none of the positives that school did.

His mother was now often surrounded by odd rectangular bottles with what looked like water or apple juice in them, but something about the way they made her talk and act made Luke certain that they were something else. Drink Posers, he called them. And these Drink

Posers were taking his mother from him as well. She slept more, it was harder for him to understand her when she was speaking and she always looked like she had been resurrected by a mad scientist like in the movies he was always too scared to watch but would sneak glimpses of anyway. Until he got too scared and changed the channel. He wished he could do that to his mother; change the channel on her and make her someone different. Someone who had managed to follow the instructions she had given him on the couch. "Don't forget him, don't stop loving him and don't forget to speak up if you need help because we'll both need that now more than ever."

The day he fell down the flight of twenty hardwood stairs in his house and broke his arm was the day he had been taken away from his mother. His socks had been too slippery on the smooth wood and before he could grip the handrail he was already at the base of the stairs, head banging and arm feeling like it had been beaten in with a hammer. It hurt too much to move so all he could do was lie on the white tiles and scream. His voice hadn't hit puberty yet so the high pitched wail was heard by most neighbors, outside their houses and in them. The only person who didn't hear him was his mother, who was once again, pulled into sleep by the Drink Posers and would only be woken up by one of her neighbors when it was too late. Luke lay on the tiles screeching, tears cascading down pale face, until a neighbor finally came to his aid and dialed 9-1-1. Luke did nothing but scream until the ambulance arrived and put his screaming, and consciousness, to rest. He might have also yelled for his father but he couldn't remember.

He woke up in a hospital room, alone. The smell he associated with hospitals was there, seeping into his nose and making his face squirm. He tried to move, felt a rigidity in his arm, looked at it and saw a blue cast covering his wrist to his elbow. There was no one to talk to so all he did was lie in his bed until someone showed up. He waited for hours, but refused to let himself fall asleep.

Eventually his grandmother came in and told him that he would be living with her from now on. Despite her expectations, Luke did not resist at all, he only asked when they could leave and when she told him it was up to him he made the instant choice to get out of there now. He didn't mind living with his grandmother, it was much better than living with his creepy mother and the Drink Posers, and his grandmother had always given him special treatment. Maybe because he was the only grandchild he had. He almost wished this change in locale could have happened earlier, but he took what he was given and slept in Gramma's big bed that night. His sleep was the best he had since his dad had died. Eight months ago.

Camilla Bradley died of an alcohol overdose two months later. When Luke found out, he didn't react, though not because he forced his bravery to keep himself from doing so. He did what he had been doing since his first parent had passed, he moved on.

But at strange moments, sprinkled throughout his life, he would think of her and start to cry. Some days he just missed her. He didn't know why, he didn't know if he wanted to, but it happened regardless. And he had no control over it. Like a forgotten alarm, ringing out at unexpected times and bringing an instant discomfort.

The thoughts of his mother and father, a difficult mix of hate and love, was interrupted by Dawn's car horn, bleating once again and tossing Luke back into his present situation. He put the photo in his back pocket, grabbed his backpack and headed down the stairs to the front door. The air that hit him when he stepped into his front yard was somewhat calming. The temperature was starting to increase slightly, from the twenties to the thirties, and despite what seemed like an imperceptible difference, it was one of Luke's favorite things to take note of. The air in Dawn's car robbed him of the feeling.

Dawn always put the heat on as soon as she got into her car. If there was a way to do it without turning the car on, she would have been the one to discover how. She watched Luke make his way through his front yard and the sight of him helped declutter her still crowded mind. Though not by as much as she was hoping for. Their morning kiss was much of the same; she wanted to feel better than she did. She didn't feel *bad* necessarily, more confused. Which she found worse.

Zoey did her best to try to make conversation, but even she couldn't worm her way through the awkward silence. It only got a little easier for her to control when Luke asked Dawn about her stomach. That was something she could work with. She didn't wait for Dawn to respond.

"She had some sort of stomach bug. But she's all better now."

She sounded certain but Luke ignored her and kept his eyes on Dawn, waiting for a response from her. Zoey glared at him from the backseat.

Dawn nodded in assurance and said, "She's right. It was just some freak sickness. I really am better. I'm serious."

Luke nodded and took his eyes away from hers, allowing her to relax.

She picked up Steph and the same question was asked.

"You feeling better?"

She took the reins this time before Zoey had the chance. "Yeah, my stomach's better now."

Steph pressed on. "What was it exactly? Like, is there a name for it?" Something about how Dawn was talking made Steph question the validity of what she was saying. People who didn't lie very often sounded distinctly odd when they eventually had to.

Dawn bit her tongue. "No, I think it was just a worse version of a stomach ache, maybe food poisoning. I threw up like half a dozen times over the weekend."

Steph faked a wince. "All right then, that's enough."

Zoey chimed back in. "Yeah, let's move on to something less gross." There were multiple reasons why she saw that as a good idea and Dawn's "vomit" was not high on the list. Getting caught was, however, top billed. She remembered the person they hadn't picked up yet and noticed that they weren't heading toward her house. "Hey, what about Myah?"

Dawn shrugged at the wheel. "She told me yesterday in history that she didn't need me to pick her up today. I didn't ask why, but she's probably getting a ride from someone else." It sounded strange to all of them and, as per usual, Zoey spoke up about it first.

"Who else would she get a ride from? We're kind of her only friends."

Steph gave a gentle slap to Zoey's thigh. Not enough to hurt but hopefully enough for Zoey to make Zoey think a little longer before speaking next time. "Maybe she has something to do today and knew she wouldn't be at school and didn't want to have Dawn drive out of her way for nothing."

But Zoey hadn't thrown her argument out of the running quite yet. "What could she possibly need? We've all seen her house. You could fit a fucking airplane in there."

Steph rolled her eyes. "Zoey, don't fight with me on this. It's too early."

Zoey said, defiantly, "I'm not fighting with you, I just think it would be best if you didn't disregard my points."

"You're not making any points."

"Not *yet*."

Luke spoke up, more so to quiet down the two bickering children than to solve the issue. "Maybe she's going for her driving test. A license is something she doesn't have and it would explain why she told Dawn not to pick her up. Can you two compromise on that?"

Steph and Zoey thought about it and locked eyes at the same time. They both agreed with the theory and stopped their discussion with a reasonable, but false, assumption.

Myah had been taken to school by her parents that day. A decision she had no say in. They had seen the girls who picked Myah up and went to school with her and found it better to keep their daughter away from them. Myah disagreed with this plan and didn't hesitate to let them know it.

"You haven't even met them yet." She kept her eyes out the window and refused to look at her shortsighted parents.

Her father responded and Myah grew more angry at the sound of his voice. "We don't need to meet them, Myah. They just don't seem like good people to hang around with."

Myah scoffed and looked at the back of his seat. "Why, because Steph is black and Zoey is confident?" Her mother made a gasp that only added more motive to her growing temper.

"Myah!"

"Give me a reason. A good, normal reason to keep me away from them." Their silence was both satisfying and more frustrating. She shook her head and moved her eyes back out the window.

Despite the fact that Oliver Rowland was a successful human service assistant and Brianna Rowland was a long time lawyer at the Wilson and Howell Law Firm in Pennston, one of the more well regarded cities in Rhode Island, they came up with nothing to say to their daughter. They had nothing against the girls they saw their daughter with on a personal level. But the two of them had never found anyone who was quite good enough for their child. And if the girls Myah had attended the Saint Thomas Preparatory School with weren't good enough then they both knew no one in this little placeholder of a school would be, either. They also both knew that if they let those girls get ahold of Myah it was almost certain that she would lose everything that made her unique and she would become just like the lesser teenagers that attended public high school.

Despite a lack of any real importance or uniqueness, the small amount of friends Myah had made at Saint Thomas were at least respectful, responsible and could carry themselves how they were supposed to. Traits that the girls who picked Myah up in the morning didn't have. Oliver and Brianna didn't need to meet them to know that. Their clothing and body language said everything that needed saying about the kind of influence they would be. There was even an easy girl in the group, the two noticed her more than anyone else. And how could they not when she was showing off so much? That was the last type of person they wanted their daughter hanging around with. But they could never tell Myah that, she wouldn't understand. So they kept silent, hoping Myah would forget this pointless argument. She didn't.

"They're not bad people." They were approaching the school now, and Myah was starting to soften her glare. She was almost with them, with her wonderful friends. She didn't care what her parents said, they were good. All of them. They didn't have any expectations for how you acted or where you lived or the things you owned like the classmates Myah used to deal with did. She didn't have to sit up straight or get her hair to look just right or smooth out every wrinkle she could find or rehearse what she was going to say hours before the opportunity came to talk so she didn't mess up and make herself look worse. Private school had its benefits, not having to worry about finding something to wear every day for instance, but things always felt a little artificial there. And here, though it hadn't even been a week, there was no pretense of a factory managed environment. Not for the school and not for her friends. And she wouldn't let her mother or father keep her from them. They'd have to make her move schools again, that was the only way. Myah knew that was already their plan, but every day they failed at accomplishing that was another victory for her. Not to mention that they would also have to take her phone away if they didn't want her interacting with them. And if they did that, Myah would send letters. Unless they strapped her into a straightjacket and locked her in her room, Myah would find a way to get to her friends. They made her feel real and odd and distinct, no longer an outline to be filled in at her parents' whim.

Brianna sighed. "We didn't say they were." They had pulled up in front of the high school and kept the gas running. "They just don't seem good enough for you."

Myah rolled her eyes, slid open the van door and hopped out. She had an idea and, before thinking it through, she looked at her mother and said, "For *me*? Has it ever really been for me?" She slid the door closed before she saw her mother's reaction and headed into the school as fast as she could.

Usually at this time Zoey, Dawn, Steph and Luke would be walking through the halls. They said they used to wait by the gym doors but couldn't anymore so now they strolled around the school until the bell rang. But finding them would be just as easy as finding a friend her parents approved of so Myah pulled out her phone and called Dawn. She picked up before the first ring was finished.

"Hi, Myah, what's up?"

"Where are you guys? Where in the school, I mean." There was a brief pause, then Dawn answered Myah's question with one of her own.

"Wait, where are *you*?"

Myah frowned. "I'm at school."

"Oh...kay." Dawn's confusion and suspicion crawled through the phone's speakers and rattled around in Myah's head. "We're walking in now, you can just meet us at the main entrance. Is that too far out of your way?"

Myah looked to her left at the main entrance doors and gave a half smile. "Not as much as you might think."

"All right, good. See you soon."

Myah almost laughed out loud when she saw them on the other side of the doors headed in, Dawn's phone still up to her ear. Myah locked eyes with her and said, "You're not wrong." The two hung up at the same time.

The day moved by as it always did for Luke, with the one bright moment being the forty-five minutes of gym, which was his very first class of the day. It was the only class where he could turn his mind off and not have to think. Every other class was nothing short of mental torture, and this torture was extremely effective. Luke's skills were just not very academic.

He was more successful socially and physically. He had used those skills to get Dawn to agree to a first date even though he knew she was out of his league. Most people called them street smarts but Luke thought of them more as "Human Smarts." And his Human Smarts were not being utilized to their full potential as he sat in Mr. Shaw's chemistry class, desperate to understand how ionic bonds were formed. He listened and took notes, but Mr. Shaw might as well have been speaking Mandarin. It would have been just as easy to comprehend. Luke always went into the class with an optimistic outlook. *Today things will change. It's a new day, a fresh start. This time I'll finally understand something this guy is talking about.* He was always let down.

Today's class only got interesting when his friend, Elijah Hamilton, bumped him on the arm and whispered, "Dude, Jonah Dunbar is dead."

Luke would have preferred if the class got interesting for a better reason, but he took what he could get. "Holy shit, how?"

"Someone found him under the tunnel on the bike path. His skull was cracked open or something. There's stuff all about it online and on the news."

Luke took out his phone and tuned out Mr. Shaw for the rest of the class. A simple search of his name proved that Elijah was right. That was all Luke needed to know. His fingers switched over to his group chat with the girls and asked them all…

L: What class are you all going to next period and what lunch do you have? Luke had animation next, another painful class to sit through, and had third lunch. He knew Dawn's schedule just as well as she did so he knew she had third as well. There were four lunches total and he could only pray the other three of them had the same one. It was a long shot but he held out hope.

S: Myah and I will be in science so we have third lunch.

Four out of five. Good but not good enough, Luke thought.

D: I'll have Portuguese which means third lunch.

He watched the phone, waiting for the final text that could make this whole situation much easier.

Z: I have boring—I mean, history. Third for me.

Luke shot his fist out in front of him and drew it back just as quickly. Elijah noticed despite Luke's efforts.

"What was that?"

Luke raised his shoulders and shook his head. "Nothing. Don't worry about it."

"All right." Elijah looked at the clock and glared at the fact that he was still in this class. How much longer could forty-five minutes go by? "Dude, I'm gonna die of old age before this class is over."

"I know what you mean." Luke didn't care about the eleven minutes left. All he cared about was getting into third lunch and explaining the recent event to the girls. The eleven minutes blinked by. As did the first hour of his animation class. Before he knew it, he was sitting at the circular lunch table the group always sat at and was trying to maneuver his way through this topic.

"Do you guys remember Jonah Dunbar?" He looked to his left at Dawn and Zoey, then to his right at Steph and Myah. As he expected, Dawn, Zoey and Steph all made faces that said two things: Yes and Ugh. As Luke also anticipated, Myah looked from person to person with an eyebrow raised. Luke explained the person he was referring to.

"Jonah Dunbar was a kid we all went to middle school with."

Myah gave a slow, single nod. "Okay."

Dawn took over from Luke. "He was this really annoying, arrogant…" her face morphed into disgust and she stuck her tongue out. Steph finished where she was headed.

"He was a fucking asshole, essentially. You're lucky you've never met him. Hopefully you'll never get the chance to."

Luke pressed his lips together until they sunk into his mouth and Zoey jumped on the Insult Express. Destination: Jonah Dickbar.

"And he wasn't even cute." A scathing insult to her, but a childish one to everyone else.

Especially Steph, who tilted her head and squinted her eyes. "Why would that matter?"

Zoey made the same *Are You Serious* face Steph had given her and explained. "Hey, cuteness goes a long way in determining how much time you're willing to spend with someone. I mean, just look at *you.*" She motioned at Steph. "If it wasn't for your dimples and cocoa powder skin who knows how much time we would have spent together."

If Steph wasn't already friends with Zoey and certain that Zoey was kidding, she would have leaned across the table and turned her face as red as a stop sign. Instead she marveled at her friend who was, more often than not, too witty for her own good. "How do you come up with this stuff?"

Zoey leaned back. "Hey, it all comes from up here." She tapped the side of her head.

Steph smiled. "Well at least *something* does."

Zoey banged her hand on the table. It was loud, even in the lunchroom, but none of the four she sat next to flinched. "See, it's not just me! You have it too!"

"What's *it*?" Steph didn't get to find out. Luke's arms waved in between them and they both stopped their conversation.

"He's dead."

The five went silent.

The sounds of everyone else talking over each other rang loud in their ten ears. What was there to say? They all came up with nothing. None of them liked Jonah, and Myah didn't like the description of him, but it felt strange when Luke said those two words. They all felt a sharp remorse slice into them. They were right about the way he acted and treated people, but, for a moment, they all hoped they were wrong about him, that there was more to Jonah that they either didn't see or chose to ignore. But there was, in fact, no other side of Jonah Dunbar that any of them had ever seen.

"How did it happen?" Myah asked. She didn't know if it was the right thing to say, but she didn't think anything was. So what was the harm?

Luke tried to remember what Elijah had said. "His skull was cracked and he bled to death underneath the tunnel on the bike path."

Myah kept on. "When did it happen?"

Luke's information had ended with the last question. Now he was just as deep in the dark as the rest of them. "I don't know. I haven't looked into it. It's online, I'm sure the details are there. I just wanted to tell you guys so we could talk about it if any of you needed to."

"What's there to talk about?" Steph asked but, even if she hadn't liked Jonah, she didn't want to be alone with her thoughts of him getting his skull cracked open.

And based on the looks across the table, she wasn't the only one who felt that way. Though she had her doubts that any of them would admit it.

"Whatever you want," Luke said. Just like his mother had on the couch many years prior.

"This doesn't seem like the best place for that," Myah said. She watched Luke nod before the blinding white of the light bulb that went off in her head obscured her vision. Her eyes widened. "But we can talk about it at my house." They all looked up at her and she went on. "It's a much better place to talk about it then here and we can talk without anyone getting in the way." *There will be two people already there, but after they meet you and see how good you all are, they won't be getting in the way either.* She didn't say that. That was for herself to enjoy. "I'll give Dawn the address and we can go there right after school. As long as everyone wants to." With every nod she got, Myah's interior smile got bigger. She wasn't happy about what had happened to Jonah, but some good was at least going to come out of it. "All right, good." She let the silence continue, but her next question was burning too hot for her to hold by herself. Not to mention that the idea was too scary for her to want to keep it inside. "You think it was an accident?"

Dawn answered with surprising anger, as if she had discovered some horrible secret. She was convinced she had. "I don't know." She looked at the four people also sharing this lunch, who sat in the corner of the room, and no one else from her group followed her gaze, which she thanked them for. "But I don't think it's the only possibility."

Amy, Evan, Heather and Trevor were the only ones occupying the table they sat at, which was no shock to any of them. The only people who ever sat at their table were new kids who didn't know any better or people who had a death wish. The latter would be especially easy to accomplish today. Amy's purchase had finally arrived in the mail and she couldn't wait any longer to show them.

"Come closer," she said. Evan on her left, Trevor to her diagonal left and Heather across from her closed in and shielded Amy from the rest of the room. It seemed a bit necessary seeing as how they sat at the far right of the table, almost in the far right of the cafeteria itself, but none of them stopped to think about that.

She reached into her back pocket and took out rectangular something that looked very similar to the something Evan had thrown away a few days ago. Except hers was better. "You can take your knife out of the trash, Evan. I won't be using it anymore." She grinned, pushed the switch up and a black feather of a blade shot out of the orange hilt of Amy's new knife.

Evan dove his hands over the hilt and buried it beneath his palms. "Shit, put that thing away. If anyone sees you at school with that, you're fucked."

Amy yanked her knife away from his hands, making sure to not cut him with it. She could have given him one little nick, to make sure he kept his hands off, but Amy didn't want to do that. To him anyway. For everyone else, the jury was still out. And that was the exciting part. She pushed the switch down and the crow's metal feather was sucked back into the hilt. The orange hilt. So perfect for her and her inner volcano. She returned it to her back pocket and enjoyed how it felt there.

"Where did you get that?" Evan asked, running through possibilities that seemed to get more and more unlikely. Her dad gave it to her, she found a magazine and sent off some cash for it, she walked to a knife store and picked it up, she found it on the street.

"Your mom bought it for me." She said it matter of factly, as if it was obvious. It was the truth only in the sense of money being paid and that money coming from his mother. In actuality, Amy had stolen his mother's credit card in the middle of the night and bought it herself but they weren't going to know that. Evan didn't chat with his mom very often already and if Amy told him not to, he would keep his mouth shut. What was done was done and it wasn't like Evan's mother was going to do anything about it. She couldn't now, not when Amy could turn the blade on her if she did.

Evan looked at Heather and Trevor and saw two people who certainly looked more excited about this than him. And although he assumed Trevor only looked as interested as he did because he thought the knife looked cool and hadn't given any thought to how much more dangerous things could be now, Evan knew that the same truth could not be said for Heather. Heather's face was glowing.

He wished was as pleased by this purchase as the other three were but he couldn't stop himself from looking into the possibilities that Amy's knife held. It was one thing to punch someone like they had done to Jonah or whip someone like they had done to Steph. But a knife was something different, a knife was permanent. The best case scenario, the least dangerous scenario, was that Amy would use it for intimidation and nothing more. But Evan knew that was impossible. "Be careful with it."

Amy rolled her dark eyes and pouted. "If anyone needs to learn how to handle a knife, it's not me." She thought back to Poodle's tattoo and almost smiled. Though that almost smile left when Heather opened her mouth.

"What are you going to do with it?"

Amy could barely look at her, the smile was too long and shark-like to stare at without getting cold. But letting Heather, who was already getting a bit under Amy's skin, see that wouldn't help anyone. She made herself look into Heather's eyes and grabbed Evan's knee under the table. Without saying anything, he brought his hand down and held hers, which gave her some much needed confidence.

"I don't have some grand plan that's thought out to the second. I won't know what I'm going to do with this until I'm doing it."

Heather's response was quick, she couldn't wait for Amy to stop talking. "I'm just asking because I feel like there should be a bigger reason behind buying a knife than just *I want it*. Maybe you should have an idea of what or who to use it on. Your impulsiveness can only take you so far."

"Well, now that you mention it, there is *someone* I'd like to use it on."

Amy and Heather stared at each other and thought of each other. Amy had, for the first time, considered hurting a member of her close-knit friend group. Badly. Her normal violent thoughts that stabbed their way across her brain like lightning strikes scorching the Earth were quick and fleeting. This time the thoughts stayed. And burned. And she saw them. And she liked them. On the other side of the table Heather tentatively added this ridiculous knife to her own plan. She didn't know if her tentative plan would work out or if Amy would use the knife for what Heather expected her to, but she would course correct if things didn't go the way she was planning them to. She didn't suffer from Amy's impulsivity.

They continued staring each other down like dueling cowboys and all Evan and Trevor could do was watch and hope they could stop one of them when they attacked the other.

"Well this is fucking awkward."

"Knock it off, Trevor." Evan didn't want to admit it, but Trevor was only half right. It was awkward, without question, but it was also something worse. Something he never wanted to feel when he was with the three of them.

It was scary. And he was scared. It felt like the world was unraveling.

Chapter 17

Myah got out of Dawn's car first and stood in between the group and the front door. Dawn, Zoey, Steph and Luke all gave her the same confused face so she elaborated.

"Before we go in, there's something you should all know about my parents." She didn't wait for them to ask. "They're really judgmental. I don't know why, but they seem to have a problem with everyone I'm friends with. So I want all of you on your best behavior. I know I sound like a mom, but I really need you guys to be as polite and nice as possible."

Everyone's eyes landed on Zoey. It didn't take long for her to notice. "What?"

Dawn put a hand on Zoey's shoulder. "Nothing." She turned her attention to Myah. "I don't think your parents will have a problem with any of us. I don't mean to brag, but we're all generally nice."

"Yes, but they tend to look for anything they can find. They're like insult vultures. And with a few of you it won't be too difficult for them to find a flaw, whether there or not." Out of everyone who could have asked the next question, it was the person Myah wanted to the least.

"Who?" Zoey asked. The sympathy Myah's face gave her answered Zoey's question perfectly. "What's wrong with *me*?" Her dad's face flashed into her brain and she kept her clenched fists behind her back.

Myah didn't want to say so she dropped her eyes to Zoey's chest.

Zoey followed Myah's eyes to her breasts and pulled her collar up to cover them. "I don't appreciate this censorship but I'll do it for you."

"Thank you." Myah looked from person to person and nodded her head at each one. "Okay, let's go." She put one hand on the knob and the other on the wood and used most of her strength to shove the door open. They went inside, one by one, and she watched as their jaws fell, also one by one, when they entered her home.

Myah lived in a recent addition to the town of Winno. It was built a few dozen years ago but, compared to some of the other houses in this town that had been established in the nineteenth century, fifty years wasn't quite so old.

Away from the quaint, small neighborhoods of moderate to tiny houses that seemed to be one more hurricane away from collapsing into a ruined mass of wood and shingles, a dozen houses stood, spaced out in a perfect semicircle. Houses that could fit one of the tiny, or even one of the moderate houses, inside of it. One house had a three-car garage which still didn't seem to be enough. One was protected by a few white columns that connected the front stoop to a third floor outdoor patio. And all of the elegance visible from the exteriors were equaled by the elegance within.

Myah's house was less elaborate than the others, but she knew all twelve buildings spoke the same message.

She hated this neighborhood and wished every house in it would burn down. Maybe the reason why so many other houses looked worn down was because all of the manpower had gone into making these beasts.

"Wow," Dawn said. The meaningless word echoed through the giant empty room. This house looked like something out of a fantasy. The polished floor that she was afraid to step on led to a white staircase that curved along the wall up to the second, but not top, floor. A chandelier, so clean it was almost transparent, hung above their heads and what she could see of the rooms down the left and right hallways seemed to match this style of living. She wanted to experience this for as long as she could. Steph and Luke were marveling as well. Zoey, however, couldn't quite contain herself.

"DAMN!"

The volume of her voice soared through the room and Myah could visualize the sound waves running along the floors and walls, cackling as they did so, and notifying her parents that an unwanted guest had arrived. She put her head in her hand.

Dawn turned to Zoey and whispered, something she hoped Zoey would take into account the next time she opened her mouth, "Keep it down."

Zoey looked down and nodded, feeling embarrassed for just a second before recovering and continuing to scan the area. "From now on I'll be good. I swear."

Myah waved her hands back and forth, passing off the promise. "It doesn't matter. Come on." She headed up the thirty-two stairs to the second floor and her four guests followed as fast as they were able. Though, even on crutches, Zoey was keeping up with them rather well.

Halfway through the staircase Steph asked, "Where are your parents?"

Myah knew where they were and knew they were close. Her mother would be in her office and her father would be in his and both rooms were to the left of the staircase. The choice she had to make was whether she took the left and showed off her friends or if she took the right and brought them to her room. Maybe having her parents confront her in her room, where she was most comfortable, would be better. Then they would be on her turf, although no place in this house really felt like hers.

She turned her head to the side and half addressed Steph as they climbed the stairs. "They're around." She turned to face forward again as she touched the final stair and her parents blocked her way, wearing the same glare.

Myah jumped back and would have fallen all the way down the steps she had spent the better half of a minute climbing up, had no one been behind her. And a mistake like that was paid in bruises, Myah knew from experience. A house like this wasn't safe for a kid and a childproof gate would have saved her from numerous falls had her parents thought to put in one. Steph caught her and repositioned her like she was no bigger or heavier than a doll. Myah got her balance back and reached the top of the steps once again. She turned around and smiled.

"Thanks."

"No problem."

The voice that cleared its throat in front of Myah made her turn to her parents and begin the introductions. "Mom, Dad, this is," she motioned to each person as she said their name, "Steph, Dawn, Zoey and Luke." Each one gave Myah's parents a handshake. They shook Zoey's hand as if it was drenched in pus and Myah grimaced at them. But before she could take any further action, physically or verbally, her mother grabbed her by the wrist and yanked her in between her and her father. It was an abnormal amount of strength and Myah held her wrist protectively once her mother let go.

"How are you all doing?" Brianna kept her left hand by her side but ran her right through the back of her daughter's hair. If this is what

Myah wanted, they would give her new "friends" a chance. A small one, maybe a fake one, but one regardless.

Dawn answered and spoke for the group so they didn't have to give the same answer again and again. "We're well. You have a beautiful house, Mr. and Mrs. Rowland."

Brianna smiled and hoped it didn't look welcoming. "Thank you, we've worked hard to make it that way."

Zoey went next. "What do the two of you do for a living?" She then, for maybe the first time in her life, caught herself as she was falling. "Oh, I'm sorry. I guess that's not something you should just come out and ask someone."

Myah's father took this one, lightly chuckling. "That's all right. We understand your curiosity."

Zoey nodded and took notice of how both of them refused to answer her question, whether it was all right or not. And that didn't surprise her. These two seemed to have rods shoved so deep up their asses that they popped out of the top of their heads like car antennas. She had difficulty believing that this was going to be a comfortable conversation when they refused to reveal information as simple as their jobs. She didn't like to think it but she already felt a queer dislike for the two of them. Them and their coldness, their artificiality. Their tight brown hair and flat clothes and studying eyes, they almost looked like cardboard cutouts. Zoey could tell when she was being spoken down to and that feeling was palpable now. And Myah had to live with these two her entire life. Zoey actually put effort into holding back a shudder as the conversation progressed. Myah's comment about them being insult vultures seemed much more believable now.

Myah's mother went on, using the smooth and confident voice that had helped her in her own field more times than she could count. Although, as far as Brianna was concerned, this conversation was already over. "What about the four of you? Are any of you employed?"

None of them were. Dawn had a car, but it was her mother's and she got gas money from Cole or her father. She didn't work for any of it. As far as Steph, Luke and Zoey, they stayed home unless they were out with each other. The four of them looked down, feeling smaller, Zoey a second time in less than five minutes, and Myah's mother said what the four of them would want to hear. Disregarding how illogical and incorrect it was.

"Well, there's nothing wrong with that. Not everyone has to go out and get a job as soon as they're of legal age. Myah doesn't have a job either and we don't pester her about it."

Myah looked down at the floor as well, feeling like a prisoner with her two guards keeping her in check. Her mother's fingers still ran through her hair and Myah noted how cold they were every time they brushed against her scalp or the back of her neck.

"I have a car," Dawn said, hopeful that that might grant her some respect but realizing how childish her comment sounded as soon as she made it.

"That's good. That's a good start."

She gaped at Myah's mother. "Seriously?"

"Of course. Are you a good driver?"

Zoey shot out an answer before anyone could stop her. "She's a great driver. She's driven us through the rain, the snow, the wind, the heat. Everywhere we've ever needed to go, we've gotten there on time."

Myah's father responded to this glowing review. "Well, if your friend's description is any indication of your work ethic, you'll have no trouble finding a job."

Dawn blushed. "Thank you."

The guards unlocked Myah's handcuffs and set her free.

"Well, it was nice to meet all of you and we hope you enjoy your time here." She let go of her daughter's hair and watched her lead her friends toward her room. She watched until all five were behind the closed door. Brianna wasn't happy with the idea of a boy being in Myah's room, especially one who looked like he could split her in half, but she let them be. She let them enjoy themselves.

Myah's room was just as visually stunning as the rest of her house. Her pastel pink walls held no posters to clutter them and the white goose down comforter on her bed looked just as soft as the furry white rug that spread over her entire floor. Dawn took notice of the full body mirror, which hung to the left of her door, and smiled. That was exactly where hers was. The walls reminded Luke of cotton candy and the floor of what he presumed a cloud would feel like. Steph took an interest in a round mirror with bright white lights lining the rim and the tackle boxes full of makeup that sat in front of it. Three of the four examined the room in silence but the fourth, to no one's shock, could not contain herself.

"Ohmygod, this room is gorgeous," Zoey squealed. She jumped onto Myah's bed and felt an enormous amount of pressure leave her body as her back rested against the mattress. Her head was wrapped in a fuzzy pillow and an extremely important question came into her mind. "Myah, are you a virgin?"

Luke mumbled, "Fucking hell, Zoey," but Myah answered with only a hint of bashfulness.

"Yeah."

Zoey wrestled with the bed she had sunken into and eventually won. She sat up, all smiles, and looked at Myah. That was the answer she wanted. "Good, because you *need* to have your first time in this bed. This is the perfect place to have sex."

Steph got up from the makeup table and stared at Zoey, who looked just about ready to have sex with the bed itself. "I just want to know why you never think before you speak?"

Zoey rolled her eyes but her smile stayed. "I do, quite often actually. I'm not telling Myah to go out and grab a boyfriend just to bring him back here and fuck him. All I'm saying is that, when the time comes, this is the optimum place for it." She looked to Luke and then, longer, at Dawn, who stood in front of the mirror checking herself out and straightening her clothes.

Myah tossed her hands around, as if trying to wave away this topic of conversation. "I hate to be the one who brings the group down, but there's a bigger reason why we're all here. And it's not to talk about me banging someone in my bed."

Everyone looked at each other and Dawn offered up her theory. "Has anybody thought that Amy and the rest of them could have done it."

Most of them didn't respond but, after a few seconds of silence, Steph gave an objection she wasn't sure she believed.

"Come on, do you really think she'd do that?" Amy was a lot of things, and Steph still had a number of welts all over her body to prove it, but this was murder.

Dawn shrugged and held her hands at the base of her shirt, just in case it decided to ride up a little. "Is it really that farfetched? Jonah treated the four of them just as poorly as he did everyone else. The difference is, we aren't violent like her. I'm sure the list of people wanted to hurt him would be miles long, but Amy would be at the top of it. It could have been accidental or not, but you can't ignore that it's at least, likely. She broke Zoey's toes for no reason, what would stop her from doing something like this?" There was a heavy pause as the four others thought it through.

"I think Dawn's right," Luke said slowly. "Or at least on to something. Anyone else?"

Myah nodded, Zoey gave a shaky, "Yes," and Steph sat on the bed next to her, arm around her shoulder and said, "There's a chance."

Looking at their faces and seeing how sick they all appeared, Dawn tried to ease their emotions as best she could. "Well, we don't know what happened and we probably never will. I just don't think she should be overlooked."

Zoey started to cry.

Myah knelt down at Zoey's feet and put a hand on her knee. Luke took the pink tissue box from the makeup table and handed it to her. Steph's arm tightened around Zoey's shoulder. Dawn sat on the other side of her and took Zoey's left hand. It was cold and shaking. "Hey, it's okay. It feels weird when something like this happens, but he's in a better place now."

Zoey looked at her with the face of anger and confusion, wondering why Dawn thought she felt much sympathy for the guy who had once called her the most orgasmic drive through on Earth. "I don't care about him." She wiped her eyes with a tissue and almost laughed at how much better even Myah's tissues were than her own. "I'm not scared of the one who's dead. It's the one who could have killed him that terrifies me."

Zoey didn't think they were in any mortal danger, but that didn't stop her mind, couldn't stop it, from envisioning the possibilities anyway. Because, if they were on to something, and if Amy somehow found out, what would happen to them? Which one of them might have an accident first? How many funerals might Zoey have to attend before Amy came for her?

She got up, avoiding Myah, and hopped to the door. "I'm sorry, Myah, thank you for this, but I think I need to leave."

Myah got to her feet and met Zoey at the door. "You don't need to apologize." She hugged her and was almost split in half by Zoey's grip across her spine.

Dawn got off the bed and joined the two. "I'll take her home."

Zoey spoke from Myah's arms. "Can we go to your house?"

Dawn gave her a smile she couldn't see. "Of course we can."

"What about Steph and Luke?" Again, her voice was muffled by Myah's body but Zoey refused to let go. Myah and Dawn looked at each other and Myah mouthed, *Take them home.*

Dawn talked into the space under Myah's arm, feeling slightly stupid as she did so. "I'll take them home first, then we can go to my house." Both she and Myah looked to Steph and Luke, who got up and met them at the door.

Myah patted Zoey a few times and pried her arms off of her back. She gave Zoey to Dawn and followed them as they went down the hall, down the staircase and out the massive front door. Myah shoved it closed behind them and smiled through the window panels. As far as she was concerned, in the greater context of what this meeting was supposed to accomplish, things went well.

She thought so.

"You know you can't be friends with them, right?"

Myah's smile was killed by her mother's voice and a glare replaced it. She turned to see the two of them, arms crossed.

"What? Why?"

Her parents looked down at her like she was an idiot for even asking. Her mother's blunt voice continued. "None of them are employed and none of them are a good influence on you. One of them is on crutches and another had bruises running up her arms and legs. Do you want to end up injured like that?"

Myah hadn't noticed any bruises, she didn't even know who her mother was referring to, but she wouldn't have put it past her to make that up for the sake of her argument. And when it came to injuries, she could have told them that she already had her own, the scratch along her back proved, but Myah thought it more important to defend those who weren't allowed to defend themselves. She could already feel herself getting angry, could feel the energy burning in her chest, but she didn't try to stop it. "What do you even think that means, being a good influence on me? What do you think will happen if I hang out with them? What do you even see in them that's so bad?" She didn't give them time to force feed her their pathetic nonsense. "And who cares if they're employed or not, they're the only thing that has made this transfer any easier. They're the only people I can talk to." Despite the emotional reaction she had been trying to get out of them with her last statement, her parent's expressions remained unchanged and she began to tear up. "You didn't even give them a chance. You can't have one interaction with someone and call it right then and there. God, you both interact with people for a fucking living, you'd think you would be smart enough to understand that."

"Myah, that's enough. It's done."

Myah turned to her father and begged, though she could already see the stony look in his eyes. "Dad, please. They're the only friends I have." She was crying now, but it didn't change anything.

"I'm sorry, honey. You can't see them anymore. And besides, it won't matter anyway. Soon enough you'll be in a new school with better people and you'll forget about them before you know it. Is this understood?" He put his hand out, waiting for her to add hers, and Myah slapped him away so hard it burned her palm.

They both watched her go up to her room, stomping step after step, and wondered when she was going to start growing up. Then they put the issue behind them and refocused their minds on something more important, like dinner. They tuned out the thunderclap of Myah's door as well as what followed.

Myah slammed her bedroom door hard enough to make her mirror rattle and she swung her small, shaking fist into the glass with no hesitation.

The sound of the shattering satisfied her and she felt no immediate pain, in spite of the very clear sensation of liquid running down her hand. She opened her eyes and saw her hand now dripping blood onto the hundreds of bits of glass that sat in a pile on her rug. Myah stared at her wound for a few seconds, then went into the bathroom, put her hand in the sink and opened her fist. Flexing her fingers hurt a bit but it was when she turned the water on that her entire hand started to sting. And every shred of glass she had to pull out of her skin added a new twinge of pain, though she didn't let that stop her.

After she had washed the blood down the drain, she put bandages on every cut she could find. Twelve bandaids later, she went back to her room, locked the door, ignored the pile of broken glass for the time being, and crumpled down onto her bed. A bed that she should use for her first time, apparently. Myah wasn't even sure if she would *have* a first time and, if she did, her house was the last place she wanted to have it in. She hated her house.

It looked nice to anyone visiting, but growing up an only child in a place of this size was nothing more than crushing. A big house was fun to play in, all kids knew that, but it was only as fun as the people you played with. And Myah had never been able to play in her house with anyone other than herself. Her parents were authority figures first and friends second, Myah had known this since she was old enough to understand the words coming out of their mouths. And the gaping doorways and endless sterile rooms she lingered through only served to laugh at her because of it. The rooms and hallways should have been filled with her friends or family, but were instead filled with false hope for a better childhood. If her parents had ever allowed her to keep the friends she made, maybe she would have been able to play with them at her house and make use of it but that hadn't been the case. She would play by herself in her massive colosseum and whenever she asked if a friend could come over or if she could go to a friend's house, she was always rejected by her parents.

When she wasn't playing in her room she was crying in it, wondering how bad of an influence someone could be when you were both eight. How much trouble could she really get into? Myah had friends whose parents actually played with them and the concept of that had fascinated her more than it should have. And when she was home and tried to get the same luxury, she wasn't surprised to always find her parents busy or tired. She wasn't even allowed to sleep in their bed with them when she had a nightmare. Instead, her mother would haul her back into her room and explain exactly how dreams worked, not knowing that the science and analysis of dreams didn't mean shit to a terrified seven year old who just wanted to be held by her mother when she was scared.

Once Myah had found herself so desperate for them to notice her that she had hid behind the living room couch, pressed between it and the wall, and committed herself to staying there until they started looking for her. She only wanted to know that they cared. She kept herself stuck on the hardwood floor, cramped between a wall and a couch, for three hours before she gave up, went back into her room and sobbed.

She was so happy to leave her house every time she got the chance that the building may as well have been haunted. But those ghosts, the ghosts of her old memories, of sobbing in her pillow because her parents hadn't noticed she had suddenly gone missing when she hid behind the couch or the the tone of her mother's disappointed voice when she had to tell Myah that there was nothing in her closet or how she had to take in a deep breath and work up the courage to ask if she could simply spend a few hours at a friend's house, those ghosts haunted her no matter when she went.

It had been nice when Myah was first brought up in it, but over the years the enticing spell of this massive white coffin had worn off. She had begun to feel as though the wood was rotting and the paint was peeling and the pristine, polished chandelier hanging from the ceiling was ready to pierce her to the floor and hold her there forever as the darkness and loneliness engulfed her.

She had been alone in the dark before, sometimes for years on end, but now Myah had found a light.

She took a deep breath, stretched her bandaged hand, got off the bed and began getting rid of the shards of glass from her rug. She had six more bandages on her hands by the time she was done.

Zoey had stopped crying once they had left Myah's neighborhood and by the time she was in Dawn's room, while thoughts of Amy and Jonah were still lurking in her mind, they had faded a bit farther from view.

"How's your stomach?"

Dawn was relieved to not have to hid behind the disguise. "It's better. The letters are healing and the skin has been turning a more healthy shade. It still hurts every now and then but, when it does, it's small and passes by." She chuckled as a test and her stomach gave her almost nothing.

"Can I see it?"

Zoey was standing in front of Dawn's full body mirror, doing what Dawn had done at Myah's house, and Dawn was sitting on her bed reveling in the lack of pain her stomach gave her no matter how she contorted her body.

Though Zoey's question straightened her out, mentally and physically. "Yeah, sure. Come here."

Zoey hopped over and sat to Dawn's right. The bed was much harder than Myah's but it was comfortable enough. Dawn lifted up her shirt and Zoey slowly reached out and touched the letters. They were less pronounced than they were the last time she had seen them and the skin around them was, as Dawn had said, more healthy. It didn't blend perfectly with the rest of her stomach but it was much closer to the apricot color than it had been before. Zoey ran her fingers along each letter and finally made reference to the word they spelled.

"Whore?" Zoey said the word as if it hurt. She had been called a whore too many times in her life to count so the word had little meaning to her now, it was nothing more than an empty sound, but it didn't make any sense to carve it into Dawn. Zoey didn't even know if Dawn had ever talked dirty before. She wanted to believe she did, considering she wasn't shy about kissing Luke whenever she damn well wanted to, but she could never tell where Dawn's boundaries were. Even when you were her friend for as long as Zoey had been. Six years and counting and she still didn't know if Dawn had ever dipped into a PG-13 relationship.

Dawn sighed and shook her head. "Yeah, I don't know either."

Zoey didn't enjoy how unfazed Dawn sounded, as if what they were talking about was no more annoying than being out of milk, but she pushed her irritation aside and spoke from a much more pleasant place. "You think she missed me and got you instead?"

Dawn smiled at her with relief and sympathy. "Zoey, you know you're not a whore. Right? It's a word you could use to describe anybody if you wanted to."

Zoey nodded. "Yeah, I know I'm not."

Dawn didn't know if she believed her, but she let it slide.

Zoey asked another pressing question. "Does your mom know?"

Dawn scoffed at the idea of her mother even being alert for more than ten minutes, much less trying to help her daughter with any problems she may or may not be facing. "No, why would she? My mom isn't like your dad who will actually be there for you if you're in trouble."

Zoey looked down and her mind didn't leave him. She saw his face, heard his voice, remembered what he had done to her foot in the car. How he purposely hurt her and smiled about it and Zoey turned from Dawn and wiped a tear away with her unremarkable fingernail.

Dawn's train of thought had its emergency brake pulled when Zoey said something that Dawn didn't know how to respond to.

"Why does he hate me?"

It sounded rhetorical, Dawn hoped it was, but she answered anyway.

"Who?"

"My dad."

"Zoey, he doesn't hate you. Yeah, he was a little brisk at the doctor's but it's probably—"

"If you say 'tough love' I swear to God." Dawn didn't finish the sentence Zoey had guessed the ending of and the lack of response made more tears fall from her eyes. For the second time in one day, she was crying on one of her friend's beds.

"He hates me. I don't try to make him, I just don't know what to do to stop it. And yeah, he doesn't say I'm a whore, but he shows it. And you could never know how much worse that is. How much more that hurts. Not only because it's my fucking *father*, but because you can do so much more if you show it. You can reveal it through the way you look at someone, or the inflections in your voice or comments that you think are super clever when they don't go over my head at all because I'm not as stupid as you think!" She sighed and brought the volume of her voice down, remembering that she was talking to Dawn and not her father. "Without saying anything, you can say so much more. As long as you know what'll hurt."

She had begun a "Talking Spree" but this one was different. This time Dawn didn't lose the thread a quarter of the way through or even *three*-quarters of the way through. She understood every word Zoey had said, first to last. And she agreed with all of them.

All and then she *saw* Zoey. She *saw* every part of her, inside and out and Dawn could feel this change deep within herself. It was as if a window, nailed shut and bonded up, had burst open and let in a light and a warmth so strong and so soothing that she couldn't put their power into words. And now, looking into Zoey's golden eyes, Dawn saw that this was what it was all about.

Guys could say they wanted to date Zoey just to fuck her as long and as vehemently as they wanted to, but when you looked into her eyes with a part of your brain you had never listened to before and saw so many different things, her weaknesses and her strengths and her smile and her intelligence and her passion and everything that made her exactly who she was, a feeling was injected into you like a drug. Looking into those eyes and feeling them looking back into you was like watching a miracle unfold. And suddenly you had to have her, you had to have that feeling running through your system for as long as possible. You had to feel like you could do anything and that everything good in this world was hidden inside those eyes and all you had to do was make a move and you would be able to experience it all. Zoey's eyes were magic.

Dawn brushed back Zoey's black hair and put a hand on her cheek. Zoey turned to look at her, her face wet with tears and Dawn leaned closer. Zoey moved her head back a centimeter. She knew what Dawn was about to do, and she didn't know if she was ready or not.

"What are yo—"

"—Without saying anything, you can say so much more, right." She leaned closer and Zoey did, too. They closed their eyes, pushed what little resistance remained away, and kissed. Their minds raced a mile a minute and Zoey felt the miserable questions and confusion that had wrapped themselves around her heart fall away in the midst of this overwhelming sense of finally finding home.

This is how it was supposed to feel with Brandon, with all of them. Zoey brought her hand to the nape of Dawn's neck and pull her closer. *I wasn't playing for that team. All these years, I just* wanted *to be.* She stopped thinking about anything else and only thought about how great it felt to kiss someone and feel it. And especially feel something so fiery and powerful and intimate as this.

There was no fear. This was her, this was who she was. She thought about that and liked it. She loved it. She could have wept with the relief of it all.

Though she didn't want to, Zoey took her lips off of Dawn's. "Did you know?"

Dawn didn't know which one of them Zoey was referring to and it didn't matter. The answer would have been the same.

"No." She leaned in again and Zoey did too, faster this time. They leaned back against Dawn's pillow and continued until another interruption stabbed at one of their minds and Dawn pulled herself back. "What about Luke?"

"Do you love him?"

Dawn did her "Zigzag Look" and didn't spot Zoey smiling at her as she did it.

Dawn didn't know how she felt about him right now. Right now she was busy.

Though there was one brief moment, most likely caused by the fact that she wasn't looking at Zoey or into her powerful eyes, where Dawn thought that she was making the biggest mistake of her life. That this was nothing more than an attempt to be happy. This wasn't her, this wasn't going to change anything or make anything better. She would probably do something like this if she was drunk, too. It was nothing more than an experiment.

But then Dawn looked back into Zoey's eyes and knew that that wasn't true. This wasn't an experiment. Nor was being with Luke. At the start of their relationship, Luke made her feel a similar way to how Zoey was affecting her now, in spite of how different they were. Maybe she wasn't black or white, maybe she had a little gray area in there, an area that had gone unnoticed or ignored until now. And maybe she just wanted to think that to make herself feel better but, regardless of who she found attractive, she knew she had to pull herself out of her head and return to the present. Return to Zoey and this eye opening experience that she was letting slip away. She stopped zigzagging and looked into the hazel paradise she never wanted to leave. "I love you." A few tears fell down the sides of Dawn's face and Zoey wiped them away. "So much."

Occasionally, an intrusive thought would drill its way into one of their minds (how she was going to explain this to Luke, what her father might say about this new development) but they were brief and swiftly passing shadows on an otherwise cloudless day. It was only five in the afternoon, but when they found themselves able to take a break, the two fell asleep in each other's arms. And woke up the next morning in the exact same position.

Chapter 18

Myah's parents drove her to school the next day, again against her wishes. She was glad it was Friday. Not because she was excited to spend another weekend living in a home she wanted to avoid, but because it meant she would get a break from being driven to school by her parents for two blessed days. Her earbuds were in, her bandaid riddles hands were hidden and her music blasted loud enough to make her wonder if she would be deaf before she made it to school. The idea didn't seem too bad to her.

She was taken away from her twisted fantasy by her mother. Myah had seen her waving around like an idiot and chose to ignore her, they had no right to talk to her after what they had done, but she couldn't ignore the insistent tapping on her knee. She ripped an earbud out and growled, "What?"

"You're going to go food shopping this weekend since you know your allergies better than we do—"

"—I shouldn't." Considering her parents were such experts at every aspect of their lives, Myah figured they ought to know what she was allergic to just as much as she did, but it seemed that such information wasn't salient to them.

Brianna ignored her daughter. "And since it will give you some much needed time to think things over and come to a more reasonable conclusion."

Myah could have laughed at the idiotic level of hypocrisy. "You're right. I should totally be more open and inviting to new things in my life."

Her mother didn't miss a beat, giving her what Myah assumed was her best lawyer's smile. A smile that had she could imagine dozens of people had seen right before they were shipped off to prison for life. "Good."

Her mother had either ignored her sarcasm or had missed it altogether, but before Myah cold waste her time trying to figure out which was worse, they had pulled up to the high school and she launched herself out of the van. She walked inside, waited by the front door for her group and thought about her assignment for the weekend.

Myah had done her own food shopping since she had gotten her driver's license the year before. Her parents only let her drive her car for errands they needed her to run. They had "made a deal" with Myah that once she got a job she could have complete control over where she was able to take her car. Luckily for Myah, she didn't feel compelled to drive and also had a friend who could take her where she needed to go if such a need ever arose. And, though she would never tell them this, she liked food shopping.

She was able to get whatever she wanted and got to take the car wherever she wanted afterwards. A few times she had left to go food shopping at noon and didn't return home until six-thirty. The food shopping usually took around an hour and a half, but the mall that her favorite grocery store was attached to took a little longer. Her father gave her his credit card to use and Myah often used a little more than she needed to. She never regretted it and they never asked her about it. With the house they lived in and the things they bought, a missing hundred or two wouldn't raise any eyebrows. And she was owed a little reward, given that finding foods she could eat was quite the needle in the grocery store haystack.

She had been allergic to Dairy, Wheat, Soy, Peanuts, Gluten and Citrus for as long as she could remember. Eating any of those ingredients, or anything that even contained them, gave her face a horrible red rash that eventually started to bleed and swelled her throat to the point of suffocation. She had learned to read at four years old to make sure she knew what she could and couldn't eat and she had gotten very comfortable having to specify this to waiters and chefs whenever she went to a restaurant. She didn't end up buying much when she went food shopping but she was at least certain that she would be able to eat what she put in her carriage without bleeding or choking. She didn't think her parents would put the same level of precaution into it.

Zoey, Dawn, Steph and Luke walked in the front door and an idea hit Myah. An idea that she was surprised took her so long to come up with. Before any of them could say anything she was talking. "Hey, do you guys want to go food shopping with me this weekend?" They all looked at her like she had an arm growing out of the top of her head and she explained the context. "My parents make me buy my own food because of my allergies and I thought it might be fun for us. It also might be nice to have the distraction and to be a bit farther away from," she gestured around her, "all of this."

They all looked at each other, getting a firmer grip on the situation, and Dawn said something that almost made Myah jump with happiness.

"Yeah, I'll come along."

The following responses from the other members of the group, even Luke's, made the urge to leap harder to resist.

Steph nodded. "I'm in."

Luke frowned. "I don't think I can make it. I need to help repaint the walls of my house. After living in the same place for fifty years, my grandmother has finally decided she doesn't like the color of her walls."

Zoey gave a minor head tilt and her voice took on an odd leery lilt. "I don't know, food shopping was always the most boring thing to be dragged along to."

Dawn put a hand on her shoulder and Zoey's expression immediately warmed up. "But most of us are going to be there."

The change in Zoey was lost on Steph and Luke, but not Myah. Though she was more concerned with convincing Zoey rather than her personality shift.

"It might help if you knew where we were going."

A smile formed on Myah's face that Zoey looked at with a keen interest. "And where is that?"

Myah's smile got bigger. She knew that Zoey's tune would change after she said their destination. "The Sapphire State Mall."

Myah was right.

Despite how few times she had been there, the Sapphire State Mall was one of Zoey's favorite places to go when she was bored. There seemed to be a store for every mood she could find herself in, but there was one store in particular that she wanted to attend this time: The Finest Fabric Apparel. The prices were a bit higher than needed, but the quality and quantity of the sweatshirts, leggings and undergarments they sold more than made up for it. Zoey wasn't interested in getting anything for herself, or at least not a lot for herself. It was someone else who needed a wardrobe update. Especially given their new relationship, if that was what it was. Zoey didn't know quite yet and she assumed Dawn didn't either, seeing as how they had yet to bring it up all morning, but she was hopeful. As long as Dawn broke the news to Luke soon to keep him from being strung along "When are we going?" Zoey asked with new excitement in her voice.

"Tomorrow," Myah said. "I assume you'll be joining us?"

Zoey almost yelled, "Yes," and looked at Myah like she was a moron to think otherwise.

But Myah Rowland was no moron. Far from it, in fact. "All right, sounds good. You should all bring money, too. You may go in thinking you won't want anything, but that mall has a strange way of coercing you. Happens to me every time."

Dawn nodded. "Oh trust us, we know. We've all succumbed to the mall's persuasion before." She squinted and her eyes zigzagged for a few seconds. "Wait, Myah, do your parents drive you there, but just leave you to shop on your own?"

"No, I go alone. I drive there." The eight eyes that looked at her all changed, some got wider, some squinted. "What?"

"You have a license?" Zoey knew she shouldn't have been surprised, given Myah's living arrangements, but it seemed like something that should have been brought up by now. "For how long?"

"Just a year. My parents only let me drive my car to get food. Until I get a job, the car is basically theirs, they just let me rent it for a few hours every now and then." Zoey made a disgusted face, and Myah hoped it wasn't targeted at her.

"That's fucking ridiculous."

Myah let go of her small fear and shrugged.

"It's your car, you should be allowed to take it whenever you damn well please."

Myah raised her hands, as if proving she wasn't holding any weapons. She could have explained that the car was registered under her father's name so technically it wasn't hers but she decided against it. "Hey, all I can do about it is take advantage of the time I get and milk it for all it's worth." She smiled, "Which I make sure to do. Meaning I'll be our driver tomorrow and Dawn can get a break. Can you all be ready around noon?" They all agreed and began their laps through the halls of the school for the fifteen minutes that remained before the bell.

Zoey could tell that today was going to be long, now that she couldn't get her mind off of tomorrow and what she might buy and who she might buy it for and how it might look on her.

Every class was slower than the last. Biology crawled by, Ceramics, despite everyone who was in it, hung for far too long, gym felt even more boring than usual, history was just as boring as usual but every ten minutes, one minute went by. Even Psychology, the class she always found the most interesting and useful, lingered on for the longest forty-five minutes of her life. And when it came to her last period, English, Zoey was so ready to leave that she thought she would be down the hall before the 2:30 bell finished ringing. And the four glares she felt when she walked in didn't help the time pass.

But After Mrs. Gardiner gave her little announcement, those glares turned from Zoey, Dawn and Steph and switched to each other.

"I know most of you are aware of the passing of Jonah Dunbar and, although he didn't go to our school, I know that many of you still knew him. If any of you need someone to talk to, I'm here."

Amy, Evan, Heather and Trevor stopped listening after 'Dunbar.' They were all busy in their own heads and reading each other's faces.

Heather saw Trevor's left eye squint and his other widen with one eyebrow raised and the other rumpled.

He looked to Evan and saw a face of both concentration and emptiness, a contradicting combination, but one Evan somehow pulled off.

The eyes below his arched eyebrows met Amy's, who made his eyebrows look like straight horizontal lines. He had trouble deciphering what her face said, eventually coming to the conclusion that it was both fury and fear. It didn't ease his anxious head, but, for a moment, he was alleviated so he took advantage of it for the one second he had it.

Amy's eyes cut through the hot air in the room to see what Heather's face would say. To no surprise, Heather wore a mask of twisted approval and corrupted interest and Amy felt an animalistic sense of danger. It wasn't because of the body that was found, it was because of the body sitting in front of her. They all looked at each other one more time, nodded in unity and raised their hands. Amy, Evan and Trevor their right, Heather her left. Another thing that gave Amy cold, or maybe now colder feet.

Mrs. Gardiner noticed them all and, with a voice that matched the mistrust on her face, she responded to the hand that belonged to the one of the four she liked the most. It took a while to decide and the winner was chosen by a hair.

"Yes, Evan?"

He responded with a tone he hoped sounded unfazed and believable. "Can we," his index finger pointed up and twisted around in a circle to involve the three he was sitting next to, "go talk to our guidance counselor? It's about our futures." Not completely wrong and not something any teacher he had used that excuse on had ever said no to. Evan had put Mrs. Gardiner in a hogtie she couldn't get out of.

Rachel Gardiner knew better than to trust any of the four students who sat looking hopeful, scared, angry, and distantly at her. It was as if, in their unparalleled arrogance, the four of them had forgotten that she had been teaching for thirty-three years and knew just as much about this school as they did. Much more, as a matter of fact. They didn't all have the same guidance counselor. There were four counselors at R.I High, assigned to students based on the first initial of their last names. There was no feasible way that one guidance counselor could have four students whose last names began with C, G, L and M. Maybe Amy and Heather shared one and Evan and Trevor shared another, but they could not all belong to the same counselor. She was ready to allow Evan to leave and make the rest stay, when it was as if the four people who sat waiting for her answer had already heard it.

And were not happy about it.

Trevor's and Evan's hopeful and scared looks turned to anger, but not enough to match Amy's, who still sat fuming, or Heather's, whose eyes looked at her from a far away place, although she was only about six feet away in the classroom. As Rachel watched those eyes, they began to grow bigger, deeper, more hazardous and, for the first time in all of her years of teaching, Rachel found herself unsettled by one of her students. And surprisingly, it wasn't the one who was always attacking her peers. Amy was a predictable pattern, awful but unsurprising. Heather was not. Rachel couldn't read anything in her eyes or on her face but that emptiness held much more room for interpretation and, being an English teacher, Rachel was familiar with interpretation. She could do it subconsciously. She felt goosebumps seize her body and when she thought about why they all wanted to leave in the context of what she had just announced, her active imagination began turning gears and pumping out possibilities. And if her imagination, her interpretation, right, who knew what might happen if they were deprived of something else they wanted.

She sent the four on their way and hoped they wouldn't be back. Watching them leave was like watching the sun finally come out after a storm. The four left in an unbroken stride and as soon as the door shut behind them and she was left with her good students, she felt secure. She knew they weren't going to any guidance counselor and she could not have care less.

"Okay, let's think about this for a second," Amy said, putting her thumbs under her chin and bringing her fingers against her mouth. The four of them stood at the doors of the empty cafeteria, far from any classroom where someone could overhear them. Evan was already reeling from the information they had been given and Amy knew now was the time to turn her brain on and think things through. It was a rare occurrence, often only happening when there was potential she could be in danger, and this time was no different. Except this time it wasn't just her. This time she had three accomplices, and that's exactly what they would remain as.

Her accomplices.

If she was in too deep, push the blame on one of the lesser two. The idea of seeing Heather in an orange jumpsuit wrapped in chains brought a grin to her face that she had to quickly scrape off. "Is there any way they could connect us to him?"

Evan answered, voice shaking. "I can't believe we killed him."

"*We* didn't. *You* did." The smile could be seen in Heather's voice.

Evan looked down and Amy gritted her teeth. The orange jumpsuit looked even better than it had before. She could almost hear the chains jangle as Heather walked.

"It doesn't matter *who* did it," she gave Heather's ankle a hateful, lava filled kick and Heather's smiled grew. "The point is, we all know. And we all need to be together on this. Like it or not, one goes down, we all go down. Deny it all you want, but when you're sitting in an empty room, a table's length away from a cop, you'll squeal like a little fucking pig. Believe me, I know." She knew this was the first time any of them had heard this information and she chose not to elaborate on it. She, instead, let the pause dangle for a bit, giving each person listening a moment to grasp the severity of their situation. She moved on when she was sure they had both hands holding on for dear life. "Now, like I was saying, is there any way they could connect us to him? We were all there, think."

Evan answered the same question, but this time had something useful to add. "I guess not. I mean, what dee-enn-ayy could they find?" There was a pause, and Amy could feel a sliver of the group's combined terror leave their bodies.

Heather, yet again, chose to hurt rather than help. "I don't know, maybe something that could be easily traced to one specific person. Something like saliva. Only one of us spit on him if I'm not mistaken."

Heather's smile came back and Amy's skin burned above the lava in her bloodstream. Whether she was joking or not, this wasn't the time for it. An example had to be made. She grabbed Heather by the shoulders, sunk her fingers in as hard and as deep as she could and hurled her against the cement wall that stood opposite them. Amy watched Heather make contact, watched her head thumped against the concrete, and pounced on her again, taking her throat in her hands. Her burning, pink hands. She looked into Heather's face and let the lava spill. She wanted to savor this moment for as long as she could. She wanted to watch Heather burn alive in the lava from her inner volcano.

"I swear to fucking God, if you say anything, I'll take my knife and cut out those buggy, massive, fuck-off eyes of yours. This isn't a fucking game. This is our lives. All of ours. You send me and Evan down the river and the police will find you in pieces. You talk, you're dead. Do you fucking understand me?"

She kept her grip loose enough for Heather to speak but, when Amy was given no confirmation, her grip tightened and her hands pressed harder as Heather's eyes began to grow. Amy hated those fucking eyes so much she wanted to strangle her until they popped out of her skull. If Heather would be conscious or alive by the time that happened became a secondary factor.

As Amy's hands squeezed her throat, Heather found her vision beginning to change. While some things began to darken, in a harsh contrast, she also began to see red and orange and it didn't take her long before thinking that what she was seeing was Hell. She didn't know if she believed in such a place, but it was hard for her to make a decision or gather her thoughts when it felt like her eyes had a few seconds left before they burst from her head. She could feel the heat from the being pushing against her and the fire and fury in Amy's face brought to Heather the realization that Amy was, plain and simple, a demon.

Her vision got more gray and Hell got even brighter. Heather thought she was almost there and she felt strange. For the briefest second, she felt her heart beat faster. What breathing she had left became rapid and dry. She felt an awful emptiness in the pit of her stomach. She didn't know it then, but what Heather was feeling is what most people call fear. While she took in her last few breaths and spent her last few thoughts trying to figure out what was happening to her, something took Hell away and she fell to the floor with the darkness leaving and sickening, bright colors from everything around her replacing it. As she took new air into her lungs she came to a conclusion; whatever had happened, whatever new thing she my have felt, she didn't want it again. She didn't want to feel anything ever again, not even the joy at torturing her family or touching her special place. Feeling was for the weak, and the weakest of all was Amy.

Evan pulled Amy from Heather when he was certain Heather would die if he didn't. As he expected from their time together, Amy fought his interference and, again as expected, almost won. But he gave it everything he had and managed to yank her away from the girl she was slowly killing and pull her into his arms.

Amy fought Evan even when Heather was out of her hands, thrashing and growling to get back to the girl whose eyes had gotten bigger than ever before. She didn't care if Heather answered Amy's question, a question Amy felt like she had asked a long time ago, right now all she cared about was having Heather's eyes on the blade of her knife. She needed them.

Before she could break out of Evan's grip and bring her fantasy to life, his voice held her back. She couldn't even hear what he said. She could only hear how he sounded. He sounded scared, again, and she let him know that he wasn't alone.

She hugged him tight and, burying her face in his chest so it could be as muffled as possible, began to cry. She cried it all out. She cried out her fear of the situation they were in, she cried out Heather and the possibility of her betrayal, she cried out the chance of losing Evan, whether by prison sentence or death row or him abandoning her in the night. She hated when she felt this way and when she started to shiver in Evan's warm arms, but she couldn't avoid the truth. She was terrified. And, outside of hope, there was nothing she could do to change whatever the outcome would be. She dug her face deeper into his shirt and cried more.

After an indeterminate amount of time had passed, Amy forced herself to regain control and, after a few wet coughs, took a step back and did her best to wipe away her dirty tears. They stained her face. When she took a step closer to Evan, she didn't put her face into his sweatshirt. This time she put her lips on his and held them there, wanting to cry again but forcing herself not to. She hoped she never would again.

She took her lips away from Evan's and bent them into the form they were so used to taking.

"So we're all in agreement. We keep our mouths shut." Her glare was very persuasive and, although they already were in favor of that plan, Trevor and Evan nodded.

Heather didn't. She was still lying on the ground, wondering if she would ever see that burning and feel that heat again. Most likely when she died, but she wasn't sure she'd be able to appreciate it at that time. Amy's voice snapped her back to the hallway she was laying down in. She glanced over at her and noticed how scared she looked. She wanted to smile as big as she could and show that ginger rat all of her teeth, but she contained herself. Her smile would come later when Amy was shipped off to prison. She instead said, "What?"

"We keep our mouths shut about this."

"Whatever."

Amy leaped for her and the new, unsettling, cold feeling jumped back into Heather's body for round two. She hated it just as much the second time as she had the first but it wasn't inside of her for long, retreating when Evan grabbed Amy and pulled her back by his side. He tried to sound tough and in control, but Heather knew she could take that tone away with just a shift of her eyes. She didn't. She let him think he was getting to her.

"Heather, we need a yes or no."

She fought back a sour smile and took a more passive aggressive approach. "Yes."

"Good."

For the first time since they left Mrs. Gardiner's room, Trevor spoke. Weird for someone like him, who often never let a quiet second go by. "Do we really have to go back to Gardiner?"

Amy and Evan looked at each other, both not wanting to, but both knowing the longer they stayed out, the more suspicious they would look to everyone else. They both said, in monotone unison, "Yes," and Trevor rolled his small, beady eyes as high as he could let them. It was last period of the day, last period of the week, and there was less than half an hour to go. They could get through it.

When the four of them came back and dropped into their seats, they thought about exactly what they had left the room to talk about.

Their futures.

Chapter 19

It was nice to not be the one behind the wheel for a change. She could sit back and talk without having to worry about the potential for a horrible, flaming death. Dawn had even gone on her phone, something she hadn't done in a car for months. She took a deep breath and tried to enjoy being a passenger.

The only downside to not being the designated driver was that Dawn was bitten by fear whenever she looked out the window. She kept thinking that Myah was speeding up a bit too fast, or stopping a bit too suddenly. Myah's driving was fine to Steph in the passenger's seat and Zoey across from Dawn in the back, but Dawn couldn't stop thinking about how this might be where she met her end. And her stomach was finally healing, too. It would be a shame to leave this world now. Although, considering what had happened with Zoey on Thursday, it would certainly make her life less complicated.

As if on cue, Zoey tapped Dawn's arm.

She blinked, surprised at having powered down without even noticing it, and saw Zoey's smile. Without thinking, only feeling, she gave one back.

"You awake?"

Dawn shifted in the leather seat, readjusted Zoey's crutches that were splayed out along both of their laps and sat up straighter. "Yeah, I was just enjoying being in a car and not driving it for once."

"Well don't get too comfy back there. I'm only giving you a break today. You're still our chauffeur to school. *You're* just lucky I barely get to drive and I really want to."

Steph's mouth fell open a bit and she forced her hand to close it. "Wait, Myah, you said your parents only let you drive to get food, right?"

"Yes."

"Well, how often do you have to go food shopping?"

Myah made a *hmmm* sound for a few seconds, then finally reached an estimate. "About once every two months."

The responses she received were so fast and sounded so similar Myah couldn't even tell who said what. Luckily, they all conveyed the same emotion so she was able to answer them all at once.

"What's the problem with that? I need to eat. What do you expect?"

Steph closed her eyes and shook her head. "We're not saying you need to go *less* often. Farthest thing from, actually."

"Yeah, how do you even manage to make the food last?" Zoey asked, anticipating the answer.

"I just eat sparingly. One meal a day, maybe two."

Dawn's jaw fell this time. "You eat one meal a day? Is that why you're built like a flimsy tree branch?"

Myah thought for a second, then nodded. "That might have something to do with it." She had always been light, ever since she was a baby. She lived now, at the age of seventeen at one hundred and ten pounds. Her bones were almost visible through her skin, her ribcage especially. It was why she had never owned a bikini. That and the fact that she thought one pieces were cuter anyway.

Myah didn't care, though. She got along just fine with the food she ate and when she ate it, though she had a feeling she wouldn't get the three other people in her car to see eye to eye with her on the subject.

"But I don't mind how I look. I know self-confidence is the first thing to go once you become a teenager, but that's never really happened for me. I've always liked the person I saw in my mirror." *Well, ex-mirror now*, she thought. Her eyes fell from the windshield to her bandaged hands and she smiled. Zoey, Steph and Dawn didn't notice. They were thinking about what Myah had said.

The three had no problem with Myah's self-confidence, but this one came at a price. And that price looked unhealthy. The small amount of food she ate on a daily basis kept her alive, sure, but it didn't put any meat on her bones.

"You might want to consider eating a little more frequently though," Zoey said. "It can't hurt." She leaned forward until her head was poking in between the two seats in front of her. She was looking below Myah's head and above her stomach. "You've got a pretty good pair, though."

"Zoey!"

Zoey recoiled. "Not in my ear, Steph. What's your deal with me giving compliments? Most girls who are really skinny don't have much of a body to work with. And, from what I can see, Myah does."

"I didn't bring much money with me, but I'll give you every cent if you stop talking."

Zoey leaned back into her seat. "All right, keep your hair up, I'm done."

They all looked at Myah through different angles, and she assumed most of their eyes were on her boobs, as she slid into a spot on the first floor of the parking garage. She turned off the car and looked from girl to girl, reading faces that were intent on helping her. And again she felt herself grateful to know all of them. "Let's get a move on. Can't buy a shit ton of food if I'm stuck in this car." She got out and slammed the door. Skinny as she may have been, she wasn't lacking when it came to strength. Shortly after, her three passengers did the same thing, though their doors were much softer. They headed through the parking garage to the grocery store entrance of the mall, all hoping the food shopping would take the least amount of time. Myah, most of all.

Zoey was happy that Myah walked in front of her, she had to find out if she had just as good of a back as she did a front. After getting her answer, she turned to Steph and gave her a smug look.

"She's got a pretty good backside, too."

"Shut up."

As the three suspected, Zoey acted like a child being dragged somewhere they didn't want to be. In part because, to an extent, she was. With every aisle they went through everyone's impatience grew, though Zoey's grew due to the endless grocery store she trudged through and the other three's grew due to Zoey. It took them until aisle five of twenty-four before all four reached a boiling point.

"Guys, they're going to find my decomposing skeleton draped over one of these shelves after old age takes me out."

Dawn, who assumed that old age wouldn't be the thing taking Zoey out today if she kept her mouth running, saw Steph tense up and she put a hand on her shoulder before Steph could unload her frustration on the girl who, Dawn did agree, was getting to be a bit much. Even on the Zoey Kay Grading Curve.

In order to keep the peace, Dawn made a decision that would better the emotional state of all four of them. "Okay, I'll take Zoey to The Finest Fabric Apparel," Dawn shot her a look and Zoey straightened out of her physical slump. "And you guys can just meet us there when you're done here. Sound good?" They all agreed before Dawn had finished her question and she led Zoey, or rather Zoey led her, out of the grocery store and into a place that they both liked much more. Even with her crutches Zoey was keeping time with Dawn, on occasion passing her.

They both walked in and Zoey became a hyperactive dog that Dawn had to keep on a leash. This was, in a way, worse than the bored and whiny child persona she had worn seconds prior and Dawn knew that she wouldn't be able to keep up with Zoey when she was in this state. So she let the leash go, but only after tranquilizing her a little. She grabbed Zoey's hands and held them until Zoey stopped scanning every inch of the store and met her eyes. Dawn's words were slow to ensure that Zoey heard everything she said.

"Zoey, I'm going to need you to calm down, all right? You've been here more times than anyone on Earth, you know this place top to bottom and there's nothing new to see. I can understand,
but far from relate to,
your excitement, but you need to get your priorities in order. It's just a store. I like it too, but it's just a store. Okay?"

Zoey rolled her eyes. "Stop talking like that, I'm not crazy." She closed her eyes and attempted to see where Dawn was coming from. "But I will settle down, all right? Don't worry about me." She slipped her hands out of Dawn's and put them on her hips. She squinted and smiled, which meant she had an idea Dawn wouldn't approve of. Dawn knew it, too. "In fact, if there's anyone we *should* be here for, it's you."

Dawn closed her eyes, sighed and asked the question she knew Zoey wanted. "Why?"

"Because I think it's time for your wardrobe to *update* a bit."

The air quotes Zoey held up around update made Dawn, who was already on the fence, definitively unwilling to go along with Zoey's plan. "Well, whatever this update of yours is, it can't happen. Neither of us have money."

Zoey's face beamed. "Oh, I do."

Dawn's face did not. "How the hell did you get money?"

"I always keep a spare stash hidden. It's important to have—"

"—Stole it from your parents?"

Zoey frowned. "Yeah," then her bright smile came back. "But it doesn't matter how I got it, the point is, we can do a lot with it."

Dawn looked Zoey up and down and decided to give her the benefit of the doubt. *Maybe it won't be that bad.* She took and step back and nodded her head, releasing the leash.

Zoey hovered over to one of the pink and white striped boxes and dug around in it until she found what she was looking for. "We can start here." She pulled out a lacy black thong and Dawn logged this moment in her brain. For the next time she considered giving Zoey the benefit of the doubt.

"Put that away. That's not going to happen." She tried to swat the thing away, but Zoey was quicker than Dawn had anticipated. Every time Dawn tried to hit it, Zoey had already moved it somewhere else. Dawn's eyes followed the article of clothing but Zoey's eyes never left Dawn's face.

Her beautiful, precious face.

Zoey moved forward with her stance on the thong debate. "Oh come on, Dawn, you would look so good in this."

Maybe for Zoey it made sense, but Dawn couldn't find any logic in her statement. "Nobody would even see me in it or know I was wearing it."

Zoey moved closer, eyes planted on Dawn's lips. "Yeah but I would know, and isn't that what matters most." Her lips shot out and hugged Dawn's. They felt cold and dry at first but, when Dawn relaxed, Zoey felt them warm up.

A few seconds following Zoey's pounce, Dawn took her into one of the changing rooms for their own privacy. The plan was to better lay the ground rules for their new relationship, if that was what Dawn had decided it was, but as soon as the door was closed and the two were alone, Zoey kissed her with a fire Dawn had not yet experienced. She fought against it, still needing to tell Zoey the truth in spite of her body telling her to put that aside and enjoy this moment, but when Zoey grabbed one of her breasts, the strength and motivation she needed was given to her. She pulled away and had to hold Zoey's head back with her hands. "Zoey, wait."

"No, I can't wait anymore. It's bad enough that we can only do this when we're alone, you can't limit it beyond that." She leaned in again and what Dawn said next made her jerk her head backwards voluntarily.

"I still haven't told Luke."

She sounded embarrassed and guilty, which Zoey found

understandable. She tried not to sound as displeased as she was. "When are you going to?"

Dawn tilted her head back and groaned. "I just...don't know how to do it. How am I supposed to explain all of this to him when I don't even really understand it myself? And how is he going to react to it? I don't want to hurt him, but I *am* by stringing him along like this." She covered her forehead with her hands and sat on the carpeted floor and Zoey, as well as her crutches, followed her down.

Dawn also had trouble telling Zoey that she hadn't turned a complete 180 like Zoey had, or at least she didn't *think* she had, but one problem had to be taken care of at a time. Right now she had to break things off with Luke and see how she felt. She didn't care if part of her thought that was a bad idea, she needed some sort of goal to work toward or the stress and questions would never cease.

"I know how difficult it can be to break up with someone, I've had my fair share of being in both positions, and while I think it's harder to do it if you know your partner well, I think that can also work to your advantage. You know Luke better than anyone else. You know how to let him down easy. And you don't have to explain the entire situation if you don't want to, you can just keep it vague. Luke's tough, he's probably been through worse. But you need to do it soon because you're right. Stringing him along like this doesn't do anybody any good. Breaking up will hurt but he'll be able to move on from that. He'll have his friends to help," she put her hand under Dawn's chin, "and you'll have yours."

She kissed Dawn's lips and Dawn didn't pull away. She felt Dawns fingers on her face and running through her hair. This time Zoey had to pull away, not because she wanted to stop but because she knew if she kept going things would get a lot more hot and heavy and a changing room in a mall wasn't the best place for that to occur. And definitely not for Dawn's first time. She took Dawn's hands and the two stood up together. They each grabbed a crutch off the floor and tucked them under Zoey's arms.

"I'm going to do it. Today."

Zoey nodded. "You can handle this. We both know it."

"Yeah." Dawn nodded back, not at all believing what she had said.

Zoey nibbled on her bottom lip for a second before coming out with it. "Can I ask you something?"

The fact that she warned her made Dawn feel a bit uneasy about the question that would follow but she gave Zoey the green light anyway.

"What exactly are we now? Like, we're clearly more than just friends. Do we have another title?" Truth be told, she was a little bit intimidated by the idea of slapping a title onto their new relationship. But Dawn, as if she had been made precisely for Zoey, told her just what she wanted to hear without any idea that she was doing it.

"Do we need a title? Or would you rather just keep things the way they are for a little while longer? We can tell people when we're ready to and we can keep it to ourselves until then. Does that sound better?"

Zoey sighed and very nearly laughed with relief. "Yeah, that sounds perfect."

"This doesn't need to be a big deal, okay? I know it's a lot to take in, but we just need to stay on the same page and we'll be all right." Dawn hugged her and felt her breasts push against Zoey's. A feeling she was most unhappy with. "While we're here, I do need to get some more bras. Ones that are actually my size might be good."

An excited and curious smile floated onto Zoey's face. "See, I told you the money was a good idea." She looked at Dawn's chest and the desire to rip off her shirt rushed through her body like electricity. "Now, I think there are some interesting things we can do with those." She pointed at Dawn's chest and almost jerked her arm back, fearing her own lack of self-control. "They're, what, triple dees? With the right bra we can make them look even b—"

"—I'll be choosing the bras." Dawn reached into Zoey's left back pocket and took the money out. Then she took her other hand and gave Zoey's right cheek a little slap. It was just for fun, she told herself, but she couldn't deny how badly she wanted to do more. "Thank you." She winked and left the changing room. Zoey followed at her heels.

Myah and Steph came into the store about ten minutes later, Steph much more unwilling, and the two stood back and examined Zoey. Even on crutches she didn't miss a beat. They watched her and Dawn chat a bit and then Zoey would go off on her own and come back a few seconds later with, it appeared, the exact thing Dawn had asked her to find.

"So, this is Zoey in her element?" Myah asked, while rubbing her hands. The grocery bags were safe in the car but the marks they had left on her hands were still red and visible. She had to talk loud so she could be heard over the blaring pop music.

Steph nodded, trying to adjust her eyes to the bright pink walls, which were almost louder than the music. "Kind of weird, isn't it?"

"Yeah, but fascinating, too."

"Yes. It is." She said it as if she were finding out something she had never known before.

Amy and Evan sat on Evan's back porch, each in a lawn chair that hadn't been used in years, thinking the same thoughts that had played on an endless loop in their heads since Friday. Evan got goosebumps and had to fight back a shiver that would have wrecked his entire body. It was the first day of March, but they would still have to deal with thirty-something temperatures for the next few weeks. He didn't know why Amy had suggested they talk outside, given her hatred for cold weather, but he had enough on his plate with Jonah without wasting time speculating on minor things like that. The more he thought about it, the better and more sure of himself he felt. There really was no evidence to tie back to him, or Amy, or any of the four of them.

As far as Heather's saliva theory, spit would harden or dry or something after spending several days exposed to cold weather. He didn't know that for a fact but it sounded right and he was too scared to look it up and be proven wrong so he decided to listen to what he wanted to believe.

Amy was thinking much of the same but her mind was more focused on the fact that there was a slight chance that there could be any evidence at all. Whether it was spit or a footprint or tire tracks, regardless of how outlandish they sounded the idea was still rooted deep into her mind. She said something aloud she didn't want to.

"I don't want to go to prison."

Her voice sounded far away and empty, like she was in shock, and Evan leaned over his chair and put his hand on hers. "You're not going to. I promise. Think about it, there's no way they could tie it back to us. We didn't leave any hair, or teeth, or even a fucking shoe size. If anyone asks, we were together and we stayed home. It was too cold to do anything outside, so we stayed in. Look at me." Amy's head shot up to see him and when he looked into her eyes, the darkness inside of them had something new in it. Something bright and shaking. They had fear. "Sweetheart, we're going to be fine."

"I just don't want to lose you." It was a whisper, but Evan had no trouble hearing it.

"You won't. I'm never going to leave your side."

"Promise?"

"The only one I'll ever keep."

Amy smiled at him, then remembered another factor that could determine her fate and the smile fell off. "What about Heather and Trevor?"

Evan glared. Not at Amy, but more at the situation Amy had created with Heather in the hallway. At times like this you needed as many people on your side as you could get. And each member of their group only had three. It would be moronic to make that number any smaller, but Amy might have done that. And, by extension, he might have, too. "They aren't going to say anything, Amy, they know how it has to be. One says something, we all take the fall. It wouldn't make any sense for either one to tell the truth."

Amy understood Evan, and agreed with him, but there was one person in particular that she was almost certain would blow it for all of them. *Should have strangled her to death when I had the chance*, she thought. "You're right. I know that, but I have a bad feeling." She looked at him and answered the question he was about to ask. "Not like my anger or the warning of it or anything like that. It's more a gut reaction. But I can't explain it. God, I can never explain anything. All my brain helps me do is hurt people." Her eyes started to water and Evan wiped them dry before the tears could fall.

"If you still have that feeling on Monday, we'll pull them aside and make sure they know how this is going to work. That is, if your method of getting the information across wasn't persuasive enough. It would have persuaded the hell out of me." They both chuckled, though Amy's was more of a choked cough. She asked if they could go back inside and Evan had no problem saying yes. They got up together and his interest got the best of him.

"Why did you want to talk outside anyway? You hate the cold and no one's even home."

Amy looked at the house carefully, as if not wanting to offend it. "I didn't want this conversation in your house. I don't want to have any bad memories in there." That was all she said on the subject. All either of them said on the subject.

The other two members of their group had much more to say.

"We can't go down with them. You know that right?"

"What are you talking about?"

God, you fucking idiot, think! "Think about it Trevor, if any of us are going to take the heat for this, it's most likely going to be Amy and Evan." Trevor tilted his head like a dog and Heather wondered if she wasn't better off working alone.

"But none of us left anything specific evidence."

"Am I the only one who remembers what happened? Evan spit on Jonah, there's your specific evidence. That will lead them to Evan and to Amy because no one would believe that he did it without her." She paused and read his blank expression. Through clenched teeth she asked, "Get it?"

"Yeah, I get where you're coming from but, if we say it was Evan's spit, wouldn't that put us at risk? How would we know it was his?"

Heather's upper lip rose and her eyebrows pressed down. She looked like a snarling animal who has reached the end of its patience with a prey that won't stop fighting back. "Evan tells you he and Amy beat up Jonah and when they had finished, he spit on him."

Trevor nodded, a bit caught off guard with how soon she had been able to come up with her response, regardless of how far away from foolproof it was. "I think it's about time I tell you that I don't really agree with the idea of selling them out. Like, you and Amy are clearly starting to have issues with each other, but I've been friends with Evan since fourth grade. It's not right to fuck them over like that. And I really don't know if we need to." Especially after his family had all changed into different people and left him behind, he didn't need to lose what few people he still had in his life.

At this point Heather was ready to put the blame on Trevor just to shut him up. She was, once again, grateful for the weaker emotions she didn't have, allowing her to be better and stronger than the people who surrounded her.

As entertaining as Amy could be when she was in her state of reckless bloodlust, she had started getting a little too comfortable for Heather's liking. So Heather found it appropriate, necessary even, to bend her until she snapped. Just bend the scrawny bitch until she went too far and then watch her be dragged to jail. However, their confrontation in the hallway had altered things and now Heather was much more interested in eliminating Amy from her life first and foremost. She needed to be put in her place, she needed to learn her lesson about what happened when she put her hands on a superior individual. For putting that black hole of fear into her stomach, even if for a few seconds, Amy was going to pay. Heather moved closer to Trevor and put her hand on his knee. He was sitting just above where her notebook was hidden beneath her mattress. She smiled at the thought of it, then wiped it off and spoke with her "Understanding/Sad" voice.

"Look, I know it must be hard to have to do something like this, but a person is dead. And the reality of the situation is that they're going to find some sort of evidence whether we say anything or not. It's possible that we'll never even need to open our mouths. But, if they find nothing, unlikely as it may be, we need to step up and do the right thing. We need to put a stop to this before it gets any more out of hand. Amy has been pushing people around for as long as we've known her but for all we know, this new bloody side to her isn't going to go away. If one of them gets mad again it could easily lead to another murder. There might have even been murders before Jonah that we don't know about. Do you want to be responsible for that?" *Cue the 'No.'*

"No."

Perfect. "Then, if it comes down to it, we need to say something. It's for the best. For everybody." Trevor nodded and Heather couldn't hold back her smile. Trevor didn't see it, he was keeping his eyes on the floor.

"I just don't want to have to do it."

An idiot and *a coward.* "I'll do it if one of us has to." She hoped she would have to. Heather could make that sacrifice and not lose a minute of sleep. "But I will need you to back me up. All you would have to do is nod and agree." *Just like you always do.* Trevor acquiesced and Heather silently moaned.

He looked at her forehead and asked her the question no one else had yet. Not even any of her five other family members. "How'd you get," he waved his hand in front of his forehead, "all that?" Her hair hid some of it, but there were still a few definitive scratch marks indented across her forehead.

Heather came up with a lie on the spot. "Oh, I was playing with Mason and he got a little too wild." Trevor snorted laughter and Heather said what she was sure most girls would say. "It's so ugly. I hate it."

Trevor reached out and followed the lines with his finger. Right to left. Once he had finished her face braille, he took his hand away. "I think it makes you look even hotter."

Oh, give me a break. Heather smiled. "Oh yeah?"

"Yeah." Trevor leaned in and Heather stopped him while feigning a fair amount of hesitation. There were hundreds of things she could have done in that moment, but she decided to play it safe. Though, of course, she had to screw with him a little. If anything, not taking advantage of a situation like this would be wrong. Before Trevor could apologize, or say whatever his sheepish face implied he might, she started the conversation in the direction she wanted it to go in. "How long have you liked me?"

He couldn't quite remember. It was possible that he had liked her from the first day he saw her, however many years ago that had been. However, it was just as possible that he didn't really like her at all and instead, wanted to take part in an activity that would relax him for a short while. That was yet another aspect of Heather that he found confusing, he could never pinpoint his exact feelings for her aside from the basic animalistic lust he might feel for any girl. "I don't really know. It's kind of hard to explain."

"But you do like me, right?" Not that she had any doubts, he just had to think she did. Though, for an odd reason, he didn't jump to answer her as she had expected him to. So, after a few seconds of silence, she pushed him farther. "Would you fuck me if I wanted you to? Just be honest with me."

He had said a lot of rather unsavory things about his female classmates in the past and some about Heather in particular, but now that it was just him and her and all he had to do was respond with a one word answer, Trevor felt a noticeable syringe suck out any strength of confidence he might have once had. His answer was just above a mumble. "Yeah."

Heather grinned and controlled herself before she could do much else. "Look at me."

Trevor did as she asked and found himself staring into eyes that often had a different depth to them. Sometimes they were too shallow or too deep, this time they were almost perfect and in that moment, he really did find Heather rather beautiful. Or maybe, in his heightened state of fear, stress and confusion, he just wanted someone to hug and talk to. Either way, Heather could see it in him and she grabbed hold of it.

"I know we tease each other now and then, but I don't think it's any secret that I feel the same way. But we can't do anything about that right now, all right? We should wait for all of this to blow over first. We have too much to deal with and too much at stake. Once everyone has figured things out we can start talking a little more about what relationship we might have, okay?" It was a rhetorical question, but she was happy with his answer just the same. She had no idea whether or not she would ever end up fucking him, she didn't particularly care either. At the end of the day, this was just one more reason why Trevor would be her pet for as long as she needed him.

Dawn thanked Myah for the ride home, got out of her car and, as soon as the three were out of sight, got into her own car and headed for Luke's house. She felt terrible.

She had sounded confident when she told Zoey she would end things today, but confidence was something that flowed fast and spilled faster, and with every passing hour since she made her statement her confidence had done just that.

And just as fast as those hours had passed, the time it took her to reach Luke's house did likewise. In what seemed like seconds, she had reached her destination and now sat in her car trying to slow her breathing and heartbeat, two things that seemed to be racing each other. Heartbeat was winning with breathing very close behind. She got a text and the sudden vibration from her phone made her scream. The two were tied now. She read the name and felt her heartbeat and breathing slow down. She read the text and they both sat down to take a break.

Z: Be honest and quick. You know you can do this. I'll be where you need me, when you need me.

Dawn zigzagged. She had told Zoey she would end things today, but she had never said when. She started texting back, asking Zoey how she knew, but before she could finish, Zoey answered.

Z: I know you would get something like this out of the way as soon as possible.

Dawn smiled with embarrassment.

D: Am I really that predictable?

Z: Afraid so.

D: I'll see what I can do about that. I'm going in now.

Z: I love you. I'm always here.

D: No matter what. I love you, too.

She turned off her phone, feeling worse, got out of her car and went inside.

The unmistakable smell of paint almost pushed her back, but after a quick head shake to clear the fumes from her mind she made her way to the stairs that led to Luke's room. She stepped lightly, hoping to make her way through the house unnoticed and put her hand on the staircase railing holding her breath. Before she could climb them, though, Luke's grandmother appeared and pushed the breath out of Dawn's body. She was faster than Dawn would have expected from such an old lady and before Dawn could react, Luke's grandmother began doing the one thing Dawn wanted to keep to a minimum; talking.

"Hi, honey. What brings you by?" She was stained with blue paint and looked at Dawn like she was her savior.

Perhaps Dawn's arrival had given her a small break, she wouldn't have been surprised. That was the sort of bad luck she found funny when it happened to someone else. Dawn gave her a fake smile and accepted the truth. "I'm here to see Luke." She pointed up the stairs. "Is he…"

"Yes, he's up in his room."

"Thank you." She walked up the stairs, each one lifting her taller than the last, and, after what felt like a while, she reached Luke's room.

A dark blue tarp was spread out across the floor and Luke was glad he had taken his grandmother's advice and used it, given how many scattered splatters of paint were now strewn all over it. Luke stood, back to the open door, shirtless and sweaty, with an orange dipped paint roller, moving it up and down the empty wall and only noticed Dawn when she knocked on the door frame.

He turned and saw a scared child for a split second, then the vision melted away and Dawn was in its place. He pushed the strange child out of his mind and warned her. "Watch it, there's paint right there. Don't step in it."

Dawn followed Luke's finger and there was indeed a bucket of orange paint near her feet. She doubted that she would have been foolish enough to step into the open bucket but, with her mind as scrambled as it was now, anything was possible. "Thanks." She took note of the color of his walls and was confused by the choice. "Orange?"

"Yeah. What about it?"

"Nothing. It's just...downstairs is blue...blue and orange are kind of opposite colors."

She noted his less than clothed appearance. On a normal day the sight would have given her more than a few ideas. She could envision that scenario now. She would stroll over, remove the paint roller from his grasp, take both of his hands and put them on her back (perhaps a bit lower if she was feeling especially saucy), lead him to his bed and let him take things from there. She would let his hands go where they wanted, as long as she stayed clothed. She would feel his excitement bulging against her waist or leg and she would consider taking things a little farther than she had taken them before, though she wouldn't end up doing so. And when they were done, both satisfied and exhausted, she would help him paint as they caught their breath. Making out took a lot out of them, it always had. But, in the end, they were always more than compensated for their efforts.

Part of her still wanted to make out with him. Hell, part of her wanted to fuck him, but she didn't have the mental wherewithal to pay those parts of her much attention. What she paid the most attention to was her growing fear and shame.

If she was in between black and white, if she was bisexual like she thought she might be, she would talk to Zoey later today and figure that out but now was not the time for it. Because she was still in the middle of them and it felt like a cheat, it felt like she was screwing over both Luke and Zoey.

Luke shook his head. "I chose orange for a specific reason. It was going to be this color regardless of what the rest of the house would be."

Dawn wanted to be out of the house within the minute but her curiosity didn't. "Why orange? Why not paint it your favorite color?" Luke responded fast and his face told her he was very passionate about the things he was saying.

"Orange symbolizes better things, like creativity, success, determination, attraction, happiness. Things that I need." He was looking at the walls and counting on his fingers, trying to remember all of the traits he had read, so he didn't notice when Dawn started crying. He did pick up on it when he heard her sniffle and dropped his roller and went to her aid. He put his arms on her shoulders and it felt like he was touching a wounded animal. "Hey, what's wrong? Orange isn't the *worst* color."

Dawn tried to laugh but her patience had reached its end. Enough was enough. The bandaid had to come off.

"I think we should take a break."

Silence. Awful, cold, mind reeling silence. Luke wanted to think she was joking, she had to be joking, but her crying said otherwise "You're serious." He didn't say it as a question, more as a way of assurance. Dawn nodded, still looking down, and Luke let his mind speak freely.

"Can I at least know why? I mean, I don't want to sound like an asshole, but I don't think I've done that much wrong. I've always protected you and respected you. I never forced you into doing anything you didn't want to or even...like, touched you when you didn't want me to. What could I have done?" He sat on his bed, mind running to find something that could have brought this fate upon him and his mind stopped running when Dawn replied.

"I know everybody says this, but it's not you, okay? It's me. I'm the one who needs time to think. You're a great guy. You deserve someone who has a better head on their shoulders. I want to be that person, but I'm not there yet. I just need some time to figure myself out. And of course I still care about you and will still help you if you need it., that will never change."

After a few seconds, Luke nodded and spoke while staring at the blue tarp coating the floor. "I think I'm going to find another ride to school on Monday."

They hadn't even been broken up for a minute and things were already descending into the bitterness Dawn had wanted to avoid. "Luke."

"I'm not mad. I just need some time to think, too. Are you okay with that?" He glanced up at her and the mixture of confusion and hate and longing he felt upon seeing her was so sickening he had to look back down. He really did need time to process this, he could barely even look at her right now.

"I am." She wiped the tears from her eyes and said something she hated saying. Something she would later think was a perfect example of the wrong thing at the wrong time. "The orange does look nice." Luke didn't respond and she left, not feeling much better. She got down to the first floor and, keeping her disgusted face hidden, ran into Luke's grandmother again. She didn't have the best eyesight so she didn't see Dawn's red puffy eyes, but she did see her.

"Oh, you're leaving already?"

"Yeah, we just had to talk about something small. It only took a little bit of time."

"Okay, honey, but you should come back soon."

Dawn nodded. "Maybe I will." She left the house as fast as she could while still attempting to look like she was keeping a normal pace. She got into her car and didn't pause to take in a breath or think. She just drove off toward home. She tried not to think during the drive and, somehow, was able to succeed at what had always been an impossible feat.

When she got home there was a note taped to the front door. She approached it and tore it off with an anger that almost caused the door itself to rattle. She was not in the mood for any other surprises today. She read the note aloud.

"Dawn. Went out. Will be home tomorrow. I told you I would give you a heads up next time. Stay safe. Cole." When she finished reading, she nodded, texted him her thanks and made her way to her bedroom.

She closed the door behind her and called Zoey. She answered before the first ring had finished.

"I take it you have a lot you want to talk about?"

It was quite the understatement but Dawn didn't tell her that. She assumed Zoey already knew. "Can you come over?"

"I'm on my way."

Chapter 20

On Monday morning, the two quartets had very similar conversations once they reached the school and parked in the student lot.

And unbeknownst to them all, the crescendo of tension began to rise.

"Okay, we need your ironclad word on this. You both need to keep this a secret from everyone. No matter what." Evan was looking between Heather and Trevor while he spoke but Amy's eyes were glued to Heather's and didn't move a centimeter throughout the entire conversation.

Heather, not interested in participating in Amy's staring contest, rolled her eyes and broke their shared gaze. "Evan, calm down. We said we won't tell anybody and we won't. What more do you want us to do to prove it?"

Amy's teeth almost shattered in her mouth. She separated the two rows before they could. "There's nothing you *can* do to prove it. We just need to trust each other." Heather gave that terrible smile and Amy, again, wished she had killed her on Friday.

"Don't you trust me, Amy?"

The feeling of contempt was something any one of them could have reached out and held in their hands, clear and solid as a rock. Evan tensed up, ready to catch Amy if she shot into the backseat to attack Heather and, judging by the hate her face was displaying, that was a very real possibility. Trevor kept silent and tried to stay as invisible as possible, the last thing he wanted was to be brought into this argument that was shifting from passive aggressive into outright aggressive. He pressed his lips together and attempted to become as small as possible, not easy for someone his size, but it didn't matter. Heather and Amy could only see each other. The rest of the world was black.

Heather was enjoying herself. Feeling Amy's anger pour out of her was like a wave of adrenaline entering her bloodstream and giving her a rush of energy. She felt like she could run a marathon. Amy wouldn't try another one of her violent stunts. She knew the consequences of such a brute action. She would have to restrain herself or risk Heather determining her future. Although Heather knew that, no matter what Amy said or did to her, Amy's future had already been carved into Heather's brain. She repeated herself. "Don't you trust me, Amy?" Her rage swept Heather off her feet and she almost giggled when she saw Amy's skin begin to turn pink.

"I trust you all right. It's what I trust you'll *do* that makes my blood boil." What was nothing more than an old saying for most was, in fact, very real for Amy. Lava was flooding through her body, reaching the surface and turning her skin into that special shade of pale pink. It felt like her skin was always pink and hot and painful now.

"What do you think I would do? We may have had our differences in the past but it's like you told me on Friday; This isn't a game anymore, it's our lives. Do you really think I would do something that would screw over your entire life and future?"

Heather's smile was smaller, but still there and still as superior and sadistic as ever. Amy wanted to rip her lips off and shred them in a blender. She took all of the strength she could possibly conjure up to fight against the volcano and did the one thing she had never done before.

Amy Cooper backed off.

"Let's go." Without waiting for a reply from anybody, she jumped out of the truck and slammed the door. She felt something wet on her face and, after touching the space between her nose and upper lip, wiped the blood on Evan's truck. It was a darker shade than his truck's red, but it would blend well enough. She wiped the rest of it onto her sleeve before anyone could see it and glanced around her at their new parking spot.

It was across the street from the school, hidden by trees that were a bit more naked now than they would have been in the summer but still did a good job obscuring the vehicle. The lot was near an old and seldom used baseball diamond and she assumed it was for the families of those who use to play ball here. The spot had been Evan's idea, hoping that parking away from everyone else would help them get away from school faster once the bell rang. Or in case something else happened that they needed a fast escape from. He didn't know what but he wanted to be prepared. Amy did, too.

The four of them headed into school. They passed Dawn's car but none noticed the girls inside. None of them cared. There was enough heavy hostility between the people in their own group, they didn't need four more girls to add to the weight.

"Does everyone still think it's a possibility that they might have done it?" Dawn asked after the four had walked past her car, into the school and out of sight. She looked from girl to girl and they answered as her eyes fell into theirs.

Zoey, across from her. "Yeah."

Myah to her diagonal right. "Yes."

Steph behind her. She took the longest to respond but eventually muttered an answer. "Yeah." But she wasn't finished there. If Dawn was going to imply that for students they went to school with every day were murderers, she needed to have a good reason for continuing to bring it up. "But what are you planning on doing about it?" She expected no response or an 'I don't know,' but what she got was much more real and straightforward.

"We tell Mr. Cleveland. All of us. Together. Today."

There was an odd level of confidence in her voice and Steph tried to reason with the outlandish idea. "I don't think that's a—"

"—Don't think. Listen. If we're right about this, we can save lives. Not just our own. And if we're wrong, no one will know it was us and we won't be at risk. There's no good reason why we shouldn't tell one person our theory. Because if we tell him and he tells the police, or if the police come to the school and want to talk to the four of them, they won't be able to get out of it. They'll have to talk. And if their stories don't line up or if one of them turns on the others, this whole mess will be over."

No one said anything for several seconds as they all thought over a situation that seemed too good to be true.

"When do you recommend we do it?" Zoey asked. She was on board with the idea, she just needed further instructions. Though the timing didn't matter to her. She would walk on broken glass at three in the morning if it meant putting Amy out of their lives. Or at least looking into her.

"As soon as we can. Ideally during first period."

"No," Myah popped out. The three heads all turned to her and she defended her opinion, feeling smaller than usual. "Maybe we should wait until last period. Just to better avoid any violent outcomes that could happen from doing it so early in the day and putting Amy's senses on high alert."

Dawn shook her head but conceded. She didn't think it was better to wait, giving the police just forty-five minutes to show up and question all four members of Amy's group didn't seem like enough time to get the answer they would need but Dawn wanted the three of them to be on her side and, if this was the sacrifice she would have to make, she was willing to do it. It was better than nothing. "Fine. We'll wait, but we have to do it today. And we all need to be there. More people, more proof, more reason to take what we say seriously."

"But there's no way of knowing if he will take us seriously."

She wondered why Steph was so against this plan, since she used to be the one most willing to go after Amy, but Dawn didn't have the time to ponder such a question. All of her time was now spent on getting Steph on the same page as the rest of them. "Steph, if a teenager was murdered and four of your students think it was someone who has shown many times in the past that they can be extremely dangerous, would you take it seriously?"

Steph answered Dawn's rhetorical question with the obvious answer. "Yes."

Dawn nodded. "We can't go soft. We need to explain everything we know."

Myah's eyebrows furrowed. "What *do* we know?"

"We know that there is a very high chance that Amy and her group may have killed Jonah. There aren't any facts that can be undisputed but, with everything we know about her, it should be enough for him to at least consider it. He'd have to be a fool not to." Dawn felt herself getting angry and extinguished the fire. Now wasn't the time or place to let it burn.

"What happened to Amy being a tornado that you get down and hide from?" Myah asked. She wasn't upset by Dawn's new, more direct approach, if anything she had been waiting for this since she saw Zoey's crooked toes, but it still surprised her how soon Dawn had turned on her previous outlook.

"She killed someone, she didn't twist a wrist or slap someone silly. Someone is dead because of her and that changes things. And I'm tired of hiding." She looked at Zoey and Zoey, understanding exactly what she meant, looked back with the same fear. When word did get out that Zoey was gay and Dawn was bi, something the two had talked about for a long time last night and now felt comfortable admitting to, though not yet verbally, neither of them wanted Amy around to figure out how this new information could be used against the two. She turned to each person in her car and said exactly what Amy had. "Let's go."

They all got out and went into the school, each thinking about the worst outcome that could arise from the oncoming situation. The beginning was different for each but all four saw the same ending: Amy with her hands around their throat.

Every class before last whipped by and before any of them could begin preparing themselves, Dawn texted the chat.

D: Everybody ready?

They were all in different classes but they could feel the apprehension from across the school. Each person answered.

M: Yes.

S: As ready as I'll ever be.

Z: Let's fuck this bitch up.

D: Leave your classes now. I'll meet you guys there.

Myah asked to see her guidance counselor, a common trick to leave class she had learned from Zoey, and went to the principal's office. Dawn, Zoey and Steph were waiting in the hall for her and the sight of them made her nerves increase a bit.

Dawn didn't give any preamble or assurances that they would be okay. Once Myah was beside her she opened the door and walked in, keeping her eyes on her principal as he three girls followed. He had been writing something by hand but at the sight of the four he dropped his pen and sat up a bit straighter.

"Yes? What can I do for you all?"

His voice sounded helpful but there was a trace of annoyance hiding under it that Myah picked up on. She was used to authority figures talking to her like she was causing problems before she had the chance to open her mouth, both at home and at her old school.

Dawn sat in the chair opposite her principal and didn't sugar-coat anything. "I think Amy Cooper may be responsible for what happened to Jonah Dunbar." Her principal stared at her with stunned silence and she added, "All of us do."

His eyes met with each pair in the room and each head nodded. "What makes you all think so?"

Dawn sat up, her elbows on the armrests and her hands joined above her lap. "Well, you know Amy. I'm sure she's spent more time in this office than you yourself have."

His eyebrows rose at the thought of the dozens of times he had sat Amy Cooper into the chair across from him and made her tell him what she did and why. At first he had been aware of the fights she started, and finished, and who they were with but, after a while, they became so plentiful and similar that he waited to get that information from Amy herself when she was hauled into his office by the Dean, breathing heavy, fire in her eyes and her skin an unhealthy discolored pink. Amy Cooper was the sole reason that, starting next year, any fights that broke out between students would be remedied with an automatic expulsion.

"Yes, I know about Amy. What does she have to do with Jonah?"

Dawn squinted her eyes and continued straight toward the goal. "You know how violent she is. And Jonah Dunbar treated everyone like dirt, including her. So we think that she might have gotten her hands on him and,

Don't hold back.

killed him."

His face told a story of a conflicted man, torn between a claim easy to disagree with and a claim that had years of injuries to back it up. "And you all think this?"

Zoey answered first. Everyone in the room turned to look at her before she did out of their sheer certainty that she would. "She's gotten worse this year. It's more likely now than it ever has been before. I'm wearing these," she gestured to her crutches, "because of her. And…other people have had things like this happen to them." She refrained from mentioning Dawn's name. She wanted her to decide when she was ready to share what had happened.

Steph tossed in her two cents to keep things rolling in the correct direction. "Zoey's right. She's been out of control recently."

They all looked at Myah and, in spite of her handicap, she added to the conversation. "I mean, I've only known of her for a few weeks but, from what I've seen and experienced, she doesn't seem very well." She thought about the nine inch, four line scratch that she still had clawed across her back. It had faded, but only a minuscule amount.

He nodded at the group. "I understand."

They waited for him to say more and he didn't. And after a few more unsettling seconds Zoey, who was starting to feel like this situation might not be as easy as Dawn had made it out to be, got the ball rolling again. "So, is there anything you plan on doing about this? About her? Are you going to look into her or tell the police to?"

Jackson Cleveland, familiar with these types of situations, fell back onto his often used strategy for conflict resolution. One that, any high schooler would tell you, only adults believed could ever be successful. "Who do you think it was exactly?"

Dawn answered fast, as if she was running out of time. "Amy and probably Evan, Heather and Trevor."

He knew the three that Amy went around with and he didn't need last names to pin them down.

"All right then, I will look into this and see if they were associated with what happened." The four students sighed with relief and he wondered how much more relieved they would be once they could put this whole mess behind them. Dawn got onto her feet and they moved toward the door, but he stopped them before anyone could put their hands on the knob and escape. "Hold on for a second, girls. We're not done quite yet." The looks of confusion and wariness from all four of them reminded him of an animal that just spotted a predator.

"Why? What's left to do?" The conversation was beginning to break out of the simple mold she had expected it to stay in and Myah felt an immediate fear seize her feeble body.

He held out his finger, a *hold on*, and reached for the intercom. He held down the button to turn it on and spoke one sentence that made the four girls who stood in front of him look sick.

"Could Amy Cooper, Evan Mitchell, Heather Grey and Trevor Logan please report to the principal's office. Thank you." He looked from the microphone to the girls. For the first time, none of them said anything. They just stared at each other, having a contest to see who could look the most terrified. He did his best to ease their nerves. "We're just going to have a simple, civilized discussion on the subject and then the four of you can get some closure."

He watched them all move to the far side of the room, standing side by side like a makeshift wall. They were all still silent. He didn't know what they were thinking but he could see that whatever confidence they may have had before had disappeared. He could understand why. It was entirely possible that their plan was falling apart before their eyes.

Less than a minute after his announcement, the four students he had called down stormed inside and their makeshift wall crumbled a bit.

The first one to notice the four girls standing on the other side of the room was Amy, who stopped dead and locked eyes with Poodle. The rest of them, one by one, noticed the girls and looked to their principal with fear or anger. Or, in Heather's case, excitement. Before anyone said anything to each other, Principal Cleveland set the stage.

"Here's why I called you four down here. Dawn, Zoey, Stephanie and Myah think the four of you had a hand in what happened to Jonah Dunbar."

Amy's hand latched onto Evan's and she held them behind her back to avoid anyone taking note of her sudden movement. Her eyes didn't leave Poodle's. Evan did the talking for the four of them.

"How could it have been us? None of us were near the area where he died." He tried to sound calm but it was difficult when he knew that every word he said was important. And a single word could ruin everything. Principal Cleveland asked the question he was anticipating and was ready to answer.

"Then where were the four of you that day?"

"Amy and I were at my house. It was too cold to do anything outside so we stayed in for the day."

"And you two?"

Amy and Evan looked at the two next to them and were prepared for everything to unfurl.

Heather loved their looks, and the temptation to drown the two was in her mind, but she chose not to. Though she didn't plan on letting them know that. She winked at Amy and saw her shake her head in a last-ditch effort for mercy. "Trevor and I did the same. We stayed at my house during the day just like these two lovers did. We talked about our futures and planned accordingly." She motioned her hand towards her principal, "You're always telling us to get our futures in line, figure out the colleges we want to go to and what our majors will be and all that. That's what we did. And probably what Evan and Amy did, too. We're smarter than you give us credit for. We're always one step ahead." Heather may have been untrustworthy but those last two sentences were nothing but the truth.

Principal Cleveland sat at his desk, satisfied and a little relieved.

He, as well as the guidance counselors and teachers he worked with, did always tell students that it was important to prepare for their futures and it looked as though their words had finally gotten through to a few people. Important people, too. Overall, he was content with how this situation unfolded and he didn't see a reason not to be. "Well then, I think that wraps this up. You are free to g—"

"—No it does not wrap this up. It doesn't wrap up a damn thing." He turned his head to the voice that cut him off.

"Zoey, that's—" She cut him off again.

"You seriously believe that? Give me a break, that doesn't prove us wrong. It doesn't prove anything. They're good liars, credit where it's due, but that's the only real thing we've learned."

Amy felt her volcano start to fill with lava and she squeezed Evan's hand tighter. He looked at her and, understanding what she meant, held her back. His left hand on her left arm and right on her hip, and it got progressively harder to keep her in place with each word she said.

"What makes you think we did it anyway?"

"You fucking kidding me?"

"Do I look it?"

Zoey smiled at her and could only hope that she looked half as angry as she felt. "Call me crazy, but I think it's likely that the same person who attacks people for asinine reasons, has been out of school more than she has been in it, and," Zoey looked at Dawn and kept the secret hidden for a little while longer. "And is getting more violent every day might have something to do with the murder of someone who she hated. Again, I'm no genius, but I know a thing or two about putting pieces together. And honey, we've got one hell of a puzzle in the works."

"Everybody hated him. There's no way to prove it was me, or any of us." She tilted her head and turned the tide. "In fact, I'm sure you all hated him, too. Or three of you, at least." She brushed a hand at Myah like she was insignificant. "Who's to say you didn't do it? You could just pin it on us because we're easy targets and get away with it like that." She could feel the lava in her blood, burning her alive and she tried to fight against it. Tried as hard as she could to not give into its acidic calling. She pressed her teeth together and clenched her toes, the way a child acts when getting a shot, and she eventually slowed its course. She took a deep breath and lessened her grip on Evan. She had accomplished what she needed to. They weren't the only suspects now. Now there were three girls who had just as much motivation as Amy had. "Can we leave, because this is honestly a waste of all of our time. Including yours." She tilted her chin toward her principal and he shrunk in his seat. She watched him stand up, probably attempting to feel more authoritative and spoke to the four wrongly accused students.

"I agree. I think it's time we end this discussion. You four," he motioned to Amy's group and felt a severe amount of hatred rise and linger in the air, "are free to go." They all left in seconds and he turned to look at the other side of the room. "You all can go as well."

But Zoey, not ready to go, continued to try to plead her case. "You have to believe—"

But to no avail.

"—Zoey that's enough. You all still have one more class before the day is over and I need you to go to it. I'm sorry if this didn't go the way you wanted it to but I can't simply call the police on one of my students because another student wants me to. I've worked with many people your age over the course of my life and you'd be surprised how many of them set each other up and try to get each other in trouble for petty, pointless reasons. Now please," He opened the door for them and they left, walking like they were on their way to the electric chair.

Once the door was closed, Zoey took the group away from anyone who could be in potential earshot and expressed the frustration that was clawing to be released.

"That's fucking bullshit! We all know it!"

Myah tried to calm Zoey down. If she got any louder it wouldn't matter how far away their principal was, everyone in school would know their location. "Look, Zoey, we tried to tell him, he didn't believe us. Maybe we were wrong about all of this from the start. It's not like we had any proof."

Zoey shook her head in furious denial. "No, we weren't wrong. Not about one goddamn detail. All they said was that they didn't do it and they got off like that. Does that seem fair?" She stomped her crutch on the floor as if it were her foot.

Dawn sighed. It wasn't. She looked down at her feet and brushed a hand against her stomach. "So we're not going to get help from anybody at school, right?"

"Right," Zoey said, almost yelled, and Myah and Steph agreed in less abrasive ways.

Dawn nodded and continued, her cold voice contrasting Zoey's flaming temper. "And will any of your parents help you if you ask or will they think you're overreacting or making something up?" She watched the three of them look down in thought and back up with their answer. She didn't need them to say it. She could read their answers on their faces and they could hers. Her voice was cold and, now, angry. "We get in my car after the bell and go straight to the police."

"Really?" Steph asked. She had seen Dawn in various emotional states before, high and low, but this one was new.

"It's our only option unless we murder her ourselves."

The three of them looked at her and didn't see any apprehension, to either idea, on her face.

"I vote police," Myah said and was relieved when Steph and Zoey agreed with her.

Dawn nodded. "I'll meet you at my car after the bell." Then, without another word, she turned around and walked back to class. She wasn't afraid. In truth, she was furious.

As was Zoey, who thought back to her idiot principal the second Dawn was out of sight. She turned to Steph and Myah and gestured her crutch in the general direction of his office. "Can you believe he didn't take our side? Steph is the only one of us who didn't get attacked and that's somehow not enough proof for him."

Steph caught something in Zoey's bitter rambling and thought it over. She wasn't surprised that Zoey didn't know about her altercation with Amy, that had been intentional, but as far as Steph was aware, she was not the only one to be spared from Amy's psychosis. Dawn had been, too. Or, at least, that's what Steph had thought.

A stomach ache?

"Wait a minute Zoey," Steph said and she could already feel her anger rising. "What do you mean I was the only one who didn't get attacked? What about Dawn?"

All of the days, all of the promises, all of the tears she and Dawn spilled over this and Zoey was still unable to fully think before she spoke. *Nice job dipshit*, she thought, *the one thing you were supposed to keep under wraps, you let slip out.*

Steph gave her a few seconds, hoping Zoey would cough up the truth and make this easier for everyone. After those seconds had passed and Zoey was still silent, Steph gave her a little vocal motivation. "Zoey?"

"I didn't...that's not what...nothing—"

"—ZOEY!"

Steph's voice took away her mumbling and replaced it with nothing. Zoey couldn't talk, she could barely even think.

"What happened between Dawn and Amy? I need you to tell me."

Her words weren't what gave Zoey chills. It was the tone. As if she was holding back an overwhelming urge to attack her, wanting to so badly that her arm might lash out independent of her brain's instruction. Her composure was falling away and leaving her untamed. Untamed with only Zoey in her sight.

Zoey lied, although she knew the odds of it sounding convincing was near impossible. "Nothing happened between them. I swear."

"I didn't ask for a lie, I asked for the truth. And I need it. Now." She seemed in control of herself but that could change at any time and Zoey figured that deflecting the issue would cause it.

"I...I can't tell you. Dawn made me promise to keep it a secret. And she's fine now, it stopped hurting." That was the wrong word to use and Zoey realized it as soon as she said it.

Implying that Dawn had been hurt by Amy only made Steph press harder. "Zoey, Dawn isn't here and we don't have to tell her we know. But if Amy hurt her, you need to tell us." Zoey still seemed to have difficulty doing what she did best, talking, and Steph decided to share her own little secret.

"Did I tell you about what happened to me a few days ago when you went to Dawn's house to talk to her?" As she expected, Zoey jumped at the idea of discussing a different topic. She would find out soon enough that this topic was related to the one she was trying to avoid.

"No, what happened?"

Steph took a step closer to her to make sure she was the only person Zoey would be able to see. "Amy dragged me into the woods up the street and whipped me with her belt. She whipped me until I bled and then they left me lying in the snow."

Both Zoey and Myah turned as pale as the snow Steph had been dropped in. Zoey asked, "Why didn't you tell us?"

Steph shrugged as if she had done nothing wrong. In addition to the shame, she had been a little too busy thinking about getting Dawn the help she needed that she didn't give herself the same amount of thought. And her damage had already started to heal, she was fine. Dawn, however, was not. "It's frustrating isn't it, Zoey? When someone is hurt and you aren't able to help them. The only difference is that I'm okay now. But is Dawn?"

"Yes she is, I already told you that."

"That means there's no harm in you telling us what happened to her, right? If she's okay, we've got nothing to worry about."

Zoey looked to Myah and Myah nodded, sympathetic to her situation but not on Zoey's side either. "We're only trying to help her, Zoey. It's for the best that you tell us. It'll be okay in the end."

Zoey began to get teary eyed, being in the middle of her friends, one pulling her left arm and two pulling her right. And no one was there to help her. She had to make the decision right now. She fought against herself for what seemed like hours and eventually settled on who's pull would be stronger. She took a deep fearful breath, wiped away the tears that were starting to form and spoke in a shaky voice.

"Just keep in mind that she's okay now."

Steph nodded, though Zoey thought her continued patience was due to the fact that she was now getting her way.

"Last Friday. Not the one that just passed, the one before it, Amy...carved the word whore onto Dawn's stomach. With a knife. The scar was there for a few days but I think it's fading." She breathed out, a quiet sigh of relief upon letting the secret into the air but tensed up again when she realized where the air would take the secret. And to who. She looked at Steph and saw her skin start to turn red, something she had never seen in real life and especially not from someone of color. Clearly her warning had gone over Steph's head.

Through clenched teeth and clamped eyes she growled, "How big is it?"

Zoey thought back to the last time she had seen it and came up with an accurate estimate. She kept her eyes on the floor. "Lengthwise it's from one side of her stomach to the other. About four inches tall. Steph, please don't be mad at me. I promised her I wouldn't tell you. She didn't want me to and I was—"

"—I'm not mad.

Maybe you should specify.

At *you*."

Zoey let out another sigh and the sides of her lips curled up. "Really?"

Steph opened her eyes and glared at her.

She dropped the corners back down.

"Really."

Steph was mad, fuming in fact, but she knew better than to explode it all on Zoey. She should have given them the information when she got it, but Steph knew that Dawn and Zoey had a connection that was more special than what either of them had with her and she knew that Zoey kept promises for as long as she could. Zoey was safe, for now at least. There was someone much more deserving of the hate and rage Steph was experiencing.

The girl who broke Zoey's toes, the girl who whipped her with a belt, the girl who clawed into Myah's back on her first day without knowing anything about her, the girl who scared and beat Kaitlin Simon out of their school. And now, the girl who carved a fucking word into the stomach of someone who had never even done anything to her. This was it, the final straw. She needed to learn that you can't go around fucking up whoever you want and getting away with it. All four of them needed to know that. And they would, Steph would make certain of it. "We need to do something about them. This has gotten too fucking out of hand."

"Steph, you're scaring me."

"You're scared of *me*, Zoey? Not the girl who broke your toes in one motion and didn't even give you a fucking passing glance?"

Zoey didn't answer.

"Myah, how much time is left until school lets out?"

Myah hastily looked at her phone and was satisfied by what she said. "Sixteen minutes."

"Great." A positive word said with sarcastic disgust. Steph continued looking at Zoey and when Zoey appeared to be slinking away, she grabbed her hand. "This has to stop. Today."

Zoey made her limp hand grasp Steph's shaking one. Quietly, she muttered, "I agree." Then she got louder and met Steph's eyes. "What are we supposed to do? I thought we already had a plan?"

"We're still going to do that, we just need to give Amy what she's been giving everyone else first. Before it's too late." Steph gave Zoey a tough, coarse smile which far from eased Zoey's nerves.

Steph spoke with a palpable passion lingering in the air around her, like the glow from a torch. "She's going to pay. For the first time, Amy is going to get what she fucking deserves."

Myah and Zoey didn't ask any other questions, Steph looked just about ready to pop and they didn't want to say anything that might cause her to. They had no idea what Steph had in mind but deep down, despite the parts of themselves saying it was a bad idea and the crippling feeling that something bad was near inevitable, they didn't care. Regardless of what Steph did, Amy was going to get what she deserved when the cops came knocking. That was all that mattered. And, in the meantime, they wouldn't hold Steph back. If the temptation grew too strong, they wouldn't hold themselves back either.

If any of them had known what would happen when Steph threw that first punch, they never would have let her out of their sight.

Chapter 21

"Did you say something? Did you fucking say something?" Amy had Heather pressed against the wall and now Heather was starting to push back. If Heather pushed too hard or started getting too arrogant, she'd knock her unconscious, Amy had decided it, but Heather only pushed enough to bring her hands to her upper body in the likely event that she would need to use them.

"No I didn't fucking tell anyone, back off." She struggled against Amy's strength and was able to send her a few inches back, but before Amy could hit her, Evan swooped in and held her arms by her side.

He whispered into her ear. "Calm down. She didn't tell anyone. She wouldn't."

Amy spoke much louder and kept her eyes on Heather the entire time. "I don't know that. I don't know what she would say. She's been on her own for the whole damn day, she's had a fuck ton of time to think about it. And more time to do it."

Heather scoffed. "Yeah, I could have, but I didn't. And if I was going to, I wouldn't have done it like that."

Evan had to hold Amy with much more strength now. She talked a mile a minute but made sure every word was crystal clear. "I swear, Heather, if you say one fucking word about it, I'll—"

But Heather was tired of the charade. "You'll kill me, yeah. I've heard this story before."

"You keep this up and that story is gonna be more real than you think."

"Shut up! Both of you!" All this back and forth, Amy verses Heather bullshit was getting old and Trevor was the only one seeing the situation through the right lens. "Can we stop and think about what just happened for a second?" All three looked at him with the same lack of knowledge and he told them what they should have already figured out. "We were only called in there because of them. Dawn, Zoey, Steph and Myah. They were the ones who said something, not any of us. They're the reason why we had to defend ourselves, why Cleveland thought, for a second, that we might have had something to do with what happened. You're all so desperate to cut people to pieces that you're ignoring the people who are literally right in front of you. Don't any of you understand that? Since when did I become the smartest member of this group?"

Amy felt like a part of her brain had been unclogged and a flood of knowledge, important knowledge, was filling her mind. "Don't worry, you won't hold that title for long." She wormed her way out of Evan's arms. "But you're right. None of us did anything." She looked at Heather. "Because we all know the punishment. It was *them*."

Heather, intrigued by this promise of violence, asked, "So what are we going to do about them?"

"We aren't going to do anything." She watched the six eyebrows leap up and she rolled her eyes. Was it really that strange for her to resist confrontation?

Ask any person, student or otherwise, in their school and the answer was a resounding yes.

"It's a bad idea to attack them half an hour after they accused us of murder? An accusation that isn't wrong, either. It makes us all look even more guilty. We need to let this one go until this whole Jonah thing blows over. Once this all passes, I might take care of them but, until then, nothing. All right?" They all nodded and Amy felt like she was back in the driver's seat. Her rightful place amongst her group. "Let's just head back to our classes and wait until the bell rings."

Heather grimaced at the idea. "I don't think so. I'll be at the main entrance. I'll meet you guys at Evan's truck." She walked down the hall and with every step, felt herself getting deeper and deeper into unforeseen territory. Like someone entering a dark, seemingly empty, cave with no knowledge of what was awaiting them within it.

The three in her group and the four opposing it understood that feeling.

No one stopped her from leaving, no one felt compelled to have her company. Once she was gone, they looked at each other, exhausted, and left without saying anything. Thirteen minutes were left and, despite none of them planning to do any work, they all knew it was safer to head back to class.

Every decision mattered now. Every decision made an enormous difference in their futures. One slip up and they were all convicted.

Just like that. They had to be extremely careful from now on.

Amy would be the exact opposite in twenty minutes.

Steph ignored Zoey and Myah while they waited in the hall for the bell to ring. She knew they were saying something, but they sounded muffled. She didn't mind though. In fact, that was what she needed. She needed to be alone in her head to make sure her anger and strength would be full and ready when that two-thirty bell rang and all bets were off.

There were seven minutes now.

She liked the feeling of not knowing what would come next or how. In situations like these, thinking would only get in the way. Actions had to take charge and everything else had to be left at the door. If Amy wanted to see how tough she was, Steph would show her. She would show her until Amy blacked out. In the middle of her fantasy the bell rang and she was moving before it silenced. "Come on." She walked past the two of them toward the main entrance and what Zoey said didn't slow her for a second.

"Steph, what are we going to do about Dawn? She'll be waiting by her car for us."

"You two go and stay with her while I take care of the problem."

The three of them burst out the front doors, Myah and Zoey trailing behind Steph and when she stopped they almost ran into her. Myah walked in front of Steph to make sure she wasn't frozen in time and once she saw Steph's face she followed her eyes to see Heather who was heading, no doubt, to Evan's truck. Steph kept her eyes on Heather but spoke to Myah and Zoey.

"Go to Dawn's car. One will bring the rest. One is all I need."

Zoey popped up next to Myah, her eyes filled with worry. "Wait, Steph, you can't take on all four of them. And you know you can't attack Amy with none of them getting in the way."

There was that overthinking again. Getting in the way, just as Steph knew it would. "Get to Dawn's car. If you're so scared then keep your eyes on me." She stormed off toward Heather and left Myah and Zoey where they stood. They weren't planning on going to Dawn's car. They would stay right where they were, where they had a perfect view of Steph. Though perfect might have been a bit too flowery of a word to use, seeing as how today Evan had parked his truck across the street in a small lot shielded by trees But, from where they stood, they could still see Steph and, farther down, Heather.

With every foot Steph stamped into the dirt, Myah and Zoey felt more uneasy.

Zoey knew this feeling and wanted to know if Myah knew it, too. "Do you feel weird?" Myah nodded and Zoey felt more assured and afraid.

"Yeah. There's this sickening feeling in the pit of my stomach. It's not stress or worry, it's more like...danger. Like a highway sign warning you of an accident up ahead. You know what I mean?"

"Yeah, perfectly." Neither of them heard Dawn come up behind them among the crowds of students that passed by but, in a way, they felt her presence.

Before Dawn could say anything they both turned around. It was a little odd, but she pushed the shock and confusion out of her head. "Hey, where's Steph?" They both looked down the road and Dawn's unflinching cold anger returned when she saw Steph talking to Heather. "What is she doing?"

"She wants to give Amy what she deserves. I think we all know what that means." Zoey looked at Dawn and held her hand. It was cold and hard. Dawn looked like she was in a trance, frozen in place, and when Zoey touched her she snapped out of it.

She looked from Zoey to Myah. "Then what are we doing over here?"

"I don't think we should get involved unless things get worse," Myah said. She knew things would but held out a small amount of optimism that they wouldn't. When Steph punched Heather across the face and knocked her back, Myah's optimism was knocked back as well.

Her hand hurt after the hit, but Steph only let the pain become additional motivation. She flexed her fingers and curled them back into the fist they were more comfortable forming. She was almost grateful that Evan's truck had been parked in this shitty extra lot. Technically it was off school property, no one else had parked here, and barely anyone could see them unless they stood within the right doorway of space. And everyone else was so busy getting on their bus, buses that were also arranged to block this parking lot from view, or into their car or walking home that no one was even glancing across the street into the tree studded parking lot. It was perfect.

"You fuck with my friends and you pay for it." She grabbed Heather by the sides of her shoulders and hoisted her up to eye level. What Steph saw made her want to knock every one of her teeth out, one by one. *She's laughing. The bitch is laughing.* That was the last thing Steph allowed herself to process. From now on her brain would take a backseat and her hands and feet would take the wheel. She brought her fist back and shot it forward as hard as she could. She expected the pain to be even worse once her hand connected with Heather's head, but it didn't. Because she never hit Heather's head. Heather's smile had dropped and she caught Steph's hand in hers, no more than an inch from her face.

She shrugged off Steph's other hand that tried to restrain her shoulder and, in one motion, Heather squeezed away the fist and turned Steph's fingers into a limp mess that looked like small, crisscrossing tentacles. She pressed hard and Steph's thumb and pinky finger touched, pushing the bones in Steph's hand into each other and making her fingers immobile. Steph tried to pull away and Heather tightened the grip. With enough strength she thought she could snap her bones like pencil lead. She looked into the scared girl's eyes and hoped she was horrified by the eyes she saw looking back.

"You've never been in a fight, you've never won one, you never will. You can't hold your own, even against one person. You really are nothing." Her right hand swung out and two of her knuckles cracked against Steph's cheekbone and sent her smacking against the dirt. Heather was one to savor moments like these, unlike Amy, so she let Steph get back up before she hit her again. Heather backed her head up an inch to avoid the clumsy attempted punch from Steph, slithered behind her and wrapped her arm around the girl's throat. She held her right elbow in place with her left arm and pressed as hard as she could. The girl went down and Heather knew that no amount of squirming or frantic movements were going to release her grip.

"Fuck, she needs our help. Myah, take these." She gave the girl her crutches and Myah almost gave them back.

"Zoey, you're already hurt."

The busses were beginning to pull out and soon enough the three of them would be the only people left outside.

"If we sit around waiting Steph could be dead. And I'm not letting that happen." After dropping her crutches to the concrete, Zoey ran as fast as she could, at first trying to accommodate for her toes before giving up and letting the pain fuel her. She ran as if there was no splint at all and, if the searing pain from her toes was any sign, she would have to wear that splint and those crutches for much longer than initially expected.

Heather pulled Steph's head up and whispered into her ear, "You want to know what I'm thinking right now?" She took the gagging as a yes and continued. "All I'm thinking about is whether or not I'll choke you until you're unconscious or until you're dead. I haven't decided yet but I think I'll just choke you for as long as I want to, maybe as long as it takes me to get off, and let the chips fall where they may." She smiled at the thought. "How does that sound?" The wet spitting and hoarse breathing made the smile bigger. "Sounds good to me, too."

Steph's eyes were turning red and beginning to bulge. She choked on her own saliva. She couldn't feel her legs and her arms were starting to fall off and join them. She tried to think of anything that would make her feel better and she could only see Heather's demonic grin. And could only hear the fact that not every fruit that grew on the tree was fresh. Now she would never get the chance to prove him wrong. She would live rotten and die rotten. Just like the other two, wherever they were. While her last breaths were being delivered a few tears fell out with them. Things got dark and Steph realized that she didn't need to prove anything anymore. Things were getting easier now. She just had to let go and everything would be better, everything would cease. Heather got to her feet and squeezed her throat tighter. Steph let go.

Zoey leaped onto Heather's back and wrapped her own arms around the girl's throat. "GET THE FUCK OFF HER, YOU FREAK!" She pulled her weight back and Heather fell back with her. Or rather, fell back onto her, letting go of Steph in the process. Heather's body pushed down on Zoey's stomach and forced the air out of her lungs. Though Zoey still didn't let go of Heather's neck. And she wouldn't, at least until Steph was breathing again. Watching her wheeze on the ground for air, taking in massive craggly gasps as she writhed in the dirt, made Zoey tighten her grip even more.

Amy, Evan and Trevor waited for each other by the main doors and shortly after heading outside, noticed the commotion between Heather, Zoey and Steph. By this point, most of the buses and accompanying students had left. If any of them looked to their right they would have noticed Dawn and Myah standing a few yards away but they were all too preoccupied.

"God, that bitch! We said we weren't going to do anything like this twenty fucking minutes ago." Amy took in a breath, channeled her frustration and tried to find a simple and smart solution to this problem. After only a few seconds of thinking, the lightbulb went off. She smiled as she said it. It felt right, satisfying, almost poetic in a way. "Let's leave her." She began to walk towards Evan's truck, aware that she was going to have to walk right past Heather to do it and reveling in that thought, when Trevor's meaty hand grabbed her arm and her smile was taken from her.

"We can't just leave her here like that." Amy's rivalry with Heather had to take a break at some point and, regardless of what the two felt towards each other, Heather was their friend. She was his friend. He didn't know if they were more than that, but that didn't matter right now. Right now, his friend was being strangled. He pulled Amy's skinny arm toward him and she slipped out of his hand like soap during a shower.

"Take your fucking hand off me! She did this to herself. We aren't her bodyguards."

"But she needs our help. She deserves it." He turned and ran to the battle between the three that would soon become four. Then six. Then eight.

Evan yelled, "Trevor, wait." Then to himself, mumbled, "Dammit." He looked at Amy and saw that she was turning pink. Any second he expected her one to start bleeding. He was afraid to, but he told her what he knew she didn't want to hear. "We have to help them."

She looked at him and her black eyes were nearly shaking, thrumming with some dark and furious electricity.

Heather was stronger than Zoey had expected and she had gotten to her feet with Zoey's still hanging off her back like a cape. She thrashed and whirled her body but Zoey kept her internal vow to keep her arms around her neck. She was flung around like a rag doll, her foot smacking against the frozen dirt, and her toes sent out a shockwave of pain that ran through her body with every hit. She wanted to let go and calm down the splintering pain, but her vow kept her arms locked where they were. Steph was right, Zoey did keep her promises. She turned the agony into a grimace and held her ground. Ground that she, most of the time, wasn't touching. Steph had been breathing fine for a while but that didn't mean shit now. Now it was about shutting Heather down. Unconscious or otherwise.

Zoey loosened her grip and planned to tighten it further when, in the instant she was at her most vulnerable place, two hands crawled in between her stomach and Heather's back, ripped the two of them apart and flung Zoey toward the much more unappealing hard brown surface. She hit hard, the right side of her head smacking against the dirt and her foot doing the same. When things came into focus and stopped looking blurry, she noticed a foot coming down onto her stomach and she rolled into a small patch of grass to avoid it. The grass felt like heaven, even with some snow still spread out in spots. She tried to shake the pain in her head away and heard a deep voice over the ringing. It was barely audible.

"Hour the toes or?"

She saw Trevor swing his leg back and had the time to translate what she had heard into what he had said (*How are the toes, whore?*) but not the time she needed to evade him. His foot hit her with full force in the worst place.

Myah put her hands to her mouth and leaked out a tear as she heard Zoey's blood thickening shriek. "Okay, we need to get them out of there." She looked at Dawn, who still appeared frozen, and Myah debated whether she would be able to take care of this on her own. "Let's go."

Dawn looked at her and felt Myah shrink away. "If I go over there, I'm not going to be able to control myself."

Myah took her hands and looked deep into her blue eyes. "That's fine with me, we just have to make sure Zoey and Steph are safe. We need to get them out off there before we can go to the cops. And, if we land a few hits on Heather and Trevor, so be it. Make them wish they didn't give you that scar."

Dawn glared at her, but it looked the same way Dawn felt; more confused than angry. "How do you—"

"—Dawn, please, now is not the time. Time is the one thing we don't have. We need to help them. Now." Dawn nodded and that was all Myah needed. She pulled her along, afraid she would hang back if Myah let go, but after three feet, Dawn was in front, leading Myah to the four of them. Myah took Heather and Dawn took Trevor.

"No, no way. Fuck them." Amy clenched her fists and felt the lava coming down her body, slow but consistent.

"Amy, I know it's better to stay out of sight but right now, the two of them are only making things worse for all four of us. We just need to get them out of there and we'll be fine, okay? We can leave just like that."

"No, if you drag me over there, I'm not going to play savior. I'm not going to drag them away and leave it at that. You drag me over there and I'm unloading everything I have on anyone I can. I want you to know that." Evan squinted and smiled. For an instant, the first instant in her life, she wanted to knock that smile off his face.

"Who says I didn't?" He took her hand and kissed her cheek. "As long as no one is around and no one will be able to see us, maybe I want to do the same thing." He licked his lips to relieve the burning and pulled her towards the six of them. She zoomed off in front of him and he broke a sweat trying to catch up. As he knew she would, she launched herself at Dawn like a lion and rolled with the girl for almost ten feet. Trevor was now handling Zoey, Dawn was more than occupied with Amy and Heather was taking on both Steph and Myah. But she was starting to lose. Evan took the opportunity and went for the one he knew he could handle. He kicked out her legs and Myah, after slamming down on the ground, turned her body over to face him and did the same thing. She was equally successful.

As soon as he hit the grass she climbed on top of him and swung her hands at everything she could. For a blade of grass like her, she packed a decent punch. But after a few too many hits, he caught her hands at the wrists and her weight became his advantage.

He scrunched his body into a ball, put his feet under her stomach, kicked straight up and pulled her arms over his head. She flew over him like a sheet and landed with a cold thud against the hard dirt.

"Get off of me, you fat fucking prick." Zoey was sure her toes were going to be broken for many more months now and the pain from the kick was still burning, but the person who was pinning her down with his knees on the left and right sides of her body took precedence. He put his hand over her mouth and leaned down to her face. Their noses were touching.

"What's the big deal? You're used to being in this position by now aren't you? You're in it ten times a fucking day, why should now be any different? Is it because I'm bigger than the guys you usually ride? Well don't worry about that, slut, because I'll be able to do you just as well." He put his hand under her shirt, on her tit, and pulled it out of the bra that only covered the lower half. It felt better than Heather's and not just because it was bigger and tanner. It felt more supple and juicy.

She struggled more but she had a human cinder block resting on the lower half of her body and it's rough, fat hands were covering both her mouth and left breast. She had no idea how far Trevor was going to go, all she knew was that she needed it to stop. She used the anger and turned it into strength. It was almost enough to save her. Trevor noted her thrusting herself up and almost laughed.

"Wow, you really do want this huh?" She rocked her head back and forth and he held it in place. "Now that I think of it, I'm sure I'm not the biggest guy you've done. After all, I'm smaller than every male teacher. And I'm most likely smaller than your father."

That single word doomed him.

The single second long image of her father made Zoey bite her tongue. Then she realized there was something better to sink her teeth into.

She bit his hand. And didn't let go. Even after he took it away from her mouth. He leaned backwards and she followed him, praying that her teeth would meet and his blood would spill into her mouth. Once he fell onto his back, she spit the taste of Trevor into the grass beside her and smacked the glasses off of his head. Part one was finished, now came part two.

She got to her feet, looked down at her still throbbing toes and decided to let her poor foot have a little rest. She had two after all, and the other one was bound to be stronger.

Zoey closed her eyes, gritted her teeth in anticipation, and swung her leg into Trevor's massive gut. It didn't hurt. She smiled and kicked him again. And again. Enjoying the lack of pain each time. Eventually she stopped thinking altogether. She kicked harder.

"You should have just stayed at whatever uptight school you came from."

Myah laughed. "I don't think so. I'm glad I came here. Even in spite of all the shit your four idiots put us through." She found it fascinating that she wasn't scared of him, or what might happen to her. He couldn't have been more than six feet away, but he would still have to charge her before he could hit her. In other words, he would give her some time to dodge him. "And you should just stick to following Amy's orders, you pathetic fucking pet. Clearly doing your own thinking isn't your strong suit."

Evan didn't want to hit her but he at least wanted to shut her up. He ran at her and she, like a delicate dancer, slipped to the side and kicked in the back of his legs once he was past. He dropped to his knees and she slammed her foot into his back, knocking him to the ground.

Sometimes it came in handy to be small and quick. She put her knees on his back and pulled his head up by his chin. She leaned closer and forced his head higher, hoping she was straining his scrawny throat. "And now I'm glad that your stupid obsession with hurting people is going to finally bite you in the ass." She shoved his face back into the dirt but before she could continue ramming his head against the ground, her weight became her disadvantage yet again.

Evan got to his hands and knees and launched himself up, knocking Myah off of him and back to the dirt. They both wondered how long the other would be able to keep this up.

The crescendo hadn't reached its peak yet. But it was close. So very close. Mere minutes away. A single digit. A single digit that could be counted on one hand.

Amy had her disgusting, invasive, interfering Poodle exactly where she wanted her; lying on her back with Amy's hands around her throat. Her three were all busy with Poodle's three, so it was just the two of them. With no one to stop her. She threw her knee into Poodle's ribs and watched her wheeze out a strained groan.

Despite the hands keeping her breathing restricted, Dawn mustered the strength and will to speak. "You killed him. I know you did. And so do the rest of them." The hands got tighter and pushed down harder and Dawn felt her throat close up. She put her hands on Amy's hot wrists and Amy let go of her throat and slapped her across the face.

"I should have fucking killed you when I had a knife to your gut. That's a mistake I won't make again." She went to put her hands back onto Poodle's throat but Poodle interlocked their fingers and let their hands drop to the ground at the sides of her head.

Dawn read Amy's face and almost felt sorry for her. But then she remembered what this girl had done to Myah and Zoey and herself and the sympathy fizzled out. Fast. "You're not going to get away from this. There's nothing you can do anymore. No threats are going to change anything. Might as well just go home and wait."

Amy glared at her and tried to pull her hands out of Poodle's, but she kept them. "You have no idea what you're talking about. You don't know a fucking thing about any of this." Her eyebrows arched up ever so slightly and her nostrils flared. "We didn't mean it."

As if she wasn't certain enough, now Dawn had a damn near confession. "But it happened, Amy. It doesn't matter if you meant it. He's dead and it's *your* fault." Amy's tearful glare returned and she tried to pull her hands out of Dawn's grip again. Which Dawn had been hoping for. Once she pulled, Dawn let go of her fingers and followed the path they took. The aggressive force of her sudden release sent Amy backwards and Dawn pounced forward, putting them in each other's positions. Dawn was now on top of Amy, doing the same thing Amy had been doing to her. But she wasn't going to kill her, she just needed her to pass out so they could get away. Though dragging Amy to the police station would make things easier.

Amy was, of course, strong, but the pure contempt Dawn felt for her and everything she had put her through over the last two weeks or so was stronger than anything Amy could throw at her. She reached for Dawn's face and Dawn moved it back an inch or two. She was in control now and felt an odd cockiness overcome her, perhaps a relative of the original feeling she had gotten that had led to all of this in the first place. And, like that first feeling, Dawn couldn't fight this one either, nor what it made her say.

"You'll survive prison. Lunatics often do. Although you deserve so much worse than jail time for everything you've done. But I guess that's the best option there is."

The smile she gave made Amy's volcano spew more lava than Amy could put into her actions. There was so much anger, so much hate, so much fear, so much loathing for this little dog. And it was so hot. For the first time, it was starting to hurt. Amy's blood and skin were starting to sting, to shake, to burn. Amy did the only thing she could. The only thing she had left. She reached down into her pocket,

her world was getting fuzzy

found the rectangle that sat there,

things were fading fast now

she pushed the switch up, *click*,

things were getting colder

and she shoved the blade into Poodle's stomach and ripped it across, just below her bellybutton. Just below the last thing she put on her stomach. An underline. A deep underline, down to the blade's hilt.

The crescendo sounded.

The hands around her throat let go and reached for their stomach. Amy looked at it and saw a waterfall of blood pouring through the blue shirt and onto Amy's white one. Her mind acted fast and she moved faster. She pushed Poodle off of her with little effort, pushing her back opened the gash even more so she fell back with ease, and Amy got to her feet, ignored her shaking legs, and ran to get Evan. He was busy with the new girl but that mattered very little now. She stood in front of him, trying to cover her soaked shirt. "We need to leave. Now."

He saw the blood as soon as he looked at her and felt nauseous at the thought of what it could mean. "What did you do?"

Amy didn't look much healthier than he felt and she knew she couldn't waste time explaining. She repeated herself and left for his truck where she hoped an extra one of her shirts would be waiting somewhere. Or one of his, that would suffice. No shirt at all would be better than this walking evidence.

Evan collected Trevor and Heather from their tussles and ran after Amy. There was no denying it now. They were fucked. Maybe not all four, but Amy absolutely was. He didn't even know what she did, all he knew was that the entire bottom half of her shirt was soaked, almost dripping, with blood and it didn't seem to be hers. When he got to his truck, he shoved Heather and Trevor into the back and ran into the driver's seat. Amy had changed into a different shirt, a green one with lace sleeves. It may have been cleaner than the one she was wearing but her blood splattered hands still stamped it in several places. She wouldn't look at him. "Where's the shirt?"

"Drive. Drive this truck right fucking now. We can't be here anymore. We need to get as far away as we can." Amy could hear how weak her voice sounded. She spoke on the verge of tears and they started to fall when Evan didn't start the truck. She looked at him and tried not to beg. "Please, Evan. I'll explain it all, but we need to get out of here." She buried her face in her hands and Evan started up the truck.

He drove off, not knowing where he was supposed to be going. They would need to go somewhere where they could be alone and where Amy could explain as she promised. She did have a great amount to explain after all. She had to explain why she was soaked with blood but perfectly healthy. She had to explain what happened to Dawn. She had to explain why she looked and acted so beaten down and miserable. Many things needed explaining, may things that all seemed to be connected.

Evan came up with a location. A location he assumed Amy wouldn't want to go to but he didn't quite care for her opinion at the moment.

"Did we win?" Myah asked, rubbing her bruised elbow as she met up with Steph and Zoey.

Steph rolled her eyes. "Myah, it doesn't matter who won, what matters is that we gave them what they all had coming." She smiled. "But yeah, if one group won, I'd say it's us." Her hand still hurt from Heather's serpent grip but it was getting better. "I'd do it again."

Myah nodded. "So would I."

"Where's Dawn?" Zoey looked around and finally spotted her.

Lying on her back, hands on her stomach, bathing in blood.

Zoey deflated and her breathing increased. "That's not real. That's not real." She knew it was, but she wouldn't tell herself that. Not yet.

"What's not real?" Steph and Myah looked to where Zoey had her eyes locked and they both saw the same gruesome sight. Steph's strategy was very similar to Zoey's. Denial at first. "No way, no way." She shook her head but the image wouldn't leave. She had a feeling it never would.

Myah had a different approach to their situation. She ran to Dawn and dropped to her knees next to her. Dawn's hands were red and draped over her lower stomach but, when Myah reached her, one of Dawn's hands moved towards her. Myah took it.

It was cold.

"Guys, she's still breathing. Get the fuck over here." She looked down at Dawn and a few of her tears fell onto Dawn's wet shirt, turning it a dark blue. Unlike the other liquid that wet her shirt which turned it to a dark purple. Steph and Zoey appeared at Dawn's other side and Zoey took the extra red hand.

"Hey, come on, you're going to be fine. You're going to be perfect, it's just a little cut, that's all. Okay? You're going to...to…." The tears she was choking on forced her to stop talking.

"I'm calling an ambulance."

Dawn tried to focus and it made her feel dizzy. "You shouldn't. It's too late."

"What? No it's not."

Dawn cleared her throat and spit up blood. It dribbled down her chin. "I can feel it spilling out, I can't feel much else. I want it to just be us right now."

Steph looked back and forth between Dawn and her phone, tears staining her sight.

"Steph, look at me."

She closed her eyes and shook her head. There was no way she would watch her friend die. She'd rather die herself.

"Look at me. Please."

Against her will, she opened her eyes and looked at Dawn. Dawn smiled at her and her teeth were red. Steph let the tears run now, she couldn't put on a brave face anymore. Zoey and Myah couldn't either. The tears felt horrible.

"I love you." Dawn forced her eyes to stay open and they darted between the three people above her, her final Zigzag Look. The taste of blood in her mouth felt like deja vu. "I love all of you." She brought her eyes to Zoey's and began to cry as well. "I wish...I could have told you...how much you muh...muh…." She forced it out. She had to finish it before her body and brain stopped her. "Mean tuh...tuh...tuh…."

Say it. Two more words. Say it. You can do this.

You can't. It hurts too much and you've lost too much blood. It's over. They can take care of each other. All you have to do is stop fighting and fall away.

I don't want to. I just want to be with them. I want to talk to them.

You're done. It's okay. Don't be afraid...

Just give me five more seconds with them.

Five seconds is all you have left, don't waste it in you hea—

Dawn stopped talking. Her stomach didn't move up and down, rapid or slow. It didn't move at all. Her eyes fell from Zoey and Zoey them turn dull. The blood continued to spread out around Dawn's stomach, falling into the grass and staining her pants.

Zoey shook her head faster and faster. The tears flew left and right like water flying from a sprinkler. She leaned her head down onto Dawn's chest and didn't hold her volume back. She sobbed into her shirt and held the cold, limp hand as hard as she could. "No, I'm not ready. Please don't leave me."

Myah let go of the hand she had held and looked down at the grass. Green, the color of growth and harmony, was becoming infested with red. Three friends had been all she needed, they had managed to feel like so much more. That was the power friendships held. She cried like Zoey, unabashed.

Steph put a closed and shaking fist to her lips and held back as much as she could. Her breathing was sharp and loud through her nose and stray snot was falling onto her knuckles. She touched Dawn's forehead with her other hand for a reason she couldn't quite discern and touching her cold, motionless face broke her. She covered her mouth and nose but her tears that came and the mouth that screamed from behind her hands were silent. Tears hit the ground one after another in three places.

Dawn Bell died surrounded by the only people she loved, fighting all the while. She hoped they knew that.

Chapter 22

Steph eventually called for an ambulance and due to R.I High School's placement within Winno, it arrived, along with several police cars and SUVs, in three minutes. She wondered if that would have been enough time but her thoughts didn't quite work the same way they used to. She heard them but couldn't understand them, as if they were in a different language.

A man and woman got out of the back of the ambulance with a gurney already folded up onto its wheels and rolled it to where the three girls sat by Dawn. They tried to pick her up and once the man touched her body, Zoey's arm slashed out and slapped him away. Her hand stung but she wouldn't give them Dawn. Giving them Dawn meant that this was real. "You're not taking her."

The woman came toward her, slow and cautious. She held her hands in front of her and looked understanding, but Zoey knew that was just an act. Zoey also knew that if she touched Dawn like her counterpart had tried to, Zoey would rip out her dyed blonde hair, strand by strand.

"Honey, I know this is scary, but we need to take her. We need to get her looked at. I need you to let go of her hand." She reached for Dawn and before Zoey could start pulling out anything, Steph came around her and held her back. As soon as her hand was out of Dawn's she wailed. She tried to push past Steph but Myah swooped down and held her where she was. With every inch that separated Zoey from Dawn she got angrier and cried harder.

"No, you can't take her! Give her back! I need her!"

Myah leaned against her thrashing friend and held in her tears as she spoke. "Zoey, stop it. Please. They're going to take her. It's their job. We can't stop them." The ambulance sped away and the lights and siren were dead air in seconds. Zoey settled down and continued to cry. Softer than before, but just as consistent.

Steph and Myah didn't hold her back. They just held her. And she returned the hold. They were all fine with staying in the same spot for the rest of the day and night and their lives, but a low grating voice rang in their ears and forced them to take part in their existence.

"Can any of you girls tell us what happened? Maybe tell us who did this? We can give you some time if you need it."

Zoey dug herself out of the arms that constricted her and got to her working foot as fast as she could. "We already know who did this." She stepped closer and pronounced the name as perfectly as she could. The mere mention of her name made Zoey want to crush something into a million pieces. "It was Amy Cooper. She goes to school with us. She—

No way. No way, I'm not saying 'killed her.'

—did this to Dawn. You can ask Steph and Myah and they'll tell you the same thing. Ask anyone, and there's a high fucking chance they'll say it was her. Even if they weren't here to see it." She spotted her crutches lying forgotten on the ground and slipped them back under her arms. She needed the support.

Lieutenant Keith Walton scanned the girl carefully and, after choosing to believe her, moved to the two girls who looked just as wrecked as their friend and asked them, "Is she correct?" Any sort of doubt that may have been hidden somewhere in his mind was snuffed out when the two girls agreed. Just as sure and honest as the first.

He nodded, took out his pad and a pen and began the grueling process that came with cases like these.

"Can I have your names?" He wrote them as they said them, left to right.

"Zoey Kay." The one who spoke with the unarguable certainty. "That's *zee-oh-ee-why.*"

He nodded and, as subtle as possible, added a Y after the E. It bled into the last name. He pointed his pen to the next girl.

"Steph Warren." He scribbled it down and pointed to the last.

"Myah, *emm-why-ayy-aitch,* Rowland."

He only got to the M before she spelled it so he didn't have to cross anything out. "All right. Zoey, Steph and Myah. We're going to need to take you three down to the station for questioning."

"How long is it going to take?" Steph asked, though not sure why. It wasn't as if she was in a hurry to get home.

"The time limit will be specific to this situation. As long as it takes for you all to tell me what happened and anything else we may need to know. But you shouldn't be there long."

"All right." Zoey put her hand up to stop his mile a minute talking. She was, for once, on the other side of a "Talking Spree." "We're going now?"

"That would be ideal."

Zoey nodded and glanced at the other officers roaming around. "By the way, you don't need to waste time looking for any evidence. We're all the evidence you need."

He gave one nod, more to show he heard her rather than that he agreed with her. "That one's mine." He pointed at the SUV he had parked along the road, one of the only vehicles that hadn't parked in the secret little lot. "I'll meet you in there once I'm done getting any last minute information."

"Okay," Zoey said. She made her way past him on her crutches and headed for the SUV. She felt Steph and Myah behind her and left the door open once she climbed into the backseat. Myah fit like a pencil in the middle and Steph took up the remaining space. Zoey's crutches were placed along their six legs like a bridge. At first no one said anything, there was nothing anyone wanted to say. They all knew any topic they could come up with would tie into Dawn. She was all Zoey thought about. How much it must have hurt, how long she was suffering, if they could have saved her if they had noticed before they did. The self-deprecating storm rained in her head and the rainwater fell out of her eyes. She tried to keep herself quiet, but all noise was mute in the SUV so her attempted silent bawling was as loud as thunder.

And in the midst of this silent hateful bawling Zoey mustered the strength to tell her friends the truth.

"We were dating."

Steph knew who Zoey was talking about she couldn't understand "What do you mean?"

Zoey cleared her hot throat, wiped the water from her pink, sore eyes and took a deep, painful breath. "Dawn and I were dating. Since Thursday." *Five days*, she thought, *happy for five days.* "After we all talked at Myah's house and she dropped you and Luke off, we went to her house and…she kissed me." The memory brought a mournful smile. "I don't expect either of you to understand this but, it just felt right. I had never felt anything with anyone else I had ever been with and her kiss," she choked on her saliva and swallowed it, "it felt so good." She stopped herself before she broke down again and stared out the dark tinted window, trying to keep the tears in her eyes and not on her face. She heard Steph give a breathy laugh and, eyes still on the dark window, her eyebrows came down.

"That's amazing."

Zoey turned to Steph, as confused as Steph had been a few seconds ago. "Really?"

Steph smiled. "Of course. I don't know if I would have caught on but I'm not surprised. You two are perfect for each other." She didn't catch on to her use of present tense. "When were the two of you going to tell us?"

Zoey looked down and sighed. "We never had the chance to figure that out." Myah pulled Zoey's head toward her and Zoey dampened Myah's sleeve.

"She would be happy that you told us," Myah said, holding back tears of her own. Zoey nodded from her spot in Myah's shirt but didn't stop crying. Until Steph confessed.

"It's my fault."

Zoey and Myah both turned to her and she was nodding to herself, convincing herself. From a face that showed no clear emotion, tears were falling. The sight was terrifying.

Myah put her hand on Steph's knee, now consoling two friends who felt responsible for something that wasn't the fault of either. "That's not true."

Steph responded fast. "Yes it is. *I* was the one who wanted to give them what they deserved. If I didn't have that stupid fucking vendetta none of this would have happened." Her stone face broke and revealed a hurt one underneath. The tears fell faster now. "I just want her back."

Myah put Steph's head on her other shoulder and lowered her own head in between the two. "I know. So do I." Her tears dropped into their hair but neither of them noticed. Nor would they have cared if they did.

Their moment of twisted comfort was interrupted when Lieutenant Walton swung open his door and slid into the driver's seat. The three separated, wiping away their tears in the process.

"You girls ready?"

They all cleared their throats in a sickening wet harmony and Myah answered. "As we'll ever be."

He nodded from his side of the metal grating that separated the front seat from the back. "Good. We'll be there in five minutes or so." He turned on the car and switched on the siren. It wasn't as loud as the three thought it would be, but it still gave them the second jump they'd had in one minute.

Myah's mouth hung agape for a brief moment. "I thought you were only supposed to use the siren for emergencies."

As he pulled the SUV into the road and looked at the few cars around him, he took a few seconds to glance at Myah and gave her a mischievous smile. "I know how little you three want to be here so, for this occasion, I'll make an exception."

"Thanks." She didn't want to say it and it sounded awkward when she did. He meant well, but now wasn't the time to try and be charismatic. She leaned her head back and closed her eyes, taking it all in. Zoey leaned her head on Myah's left shoulder and Steph did the same on her right. They looked like a picture a mother would take of her three kids that fell asleep during a long car ride. Before any of them could figure out what they were going to do when they got home and how much they didn't want to be alone, the SUV came to a halt and they opened their eyes to see the Winno Police Station.

It had felt like seconds since they closed their eyes outside of their school, but that was how resting worked. Ten seconds in resting time was equal to five minutes in the real world. Zoey, Steph and Myah would be in the police station for half an hour.

The three of them sat across from Lieutenant Walton in a dim little room. From the look of the empty walls, the two way mirror and the table and four chairs they sat in, it seemed to be an interrogation room. The thought of it made Myah keep her hands in her lap, hoping she wouldn't have to touch anything.

"So you three were there when it happened?" He didn't feel the need to specify where and what, he had a feeling the three knew what he was referring to.

Zoey sighed. "Yes, we were all there. We all saw everything."

He nodded and pressed on. "And can any of you tell me what happened?"

There was dead silence from the three of them as they all thought about who was strong enough to say it. After half a minute of quiet, and mental preparation, Myah was able to speak. Her teeth were closed and she looked into her lap the whole time.

"The four of us got into a fight with a few people from our school.

And one of them...stabbed Dawn and killed her.”

“And who were these people that you got into this fight with?”

Zoey answered before Myah could. This information she had no problem giving.

“Evan Mitchell, Heather Grey, Trevor Logan and Amy Cooper. Amy was the one who did it though.”

He wrote all four names down and hovered his pencil over the supposed leader. “Can you describe Amy? Is there anything particular about her that might make her stand out?”

Steph took over now. “She’s a ginger, she has black eyes and her skin is always pink. She looks like she was kicked out of Hell.”

He nodded for a few seconds before stopping and furrowing his eyebrows. It looked as though he was having some sort of PTSD flashback. Zoey’s eyebrows mimicked his. “What?”

The name was hard to pin down but the description, that was memorable. Still though, Keith put his face back into its previous deadpan form. “We’ve...interacted...with Amy Cooper before.”

“For what? Why?” Steph asked. He shook his head and her frustration expanded.

“That doesn’t relate to this situation.”

Steph let some of her dissatisfaction spill out. “Well, maybe it does, because she’s the one who stabbed Dawn and what you know might make this” air quotes around her next word “investigation a lot easier to solve.”

“We don’t need the three of you to help our investigation. Right now we just need you to answer a few questions.” None of them responded and he continued. “So your friend, Dawn Bell, is that correct?” They all nodded. “Is there any reason she would be targeted in the way that she was?”

Zoey’s voice cracked like glass as she spoke. “No. We don’t even know why she was targeted in the first place. Amy carved the word whore onto Dawn’s stomach but, from what all of us know, she had never even,” she paused, feeling embarrassed, and chose a different phrase, “done it...with anyone. And in terms of what just happened? Again, we don’t know. Dawn stayed out of Amy’s way, we all did. But she had taken a particular interest in us over the last couple of weeks and the only person who would know why is Amy. Maybe what she did was planned out from the beginning or maybe it was an accident.” She cringed at the thought that what happened to Dawn could be justified under the excuse of it being an accident. If that was the case, Zoey would make sure that Amy would have an accident of her own. If she could get away with it, so could Zoey. "But whatever the reason, none of us know why she did what she did. We're really not the best people to talk to when it comes to her. We tried to know as little about her as possible."

"But you know more about her than we do, right? After all, you've apparently interacted with her before, you had to get some information on her then." Steph sounded and looked betrayed and Lieutenant Walton ignored her tone and focused on what she said.

"It may please you to know that, yes, we do have information regarding her. But, like I said before, that doesn't pertain to this issue or any of you. We will look into Amy and her friends and, depending on what happens, we may need to ask you all a few more questions but, as of now, the three of you are free to go." They all sprung up, Zoey with a bit less grace, and headed for the door. He realized something and asked them to wait. And by the looks on their faces he didn't think he would get away with such a request a second time.

Steph's hand squeezed the doorknob, wishing she could break it and relieve some of her anger. "What?"

"Do any of you have rides home?"

They all looked at each other, realizing that none of their parents knew where they were, and Myah offered a solution. "Yeah, I can call my parents, they'll come get us. It won't take long." He looked satisfied with her answer and Myah was relieved that she wouldn't have to go into any further detail on her, depending on her parents, potential lie.

"All right, good. Now I suggest that the three of you go home straight away. Whether you want to stay together or be alone is up to you, but it's best if you all go home and rest." He didn't know how much rest they would be able to get seeing as how it wasn't even four yet, but he hoped they would take his advice nonetheless.

Steph nodded and her hair bun rattled on her head. "Okay we will. Thank you." She swept out of the room like a breeze and didn't wait for Myah or Zoey. She knew she wouldn't have to. They looked just as antsy to leave as she was. With the two of them on her heels, she moved through the halls like water and pushed through the big glass doors. She heard the door creak as she opened it, heard two more creaks after her and she turned around in the parking lot to face Zoey and Myah. "You both know we're not doing anything he just told us to, right?"

Zoey squinted her eyes, looking accusatory but much more confused than upset. "Then what are we supposed to do?" Steph moved toward her and Zoey took a step back before her mind could tell her to, crutches and all. Steph didn't notice.

"We go after the four of them."

Myah pinched her eyes together. "No, Steph, that's not a good idea." It almost sounded like a whine but Myah didn't care.

"Why not?"

Myah closed her eyes and took a deep breath, as if dealing with a petulant child. This was the same girl who blamed herself and her vendetta for everything that had happened and now she wanted to go after them again. Apparently Steph only allowed herself a few minutes of understanding before she relapsed. "Because, we don't know where they are and we don't know how to find out. Not to mention that going after Amy and her group is the reason why we're in this position to begin with. And what would we even do if we did find them? We aren't murderers."

Steph's voice was low and deep and surprisingly assured. "We could be."

Myah and Zoey glanced at each other and read the same fear on each other's face. Though it wasn't just fear. There was some temptation underneath it, hiding like a snake in tall grass. The two ignored the latter and brought the former to the surface.

"I don't think you really mean that," Zoey said. Steph glared at her and Zoey wore both her fear and her temptation. She wasn't showing it as much as Steph was and she was still more tired than anything but she couldn't deny it. She was angry, too.

"I don't think I do either. Or, at least, I *hope* I don't. But at the same time...what the fuck, right? An eye for an eye. She doesn't deserve to be thrown in jail, she deserves to burn in Hell. It can't just be me who thinks that, right?"

It wasn't, but neither Zoey nor Myah were willing to admit it. Myah was willing to admit something though, despite her plan not being fully formed. "Maybe a compromise can be made." Steph glared at her and she put her hands together. "Just hear me out." Steph gestured for her to continue.

"If we, or you, kill Amy, we'll go to jail and she won't suffer at all, nobody wins. I'll tell you what we can do, though. We can come up with a plan and get the police in on it. We can corner her, trap her and force her into their handcuffs." Myah was getting into her fantasy now. Enjoying the idea of it. "We can be responsible for bringing her down and letting her rot in prison for the rest of her life. Is that good enough for you? Because I think being in jail for life is probably a worse fate than death." She inhaled the breath she had been putting off while she spoke and as she simmered down she gave a few glances to Steph, who's face had shifted and, lucky for Myah and Zoey, became much more open to the idea Myah had given.

"What kind of plan?"

Myah raised her eyebrows, looked down at the concrete and thought out loud. "Well, first we have to get all of the information we can on Amy. That's where the two of you would come in. Anything you know about her will help. Where she lives, where Evan and Heather and Trevor live, where she goes, where she hides. Right now all information is good information. If you don't know anything, go on Lens and ask people for information. I'm going to call my parents. We'll continue this when we get to my house."

They aren't going to let you take the two of them home. They don't approve, remember?

Well, I think I've got a pretty good reason for needing to be with my friends right now. Let's see them talk their way out of that one.

The three of them sat on a wooden bench outside the police station for twenty minutes waiting for Myah's parents. Myah thought about what she might say to them and Zoey and Steph thought about anything remotely connected to Amy Cooper. They both sent messages to half a dozen other friends who had known about Amy for as long as they had and, while they waited to see if they could offer anything useful, Steph and Zoey combed through their memories. They had both known Amy since elementary school, almost a decade now, one of them was bound to remember something. And eventually, one of them did.

The memory struck Zoey like an arrow, but she didn't let her realization be known. It was possible that it was a dead end but it was also possible that it wasn't. She would tell them about it when they were in Myah's room. For now, she just thought about it. Over and over.

Chapter 23

"Amy, we need you to tell us what happened," Evan said. "We all need to know. No one will hear you but us." They were in the laundry room in the basement of Amy's house. The four of them were the only people there but her voice was still soft, timid, as if she was scared of herself.

She held Evan's hand as she unburdened herself. Her other hand rested, palm down, on the washing machine she was sitting on. "Dawn was on top of me and she was choking me. Whether or not she was going to kill me or knock me unconscious I don't know. But she started talking about how I'd end up in prison and…I did the only thing I could." She took a deep breath and looked Evan dead in the eyes. "I stabbed her. In the stomach." Saying it made it so and she hugged him, tears staining her face, and he returned it.

His thoughts raced through his head. "Okay, maybe there's a way to get out of this." His doubt was picked up by Heather.

"No, Evan, there is no way out of something like this. We weren't the only ones who saw it. Everybody from their little group did. It's only three people but it's more than enough." She turned her annoyance from Evan to the idiotic redhead that curled around his body. "You went too far this time, Amy. You're done. You're going to jail for this."

Amy unlocked herself from Evan's chest and faced Heather, who stood leaning against the doorframe with her arms crossed and a face of disapproval shining bright in the dull room. Amy's glare was so intense it hurt to wear, but it was all she had left. "No. No fucking way. I'm not going to jail. I'd sooner die."

Heather made a face of curiosity and said, "Well, who knows? Maybe this state approves of the death penalty. But I guess you won't know until you're there, huh?"

"I'm never going to end up there."

Heather rolled her eyes at Amy's childish behavior and set her cards on the table. "Amy, you killed somebody. That blood is on *your* hands.

272

And shirt, and knife. You literally cannot get away with this. They're going to find you and when they do, they're going to haul you away and I'm not going to stop them. I'm not going to live my life on the lam because you're too weak to control yourself. Dawn, Jonah, Dawn again. Someone is going to speak up. You can't keep everyone quiet. I have half a mind to speak up." It wasn't a lie, just an altering of her previous plan. She had wanted to wait for all of it to blow over, wait for Amy to feel comfortable, before she sent her to jail, but this could be better.

"Heather, hold on."

"Look, Evan, I know you really *love* her," she said love like the word disgusted her, "but you can't let something like this slide. You know she won't be able to get away with this. And you'll still be able to see her. You know, during visiting days." She added that last part just for fun but Amy's reaction disappointed her. There was nothing. No emotion she could feel, no expression she could describe. Amy's face was dead.

"Evan, can you and Trevor give the two of us a minute alone, please?" It may have been a question but she stated it like an order.

Evan nodded at the back of her head. "Yeah, sure." He motioned Trevor out of the room and the two left Amy and Heather alone. Although he was prepared to barge back into that room soon, he was more than happy to leave it for the time being. The air was old and stale and humid. And strained.

Trevor asked, "Do you really think she could get away with this? I mean, seriously dude, this is really bad."

"I don't know." Evan kept the fearful tears in his eyes and refused to let them spill down his face. "Stand by the window. Tell me if the police show up."

"Amy, you're not going to talk me down from this. Or intimidate me or succeed at whatever you're planning on doing. There's nothing you can do this time." Heather crossed her arms again and gave her a cold scowl. She was ready to leave and not because she was scared. Once she was away from this reckless little rat, the truth would be known and Amy would be out of her life.

Amy's face was just as empty as it had been before but a hint of color was starting to fill it. A hint of life. She licked her dry lips and, with a voice just as dry, said, "Yes there is. There is something I can do." Her voice sounded hollow and deeper, like she had been possessed, and then her face changed. Her eyebrows fell just a tad and the corners of her mouth fell with them. She wasn't angry, she was determined. Heather's macabre interest overcame her and she asked something she knew she shouldn't.

"What's that?"

Amy gave her a clear answer without saying a word.

Before Heather could react, Amy's hand slipped into her back and then into Heather's throat. At first she felt nothing, but when Amy pulled her hand and the wet blade out of her neck, Heather noticed the difference. Her neck was wet and when she put her hand up to where it hurt, she felt a tiny slit in her throat. As her hands were covering it Amy put the blade deep into her left thigh. One hand fell to grab the new pain and her legs gave out all together. She fell to the floor and, while still holding the deep-rooted cuts in her body, attempted to crawl away. As she wiggled to the door she felt a foot stomp down on her back. Nothing cracked or broke but it felt like something had. She wheezed out one of her final breaths and made a pleading reach toward the door that separated two very important people from helping her. She heard Amy's voice, just as apathetic and unrelenting as before, but this time Amy's voice terrified her. She squirmed under Amy's shoe and began to do something that was, as far as she could remember, completely new. Heather began to cry.

"I'm not going to jail, Heather. And no one is going to make me."

Heather felt Amy's knees drop onto her spine, there was another burst of pain from the back of her neck and then everything went away.

It was fortunate that they were in the laundry room. *One bed sheet should do the trick*, Amy thought. It did. But she did one more thing before wrapping Heather up. She had made a promise to herself that she would have Heather's eyes and she wanted to fulfill it.

She walked out of the laundry room, closing the door behind her, and Evan took note of her appearance. She was wringing her hands as if she had wiped them on something, but that wasn't what made him concerned. Amy looked the same, clothing wise, but her face looked different. It was small but noticeable, like someone who had switched to contact lenses after years of wearing glasses. He took in a silent breath and spoke, hiding his growing panic. "Where's Heather?"

She looked down at her hands and held them out to him. He took brought them into the light and saw how pink they looked. So pink they were almost red. Red. That was all he needed to know. He held her hands harder and his fear slipped out.

"Amy, please tell me you didn't. Don't lie to me, but please tell me you didn't."

She looked at him, her bottom lip quivering but looking far from scared and she responded. Her voice was still soft as feathers. "I'm not going to jail."

The breath was taken out of Evan's lungs and he did what he always did when he was scared; he embraced her. She embraced in response and she stroked his hair once she did. Her voice remained soft so only he could hear.

"It's okay. I did what I had to do. We'll be fine." She sounded calm, almost pleased, and the terror he felt made him hold her closer.

Trevor, who had been fulfilling his role and had yet to find any vehicles coming down the street, took his eyes off the window and turned to the two. "Where's Heather?" He started to move toward the laundry room.

"Trevor, don't."

But it was too late. He opened the door and saw a white sheet on the floor, spotted with dark red patches, wrapped around something that very much resembled a human. He wasn't the smartest in the group but he knew who was under the blanket. What he didn't know was what to do about it. He closed the door and looked at Amy, who had ended the embrace and was now standing beside Evan. "You killed her?" He knew she had but it came out like a question regardless. A question Amy was not happy to hear, if her sullen face was anything to go by. She stood up straight and her voice was firm. "I did what I had to do. I'm not going to jail, Trevor."

He looked at Evan for help and only received a small head shake. "You're okay with this?" He gave no answer. "Well I'm not, no way. I'm done." He started to move to the door and, like lightning, Amy's hand slammed against it, keeping it closed. The sound made Trevor jump back. Her eyes got wider and, for a moment, he saw Heather looking at him. With a bleeding slit in her neck and gray irises. The vision made him start to sob and as the tears clouded his vision, Amy took Heather place. The blood and gray were gone, but her eyes still looked just as dead as Heather's had.

"Nobody is done. Nobody can ever be done. We're in this forever, now. It's our lives."

"No it's not. It's your life. I never killed anybody. Never even got any blood on my hands. Amy, I won't tell anyone. I'll make something up, I promise." He saw her eyes shrink and her head tilt. Her mouth turned upward in a demented and lethal smile that almost made his jaw fall.

"What are you going to say, huh?" She was walking toward him and he knew his back was going to be up against the wall at any moment. And once that happened, he wouldn't be able to get away. He would be cornered. He would be her prey. "What story are you going to make up?" There was no trust in her voice, he didn't think she would believe anything he said. And it didn't matter anyway because Trevor couldn't think of anything to say. His mind was empty. All he could think about was Heather. And the wall was getting closer.

"I-I don't know." Six feet from the wall.

"You don't know?" Five.

"I don't know yet." Four. "But I'll think of something. I just need some time." Three.

She moved faster now. "We don't have time to spare, Trevor. We don't even have time for this conversation. You need to come up with something now."

She still had no faith in him, but it didn't matter. Now he *had* come up with something.

He stopped walking, a foot from the wall, and stood his ground. Amy stopped as abruptly as a wind up toy. Her face and mind were still set on her next move.

"I've got something, all right. I've got *this*." He moved to shove her wherever he could but Amy slipped in between his arms and he felt something small pierce his gut. He looked down and saw an orange rectangle sticking out of his stomach. He looked back up at Amy's face, hoping it would be different, but it wasn't. There was nothing. She backed away, taking the orange rectangle, as well as the black wet blade, with her and the first thing Trevor noticed was that she wasn't blocking the door. He was still able to stand so he made his way to the exit.

As soon as his hand turned the knob he felt a finger bury itself into the hole in his stomach. He screamed, letting go of freedom and safety to grab the burning pain, and was thrown to the ground by another hand. He shook off the pain from hitting the hard carpet and, hand on his bleeding gut, backed away from Amy as much as he could. He didn't get far. She stomped on his ankle and a different pain came from there. It didn't bleed but it began to swell.

Amy, with her foot on Trevor's broken ankle, turned to face Evan who had backed himself away from what was taking place. "Come here." He shook his head, as if in denial. Her fists clenched and she pressed her foot harder, getting another scream from Trevor as a result. *He needs to do this with me. If he doesn't, he won't be able to understand. We do this and we're both on the same playing field.*

"Evan, honey, you need to come here. I need you." Her voice sounded sweet, loving and scared. On purpose.

Evan complied. His movement was slow but he stepped one foot every second. When he got to her side she smiled. The first real smile he had seen from her in days. It gave him hope and what she said next took it away.

"I need you to hold his head back. Leave his neck open." He blinked wide eyes and looked at Trevor, who saw an opportunity and lunged for it.

"No, Evan, please don't. Come on, please don't do this." The tears and phlegm made it difficult to speak, and the bloody stomach and broken ankle didn't make it any easier, but this was his last chance for mercy. He had to go for it with everything he had. "It doesn't have to end this way. I can make up a lie, I won't tell anyone, I swear."

Evan looked from person to person. Trevor sounded horrified and what he was saying was convincing, but Amy still had a greater hand in Evan's decision. No matter how much Trevor begged and pleaded, Evan looked at Amy's face and they both knew he had chosen a side.

"Just hold back his head. It'll be quick. I know what to aim for. He won't suffer for long." Her voice, again, sounded harmless and innocuous. Maternal almost, and Evan nodded.

He walked around to Trevor and, despite his screaming and clawing, Evan held his arms down with his legs and held his head back by the chin. The chin was wet, but not wet enough to slip out of Evan's grip.

Amy climbed onto Trevor's body, eyes on his neck, and flicked out her knife. The screaming and kicking continued, getting louder and more aggressive, but he was immobile and they all knew it. He was just desperate. Amy moved Trevor's head to the side and found the vein. She held the blade out horizontally and, if Evan had blinked he would have missed it, shot the knife into Trevor's neck and pulled it out in one swift straight motion.

Blood sprayed onto Amy's face but she didn't move. She didn't react. She didn't close her eyes or even squint them. She sat perfectly still as she was painted red.

After a few seconds had passed, his body began to slump and Evan released his grip around Trevor and pulled Amy off of him. She was dripping with blood. He swore he could see beads of blood on her eyeballs.

Amy took Evan's shaking hands and stopped him before he started. She knew his mind was a blank sheet of paper and the words written on it would determine how he felt. "We had to do it. They were going to get in the way. We did the right thing." She squeezed his hands a little harder, until he reacted, to make sure he was paying attention. "It's just the two of us now. We're all we have left. And," she chose to say 'we are' instead of 'I am,' "we are not going to jail. Do you understand that?" He nodded and his scattered eyes bounced around as he tried processing the information around them. She let him have his time. This was a lot to process so soon and she knew it would be tough for him to leave his life behind. But with the right words, tough could be made flexible. When his eyes slowed down and settled, Amy planned to continue but he spoke before her.

"We need to get you cleaned up."

Amy looked down and saw her shirt, red and green, and thought of Christmas. She felt her face, wet and sticky, and wondered how she hadn't noticed either until Evan mentioned them. "Okay, I'll jump in the shower and clean it all off. Then we can go." She turned to leave but Evan grabbed her arm and spun her around to face him.

"Go where?" He sounded lost and she took his hand and kissed it, leaving some of Trevor's blood behind.

"I don't know yet. But I'll think of something. I just need some time."

"What about them?"

"Why does that matter? We're never coming back here." She sounded certain but felt far from safe. Her face showed this better than her voice did.

"Are you okay?"

She looked at Evan's timid face and saw herself for a brief, chilly moment. She shoved it aside and smiled. "Yeah, I'm fine." She had an idea that would take his mind off of what had happened and a sly smile spread across her face. "Want to help wash it off?" He smiled at her and she felt more relieved.

"That sounds good." His voice was found.

"Perfect." She took his hand and led him up the stairs into her bathroom. She could feel the blood on her face and in her hair. "This may take a while."

"Good."

Amy giggled. Whether it would happen before or after she was clean she didn't know and she didn't care. Sex always brought them together and cleared their minds. They needed that now more than ever.

The second her shirt and jeans hit the white tiles they did it. And as she reached the peak of her orgasm, she could no longer keep her needling question inside. As she tried to control her breathing, she asked him, in a voice that was more shaky than she would have liked, "Do you still love me?"

In the midst of everything that had happened recently and the fact that he hadn't been prepared for the question and the fact that he was already starting to think about their slim chances of getting away with all of this, Evan had to take a few seconds before he could answer her. But even in spite of everything, the answer he gave her was true. Which might have been the biggest problem he was dealing with. "More than anything."

Once they had both finished, they showered. And, after the sex, both of them needed it. Once the water was off and they were drying themselves, Evan's brain began working again.

"Have you thought about what our plan is? You know, where we can go?" Evan didn't sound anxious or scared, he sounded calm. Somewhat prepared. He wasn't.

As Amy dried her hair and turned the white fabric of her towel more red than she would have wished, even after washing it there still seemed to be a fair amount of blood everywhere, even in her bangs, she answered him.

"Yeah, I actually have thought of a good place to start." She prided herself on the idea. Surely no one would know to look for them there. The last time she was there was a decade ago.

"Where?" She paused, making him wonder if there was a trace of skepticism in what she was thinking, but she answered him anyway.

"The Forbidden Path." She wished it would have sounded as convincing as she wanted it to, but it came out of her mouth with a dangerous amount of self doubt. The lack of response from Evan made the self doubt lethal. She glanced at him and the raised eyebrow he wore gave the self doubt a loaded gun. "What?"

"The Forbidden Path?"

"Yes. And don't say it like it's the worst idea I've ever had."

"Well it kind of is, Amy. The Forbidden Path is a jogging trail in the frog park. We can't live there."

"God, Evan, I didn't think we would. That's not what I'm suggesting."

Evan crossed his arms and leaned back against the wall. "Then what are you suggesting?"

Amy took a breath, hot and humid from the wet shower air that lingered in the bathroom. "We can't live there, but it's a good place to think. Nobody goes there anymore since the new bike path was built around the park. Even when my second grade class was there a decade ago our teacher said that people didn't use it very much. And if someone did, they wouldn't use it in March. We go there and we're safe to plan ahead. No one will get in the way. And if they do...I'll take care of them." Evan nodded and the gun that the self doubt was holding turned the barrel to itself and pulled the trigger.

"That's good. That's a good start, but we can't be there long. What time is it?"

Amy turned on her phone. "Four fifty."

"And at this time of year, the sun goes down at around six thirty. We'd have to be out of there before that. That's an hour forty right now."

"Why?"

"We can't be in the woods, alone, at night. There's no way we would be able to make it out unharmed."

"We'd be the only ones."

"We'd be the only *people*. Nature is full of deadly shit, Amy. Spiders, snakes and foxes aren't exactly alien to places like that. And since, apparently, no one has been there for a long time, no one has been keeping tabs on what could be out there either."

She gave him a nod. "Then we have to leave. Right now. I'll get some things from my room and then we can go to your house and you can get whatever you need. We need to travel light. What? Why are you shaking your head?"

"I don't want to go home before we leave. From here, we go straight to the path. No pit stops. We need all the time we can get." He figured it might be easier for him to accept what they were doing if he wasn't given an opportunity to think too much about it. And going home, avoiding his mother and packing a bag as if he were going on vacation seemed like the best possible way for him to start overthinking. And he was already starting to overthink this.

He looked serious and Amy took him as such. "Okay, if that's what you want." She began to walk past him to the door but he stopped her before both feet were in the hallway. "What is it?"

He spoke with a tone that made her think of metal. "We're leaving everything behind. You know that, right? We walk out of this house and we're never coming back. You have to let all of your relationships die. Even your one with Elizabeth."

For the first time since her plan was set in her mind, Amy felt apprehensive. Severing everyone else she was fine with but, once she left her house, killing her bond with her sister seemed like something she couldn't do. Even though she hadn't seen or heard from her in years. Because if she did get the chance to talk to her, she would learn about what had happened to her family, learn that it wasn't her fault. The grip on her guilt would loosen. But the small chance of speaking to her sister one more time wasn't worth going to prison. Nothing was worth going to prison. And since Amy had nothing left, she had nothing to lose. And if Liz wanted to forget about her, Amy would do the same. "I know. And I'm willing to let it all die. It's worth it if it keeps us together." He let go of her and she went to her room. She didn't hear the cowardice and hesitation in his voice or see it in his face.

There wasn't much she needed. She slipped into a tight black V neck, a shirt that thankfully wasn't sopping with blood from two different people and, in spite of the hurry she knew they were in, she checked herself out in the mirror hanging on her door. She moved her hands up and down her body, feeling the two things in her pockets that she needed. Her phone and her knife. Though there was one more thing that would be helpful, but it wasn't hers. It belonged to the person across the hall. She opened her door for the last time and went to get what she should have taken a long time ago.

"What are you looking for in your dad's room?"

She didn't answer. She found what she needed, held it up and let the rolled up wad of money do the talking.

"How did you know that was there?"

Amy shrugged. "I liked to snoop when I was a kid."

"How old were you?" Evan asked it through a laugh.

"Six. Don't judge me, I was bored a lot. After Mom left, I didn't have anything to do. Liz had her big eleven year old friends and Dad treated me like I was another piece of furniture." There was a brief sad silence but Amy was able to end that. She was tired of feeling sad.

"And besides," she waved the roll around like a flag and smiled, "it came in handy, didn't it." She closed her father's sock drawer and stood up, ready to leave, but Evan hadn't finished their new, ill-timed game of twenty questions.

"Why haven't you taken it all before?" Amy gave him a look he had seen on his mother's face before, whenever he asked a question that showcased his lack of experience with the real world.

"If you take one or two bills, the roll looks the same. If you take half of it, it looks very different. And I'm the only other person who lives here so I couldn't have pinned it on someone else. I took them only when I needed them. But now it doesn't matter. It's my last fuck you. I just wish I could see the look on his dried up face when he finds out that it's gone. And that I was the one who took it." She stared at the money and almost wanted to rip it to shreds.

Evan took her hand, bringing her back to their present. "How much is it?"

She looked down at the roll, not knowing for sure but knowing enough to satisfy herself and hopefully him. "Don't know, but the lowest bill in this is a twenty. Everything else is the same or bigger. This will be enough for a while." Evan nodded and kissed her forehead. It felt like a kiss you would give a dog, like a pat on the head for good behavior, but there were bigger issues than that so she ignored it. "We need to go."

"Yeah we do," Evan said. Then he was reminded of something that could become a very big problem if it wasn't dealt with. "Wait."

Amy blew smoke out of her nose. "What now?"

He knew she hadn't thought of this so he pushed her annoyed tone to the wayside. "You said your second grade class went to this path, right?"

Amy crossed her arms, pressing her breasts together, and leaned on one leg, jutting out her right hip. "Yeah, what about it?"

Her tone needled him a little bit more but, again, he ignored it. "Was there anyone in your second grade class who might have remembered it, too? Someone who might think to look for us there?"

"What, one of the thre—" she looked to the right and looked back. "—two of them? Steph and Zoey?"

"Yes. Were either of them in your second grade class?"

Amy tried to remember, but she had done her best to block out large pieces of her childhood so thinking back to the specific people in her second grade class was a bit like trying to put together a puzzle without knowing the image it was making. "I don't know, Evan, I think Zoey might have been. But she was just as big of a dumbass then as she is now so I don't think it'll be a problem." She put a hand to her head, feeling the heat from her skin, and she bit down on her bottom lip. Shortly after, Evan took her hand off of her head and put it in his.

"It's okay, sweetheart, don't hurt yourself." He kissed her lips and this one felt much more passionate and loving than the one he had given to her forehead. "I trust you. Let's go."

"Our new lives start now." As she got into Evan's truck, a truck that still had her blood smeared on it from that morning, she thought of The Forbidden Path and one girl from her second grade class.

She won't remember. She won't look for us there. She won't look for us at all. She went through a lot today. She'll probably be MIA for the next few weeks, minimum.

Out of the five statements Amy thought to herself, only one was true.

Zoey had gone through a lot today.

A lot to motivate her.

Chapter 24

"Hey, Myah, is that them?" Zoey asked as a white van pulled into the otherwise empty parking lot and slowed to a stop in front of the three of them.

Myah looked at the van and glared. "Yep." She got up, almost jumped up. "Let's go." Zoey and Steph got up after her and they headed to the van. Myah got there first and pulled the door open, but stood to the side. "You two get in first." They climbed in and sat in the back. Myah followed suit.

"Myah, do you want to tell us why you were at the police station?" Brianna asked, trying hard to sound demanding without sounding weak.

Myah shrugged and used one of her mother's lawyerly sayings that she had heard for years. "I'm sorry, but I'm not at liberty to discuss that information."

Brianna turned around in the passenger's seat with a mixed look of awe and disapproval and those feelings only grew when she saw her daughter's self-righteous smile. But, for the time being, she pushed the concerning expression aside and asked another question. She was met with another upsetting answer.

"Where are we dropping off your...friends?"

Myah's voice was blunt and deadly. "The same place you're taking me. Our house."

"No. I'm sorry Myah, but we can't do that. We've been over this."

When Myah clenched her fists and replaced her level-headed smile with a twitching glare, Zoey's and Steph's watchful eyes told them to keep her calm. When she unbuckled her seatbelt their eyes and mind told them to move. To stop her. To hold her back. But they didn't.

They didn't want to.

"Really? We've been over this, have we?" Myah climbed through the moving van from the back seat, to the middle and dropped to her knees in between her two parents in the front. Her father kept his eyes on the road but his head turned towards her.

"Myah, get back in your seat right now. Do you know what could happen if a police officer saw you?"

"I don't care. Not anymore." Her voice described someone who was beyond reasoning with. "Now, like I was saying, we haven't been over shit."

"Myah—"

"—SHUT UP!" Silence washed over the entire van. "Don't say anything. For once, just fucking listen to me." Myah took a breath, told herself to calm down, ignored herself and went on. "I have been through more today than either of you have in your entire lives and Zoey and Steph are the only ones who can help me through it." She felt tears coming again but she didn't let them out. Her mother tried to reach for her but Myah pulled away. "Don't touch me!" Her mother brought her hand back and Myah ended the conversation with complete honesty. "If you don't take them to our house, I swear on my life, you'll never see me again after today." The stone of her mother's emotionless face started to crack, revealing a fear that almost looked real, but it didn't affect Myah in the least.

Brianna again tried to reach for her daughter. "Myah, what happened?"

Again, Myah pulled her face away and wiped her eyes, revealing her hardened glare. "Take us home." She turned around and crawled back to the end of the van, where another duo of concerned people looked at her.

She strapped back in and looked over at them. "What?"

Zoey opened her mouth but nothing came out. Steph remained silent and Myah moved on. Her commanding tone was welcomed by the two of them.

"We're going to my house. We'll come up with a plan there. Have either of you thought of anything that we can use?"

This time when Zoey's mouth opened, satisfaction poured out. "I think I've got something that can help us. Back in elemen—" Zoey's information was cut short when Myah put her hand over her mouth. Myah shook her head and Zoey nodded. Despite the opposite gestures, they both knew what the other meant. Zoey's eyes dropped to Myah's hand and she let go. "You know, you could have just told me to stop talking."

Myah raised her eyebrow.

"What?"

"Has that ever worked before?"

Zoey took a longer time to think about the answer than she needed to, primarily to make Myah think there was a lot more to consider than there was. "No."

"Exactly." Myah rested her head on Zoey's shoulder and sighed. Zoey leaned her head against Myah's and did the same. They fell asleep and stayed that way until they got to Myah's house. Steph, who didn't think she would ever be able to sleep again, woke them up and Myah led them into her room.

"Watch where you step. And don't take your shoes off when you're in here."

They both nodded and didn't ask why. Myah sat on her bed and gestured to Zoey. "What have you found out?"

Zoey got up to pace. It always helped her think. Even with the splint and crutches, which she would indeed have to wear for several more weeks thanks to Trevor, she needed to move for her brain to work at its best.

"Okay, so, in elementary school my second grade class went out on this kind of nature walk on this dirt path in the park. My teacher called it The Forbidden Path, which doesn't make sense because it wasn't forbidden, but I know where it is. And I know how to get there."

Steph held her hands up and waved them back and forth. "Wait a minute, Zoey, how does this help?"

"Amy was in my second grade class. It was the only field trip we went on throughout all of elementary school, that's why it sticks out in my mind so much. And because I thought the path was gross and scary." She took her phone out of her pocket and tapped the screen. "I went on Lens and asked a few people who were also in our class if they remember it and they all did. So, if we still know about it, there's a chance that she knows about it, too. Meaning she knows that it's essentially abandoned. Nobody ever uses it. Which makes it a pretty good place to hide out. For a little while, at least."

Myah stood up and hugged Zoey, who returned it instantly. It wasn't like Dawn's, she knew nothing ever would be, but for now it might be a good enough substitute.

"That's good, Zoey, that's really fucking good."

"Thanks." Zoey ended the hug and clarified some things. This wasn't a flawless idea, after all, and there were bumps in the road she knew needed addressing. "But this isn't foolproof. We don't know for a fact that we'll find them or that they're even going to be there."

"It doesn't matter," Myah said. "It's a good place to start and it's a place the police probably won't think to look." Her appreciative smile was lost in a new sea of disgust. "That means we have to leave now. And I have to get the keys to my car."

"You want us to get them with you?" Steph asked, ready to be as blunt and aggressive as Myah needed.

"I appreciate it, but you guys don't need to do that. Just go outside and wait. I can handle them."

"You sure handled them on our way here," Zoey said, still a bit awestruck by it.

Myah smiled at Zoey. "This isn't the day to try to fuck with me. With any of us. I'll be fine, I swear. Now, we need to go."

They all left her room and, with a final nod of assurance at the front door, Myah separated from the two and went into the dining room where she found her mother. It would just be the two of them. Myah had noticed her father's office light was on before she came downstairs but that wouldn't deter her. Even the fear Myah felt at seeing her mother was light and she was able to kill it as she pressed her nails into her palms. "I need my keys." Her mother didn't look up, but she did respond. And, based on the tone of her voice, Myah didn't think she was being taken seriously.

"What was that?"

Myah gritted her teeth and spoke louder than she needed to. Louder than she ever had. A part of her wanted to take it easy, her mother didn't know what she had been dealing with today, but another part of her didn't see that as very fair. Myah had broken down a little in the car and both of her parents must have known something had happened to her but now her mother was going right back to her old self. Myah might have surprised her in the car, but now her mother was back in her awful ugly waste of space of a house and her strength was replenished. She had gone back to her old ways, where Myah's problems were secondary to her opinions. But Myah was not going to let her mother sail away from her now. That ship was about to sink. "Give me my keys. I need them. Now." Her mother scoffed and Myah's eye twitched with fury.

"After the way you spoke to us in your father's van you won't be getting those keys for a while young lady." Myah was creeping closer, not thinking at all about what she was going to do, but her mother didn't notice. Her magazine was apparently more important than her fuming daughter. "You need to take a long look in front of a mirror and—"

Myah slapped her across the face. Slapped her right out of the chair she was sitting in. Slapped her onto the wooden floor of their kitchen. She wanted to do more but her burning hand prevented her from it. All she could do was take her physical anger and transform it into its verbal equivalent. So she did.

"And you need to hear what I'm saying. Give me my fucking keys! My friend was murdered today and the last thing I need is you treating me like I'm a fucking obstacle that's in your way! So be a mother, help your kid and give me my keys."

It felt strange to yell. Myah was very soft spoken and, after years of being that way, found it hard to even raise her voice at all. But it felt somewhat therapeutic to reach that volume. Though if she was only going to raise it in situations like these, she never wanted to scream again.

Brianna held a hand to her red cheek feeling surprised, enraged and impressed, but after a second or two she realized what her daughter had said. "Your friend was what?"

"Where are my keys?"

"How did it happen? Was it the blonde?"

"Son of a bitch, where are my fucking keys?"

"If I give them to you, you have to promise to stay here for a minute and explain what you're talking about."

Even now she was still trying to bargain so this wouldn't be a complete loss on her side. It wasn't enough to do what your daughter asked, you had to get something out of it as well. Myah nodded. "I promise."

Brianna brushed herself off and went into her purse, bringing out a very familiar looking silver key. She handed it to Myah and put a hand on her daughter's shoulder. Much like Myah was to Zoey minutes ago, Brianna Rowland was proud. Proud of Myah's strength. Physical, mental and emotional.

She could make an extremely effective lawyer someday.

"What's this about your friend?"

Myah backed up, away from her hold, and shook her head. "I can't tell you right now. There are too many things that I have to take care of. And one of them being the motherfucker responsible." She turned and started walking away.

"Myah, what are you talking about? Whoever this is, you know violence isn't the answer. We raised you better than that."

Myah screeched to a halt and her shoes screamed against the smooth wood. She turned around, as slow and as calm as she could manage, upon hearing this baffling statement. "Since when did you fucking raise me? I've learned more about who I am with Zoey, Steph and…Dawn in a week than I ever have living with you two for seventeen years. You've never treated me like a daughter. You've treated me like a witness. A means to your end. Maybe you're the one who needs to take a long look into a mirror and decide if you'd rather be a mother or a lawyer. Because right now, you're only one." She turned around and left her silent mother.

An effective lawyer indeed. Brianna smiled at the thought.

Myah pulled open the massive front door and ran to her car where, like they had said, Steph and Zoey were waiting. She unlocked the doors and slipped into the driver's seat, with Zoey to her right and Steph to her diagonal right. The thought of the empty seat behind her made her tighten her grip on the steering wheel. "Are we all ready? Because this is happening. Right now." They both nodded and Myah did the same. "Zoey, you know where this forbidden path is?" Zoey's smile put her into a much needed internal repose.

"Just call me your jee-pee-ess."

"I will when we need you. Right now we don't."

Zoey's smile vanished. "What do you mean? Where are we going now then?"

"Back to the police station. We can't bring them all in by ourselves, we need all the help we can get. We'll explain our plan to them and they'll see it through with us." Myah sounded more sure than she was.

Steph noticed that. "And what if they don't go along with it and tell us to go home and get more rest?"

Myah looked through the windshield and into the future. "Then we'll have to bring them in ourselves. As many of the four as we can. Dead or alive." She put the car in drive and zoomed down the road. All three were thinking the same thing.

Dead or alive.

None of them had a problem with it. They might have before, but not now.

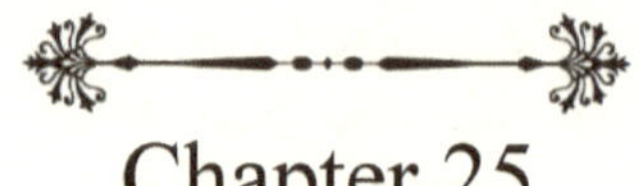

Chapter 25

"And you're absolutely sure that almost nobody knows about this place?"

"Yes, Evan, I'm sure. The only people who know this place exists probably forgot about it years ago. Now stop looking around like a prairie dog searching for predators. Calm down, and sit." She patted the dirt to her right and Evan walked to it and sat beside her, leaning the back of his head against a vine wrapped tree behind him. He slipped his hands into the sleeves of his shirt and gave a wary look to the girl next to him.

"Aren't you afraid of getting cold? Or getting poison ivy or something? Some of these plants are taller than us, even when we're standing."

"I don't get cold. And it doesn't matter anyway, we can't go back."

Evan remembered the reason why they were there. "Right, so, we have to come up with a plan?"

There was a hint of regret in his voice and it made Amy stick her fingers deep into the dirt. "Yes. We do. You are all right with that aren't you?" She asked to be nice. The sadness she heard enraged her and it didn't matter what he said, she was leaving. She didn't want to go without him, but she wouldn't stay to await a jail cell.

Evan made a motion that combined shaking and nodding his head and the way in which he said his next words vocalized his conflicted body language. "Yeah, yes, I'm with you. I promise."

She knew he was lying, or at least not believing what he was saying, but she pretended to believe him. When the time came, he would come with her. She just had to wait for him to repair his torn morality. "Good. So, where should we head?" She expected no answer from him and she got it. She couldn't be too upset with his failure to plan ahead, however, because she had fallen into the same pit. She had no idea where to go either. She almost thought it would be a better idea to not plan ahead at all.

Just keep moving away from here, that's all that needs to be

The two of them thought with their heads to the back of the tree as the sun continued to sink. It was five ten. They had an hour and twenty minutes before it would be down completely and they would have to leave for their own safety.

Evan's mind continued to bring him to the same question he didn't want to ask. He knew he would, he hadn't been able to forget about it since she had brought it up, and figured it might be better to just come out with it. He closed his eyes and got it over with. "Are you ready to tell me why you've been involved with the police before?"

Amy closed her eyes too and sighed. She didn't want to answer, but she needed him as happy and content as possible, so she did.

"This was before we met. I was twelve. And there was this girl," she gave an empty laugh, "I don't even remember her name. Or what she did that I found to be so fucking irritating, but I had had enough of it. I wasn't violent back then but something about that girl just pissed me off too much to ignore. Maybe that's when my volcano erupted for the first time. Once school ended, I waited for her and when I saw her...I attacked her. Like we did to Poodle. She stayed late, probably to tutor other students or something, so there was nobody there to stop me, it was the first time I had ever given myself to my anger, so I was finished when *I* wanted to be."

She moved her fists up and down like she was beating on a drum. "And I just lost it. I just hit and hit and hit until my hands were drenched with her blood. I fractured her jaw, broke her nose, knocked a few teeth down her throat." She spoke like she was reading items off a grocery list. Like she was bored. "I had put a bag over her head so she wouldn't be able to see me as I...did it and I warned her not to say anything but, of course, she did. I was brought in, but they couldn't take me away or put me anywhere because there was no evidence to prove it was me. I mean, I basically got away with it, but sometimes I wish I hadn't." She didn't notice the tears that were running down her face. "Maybe if they had put me somewhere I wouldn't have ended up like this. And I wouldn't have dragged you into it."

Evan moved her back away from the tree, hugged her and she sobbed into his shoulder. "But if you were taken, we never would have met. Maybe it was more worth it than you think."

She chuckled from his shoulder, then felt cold again. "It was so scary, Evan. At that age, having all of these people in your face, wanting you to be guilty, almost forcing you to confess. It wouldn't be hard if you were innocent, but I wasn't. I had to stand alone and try to convince everyone that it wasn't me. That kind of timid loneliness could kill you all by itself. It almost did. Maybe it should have." She sobbed harder at the realization that she wanted to tell herself wasn't true, that she was just stressed, but she couldn't deny that everything she said she meant. And her momentary desire to be dead wasn't different.

Evan's mouth was aligned with her right ear and he spoke into it. "None of that stuff matters anymore. We're starting over. You are who you want to be. You're stronger than you think." He heard her sobbing soften and stop but he didn't let go of her. He tightened his grip on her and she nuzzled her head closer into his shoulder.

A plan was the last thing either of them were thinking about.

As soon as Myah's parked in the lot at the Winno Police Station, Zoey hopped out of the passenger door, leaving her crutches, and hobbled to the entrance.

"Wait, Zoey. Dammit. Steph, can you go after her? Stop her before she does something stupid."

"Yep." Steph barreled through the back door and took off.

After taking the keys out of the ignition and taking a few deep breaths to calm herself down, Myah got out, grabbed Zoey's crutches and met the two at the front entrance where Zoey had been caught. Steph's arms wrapped around her stomach and Zoey was leaning the back of her head against Steph's face.

Steph smiled at the girl who sulked in her arms. "For someone with one good leg, you're pretty damn fast."

She loosened her grip and Zoey took the advantage, releasing Steph's hands and arms and backing away from her captor. "You didn't have to hold me down like that. We're all on the same page here."

Myah looked at her and was relieved to see Zoey shrink down a little. "Zoey, this is important. We all have to know what we're going to say and we all have to do it together. You can't run off and leave us behind. One slip up, and we're on our own." Zoey nodded and Myah put her hand on Zoey's shoulder. "I don't mean to be bossy, but this isn't a joke. You know what I mean?"

Zoey nodded again and held her elbows for comfort. "Yes, I do. And, just so we are on the same page, the plan is to tell Lieutenant Walton what we know and hope he goes along with it, right? And the rest is up to fate and hope?"

Myah looked down and felt, for the first time, like this was destined to fail. "Yeah. That's all."

"That's all we need," Steph said. "Fuck fate and hope." She opened one of the doors, motioned the two inside and followed after them. Myah walked up to the front desk and spoke before the woman on the other side of it got the chance to.

"We need to talk to Lieutenant Walton."

The woman looked at her like she was an infant. "I don't know if he can see you right now."

Myah was prepared for something like this and was already forming a backup plan as she addressed this dismissive receptionist. "Tell him if he's interested in finding Amy Cooper to talk to us. And we're pretty pressed for time so I'm going to need you to do that right now."

"Who is Amy Cooper and why is she important? I can't let you see him if this is about a little argument that happened at school, honey."

Myah nodded, eyes scanning the room she was in and the rooms she could see. In another instance of her small stature and speed being an advantage of hers, she pushed past the desk and raced into the gut of the police station, hoping she could find his office. She heard Zoey, Steph and the receptionist call out to her but she pretended she didn't. She scanned each room she passed until she found an office with Lieutenant Walton at the desk. She didn't have time to see if anyone else was in there with him or if this was even his office at all, she was already in the room before she thought of it. He looked at her, alarmed, but she had come this far and wasn't about to be shooed away. "We need to talk."

"What is this in regards to?"

He sounded slightly annoyed but Myah could live with that. "It's about Amy. We know where she might be."

Just as she said that, Steph and Zoey entered as well. Followed with haste by the receptionist, who stood in the doorway and gave her side of the story first.

"Sorry, Lieutenant. They got past me and I couldn't stop them. Do you want me to call security?"

Zoey and Steph looked anxious but Myah knew they were safe. And when Lieutenant Walton shook his head, Zoey and Steph joined Myah.

"No, that's all right. They have some important information for me."

Zoey turned to the receptionist and took a step toward her, pushing her out of the doorway and into the hall. "Well, you heard him. Looks like we're safe. Nice seeing you and have a great damn day." She slammed the door in the receptionist's face and then turned her attention to the much more pressing matters. "We know where Amy is. All of them. And we need your help to get them."

Lieutenant Walton sat back in his seat, prepared to both soak in what they would say and decide if he would take them seriously. "Then tell me everything you know. Everything important, you know."

Myah stepped up. Literally.

"We've come to understand that there is a secret hidden path that a few people know about but nobody ever goes to. That's where we think they might be hiding."

"And why do you think that?"

Zoey stepped up beside Myah.

"My second grade class went there and no one has been there since. Amy was in my class and we both were told about how desolate and empty it was. It's a pretty good place to hide out. Aside from us, I don't know if anyone else even knows it exists."

"And where is this path?"

"It's in the frog park, on the far east side of town. I can't describe its exact location, but if I was there, I'd be able to find it."

Steph took note of his skeptical face and moved a step forward , standing by her girls. "We can't say for sure that she's there, but it's a good idea to take seriously. So I suggest you do. Or we'll go down there and take them out however we can." She could tell he understood her meaning and was glad his expression became as serious as it did. Because they were serious, too.

"All right, we'll send a car down there to see if there's any truth to this theory of yours." When Myah spoke, it startled him.

"No. We have a plan. It doesn't involve any murder so you don't have to worry about that, but we know what we're doing. And if you want to get her, you'll have to trust us on that. But you can't doubt us.

If you do, our whole plan will go to shit and you won't be any closer to getting your hands on her. Are you willing to do that?"

For once, Keith Walton felt like he was the perpetrator. He didn't like it, but he knew these girls were onto something. And bringing in Amy Cooper would be an immense help. "I am not willingly to blindly follow you, no, but I am willing to offer what services I deem necessary depending on what your plan is."

Zoey grinned. "We'll take that as a yes." She leaned her upper body over the table, snatched a pen and paper from his desk and began scribbling words onto it. "Here's how this is going to go."

Lieutenant Walton listened with prepared ears and, lucky for Zoey, Myah and Steph, found relief in knowing that their plan wasn't near as childish or outlandish as he thought it would be. If anything, he was surprised at the simplicity of it. It wasn't flawless, but the plan the three came up with could work.

Once she had finished, Zoey took a step back to be in line with Myah and Steph. She felt good about the plan, she just hoped that he did as well.

"It's not perfect, it's not bad either. But this involves a lot of trust. And trust goes both ways. I can only give you as much as you give me."

Myah, Zoey and Steph stared at each other for a few long seconds and all looked back at Lieutenant Walton with eager, serious faces.

Zoey nodded. "Then I guess you'll be giving us a lot."

He nodded back and hoped that this all would work out. He was taking a risk letting the three of them have as much power as they did and, even though he did trust that they would fulfill their part of the plan, it didn't reflect very highly on him that he needed their help. Though maybe the time for self image issues had passed. A car had just arrived to Amy Cooper's residence and found no one living but more than one dead. Maybe they needed what help they could get. "We should leave now. The sun's going down and we don't know how long they'll stay there."

Steph pulled out her phone, read the time the sun would set, read the current time and did the math. "We have one hour and six minutes left."

Lieutenant Walton stood up, rising a foot above them and headed to the door. He opened it and looked back at them. "Then let's move. I'll bring an extra car just in case we need a few more officers and we'll keep the sirens off."

The three filed out of his office and Zoey, feeling an abrupt and powerful ache for Dawn, slowed down to be in line with the other two and took Steph's hand once they were beside each other. Steph held her right back. Zoey was grateful. She thought that, if she was going to have to deal with this emotional whiplash for even half as long as she thought she might, it was good to have a few people who could understand her. Even if no one would be able to understand it perfectly, she still felt lucky to have what she did.

After the three left, Keith swung his office door shut and went to gather what officers he could. He had, presumably, two people to apprehend and it was very likely that one of them had murdered three others, maybe more. Maybe the Jonah Dunbar case was related to this. The plan was simple but there was still an unpredictability that hung around it. And the three girls at the head of this pan seemed more unpredictable than any other aspect of it.

When the three doors to Myah's car slammed shut there was a brief moment for the three of them to come to terms with what they were all about to do. They were all ready.

Myah turned the key in the ignition and as the vehicle came alive, she looked to Zoey. "You're up, *gee-pee-ess*. Where are we going? Where is this frog park?"

Zoey thought about it and ran her finger in front of her, left and right and up and down, as if tracing the car's path. "If I'm remembering correctly, take a right out of the parking lot."

Myah did so. The car cut through the streets, most of which she was unfamiliar with, rarely ever faltering or stopping and by five-thirty, six minutes after they had left the station, the three of them parked in the front lot of the frog park.

Myah found the name strange when Zoey had said it, she had passed it off as a nickname, but, to Myah's surprise, the sign to the right of the main entrance read, in green letters, WINNO FROG PARK.

"It's really called that? The frog park?"

"Yep." Zoey said. "There's used to be some special frog species that lived all around the park, but they all either jumped ship or died or something so the town made a big frog statue as a…memorial I guess. I don't know, I can think of a few better things to spend money on but I'm not in charge."

"Here they come," Steph said.

Zoey and Myah looked at her and followed her eyes to see two police cars pull in and park beside them. The sight of the police cars gave Zoey a twisted feeling of nostalgia and she shook it off as the three girls swept out of Myah's car and met Lieutenant Walton at the gate. Zoey kept one crutch in the car but used the other for her weak foot, hoping using one instead of both might make her faster. Just in case speed became something she needed to have.

"Do your officers know what they're supposed to be doing and what they're *not* supposed to be doing?"

Lieutenant Walton sighed, tired of being treated like a child, and focused on the matter at hand. "Yes, I've explained how things are going to go. You don't have to worry about me."

"I hope not," Myah snapped.

"Hold on a minute," he said and hoped that they would listen. "I believe it's smarter if you all step aside and let my officers handle this."

All three of them wore the same face but Steph was the first to let their irritation be known. "You're trying to push us to now? When we're already here?"

Lieutenant Walton put his hands out in front of him, already losing faith that they would hear him out. "We're not pushing anyone out, we're just looking out for everyone's safety. You're putting yourselves in danger by doing this and, if you're right about this theory, then you've already gone above and beyond in terms of helping us."

Zoey squeezed her crutch to relieve some of her anger and did her best to remain calm. "But if Amy sees cops closing in on her, she's going to run and the only way you'll be able to bring her down is by shooting her. I assume a seventeen year old is faster than four forty year olds but I could be wrong. However, we can sneak up on her more effectively since we're smaller and we can blend in better. As a bonus, we can drag her out of the woods without putting a bullet in her. And you guys are already going to be guarding the only exit there is, why isn't that enough for you?"

His patience had run out and his voice reflected this. "This isn't about evening the load between my group and yours. I appreciate what you're trying to do, but our officers are trained for these situations. We're not going to let her get away. We'll still be on the exit, we'll just lead her there so you don't have to risk getting hurt. This isn't something you have to agree with, but it's something that's going to happen whether you like it or not." He watched the three of them, all too angry to put their thoughts into words, and wondered what they, might say once they were able to again.

Myah looked down, nodded, and looked at Zoey, who seemed ready to break her crutch over her knee. "Zoey, where is the path?" Zoey and Steph looked at her with the same angered betrayal and she nodded, hoping they would understand her meaning. Even if they didn't now, they would soon.

Zoey shook her head and stumbled into the park, though just a few feet. It wasn't far. She scanned the surroundings, the walking path to the right that took people through a few well kept gardens, the half dozen benches that lined another walking trail in front of them and the wall of woods to their left. She spotted the tree and made no motion towards it. It was possible that she had understood Myah's nod but now wasn't the time to ask her about it. She would know when they started moving. "Found it."

"Where is it?" Lieutenant Walton asked.

Zoey made her way over, noticing how close Steph and Myah were, and had a feeling Steph knew the new plan as well. She led the two and the few who followed to a massive pine tree. She pushed a few branches up, ignoring the needles digging into her arm, and uncovered a spot that, to anyone else, wouldn't have looked any different from the rest of the wall of grass that separated the woods from the park. But Zoey could see the difference, she knew the path. "Right there."

Myah faced Lieutenant Walton and felt a bit more brave than she had been expecting. It felt nice. "You're really not going to let us do this?"

"It's not a risk worth taking. We'll find her."

"Are you going to shoot us if we try to help you?"

He almost laughed. "Of course not. You've all been a great help."

"We're not done helping yet," Myah said and she reveled in the confusion on his face. "No one ever listens to us. You should have. Yell and you'll ruin everything."

The realization dawned on him a second too late.

Myah threw herself to the ground and climbed through Zoey's opening, Steph did the same and Zoey followed, dragging her crutch in with her. Noe of them stopped to wait, they couldn't afford to. They ran, Zoey leading the pack and following the path as if it were freshly carved into the dirt. After a few seconds of running she hid behind a tree and Myah and Steph met her there.

Zoey looked back, spotting the pine tree with ease, and saw nothing more than a wide shield of trees running left and right as far as she could see, covering them from the rest of the park. The plants and trees and foliage were far more overrun on this side of the trees and, unless the officers were very well hidden, no one had followed them in. They may as well have entered a forgotten world. Though not forgotten by everyone. "They're in here, somewhere. They have to be. I think it's best if we stay low, stay together and cover as much ground as we can before the sun goes down. Sound good?"

Steph nodded. "Yeah."

"I'll lead."

"We'll be right behind you," Myah said. She nudged Steph's shoulder and spoke to both of them. "And if anyone sees anything, we silently let the others know. You both got that?" They both nodded and Steph gave a small look of weariness to Zoey, who didn't notice.

Zoey stepped in front of Myah and Steph and, before moving any farther, informed them of information she was sure they'd need to know.

"Don't lose each other. It's a goddamn labyrinth in here." The two nodded and moved in a bit closer. Zoey started down the old path and traversed through the overgrown foliage. She remembered where her second grade class had stopped walking and sat down. At the base of some gigantic tree. One that, to them at that age, looked like it stabbed through the sky. If Amy's group was anywhere, it would most likely be there, where she was most familiar. Zoey didn't know if Amy knew the path and pathways that made up this section of the park but, if she knew how to get around as well as Zoey did, this problem could become much harder to deal with.

"Do you think the cops will fulfill their end of things and wait at the exit?" Steph asked, looking around the ocean of brown and green for anything orange.

"I don't know," Zoey whispered. She really didn't. Myah was right, no one ever believed them.

Luckily, the place hadn't changed much since Zoey had last been there. The trees and plants were taller and there was no spot of ground that wasn't covered with grass or leaves but, in terms of getting around the Forbidden Path and knowing what came next, it was like she had been there yesterday. The trees covered any sunlight that could obstruct her view. They stood tall and the leaves seemed to hold hands with those from other trees, creating a dome over the pathway and the woods in general.

As Zoey walked, she took a hairband out of her pocket and tied her sleek, black hair into a ponytail. She didn't often wear her hair this way, but the air in the forest was much more humid than the air outside of it and the ponytail made her head feel less hot. Her toes still hurt and every step she took sent a new blast of pain through her body, but she put her own complaints aside and focused on finding the tree. It was close. A few more turns around the bushes and trees and the three of them would be there.

So would Evan and Amy.

Chapter 26

"Neither of us have a plan, do we?"

Amy didn't want to admit it, but she knew they had to face the truth at some point. "I don't think so." She looked down at the grass, feeling, careless and stupid, but before she let her negative thinking overtake her, she offered up what little plan she had thought of. "We can just go and see where we end up at the end of the day. As long as we're away from here, what's the harm?" Amy glanced at him, hoping she didn't look as desperate as she felt. "How does that sound? It's better than nothing."

Evan nodded. "That's true." He didn't want to say anything more positive than that. And Amy didn't need him to.

With a content sigh, she stretched and sat up. "We should get moving then."

There was the tree. Zoey could see it from where she crouched. It was hard to miss. Myah and Steph were still right behind her and it didn't take them long to figure out why they had stopped. The two gave the tree a long, considering look and turned back to Zoey, nodding. Zoey pointed to their right and they all skulked in that direction. After a few feet, the two who sat at the base of the tree came into Zoey's sight so suddenly that, for a second that turned her blood to ice, she thought they had spotted her. And because of that she dropped to her knees. She glanced at the two behind her and pulled Myah down with her. Steph took the hint and did the same. Zoey spoke softer than she ever had before.

"I was right. They're here. Right around the corner."

Myah spoke like her life depended on it. "Who? How many of them?"

"Just Amy and Evan."

Myah nodded at the ground, thinking out loud. "Good. The less the better. Now we have the numbers advantage."

"What comes now?" Now it was Zoey who sounded like her life

depended on Myah's answer.

Myah's eyes ran along various branches and vines as she spoke. "We'll spilt up and corner them. Zoey stay here and come in on their right, Steph, go around and come in on their left. I'll go right and come in in front of them." Steph and Zoey nodded and each one headed off in their assigned direction.

Myah continued on her knees, shielded by the bushes and grass and was once agains grateful to be so small. She thought about this new plan and hoped it would work out. *The only place that won't be covered by one of us will be covered by the tree. And Amy will have an easier time getting through that than any of us.*

She felt like a lion sneaking up on unsuspecting prey, blending into the tall grass, alert and ready and hungry. She was in position, no more than ten feet away from Amy and Evan, she could see them and she could tell they couldn't see her. She wondered how they were going to make themselves known but Zoey answered that question for her.

Myah watched Zoey pop out of the grass like a Jack-in the-box and she followed, revealing herself and burying her heels into the ground for any extra support it could bring her. She watched Evan and Amy spring up and she was glad that they looked so caught off guard and afraid.

They fucking should be.

Amy turned to run to where she thought she could, but Steph swept in front of her and kept their little virus contained. Unlike Zoey and Myah though, who were a few feet away, Steph was no more than a foot from Amy. "Nice try." She shoved Amy back and almost took her off her feet, if not for Evan catching her before she could fall.

She recovered quickly and Zoey stepped closer, letting her crutch stab into the ground. "Make this easier on yourself and come with us. You fight back, so will we. Don't tempt us, bitch."

Amy backed up until she was against the tree. "I'm not going anywhere. And none of you are going to make me."

"Oh yeah? You think so?"

"Yes. I've done more today than I ever thought I would have to and I'm not about to let it all be for nothing. I'm not going to fucking prison."

Zoey was, at this point, close enough to Amy to not have to run towards her to pin her against the tree. She only had to take one step and she was on top of her, arms pressed against her neck and chest.

"Yeah, I know you've done a lot today. We all know what you've fucking done today." She felt tears coming but held them back. Now was not the time. "And soon enough, a judge and your cellmate will know what you've done, too." Amy kicked her splint and Zoey turned the pounding, screaming, burning pain into fuel for the fire of her anger. With a hateful smile, she said, "You'll have to do better than that."

"Not a problem." Amy glanced at Steph, remembered what she had done, and slammed her forehead into Zoey's. She had a surprising amount of strength holding Amy against the tree, but once Amy hit her, she launched back like a scared child. Amy took the opportunity, flicked out her knife, dotting the grass with a few drops of blood, and swung for Zoey's throat.

Zoey moved back, shielding her face, and felt fresh blood run.

Amy and Evan knocked Zoey out of their way and ran, Evan hot on Amy's heels but having to put in a lot of effort to keep himself there.

Myah and Steph picked Zoey up off the ground. She held her bleeding left arm. The horizontal cut wasn't a gash, but a substantial amount of blood did come from the wound. Enough to soak the cloth that ripped open around it. "I'm fine. We need to go after them."

"Maybe we should make sure you're going to be okay first," Myah said, trying to examine the cut.

Zoey pulled her arm out of Myah's hands. "Fuck that. I'm not letting them get away. We'll deal with my cut later. Let's go. Now." She ran through the pain in her foot and arm. The pain didn't matter. And neither did the dirt and grass that her back was covered in. In this real world situation, how you looked and felt meant nothing. All that mattered was how you wanted to look and feel and how you could let that future you bring you into the future you wanted to see. Zoey knew how she wanted to look and feel, but feel was much more important.

"Do you know where you're going?" Evan asked, through quick and raspy breaths.

"Down to the inch." And she did. In spite of how busy and random these woods were, Amy knew where the exit was and knew how to get there. She found it odd that she remembered but perhaps it wasn't too surprising. The path ended where the park ended and she was able to envision her seven year old self looking out at the rest of the town and wishing she had someone to explore it with.

"So there's a destination in your mind?"

"Yes, don't worry about it, Evan."

But, as they both knew, worrying was Evan's specialty and worrying was what he did once more. His thought process and morality finally caught up with him and he slowed down. He was surprised it had taken him this long, but something about the fact that they were running again and that they would be running for the rest of whatever remained of their free lives made him realize how small any positive ending for them seemed. And despite how supportive he could be, and how supportive he could pretend to be for Amy's sake, he knew they wouldn't be able to live the rest of their lives running and hiding and never get caught. At this point they were just circling the drain.

Amy noticed him and forced herself to slow down as well, though she was in no mood to take a break. They were far ahead of Zoey, Myah and Steph, but that was no reason to let their gap decrease.

"Evan, we need to keep going. We can't stop."

"I need to."

"What are you talking about?" She didn't want to, but she sounded scared.

"Amy, I don't think we can do this. Maybe it *is* better if we just give ourselves up. We don't know if they can blame us for everything, or anything, honestly. There's a chance—"

"—A chance? A chance that we may make it out of all of this without anything bad happening?

"I didn't say that."

She ignored him. "What is that chance, Evan? One in ten million? I'm not taking a chance that gambles freedom with life in prison." She took his hand but he pulled it away. She held back her fear and tears but she couldn't for long.

"I'm sorry, Amy, I really am, but this is too much for us. We can't just run away from everything. I thought I could handle it, I tried not to think about it, but our odds of succeeding are so small. We haven't even left the town yet and we're already running. We're trying to escape the police. That's damn near impossible for adults to pull off, how are we supposed to do it? We'd be caught within a week and we'd be put in the exact same situation we're in now. You have to understand that. We have a chance to give up willingly, and maybe get a lighter sentence. It could work if we play our cards right."

All of that fear of his that she had spent so long trying to get rid of, all of his wary comments and looks throughout the day, all of the times he told her he would stand by her no matter what and refused to do as he promised. No matter what they went through he could never just be there for her in the way that she needed him to be.

Amy was crying. Her tears were hot and they stung but she didn't stop. "I'm not playing anything. I'm not going to prison, Evan. Please."

He gave her a look of certainty that made her shiver and he took another step back, his hands behind his back. "We don't know that we'll go to prison. I'm sorry, Amy, but we can't live like this. And I'm choosing not to."

"Evan, please don't leave me. You're all I have. You can't quit on me, too."

"If you choose to run, I won't tell them where you're going. I'll help you however I can. I'm sorry. Do whatever you got to do, whatever you think is right." He closed his eyes and waited to hear her run. But he didn't. He heard sniffling, a deep slow breath, a few steps that seemed to be coming towards him and he prepared himself for a kiss. He heard a very familiar flick and realized that wasn't what he was getting.

"I love you."

Before Evan could put a hand to his throat, which felt like it had just been pierced by a doctor's needle, he fell to the ground. He rolled to look up and saw nothing but a ceiling of leaves. The ceiling started getting blurry and he thought briefly about how she could have done this to him. And what else she would be willing to do.

His blurry surroundings went from green to gray to black.

Myah and Steph caught up to Zoey but it took longer than they thought. Even with a bad foot, she was keeping a fast pace.

"Do you think Amy knows where she's going?" Myah asked "Does she know this place as well as you?"

Zoey didn't break her stride as she spoke. "I guess so seeing as how we haven't run into her."

"Do you think Evan does, too?"

Before Zoey could respond they ran into an answer.

They looked at him for a few seconds, the way someone might look at a piece of roadkill. Steph's voice was careless. "He's dead."

Zoey turned to look at Myah. "I guess not." Her unaffected expression turned more serious and she looked all around her. Myah and Steph did the same, though she knew they weren't seeing what she was.

"What's wrong?" Myah asked.

"She's trying to get out through the other side. I guess she doesn't know who's waiting for her there." She might have killed Evan, but Zoey doubted that Amy would be able to take on multiple cops.

"That's assuming that the cops actually went there," Steph said. "And that ignores the fact that we deserve to be the ones who take her down."

She thought for a moment and a wise smile spread across Zoey's face. "That can be done. I know how we can get to the end before her." The smile left. "But we have to run, like, a minute ago."

They all ran as fast as they could to make up for that minute. After a while it became obvious that Myah and Steph had slowed down to keep Zoey alongside them and, at this rate, Zoey knew Amy would be out of their hands. The thought of it gave her an idea.

"Steph, I need you to hold out your arms. Like this." She held her arms out, palms up and Steph duplicated the move. "All right, great. Now here comes the hard part. You have to hold them out for the next few seconds, okay? No matter what, do not fold."

"Okay, Zoey, I've got it. What are you thinking?"

Zoey twisted her body and ran with her right side in front of her. "I'm thinking that Amy will be a free bird at our speed. I know that I'm the one causing us to slow down so I'm going to kill both problems." Without another word she jumped into Steph's arms and, like she had said, Steph kept her arms outstretched and didn't let them fall when Zoey's weight was added. She stumbled a bit, understandable, but once she recovered she and Myah sped up a significant amount. And now Zoey's leg didn't bang and burn as much. Everybody won.

Zoey looked up from where she was being cradled, at the person doing the cradling. "It's a good thing you're strong."

"It's a good thing you only weigh, like, one-twenty. I've had to lift heavier." Steph glanced at the foliage they were running through and trying to avoid getting tangled up in. "Have we been going the right way this whole time?"

Zoey looked forward from Steph's arms and felt safe knowing that they were still on the right track. "Yes. But we have to turn left soon. Then we're there."

Zoey's weight, while not being the heaviest thing Steph had ever held, was now becoming an unfortunate burden. And the running was starting to slow her down. "Okay, so when is this turn?"

Zoey was quiet, curled in Steph's arms like a sleeping cat. Then the cat woke up and she shouted, "Right now." The urgency in her voice acted as extra motivation for Myah and Steph, who yanked themselves left as soon as Zoey piped up. They continued running, not knowing where Amy was or where they were going or where they would have to stop and Zoey eyes every tree and bush and vine as she passed them, waiting for the exit. She almost let it pass her, but she remembered the two trees that guarded it on both sides, long and lanky, one bending to the left and the other to the right, and told Steph and Myah to stop. They did and when Zoey asked her to, Steph let her go with very little hesitation. Zoey looked through the trees and, like Myah, could see the officers on the other side. She was glad they had listened but she hoped they wouldn't interfere. She had earned this moment and she was going to see it through. She turned back to the path and started down it. "Let's create some distance between us and the cops. Don't want them hearing anything and getting in the way."

Steph and Myah followed her, feeling similar sentiments. They made it only a few feet before Zoey stopped them. "She's coming. Listen."

They did and, after a few seconds, heard the rapid thumping of approaching footsteps. Neither of them had any idea how Zoey had managed to hear those footsteps before they did.

"Get down," Zoey said and, again, Steph and Myah did so. Zoey did as well, but she didn't crouch as low as the other two had. She couldn't, she had to shoot up as fast as possible. She removed her crutch from under her arm and held it like a baseball bat, waiting.

After a few more seconds of listening to the footsteps and a few unpleasant seconds of wondering if Amy was going to end up running in this directional all, Zoey could see her legs zipping around trees and bushes and, without waiting to take aim, jumped up and swung her crutch, hitting Amy in the chest and sending her onto her back.

Something as lightweight as a crutch would not have been able to knock Amy down on a normal day but, whether it was Zoey's strength or Amy's distracted mind, it did the job today.

Before Amy could get up, Steph pounced on her, digging her hands underneath Amy's arms and dragging her to her feet.

Amy squirmed and contorted, her hair flying in all directions and looking like an actual raging fire for a second, but Steph's arms had been prepared for the fight, and her drive to keep Amy prisoner turned her grip to stone. "Stop fighting it, bitch. You're done."

"She's not done," Myah said as she approached their bloodstained guest. "Not yet." She kept a distance of several feet, just in case Amy might try to attack her like she had to Zoey. "Where are Heather and Trevor, Amy? We know where Evan is, but where are the two of them?" There was a pause and she continued asking questions she knew the answer to. "What did you do to them?"

Amy still tried to shake herself out of Steph's grip but when the three of them were mentioned, her strength left her body. She responded, sounding surprised and confused. "I killed them." Once she heard herself say it, her twisted logic came back. "They couldn't handle it. They were going to try and turn us in. I had to. Heather and Trevor were just going to get in the way."

"You had to, huh? You had to kill Evan?" His name made Amy shrink, as if she had just realized what she had done. "You had to kill your boyfriend? I doubt he was going to turn you in. He was probably the only person on Earth who cared about you. And to repay him, you stabbed him in the neck and let him bleed out a slow, painful death."

Amy shook her head in bitter denial. "No, you idiot. I knew what to aim for, and I hit it. The carotid artery. You're dead in, like, a minute."

"A slow, painful, never-ending minute knowing that you're going to die. Not knowing when, just knowing. And he had to die knowing that his beloved girlfriend was the one who killed him and left him for dead in the middle of the woods. How fucking considerate of you."

"I'm sure Dawn was thinking the same thing."

The mention of her name made Myah's hands become fists. "You're a fucking monster. I wish you could suffer as much as we have. But I guess this is a start." She closed the gap between them and sunk her nails into Amy's back, scratching along her skin. She cringed and grunted and Myah went slower. "How does it feel to be on the other side of the abuse? Hopefully your scar will stay longer than mine." She swung her leg at Amy's ankles, Steph let her go and she fell hard against the dirt.

"Hold her," Steph said to Myah and the two switched places. Myah brought Amy back to her feet and braced herself.

"You deserve so much more than we can do to you. But I think we all should get in at least one hit." She swung her fist at Amy's face and cracked her knuckle against Amy's cheekbone. She would have hit the ground again but Myah didn't let her fall. She kept her prisoner in her arms. A red line became visible where Steph's knuckle had scraped skin. A red line that soon began to leak red down her face. "Maybe two hits." She drove her knee into Amy's stomach and she could feel the air shoot out of Amy's mouth. Again, Myah held her as still as she could. Steph leaned towards her and let out a bit more of her hatred.

"I want you to remember how this feels, not just the pain, but the feeling of being held down. Of feeling powerless and weak and useless. Feeling like you can't do anything. How do you think I felt? Or Myah, probably Dawn, too."

When she said Dawn's name Amy lifted her head up with the fruit smile Steph had ever seen from her. It looked hideous. "When I carved that word onto her stomach she cried like a fucking baby. I wish I could do it again."

Without telling herself to, Steph punched her again and sent her head flying back into Myah's shoulder. Steph flexed her fingers and reveled in the lack of pain she felt. She stepped to the side and let Zoey finish.

Zoey walked toward Amy with tears in her eyes. "You harass my friends, you break my toes, you kill my...my best friend, my girlfriend." They hadn't planned on using a title but Zoey wanted to now. And saying it felt nice, like getting a hug when you needed one.

Amy squinted and spoke through a chuckle. "You're what?"

Without planning to, Zoey shot her fist out and cracked it against Amy's mouth. It hurt, but she knew Amy's hurt more. "No, you don't get to talk now. You do this to all of us and for what? What did any of us ever fucking do to you?" Amy didn't respond and Zoey wasn't shocked. Zoey knew there was no good answer to give, Amy just enjoyed hurting people and that was all. Zoey continued. "I'd like to hurt you, I'd like to kill you, I'd like to slit your throat with your own knife and bury it up your ass. But I won't. Because that doesn't put you through what you put us through. Nothing does. But the closest thing would probably be you, in jail, for life. So you can have as much time as possible to think about everything you've done to all of us. Alive and dead. You're going to grow old and rot. Alone. No one will waste their time thinking about you and you'll disappear like you never existed. That's what you deserve." She looked away from Amy and spoke to Myah and Steph. She wiped her hate filled tears and cleared her throat. "Let's go. If we leave through there," she nodded her head at the exit, "this'll be over too fast. I want some time alone with you guys. Let's go back the way we came."

"What do we do with her?" Steph kicked Amy's ankle to add unneeded emphasis.

Zoey answered, appreciating the kick. "We bring her with us. Knock her out." Amy struggled again and Myah held her in place, maneuvering her arms behind Amy's back to grab a handful of tangerine hair and yank it down, keeping her head immobile.

Steph nodded, reached for Zoey's crutch and wound it back. She let her fingers find the best position, very close to the position Zoey had, and swung it against Amy's temple. The instant the crutch connected, Amy's head dropped. Myah put her hand to Amy's heart and, to her surprise, she found one.

"She's alive. She'll probably have one hell of a headache when she wakes up though."

"That won't be too important to her when the time comes," Zoey said. "Come on, let's get rid of her." They started walking back to the entrance, Amy's unconscious body hauled over Steph's shoulder like a duffle bag, and Zoey felt the need to try and ease the tension.

"God I hate these fucking woods. If I never have to come back here I'll die happy."

"Let's hope we never have to," Myah said, looking through their claustrophobic yet very open environment. "How do you know this place so well, anyway? Wasn't the last time you were in here in second grade?"

"That field trip was a very big day. Our teacher prepared us for it weeks ahead of time, she had mapped it out and given all of us maps of our own and she made sure we'd all know where to go in case we got lost. It was basically designed to be remembered."

Myah understood that type of unwavering memory. She still remembered the specific pattern of stitching on the couch she had hidden behind as she waited for her parents to remember her. "Did anyone get lost?" she asked.

"No. We did lose Amy for a bit but she was just at the exit staring out at the rest of the town."

Myah glanced at Amy's body, dangling over Steph's arm. "What was she like back then?"

Zoey answered fast, as if wanting to get Amy out of her head as soon as possible. "Better. Mostly just quiet though. She cried a lot. At least once a week our teacher would have to take her into the hallway and calm her down."

"Boo hoo," Steph spat and changed positions so she was now carrying Amy like a bride being carried into her new home. She felt Amy's knife and was grateful to the idiot for not disposing of it.

"That's kind of a relief," Myah said.

Zoey glanced at her. "What do you mean?"

"I thought you might say you know this path well because you've had sex here or something." When she saw their faces, she explained. "It's a secluded space, no one would ever know you were here, it's not that crazy."

"It's not crazy but it is gross. I would never do that, although it wouldn't be the worst place I've ever had sex." She looked at Myah and smiled. "I mean, it's certainly not as good as your bed, for example."

Myah smiled and her face felt hot. "I think you want to have sex on my bed more than I do."

"You'll understand why once you get laid. You don't know how it feels." She realized something and accidentally said it aloud. "I don't even really know how it feels." They both looked at her and she looked down. "I mean, how it would feel for you two is different than how it felt for me. Because...." She found no good way to end her explanation so she left it at the word it started with.

"Because you've changed," Steph said. She put the side of her head against Zoey's. It was the best she could do with her arms occupied. "And for the better, I think."

Zoey nodded and thought she felt a slight blush running up her cheeks. It may have been the first time she ever felt a little bit embarrassed to receive a compliment. "Exactly." She noticed that they were approaching the pine tree and sighed. "End of the path."

She pushed up the bottom branches for Myah and Steph, who threw Amy's body to the ground and dragged her through the underbelly of the tree as they passed through. Zoey gave one last sickening look to the Forbidden Path and followed.

Steph picked up Amy and dropped her into the arms of Lieutenant Walton. She was prepared for some big pointless speech from the man so she cut him off before he could get going. "You can thank us later." Zoey and Myah came up next to her and Myah gave the same commanding tone to him that she had given before.

"She's unconscious and we're all okay. Now do whatever it is you do with people like her, but make sure she can't get away. Lock her up if you have to, but keep her with you."

Steph remembered something that would help their case and added, "There's some evidence in her back pocket that' should help you figure out who she killed. You can ignore any of Zoey's dee-enn-ayy you may find."

Zoey moved her cut arm into his sight. She hadn't felt any pain until now. "Yep. It stings, but I'm still here. What am I going to have to do for this thing to go away? Because I really don't want to have to go to the," she put her fingers up in quotes, "Rhode Island Medical Center," the quotes fell, "for the third fucking time in less than ten days."

Lieutenant Walton was still very upset at how this plan had unfolded but he didn't stop himself from helping her with her wound. He took a look at Zoey's arm and scrunched his nose. "I think you'll be fine. It's not deep enough to require stitches so you just need to pour some rubbing alcohol on it, wrap it up in some gauze and give it a few days to heal itself."

"Wouldn't be the first time."

"What happens now?" Steph asked, anticipating his answer.

"Well, I'll have some people go out through the path just in case there's any additional evidence," he looked at the woods and didn't notice any of the girls glance at each other as they realized just how much evidence there would be, "Ms. Cooper is going to come with us and, once she comes to, we'll follow our usual procedure. And where that's going to go is dependent on what we find and our possible options.

"Will she go to court?" Myah asked.

"How old is she?"

"Seventeen." Zoey's voice was almost desperate.

He nodded. "If the crime is severe enough, seventeen year olds can be classified as adults and charged as such. You should all also be prepared to testify."

Zoey put her hand up. "Okay, but maybe give us a few days. I don't need to think about all of that shit right now."

"Fair enough. As for you three, you'll have to answer some questions, we'll want to make sure you're all okay and after that you can go." They all nodded and waited for it to begin.

It took a while, each girl gave her version of the story, Steph admitted to knocking Amy unconscious and felt a little more proud of herself each time she said it, they all gave half effort apologies for ruining the plan, Zoey's arm was bandaged in spite of her desire to do it herself, and after a while the three were free to go. They left the police, and the Winno Frog Park, as fast as they could. Once they got in Myah's car, closed the doors and cranked up the heat, they all sat back and absorbed everything that had happened. For a few seconds.

"I want to have a funeral for Dawn."

Myah and Steph looked at Zoey and, after realizing that she was serious, they both agreed. With a heavy heart and a hollow stomach, Steph said, "Then we should start planning it."

They drove to Myah's house, sat on her bed and planned everything out in one night. They made the calls the next morning when they woke up at noon and got all of their parents to help where they could. Most of their help came from paying for the expenses, Zoey's father gave them more than anyone else, and during this planning process, a process both stressful and miserable, a process that felt like it was draining them of whatever youth and happiness they had left, they were all glad to have the families they did.

Zoey, Steph and Myah put the information on every piece of social media they had and they prepared themselves for the Friday when it would all happen.

In four days they would let her go.

Chapter 27

Dawn Bell's funeral was held on Friday, March seventh from five o'clock in the afternoon to eight o'clock at night at the Soaring Dove funeral home. Zoey, Myah and Steph, pulled into the parking lot before anyone else had and were escorted into a parking spot right in front of the main doors by an older man. They got out of Myah's car, thanked the man and trudged inside.

To the right was a massive curved desk. There were several chairs on this half of the funeral home that were angled to face an unlit fireplace. To the left was a staircase that went to the second floor, but things would be held within the two rooms on the first so none of them paid the staircase much attention. There were two white sliding doors, an entrance and an exit, that were half open to reveal some of the second room and in between both doors was something only one of them had seen prior to this day.

"Steph?" Myah asked, nearly breathless. "Is that the piece you told us about?"

Propped up on an aisle was a sixteen by twenty inch portrait of Dawn. It was just her face and her name below it, but that was enough. Neither Zoey nor Myah were aware of Steph's abilities as an artist but even Steph had surprised herself with this one. She had drawn and created it with colored pencils to give it a softer feel and had spent days trying to get it as perfect as she could. And when she realized she wasn't going to be able to get that, she instead tried to make something that would please the two of them and would have pleased Dawn. The background was a simple blue and had been the last thing Steph had added. After getting lucky when it came to drawing Dawn herself, Steph was not willing to mess things up by trying to go overboard with the background. The photo itself was an imitation of the one Dawn had taken for picture day. Which meant that Dawn was dressed and made up to the nines. Something that Steph had managed to capture. Her makeup, the contour of her face, what little there was to see of her shirt and her silky, wavy hair that nearly ran off of the canvas itself. It looked just like her. But that bordered the line of comfort. You couldn't eat too much sugar without getting a cavity.

Steph thought back to her conversation with Clifford, thought about how dismissive she had been of her abilities as an artist, and started to rethink some things. Making this piece had helped her, in spite of how many tissues she had used during its creation. Maybe this could be her future, or some small part of it. It had brought Dawn back to life and kept her alive for a few hours, and it had made Steph feel more alive as well. She craved that feeling, she needed it.

"Do you guys like it?" Steph asked. As nervous as she had been to start it and in spite of the minor faults she could still pinpoint in it, Dawn's eyes still didn't have that spark she had tried to give them, she assumed Myah and Zoey would be more optimistic. She hoped so, anyway.

"It's amazing," Myah said, again speaking through gasps. She had expected something small, maybe even something a little less than passable, but she hadn't been expecting what looked like a towering image of one to one accuracy. From the light of her eyes to her sharp nose to her smooth hair and the slight curve of a smile that almost made Myah feel warm, even now. She had a feeling, even though she hadn't seen any other pieces Steph had done and hadn't even known she was an artist, that this would be her magnum opus. At least, as far as the three of them were concerned.

"What's going to happen to it?" Zoey asked after she caught her breath. In truth, it was a little hard to look at it while keeping herself under control but in time she didn't think that would be a problem. She just hadn't been expecting it and certainly hadn't been expecting it to look as good as it did.

"We can figure out who gets it once all of this is over. I've seen it enough to last me the rest of my life so I don't really want it, but you two can discuss ownership if you want to."

Myah glanced at Zoey and was very was aware of which one of them was going to end up with Steph's piece. She was content with that. Happy with it, even.

They started walking towards the sliding doors but before any of them could reach it, a woman jumped in front of them. She seemed to have appeared from thin air. "Hi. Can I help you?"

She sounded oddly cheerful considering her profession but Myah ignored that. "This is Steph, Zoey and I'm Myah. We were—"

"—You were the one I spoke to on the phone. You three were the ones who set this all up. Is that correct?" Her chipper tone now had an air of amazement and surprise but, again, Myah chose to ignore it.

"Yes, that's correct." The woman took Myah's hand and Myah fought a powerful urge to rip it away.

"I'm so sorry for your loss." Her face and voice finally matched their current setting and Myah found it an appropriate time to pull her hand back.

With a forced smile, she said, "Thank you." *I hope I never hear that again,* Myah thought.

She would hear the words, I'm so sorry for your loss, many times before the funeral was over. She would stop keeping count at twenty-five but she would hear them long after that. Keeping track would just become too much for her to think about.

The woman's voice went back to its positive roots and Myah gritted her teeth. "Well, I'm Diane. I'm the curator here so anything you want, you just need to say my name and I'll be there to help. If someone's here who you don't want to be, if someone isn't here who you *do*, whatever it is, I'm your go to for help."

Myah nodded. "Okay, thank you. We'll remember that."

The woman's voice got softer and she moved in closer. "She's in there, if you want to see her." She pointed at one of the sliding doors and headed back to her desk.

In a flash, Steph's piece left all of their minds.

Myah heard a shaky groan come from behind her and she turned around and saw Zoey, tears starting to form, arms limp, fingers rubbing her black dress, shaking her head. "No."

"Zoey, we have to go in there."

"No, I can't. I'm staying out here."

"Zoey, I know this is hard, but—"

"—Don't feed me that shit, Myah! You know better."

Myah nodded. "Sorry."

Zoey took a deep breath through her clogged nose. "Going in there and doing all of this is going to put an end to everything. This'll be the last time I see her. I'm not strong enough to handle that. I can't. And now my makeup is going to run."

Myah took Zoey's hands away from her face and wiped away her tears. "Zoey, we have to do this. We set all of this up and we have to follow through. If there's one thing I've learned about you, it's that you're one of the strongest people I've ever met. You ran through the woods with three broken toes, for God's sake. I know you don't want to hear this, but you have to. I know it's hard to say goodbye. But we'll be by your side every step of the way. Don't forget the people you still have. I'm sorry, but you have to go in there and you have to say goodbye. We all do." She hugged Zoey and Zoey's crying got louder, though Myah's dress muffled it. Myah took her right hand and motioned for Steph to come. She did without hesitating and joined the hug. Though, after a few seconds Steph broke it up.

"All right, we should...get this over with now." Steph took Zoey's hand and led her through the door.

Apparently they entered the exit doors, because all they saw when they stepped in were rows of chairs, all aimed towards the front of the room. Their eyes followed the white seats and saw more flowers than the population of Rhode Island covering almost the entire front half of the room. And placed in a smooth white box, in the middle of all of them, was Dawn.

Zoey heaved a painful scared sigh, squeaked out a small groan and held Steph's hand tighter. "We have to do this."

Myah took her other hand and didn't know if she was asking a question or making a statement. Either way, Myah answered. "We do." She and Steph led Zoey to the piles of potted flowers and stopped at the coffin.

The lower half of her body was covered by the smooth wood, but the upper half was out for all to see. Her hair was in its usual curly state and it was spread out around her body. Her skin was pale, but not paper white, more a dull cream. Her skin didn't blend in with her white dress, thankfully, with its puffy shoulders and gold rivets along the chest and sleeves. Her hands were draped across her stomach with her nails painted a baby blue. She looked exactly like she had when Zoey had seen her zone out for the first time, save for the dress. Which Zoey had done on purpose.

"You picked a beautiful dress."

"Thanks, Myah. It was going to be hers. I bought it for senior prom. I know it's a year away, but I wanted to be prepared. I thought about it being mine but it seemed to suit her more than me. It's not the best circumstance, but at least she got to wear it." Zoey smiled but the tears still slid down her face. "Just imagine how good she would have looked in it at prom, in front of everyone. I would have been so proud to be with her. Why did I take so long to figure it out? I could have been with her for so much longer."

"What's important is that you made the most of the time you had." Steph thought for a second and realized something. "And weren't the two of you, kind of, always dating? I mean, you two had a relationship that wasn't like any other of Dawn's or yours. You were always together, you trusted each other more than anyone else. Really, all that changed when you started dating was that your friendship had a different title. Other than that, your relationship was basically the same. Maybe that's a better way to look at it. You were always dating, in a way. It just took a little while for both of you to figure that out."

They all heard someone say "Hey," and turned to their right in unison to see Cole, wearing a black suit and a strong face.

"Hi," Zoey said with a genuine smile.

Cole looked to Zoey's right, at the white box and his face got weaker. "Is that?"

Zoey nodded and hugged him when he reached the coffin. "I'm so sorry, Cole." She could feel his tears melt into her dress and she hugged him tighter. After a while he let go and looked down at Dawn.

"She looks beautiful."

"You can thank Zoey for that."

Zoey looked at Steph, understood what she was trying to say, but shook her head. "No. All I did was give them the dress and demand they put her in it. Everything else is just her." She looked at Cole and remembered the other Bell family member. "Is your mom coming?"

Cole glared through his tears. "No."

Zoey did the same. "No?"

"Well, maybe I should rephrase. I don't know. I didn't tell her, because she doesn't deserve to know. She doesn't deserve to fucking be here." Then his voice got softer. "We were so close."

"Close to what?" Myah asked.

He looked at his hands while he spoke, finding it easier than looking at Dawn. "I don't know if Dawn every told you guys that I had a bad habit of disappearing, but the reason I did that so much was because I was looking for a place where we could live. We needed to get out of that house, away from that woman. And I just left her there."

"It's not your fault," Zoey said. She doubted that saying such a thing would work, and from Cole's face it didn't, but it was all she had.

Cole composed himself and cleared his throat. "When is everybody supposed to get here?"

Myah looked at the wall clock. "Pretty soon. I think all of our parents are on their way."

Myah was right. Just a handful of seconds after mentioning them, their families arrived. And arrived in one big clump, although they had all taken separate cars with no knowledge of when the others would show up.

Myah accepted the hugs from her parents and accepted their compliments for how well the service had come together, but she wasn't interested in talking to them. Not today.

Steph hugged her mother and was very happy to accept Emily's condolences drawing. She didn't know what the drawing was of but she kept it in her hands the entire time. Arnold may have been there but she didn't think to look for him. There was no point.

Zoey's mother gave her a hug so strong Zoey lost her breath for a few seconds. Once it returned she was able to squeeze her mother tighter and missed the feeling of being accepted by a parent. Once their hug ended and Zoey saw her father, she didn't know what to expect. He gestured for her to come towards him and when she did, he led her through the doors and into the much less crowded half of the room. She limped after him, her crutches weren't something she wanted to use today, and balanced on the heel of her right foot.

She didn't say anything. She just waited, enjoying watching him squirm.

"I don't really know what to say, but I'm sorry about Dawn."

They both knew that he did, in fact, know what to say and Zoey stared at him until he said it.

"And I'm sorry for how I've treated you. I haven't been the person you've needed and I want to try and change that. I don't know what I'll have to do for you to forgive me but I'm willing to do it. I love you, I do. I just haven't shown it properly, but I want to. I don't want to cause you any more pain, you've already had to deal with too much, I just—"

"—It's okay."

He looked at her and could have dropped his jaw if he had less self-control. "Really?"

Zoey shrugged and made sure the tone of her voice did not sound sympathetic in the least. "We'll talk later. There are some things I have to tell you. But I'm not going to lay down and accept your apology immediately. If you love me like you say, I want you to show it. I deserve it."

He nodded and looked at his feet for a moment, embarrassed but accepting it. "Can I hug you?"

"You can."

It was an odd hug, the first one they had shared in years. But as they embraced, Zoey remembered all of the hugs they had shared when she was a child, after she got hurt or after she came home from school with exciting news, and wanted this hug to be their last odd one. She wanted her dad back and, if he was willing to put in the work, she would let him back in. She needed every ounce of love she could get now.

Once they let go of each other, they joined everyone else and Zoey noticed a prideful look in her mother's eye when she looked at both Zoey and her father.

By four-fifty, the twelve rows of eight chairs were filled. After all of the I'm Sorry's were out of the way and everyone had sat down, Zoey, Myah and Steph walked to the front podium and looked out at the crowd. They only knew the people in the second row, their parents, Cole and Luke, some other friends from school. Everyone else was a relative of Dawn's and, although Zoey recognized a handful of them, there were far more that none of them knew. Zoey took a deep breath, held Myah's and Steph's hands, looked out at the sea of strangers and spoke.

"Dawn Bell lived a life that was important to all of us. That's why we're here. Regardless of what traits of hers you saw, she was important enough to you for you to come here and say goodbye. Personally, I saw someone who just...cared. More than anything. She would always be there to help you and listen to you when you needed it, even when you didn't have much to say.

"There are some memories with her I'd like to forget, but there are so many more that I'm so grateful I'll get to remember. She made me the person I am. Just being with her made you feel special, like you could do anything as long as she was by your side. She was a good person, a good friend, a good...therapist when I came to her with my stupid problems...and I loved her. She made me feel like I was home. And even though we're saying goodbye and putting her to rest, even though, in person, we'll never see her again, that doesn't mean she's gone. Her memory will always be with us. Each one of you, in being here, proves that a part of her lives in you. All we have to do is remember her. It doesn't matter the memory, it just matters that there is one to remember. So this is to her memory."

She gave a half nod and her hands let go of Myah's and Steph's. As the seated strangers applauded and Myah spoke about her limited experience with Dawn, Zoey turned to face the coffin and got down on one knee in front of it, speaking in a shaky whisper.

"I'll remember you. Every day for the rest of my life. I promise."

She kissed her index and middle fingers and put them to Dawn's purple lips. They felt warm, almost lifelike and she grimaced at this final sick joke. Zoey took Dawn's right hand off of her stomach and held it. She interlocked her fingers and, with her other hand, bent Dawn's fingers around hers.

"I'm always here."

She knew Dawn wouldn't respond so she responded for her.

"No matter what."

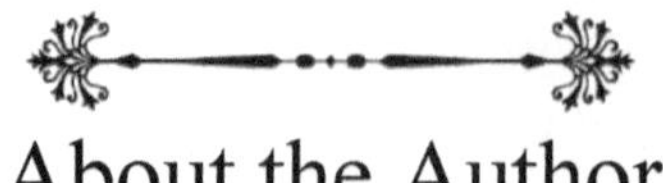

About the Author

Dylan Hubbard was born and raised in Rhode Island. He graduated from the University of Rhode Island, where he spent his senior year as a contributing reporter for the university newspaper, with a Bachelor's degree in Writing and Rhetoric and a minor in English.

9 798330 309788